ABSOLUTE RAGE

ALSO BY ROBERT K. TANENBAUM

FICTION
Enemy Within
True Justice
Act of Revenge
Reckless Endangerment
Irresistible Impulse
Falsely Accused
Corruption of Blood
Justice Denied
Material Witness
Reversible Error
Immoral Certainty
Depraved Indifference
No Lesser Plea

NONFICTION
The Piano Teacher:
The True Story of a Psychotic Killer
Badge of the Assassin

ROBERT K. TANENBAUM

ABSOLUTE RAGE

ATRIA BOOKS

New York   London   Toronto   Sydney   Singapore

ATRIA BOOKS
1230 Avenue of the Americas
New York, NY 10020

Copyright © 2002 by Robert K. Tanenbaum

All rights reserved, including the right to reproduce
this book or portions thereof in any form whatsoever.
For information address Atria Books, 1230 Avenue
of the Americas, New York, NY 10020

Library of Congress Control Number: 2002104605

ISBN: 0-7434-0344-4

First Atria Books hardcover printing August 2002

10 9 8 7 6 5 4 3 2 1

ATRIA BOOKS is a trademark of Simon & Schuster, Inc.

For information regarding special discounts for bulk purchases, please contact
Simon & Schuster Special Sales at 1-800-456-6798 or
business@simonandschuster.com

Printed in the U.S.A.

DEDICATION

To those most special, Rachael, Roger,
Billy, and Patti
and to the
memory of my boss, Frank S. Hogan

ACKNOWLEDGMENT

Again, and yet again, all praise belongs to Michael Gruber, whose genius and scholarship flow throughout and who is primarily and solely responsible for the excellence of this manuscript and whose contribution cannot be overstated.

ABSOLUTE
RAGE

1

KILLING PEOPLE IS SO EASY THAT THE IRON LAWS OF SUPPLY AND DEMAND
*make it hard to earn a decent living doing it. As a result, murder for hire
is almost always a sideline, and the people who engage in it are by and
large stupid losers, quickly caught, and quicker still to rat out the idiots
who hired them. The very few real professionals in the business are careful never to meet their clients. Instead, they deal through people like Mr.
Ballantine. Mr. Ballantine is sitting in the driver's seat of his Mercedes
sedan at the corner of Gansevoort and Washington Streets at 7 P.M. on a
Sunday evening, about the loneliest place you can be on the island of
Manhattan. This is the old meatpacking district, deserted at this hour,
except for the occasional street person. It's early summer, the sky is the
dull color of galvanized metal and seems to reflect the heat of the day
down upon the City. Although the river is close by, there is no breath of
air. The bits of trash on the street do not stir. Mr. Ballantine has the air-
conditioning on high. He is listening to a Frank Sinatra CD. Frank is
singing "Fly Me to the Moon."*

*A white car goes by, brakes at the end of the street, and does a clumsy
U-turn. Its driver parks behind the Mercedes and gets out and, as he has
been instructed to do, enters the rear seat. Mr. Ballantine does not turn
around. His dark eyes meet the watery blue ones of the other in the
rearview mirror.*

"Ballantine?"

"That's right. Did you bring the money?"

"I can get it. I wanted to discuss the details."

Ballantine allows himself a small sigh and glances at the dashboard clock. He had hoped that this would go smoothly, as he has an appointment downtown, but obviously he was wrong. He studies what he can see of the man in the mirror. A pale disk of face, late forties, running a little to fat. Stiff sandy hair, sideburns somewhat longer than the current fashion in New York, a dark suit jacket with a gold pin of some fraternal order in the lapel, a thick tie with a heavy, mixed pattern. An out-of-towner, a hick. A little cornpone in the voice, too. A Southerner? That would be unusual. Southerners usually did it themselves.

"No, we don't discuss the details," Mr. Ballantine says. "You give me twenty-five now and it gets done and you give me twenty-five again. That's it, end of discussion."

"I don't know. That's a lot of money, you know. Just to hand over to someone you never seen before."

Not Southern; a hillbilly of some kind. Mr. Ballantine is tempted to cut it off right there, tell the hick to get lost, but he has already invested some time and money. He has paid the bartender who picked up the job, and the guy the bartender told, who told him and set up the meeting. He could write that off as overhead, but still . . .

"Look," says Mr. Ballantine, "you never did this before, am I right?"

"Yeah, but . . ."

"I've done it a lot, which tells you something. That I know what I'm doing. Because, you know, this is illegal."

A short bark of a laugh from the rear seat.

"Right, and I'm still here, on the outside. Also, think about it for a minute: I'm dealing all the time with people who want to get rid of other people, they're not going to sit down for getting ripped off. I wouldn't be in business if I did that. This is the way it has to be. No questions. I don't know you, you don't know me. You don't know who I'm going to get to do the job. He doesn't know you. Me, I'm just a voice on the phone and an envelope full of cash in his post office box as far as he's concerned. Everyone is sealed off from everyone else, you understand? Seal-off is the main thing. That and the professional job, experienced personnel, guaranteed operation, and so forth. Now, I'm not saying there's not cheaper ways to go."

"For example?" said the man in the backseat, his tone avid. Mr. Ballantine checked his mirror. The man's eyes were wide with interest.

"For example, you could find some guys in a bar around where you come from, a couple of tough guys, what d'y'call them, good old boys. And you could give them a couple of grand and they'd go do it for you. Assuming they do it at all and not get drunk and fuck it up, it'd take maybe three, four days before they told someone, or the cops traced something they dropped at the scene back to them, and a couple of hours after that, they'd come and arrest you, because those boys'll give you up quicker than shit. On the other hand, you saved all that money."

"I'm not that stupid, Mr. Ballantine," said the man coldly, after a brief silence.

"We don't know that yet. If you're not stupid, either you're going to forget about the job, kiss and make up with this fella, or you're going to give me twenty-five large in assorted unconsecutive currency. Those are the two nonstupid options. Up to you, Jim. I could care less either way."

"I'll have to think about it," said the man, easing across the seat. "Other people are involved in this."

That would be another mistake, thought Mr. Ballantine, but said nothing as the man walked back to his rental. When the car had disappeared, Mr. Ballantine got out into the heat and snapped off the magnetized fake New York plates and tossed them in the trunk, revealing the authentic Jersey plates underneath. Sealing it off.

The voices of children woke her out of a sun-dazed nap and she sat up in the beach chair, checking first of all to see if Lizzie was there, and of course she was, building her sand castle where the sand got damp. There were two boys, about ten years old, both dark-haired and lean, one in a red Speedo suit and one in baggy cutoffs. They were splashing in the shallows of the Sound, playing with something big and black, a truck-tire inner tube? In the distance was an adult, obscure now in the glare and salt haze. A woman.

Rose allowed herself a moment of annoyance. Crab Point was a private beach, although who it actually belonged to just now was a lawyer's guess. But it had been in her family for generations. She had come here as a child, to the big white house on the beach, and she had brought the boys here when they were babies, and now, after a long hiatus, she had brought Lizzie, and who was this woman to come here as if it were a public park, with her two noisy kids and her—

Dog. The thing was the size of a calf, black, dripping sea spray and slaver, and it was rushing directly at her and Lizzie. Her belly jumped with fear. She started to get to her feet to get between the monster and her little girl, who was kneeling next to her sand castle, her back to the onrushing dog, oblivious.

There came a piercing double whistle and the dog, now not more than three yards from Rose, spun instantly around like a mechanical toy, throwing a gout of sand as it skidded, and immediately began to race back toward the other woman.

Who waved and called, "Sorreeee!"

Rose experienced a rush of anger, at the woman and that animal, but also at herself, for her appalling cowardice. She had never been frightened of dogs before.

"Can I go in, Mom?" asked Lizzie. "It's boiling." She had her little red tube around her waist.

"Sure, honey, I'll come with you." Rose was afraid of the water, too, afraid of letting the girl go in by herself, although Lizzie had been a good swimmer since the age of five. When had she become a coward? As soon as she asked the question, she knew.

From the water, floating on her back, she watched the other woman spread her blanket and set up her backrest, and, with somewhat more interest, her undressing. She wore a small, blue-striped bikini, although she was rather mature for a bikini—late thirties, early forties, Rose judged. A terrific, lithe body though, obviously one of those disgusting women who could eat anything and went wiry rather than slack with age. Another reason to dislike her. Rose rolled over and began to swim back and forth on the gentle swell. Maybe she could work off a few pounds before Red got here.

The next day, the woman was there again, with the boys and the dog, although the dog did not repeat its threatening dash. It played with the boys or sat like a basalt sphinx by the woman's side. She waved, and Rose returned a barely polite one. The next three days were the same. They arrived around four and stayed for a couple of hours. The woman rubbed herself with baby oil, but did not apply sunblock, nor was she apparently worried about her children burning up, unlike Rose herself, who was constantly laving her own skin and that of her daughter with Plus 20.

The boys were identical twins. Through her covert observations,

Rose learned that the one with the red Speedo was called Zik, and the one in the baggies was Zak. They were oddly different: Zik spent his time making elaborate sand sculptures; Zak spent his chasing shorebirds, and throwing sticks for the dog, and building crude sand castles, which he demolished with thrown clods as soon as built. Eventually he would squash part of his brother's work and there would be a short, noisy brawl.

Rose was glad the woman kept to herself, but she could not help her curiosity. On a trip into Holden, she'd asked Donna Offut at the grocery, who knew everything, and learned that the family was from the City and had bought the old Wingfield farm. The woman raised big dogs and trained them for guard work. There was a husband, too, who worked in New York and came out on the weekends.

The woman was named Ciampi. Apparently she'd made a pile in the market and spent a chunk of it buying and fixing up the derelict place. In all, thought Rose, not the sort of person she particularly wanted to know. The South Shore was, of course, loaded with that type, but up until now the less attractive, less accessible far North Shore had been relatively unscathed by nouveaux hordes. But maybe that was going, too; another little gritty bit of sadness.

On the fifth day, the Ciampi woman arrived without the dog and with only Zik in tow. She waved, and Rose waved back and watched the usual baby oil routine. Rose was again astounded. Had the woman never heard of cancer? And letting that boy run around in this blazing sun was close to child abuse. Had she appeared stark naked, Rose could not have been more shocked. On the contrary, she might even have approved, as long as a reasonable sunscreen had been applied. Rose adjusted her position under the shadow of her beach umbrella to leave no skin subject to the toxic rays. Taking up her *Harper's*, she read four pages about the horrendous state of agricultural inspection before dozing off.

When she opened her eyes, she found Lizzie and the boy were building a sand castle of prodigious size, not the usual lumpy kid construction, but something far more sophisticated, with sheer, smooth walls pierced by arched gates, buttresses, and high, round towers. The boy was dabbing wet sand onto the structure and talking, weaving a story about the tiny lead figures they were arranging on the walls, a dungeons-and-dragons sort of tale: wizards, warlocks, imprisoned queens, dark riders, heroic elves. Lizzie was chattering along with this, as if she had known the boy for years. Rose listened, fascinated and amazed. It had never happened in her experience that a ten-year-old boy had volunteered to play with a girl of the same age. Then Lizzie became aware of her mother's stare and grew self-conscious enough to break the enchantment. She stood and walked over to Rose's blanket, the boy following.

"We want a drink," said Lizzie, reaching into the insulated bag.

"Drink, *please*. And offer one to your friend, Elizabeth," said Rose, smiling at the boy, and getting her first close look at him. He was at the very peak of his boyish beauty, and the peak in his case was remarkably high. Dark curls, bisque skin, large black eyes with thick, unforgivable lashes, a cupid-bow mouth, and the germ of what would become a straight Roman nose.

"What do you want, Giancarlo, Coke or Sprite?" asked Lizzie.

"Coke, please," said the boy, and Rose said, "I thought your name was Zik?"

"Oh, that's my baby name. My brother is Isaac or Zak and so I had to be Zik. Parental humor, ho ho. My brother is the only one who still calls me Zik." He lowered his voice and looked grave. "He's profoundly retarded."

Rose's brow twisted in sympathy. "Oh, how awful. I'm sorry."

"Yes, well, we try to cope and all. That's why he's not here today. He had to go to Creedmore for his . . . you know, his treatments."

Lizzie said, "Their dog killed all their rabbits, Mom."

"Yes," said the boy. "It was a huge mess. He ravaged them. There were bunny parts all over. That's why he's not here either. My mother flogged him with the dog whip and locked him in the cellar. She might shoot him, or sell him to, you know, a dogfight man." He took a long sip from his Coke as they stared. "Boy, I was really thirsty. My Mom never brings anything but beer, but, you know, a couple of beers on a hot day and I get a headache and Zak is uncontrollable and has to be whipped."

"Whipped?" said Rose with a gulp.

"Oh, sure. My mom's quite the flogger. Look!" He half-twisted to show his upper back. Two thin parallel scars ran from his shoulder almost to his spine, pale against the tan. "I overturned a pitcher of martinis and she got out the dog whip on me. She's totally out of control when she gets plastered. I think she feeds us beer to destroy our brain cells. She's really quite sadistic. She used to give my sister sherry in her baby bottle."

"Did it work?" asked Lizzie, openmouthed.

"Partially. My sister speaks forty-eight languages perfectly, but otherwise she's a complete idiot. She sometimes puts her shoes on the wrong foot."

Rose sighed and said tartly, "You know, it's one thing to make up stories and another thing to tell fibs. I'm sure your family would be very unhappy if they heard you talking about them that way."

Giancarlo's response was a smile of such devastating charm that light seemed to leap from his face, and Rose's irritation melted away and she laughed, reflecting in the moment that laughs had been few and far between recently. Lizzie broke into giggles, too. In a moment they were all three roaring like a sitcom laugh track.

"What's the joke?"

Rose looked up and saw that Giancarlo's mother was standing at the edge of their beach blanket, holding a long-neck Schlitz.

"I was being amusing, Mom," said Giancarlo.

"I bet," said Marlene. She nodded to Rose. "Hi, I'm Marlene Ciampi. I'm more or less responsible for this creature." Rose introduced herself and her daughter, who asked, "Did your dog really eat up all the rabbits?"

Marlene gave her son a sharp look. "A rabbit got out and Gog chased it. Gog is not built for chasing rabbits. The rabbit is safe. What other lies did he concoct?"

"He said you flogged him with a dog whip and gave him a scar," said Lizzie.

"That's more of a prediction," said Marlene. "In point of fact, he got those scratches falling on a bale of razor wire he was told more than once not to go near."

"And I assume his brother isn't retarded either," said Rose.

"*What!*"

"He *is*," insisted the boy. "She's in total denial about it."

Marlene went after him with an openhanded roundhouse aimed at the red Speedo, which he easily dodged. He danced away, laughing maniacally. "See! Child abuse! That proves it, Mom."

The children went back to their sand castle, chortling.

"Pull up a beach," said Rose, and Marlene sat. Rose noticed with a distinct shock that the woman was missing several joints of the small fingers of her left hand. Otherwise, she was remarkably beautiful, in a Mediterranean way. "He must be quite a handful," Rose said, "with that imagination. Is his brother the same?"

"Completely different in every respect. You can barely get a word out of him. Gianni, as you see, is an artist." Giancarlo was carving a delicate arch in a thin curtain of sand.

"I don't see how he gets it to stick together," said Rose. "It's marvelous."

"Oh, yes. Sometimes a little too marvelous for daily use. Zak never picks up a crayon. His thing is war, guns, blowing things up, taking things apart, heavy machinery. That's why he skipped the beach today. We're having a backhoe in to rip out and replace a water pipe to the kennels. Watching a backhoe is his idea of paradise."

"He should meet my husband. They'd have a lot to talk about."

"Your husband runs a backhoe?"

"A dragline. Or did. He's with the union now."

"Really? I'm not sure I know what a dragline is."

"It's an excavation machine. The bucket can take a hundred and fifty yards at a bite, three hundred tons or so. The powerhouse is the size of a small office building. They use them in open-pit mining."

"Presumably not on Long Island, though."

Rose laughed. "Oh, no. Robbens County, West Virginia. That's where we're from. Or that's where Ralph is from. I'm from next door. The big white house."

"There's a story there."

"Oh, yes. Oh, yes, indeed."

"I want to hear it. Let me get the beer."

So Marlene dragged her cooler over and they sat under the umbrella and slowly drank and rubbed the icy bottles against neck and forehead, watching the slow, remarkable extension of Giancarlo's sand palace, and talking. Rose talked, rather, and Marlene listened. She seemed good at it, professional even, and Rose was not surprised to learn that she had been a prosecuting attorney in New York and later a private detective.

Marlene, for her part, after offering the minimum personal data, was content to let the other woman ramble on. Rose Heeney was the sort of woman she had never been much interested in, a type she privately called the Cheerleader. She had been exposed to a number at Smith. They had golden hair and blue eyes and were fair and round of limb. They wore kilts and circle pins and had bright, straight teeth. They strolled in laughing gaggles, dated fraternity boys, and married early—she read their names (invariably triple-barreled) in the alumnae news. And Rose Wickham Heeney was what they became, it seemed. Or not quite. Heeney had not been in the master plan of the Wickhams. They had not envisioned an Irish roughneck dragline operator for their golden girl.

They focused, naturally enough, on the kids. Besides Lizzie, there were two sons, Emmett, twenty, and Daniel, eighteen. The former had gone to Wheeling for a couple of years, then dropped out to work in the pit. Dan was at MIT. Marlene detected regret in her tone, and a pride in the younger that could never be fully expressed lest it hurt the older boy.

"Do you really have a daughter," Rose asked, "or did he make that up, too?"

"No, Lucy's real enough. She's in Boston, too, as a matter of fact, at BC, a freshman."

"Oh, good," Rose said, smiling. "And I assume she doesn't speak forty-eight languages and can put her shoes on right."

"I don't know about the shoes, but she does speak something like that many."

"You're kidding me!"

"No, actually not. She's some kind of language prodigy. Scientists come in from all over the world to study her, and good luck to them. I have not been blessed with normal children. Although, Zak seems normal enough, except for being Gianni's twin. I think he makes a practice of it. So how did you and . . . ?"

"Ralph, but everyone calls him Red."

Marlene glanced at the blaze of copper on Lizzie's head. "I should have guessed. How did you and Red hook up?"

"Oh, you know, my social conscience. After I got out of Vassar I messed around in New York for a year, working for a magazine, which folded, and I guess I was supposed to get a job at another magazine and wait around to get married. I mean that's what Mom did, right? That or be a modern woman and go to professional school like you. But I didn't want to go to professional school, and I wasn't exactly sure I wanted to be a modern woman. The guys I was dating . . . I mean, they were all right, but you know . . ."

"Bland."

"Bland, or totally focused on the greasy pole, or . . . I dated a sculptor with a loft in SoHo for a while, but honestly, all those people . . . I couldn't take them seriously, the black clothes and that attitude and the constant backbiting about everyone's work. And so I applied to VISTA."

"After the sculptor broke your heart."

Rose laughed longer than necessary and drank some beer. "Yeah, you got me pegged. The Foreign Legion of the white girls. They sent me to Haw Hollow, West Virginia, to help run a craft cooperative. It mainly involved bookkeeping and writing grant applications and arranging child care so the women could quilt and weave. Well, you can imagine it was quite a shock. You don't think people live like that in America anymore. I mean white people."

"Poor."

"Is not the word. The whole county is kept alive by miners' pensions. They won't take any help from the government, you know. Extremely proud, living in these little hamlets up in the hills—*hollers* is what they call them. The water's all rotten from the acid drainage. Half the county looks like moonscape from the strip and pit mines. They're supposed to rehab the land, but a lot of them don't—the coal companies. And they won't just leave and go to the cities for work. They want to stay by their home places." Rose sighed. "And so there I was, a little middle-class girl doing her social obligation, and one night I drove down to McCullensburg— that's the local metropolis, population twelve thousand, a Mickey D, three gas stations, and a Bi-Lo—for a meeting of all the various do-good types, and after all the social workers had droned on for a while, this guy steps up to the mike, and he gives this incredible, incredible speech, all about the hard lives of the people, and how bad they'd been treated by the mine companies and the government, and how they deserved dignity. He said the mountain people were the best people in America, how they were the only ones still living the original vision of America. I mean, it was a stem-winder, and you could see he really believed it."

"It sounds like a Pete Seeger concert."

"Oh, right, I was the same way—nobody's more cynical than an idealist trying to deal with twenty kids and a busted toilet. I guess you had to be there. We gave him a standing ovation. We were in the Methodist church hall and they had coffee afterward and I went up to him and told him how much I liked his speech, and he said something like, talk's cheap, and I said, no, he inspired me, and he gave me this look, I can't explain it, but no one had ever looked at me that way before. Penetrating, like he could peer into the bottom of my gas tank and see it was more or less empty. And he pointed to all the various social-work and church-lady and government types in the room and said, you think I inspired these people? Yeah, to applaud for a minute or two. And then they're going to go back to doing what they've always been doing, taking a middle-class paycheck for helping the poor and downtrodden. They're not going to change. They're not going to put their bodies on the line for something."

Rose paused and took a gulping swallow of beer. Marlene saw that she was flushed, but whether from the beer or the sun or the rush of memory, it was impossible to tell.

"He wasn't just posing either, like a lot of lefties were back then, like college lefties, who you just knew were going to cut off their hair in a few years and go to work for some company, or keep it long and get tenure. He was the real deal. And it was Robbens County, too." She looked at Marlene and saw the incomprehension she expected.

"No, you never heard of it. Neither had I before I got there. They used to call it Red Robbens. The unions against the owners, like it was all through the coal country back around the turn of the century, but in Robbens it was different, and worse. The labor stuff was just overlaid on top of a kind of low-level tribal war that'd been going on there for a hundred years. Some families sided with the owners, some were union, so the violence was particularly bad. For a while there were whole hollers up there with no males over twelve in them. All the men were dead or in prison. They sent in the National Guard for a while, but it didn't stop the killing. The soldiers were afraid to go up into the hills, and there weren't any decent roads to get them up there, either. The area didn't really settle down until the war and the government made sure that the coal kept flowing and made the companies settle with the union. Then they started pit mining and the whole thing collapsed." Rose stopped and laughed nervously. "Oh, God, I'm being a bore, aren't I? You don't want to hear about the industrial history of Robbens County, West Virginia."

Marlene laughed, too. "Since you asked . . . but I take it there was an attraction. I mean that night."

"Oh, God, yes. I wanted to throw my body into the cause."

"So to speak."

Rose chuckled. "Right, that, too. It's such a cliché, I know—well-brought-up girl from Long Island meets working stiff. But the work—he made it seem real, not just theory but real, about really helping suffering people find their dignity. Anyway, that's the story. After my VISTA hitch was over I moved into his place. A trailer. My parents went nuts, of course, but they had to stand for it, given the times, and the fact that in three months I was pregnant with Emmett. At least he's white, as my father charmingly said, more than once." Rose fell silent and looked out past the kids, to the Sound.

"So, is it almost heaven?" Marlene asked lightly.

"West Virginia? Formerly. The parts that aren't scarred, they're really lovely—blue hills rising out of the mist, the woods full of flowers in the spring. But the damage is awful—whole mountains reduced to slag. Majestic is less than responsible in reclamation, and they have, let's say, a good deal of influence with the legislature." In response to Marlene's inquiring look Rose added, "Majestic Coal Company. They're practically the only employer, so as you can imagine, there's not much environmental consciousness, except for the Robbens Environmental Coalition. Which is me, and a bunch of high school students and the Presbyterian minister. And"—here Rose waved her hands and rolled her eyes—"and, McCullensburg is a little sparse culturally. On the other hand, there's not much money. Union officials are not the best paid, if they're honest, and Red's as honest as they come. I got a little inheritance when I turned thirty, and we bought a crumbling farmhouse and fixed it up. Talk about stories . . . if you ever want to be truly bored, I'll tell you about the bats, and the hornets in the well house."

"It sounds like a good, if unexpected, life."

"Oh, sure, it was . . . *is*, I mean."

She's going to tell me now, Marlene thought, with a certain sinking of the heart. The guy's having an affair, the oldest boy's on drugs, something. Marlene's husband said that Marlene could take a stroll down Grand Street and before she'd gone two blocks, forty-three women in trouble would have leaped from doors and windows into her path. She knew the signs, anyway, a pinched look, the eyes drifting, the speech a little too positive. This one was on a tight rein, kept it in mostly, would probably come to regret this impromptu, overly casual intimacy with a stranger.

But at that moment, the kids came running up with demands to be fed, and consulting Marlene's watch, the women realized what irresponsible sluts they had been, for it was past six, and Lizzie, although slathered with enough sunscreen to render harmless a smallish nuclear device, had developed a burn around the edges of her suit. So they packed up, pulled on shorts and tops, and walked through the dunes to the sandy blacktop road. A red, late-model Dodge pickup was parked on the shoulder.

"We walk from here. We're just down the road," Rose said, pointing.

"Get in," said Marlene. "We'll drop you off."

Rose objected that it wasn't necessary, but Giancarlo had already let the tailgate fall and was helping Lizzie up into the truck bed.

"Let's go for pizza, Mom," he said.

"Another time," said Marlene.

"That means yes," he said to Lizzie, and started to chant, "Pizza pizza pizza," jumping up and down and making the truck rock on its springs.

"I can't imagine what's got into him," said Marlene to Rose with feigned innocence. "He's usually *so* well-behaved." To her son she said, "What about Zak? He's probably starving, too. And we're all too covered in sand to sit in a restaurant. I want to take a shower and I'm sure Mrs. Heeney does, too." Marlene was demonstrating motherly reasonableness to the civilized Rose Heeney. Had she been alone and had Giancarlo pulled a stunt like this, she would have leaped into the truck bed and tossed him out on his butt, which Giancarlo, being his mother's son, knew very well, and which was the reason he felt free to be as brazen as a pot now.

"We can pick him up," the boy protested. "And we can go to the Harbor Bar and sit at the outside tables. *Puleeeze,* Mom?"

"Oh, the dear old Harbor Bar!" said Rose. "Oh, let's! As long as you promise to pour me home and not get dangerous drunk yourself and protect my daughter's virtue and mine and leave 15 percent and floss after meals. *Puleeeze?*"

So they got into the truck and Marlene drove down the peculiarly named Second Avenue, which is what the beach road is called in that part of the North Fork, and turned at the sign that read Wingfield Farm in incised letters touched with flaking gold. It was the same sign Rose recalled, except the picture of the Holstein had been replaced by a laminated photo of a black mastiff, and where it had said Registered Holsteins, it now said:

AKC Registered Neapolitan Mastiffs
Guard Dogs Trained in the Kohler Method

They drove past it down a rutted, grass-grown path, through a thick stand of low pines, and into a large yard, shaded by a huge, dark persimmon tree and a row of ragged lilacs. At the head of the yard was a large clapboard house with a brick-colored tin roof and a screened porch. Its white paint was peeling and gray with age. A rambling rose with new flowers grew untidily up one side of the house and onto the roof. Just visible behind the house was the top of a barn, from which came the sound of mad barking. Rose cried, "Oh, it looks just the same! We used to come here for fresh butter and eggs. I haven't been here in years."

Marlene got out and went to the front door. The mastiff Gog was there; he whined and greeted her in the manner of his kind by shoving his wet nose into her crotch and drooling on her foot. She let him slip by her and shouted into the house for her son. Silence. She went through the house into the kitchen, once again reminding herself that she absolutely *had* to get rid of that flowered linoleum and the pink paint job, and went out the back to the barn. The dogs in their kennels set up a racket, and she calmed them and greeted them by name—Malo, Jeb, Gringo, all young dogs in training, and Magog, the brood bitch. Magog was lying on her side, looking dazed as five newborns tugged at her teats. "How are you baby?" Marlene asked tenderly, and allowed the animal to lick her hand. "I know *just* how you feel."

Behind the barn, she saw that the yellow backhoe was still there, although deserted, together with the flatbed truck it had come on. She inspected the trench that ran from the concrete pumphouse halfway to the barn and saw, with dismay, that the project had been stopped by an enormous boulder squatting in its depths like a petrified rhino. She shouted out for Zak and made a perfunctory check of the other buildings—a long, swaybacked, decayed chicken coop and a dusty greenhouse—and was not surprised to find them empty of all but the lower forms of life.

Back at the truck, she saw that Gog was on his hind legs at the passenger-side window, trying to get at Rose, who had rolled up the window; her face was nearly obscured by the dog slime on the glass. Marlene called him off and dropped the truck's tailgate. The dog leaped in, amid shrieks from Lizzie and giggles from the boy.

"That dog!" said Rose. She looked a little pale.

"He's perfectly harmless," said Marlene. "Mastiffs produce more saliva than any other living creature, and being naturally generous animals, they like to share it with us drool-deprived organisms."

Rose giggled. "You're something else. I swear, I feel like I've joined the circus today, our little lonely existence transformed. Where's your other boy, by the way?"

"I have no idea, but my guess would be alien abduction."

"You're not worried?"

"Oh, no. They almost always bring them back after they've implanted the spores."

"Seriously . . ."

"Seriously? He's undoubtedly with Billy Ireland, my trainer, probably at a hardware store looking at flanges or valves and having the time of his life."

Holden was little more than a half mile from the farm, a wide place on Second comprising a gas station, a grocery and general store, a miniature marina with a boat-livery/bait-'n'-tackle appendage, three motels, one with a coffee shop attached, four houses (summering as bed-and-breakfasts), and the Harbor Bar. Stuck on the narrowest point of the North Fork, Holden offered access to both the Sound and Southold Bay. It looked like old Long Island, the sort of tiny beach town that had long vanished on the South Shore or farther west; people in Holden still pronounced *Montauk* with the accent on the second syllable.

The Harbor Bar was a low, green-roofed white building with beer signs in the windows, backed right up to the water, with a weathered deck built out on pilings trimming it on one side and at the rear. White tin tables with beer-company umbrellas flying from them were set out on the latter, each accompanied by an odd assortment of chairs.

"'For men must work, and women must weep,'" Rose intoned as they followed the trotting children down the deck, "'and there's little to earn and many to keep, though the harbor bar be moaning.' My dad used to say that whenever we came here. He claimed it referred to the drunks at the bar. God! Maybe they're all still there, still moaning."

The children ran to a table and the women followed. The place was nearly full with an early-dinner crowd, mostly sun-reddened tourists on their way back from Shelter Island or Orient Point. One table, however (its top nearly covered with empty beer bottles), was filled with locals— two dark, tanned thirtyish men, one burly and tattooed and balding, the other ponytailed, both in cutoff jeans, muddy work boots, and wife-beater shirts, plus an older man, slim, well-knit, blue-eyed, florid, with a fine dust of graying gold on his head, and next to him, a very dirty little boy with a white hard-hat flopping on his head. The blond man caught sight of their group and nodded, smiling, at Marlene, a deep nod, nearly a bow, but nothing mocking about it. The boy saw her, too, and Marlene was not surprised to see appear on his face an expression far from that which ought to blossom on the face of a lad observing his beloved mom, but something much more like dismay. Marlene ignored him and sat down. The children did the same, immediately grabbing the crayons and starting the paper games thoughtfully provided on the place mats.

"The prodigal son is getting his bag on after a hard day's work," Marlene remarked, and, following Rose's look over at the other tables, added, "The Damico brothers, Gary and Phil, general contractors, and Billy Ireland. I think I'll just leave the four of them alone. They look too crude for the likes of us."

"They would be the Shelley Society in McCullensburg," said Rose.

Marlene picked up a little card stuck to the chrome stand that held packets of sweetener. "Gosh, anchovies and artichokes is the special pizza and they're doing crabcakes, by which I can tell it's Friday." She waved to flag down a waitress. "I'm sorry to say we can't get shit-faced. I have to pick up my husband at eight oh seven."

"I bet he's not crude," said Rose.

"Oh, he has his crude moments. But generally he's the Shelley Society compared to me."

"Your trainer is staring at you. Not necessarily an employee-employer look, if I may say so."

"Yes, well, that's partly why I keep him around," said Marlene. "And he's terrific with the dogs."

2

MARLENE SAT ON A WOODEN BENCH OUTSIDE THE LITTLE SOUTHOLD railroad station and stroked her dog's velvety ears as she waited for her husband's train to appear. Marlene was a Romantic, like many people who were highly religious in youth and are no longer so, and all Romantics love trains, even cheesy commuter trains. Although she knew her husband as well as she knew herself (better, if truth be told), she still wished for him to be ever a dark stranger. So, waiting in the gathering dusk, and nearly alone on the platform, she amused herself by striking different poses before her reflection in the glass of a trade-school advertisement while entertaining fantastic thoughts.

Such as getting on this train and staying on it to the end of the line and then back to the City, and staying on trains and getting off in strange cities, and staying in hotels, always second-class hotels near the station, and then boarding another train for another city, and living an anonymous life, and dying, finally, on the Orient Express. Marlene loved her family, of course, and the main attraction of this fantasy was that it would remove them all from the sphere of danger and catastrophe that she felt she dragged around with her. She had been lucky so far, but she understood that good luck builds up like an electrical charge and that at a certain point it sparks over into the bad kind. Although she now tried hard to be good, she believed that the pattern of her life almost demanded this result: that when confronted with certain kinds of situations—arrant injustice, for example, or certain forms of cruelty—she would make decisions and take actions leading to violence. She had personally killed three people and caused the death of several others, and while she hoped that this aspect of her life was over, she had no real confidence in a permanent escape.

She shook herself like her dog to put these thoughts aside and turned her attention to her business, humdrum thinking about accounts and vet fees and three-inch galvanized pipe and diesel pumps. She wished, really, that she were a struggling businesswoman supporting her children by honest labor and frugal housekeeping, but this was not the case. The kennel and training operation was a tax dodge. Marlene had made a great deal of money in the way that such money was often made in the midnineties, by being in the right place at the right time. She had been a partner in a security firm that had grown rapidly and gone public, and which had profited vastly from a spectacular rescue of a kidnapped client on the eve of its initial public offering. The stock went up and up, on its merits and on the publicity, and later as a refuge for the smart money when the dotcoms tanked. Marlene had, however, discovered that the spectacular rescue was a scam, although the people killed in it had been real enough, and had demanded a buyout, to which her partners reluctantly acquiesced. She assuaged her Godzilla of a conscience by giving almost all the money to the Church, stashed in a religious foundation. A Jesuit named Michael Dugan ran it for her, as Billy Ireland ran the dog farm. So she could slip away without anyone really noticing she was gone. The twins had each other, Karp had his work, Lucy had her fifty-seven languages. They would all sit down to dinner and wonder why there was no food. No, that was unfair to Lucy; she could cook as well as Marlene herself.

Idiot thoughts. Demonic ravings. She was a little crazy, too, tried to keep it under control, mostly a success, except when she drank. She shook herself again, and this time the dog took this as a cue to shake, too. Unlike his mistress, he sent long streamers of white drool in every direction. She stared at her reflection and made gargoyle faces, crossing her eyes. She could really cross them now that she had been fitted with the latest high-tech socket for the left one, which was fake. Now they tracked together, instead of, as before, the fugazy staring out motionless like the orb of a dead mackerel. Most people no longer thought she looked odd, which said something about the perceptions of most people.

She checked her watch, arose, and looked down the track, into the reddening west. Tiny twin balls of light hovered above the rails out at the limits of vision. It was rather nice having a little summer vacation from being married, she thought. Karp came only on the weekends, so it was almost like college dating again, except you knew the guy wouldn't be a complete asshole, assuming one's husband was not one and you still loved him. Hers was not, by and large, and she did, by and large, although she was not adverse to having an attractive stranger around on the weekdays. Not that she would ever *do* anything, knowing herself to be the kind of woman who, once unfaithful, would bring her whole life crashing down and end up penniless and drunk in a trailer park in Tempe, Arizona.

She sat down on the bench again. The dog hadn't moved, since she had down-stayed him and hadn't spoken the release. The dog would have stayed there had a butcher's cart overturned before him and strewn the platform with prime rib. Billy Ireland was a hell of a trainer. She smiled and cooed at the dog, who wagged his tail, but still didn't budge. The train pulled in and a woman and two men got off. One of these, very tall and broad-shouldered, carrying a canvas overnight bag, and dressed in a beautifully cut tropical-weight blue pinstripe, was her husband, Roger Karp, universally known as Butch. She watched him look up and down the platform. He saw her coming toward him with the huge dog at her heels, and she observed, first, how tired he seemed, his face gray and heavy with the City, and then how it lit up when he saw her. Oh, good! They embraced and kissed, not just a suburban-wife-at-station peck, but a real kiss with plenty of chewing, like teenagers. It was always something of a surprise to both of them that they were still interested although they had been married since the Carter administration.

They walked arm in arm to the truck. "So how was the week that was?" she asked.

"Don't ask." He settled himself in the passenger seat and waited as she let the dog into the back and got in behind the wheel.

"You look tired."

"You look great. You're tan. You've been lounging on the beach."

"Uh-huh. I met our neighbor there this afternoon. She's got a little girl the twins' age."

"Our neighbor? That old couple?"

"No, on the other side. In the big white house."

"I thought that was empty."

"Me, too, but she's opening it up. They're going to sell it. Her dad kicked off and there's some kind of inheritance tangle. I got her drunk and pried out her secrets. They're a fine old Long Island family fallen on hard times. A nice woman, though—Rose Wickham Heeney."

"Heeney?"

"Yeah, it doesn't go with the other names. Apparently she married a working stiff from Appalachia, which didn't fly too great with the folks."

"So you have a basis."

She gave him a sharp look. Karp's family was a sore point. "Yes, and not only that, there's something worrying her. She'll be talking away and then kind of freeze and look around for the kid, a little panic reaction."

"Well, you know how to pick 'em."

"I'm not getting involved. Meanwhile she's someone to talk to, and the little girl's a doll. GC is smitten."

"How are they?"

"Thriving. Zak has his rat gun and Billy to tag around after, Gianni is building sand castles of ever greater extent and complexity and he's farming up a storm. They stay out of each other's hair."

"And your felon?"

"My felon is fine, and I wish you wouldn't call him that. He did his jolt and he's a citizen now."

"Aren't there any *girl* dog trainers?"

"Women. Of course, but I haven't found anyone as good as Billy Ireland." She slowed the truck for the turn off Route 25. The sun had sunk at last into Queens and the world had turned pearly blue. She switched on the truck's lights. "You're just jealous. You think we're doing it on the kibble sacks."

"Are you?"

"Not on the kibble sacks. And again she asks, changing the subject, how was *your* week, darling?"

"Hot. It was over ninety all week and it's only June."

"I mean work."

A cloud came over his face. "Fine. The usual." Which meant, not fine. Unusually awful.

But he greeted the boys cheerfully enough when they ran out to mob him, and he seemed more relaxed, later, at the table, dressed in worn jeans and a T-shirt. The twins filled him in on the week's events, including a detailed description by Zak of the backhoe operation and of each of the four rats he had stalked and killed, and from Giancarlo, a long summary of the rules of a swords-and-sorcery fantasy game he had invented, and a crop report, corn and carrots, tomatoes, potatoes, lettuce. She noted, however, that Karp drank two beers, as much alcohol as she had seen him consume at one sitting, and that, try as he might, his attention was drifting.

"Zik has a girlfriend," announced Zak when they were clearing the table.

"I do not!"

"Yes, he does. She has red hair. He *loves* her." A snarling chase through the house, which Karp broke up by grabbing each boy under an arm and dragging them out to the porch, where he plopped the three of them down on the rusty glider.

"It's true," Zak insisted.

"Is it true, Giancarlo?"

"No. I have a friend and she's a girl, but she's not a girlfriend. I'm too young to have a girlfriend."

"I see. When had you planned to start?"

"When I'm sexually mature, Dad," said Giancarlo, which reduced his brother to choking giggles.

After this had subsided, Zak said, "Billy Ireland taught me how to drive the truck. I can put it in second."

"Really? Does your mom know about this?"

"Oh, you know—Mom knows everything."

Later, when the boys were in bed, Karp sat on this same glider with his wife, who was drinking Rémy out of a juice glass. The night was humid and warm, but there was a comfortable salt breeze from the Sound. Crickets sawed away in the surrounding trees, invisible in the country dark, real darkness, which Karp always found disconcerting after the City's perpetual glow. They had turned off the lights in the house. Then a light appeared from the small window under the barn's eaves. It came from the small apartment occupied by the dog trainer.

Which reminded Karp. "What's this I hear about Ireland letting Zak drive the truck?"

"Oh, it's just on the property. He's thrilled about it. You know how he is."

"It's still dangerous."

Marlene shifted to look directly at him. "No, it's not, and you don't really think so, either. You're pissed off about something at work and you are about to start a wrangle to get your ya-ya's off at me."

"I'm not."

"Everything's perfect at the office?"

"Yeah, it's fine."

"Oh, bullshit!"

"Marlene, forget it. I'm just tired."

"What are you tired about? I thought you conquered crime up there. You're not a kid ADA running around Centre Street with fifty open cases. You have a nice office, a glamorous secretary, minions at your beck and call . . ."

"Marlene, be serious. I'm chief assistant district attorney of New York County. There are a lot of pressures . . ."

"Like what?"

"Nothing." Long pause. A release of breath. "Jack's calling me off the congressman."

Marlene raised her eyes to heaven and her palms upward. "Thank you!" And to him: "Why do I always have to worm it out of you?"

"Because it's *my* problem, okay? Why should I bring that shit home?"

"It's *not* your problem. It's *our* problem, because when you're pissed off at that fucking office, you snarl, and pick nits, and get on everyone's nerves. My nerves, to tell the truth. The boys are so glad to see you, you could whip them with coat hangers and they wouldn't mind. So give! What's with the congressman?"

Karp cleared his throat. His childhood memory did not recall a single scene in which his father had talked business with his mother, and despite the years he had lived with Marlene the process remained uncomfortable, unnatural.

"Well, you'll recall we had that election last year, and I think that's what's behind this. McBright got 48.6 percent of the vote against Jack, including nearly 80 percent of the nonwhite vote. The congressman campaigned very hard for McBright."

"Being a black guy himself."

"That is a racist comment and unworthy of you," said Karp primly.

"I'm sure the congressman thought he was the better man for the job. However, that's the fact. Given the demographics of the City, in the future it will be very hard to win office in New York County conceding 80 percent of the nonwhite vote. Are you sure you want to hear this?"

"I'm riveted and would be even more so if you would tickle my head."

Karp started to massage his wife's scalp and continued. "Okay, this started with looking at dirty money uptown. The congressman naturally has a campaign fund. Many uptown notables and businesses contribute to this fund. Among the biggest contributors is a firm called Lenox Entertainment Enterprises. They own clubs and restaurants and movie houses, uptown mainly but also all over the City. The firm makes a corporate contribution, as do a large number of its employees, up to the personal max. This is hard money, by the way, right into the congressman's coffers. You wouldn't think that a guy who cleaned up a movie house after the show could afford to drop a grand on a political campaign, but it is so. And not just one, either."

"That's America, God bless her!" said Marlene. "Lower, please."

"Okay, shady campaign funding . . . not our problem, really. But it turns out that one of the partners in Lenox is a person named Waylin Pennant, aka Beemer Pennant. Or Pimp Pennant, as we like to call him. Who is definitely our problem. This campaign stuff is what tickled our interest, in fact."

"Gosh, Butch, if pimps can't give money to politicians, they'll have to shut down K Street. Or Texas."

"True, it's Mr. Pennant's right to support the candidate of his choice with money beaten out of whores. Pennant, by the way, is not just your average street Mac. He seems to have industrialized the process, like the Mob did back in the old days. Basically, he doesn't run girls himself— pimps pay him for territories, and he probably gets a rake-off out of most of the fleshly commerce in the City. And he does the usual loan-sharking and so on. No drugs, though. He's a smart cookie."

"Yes, I would stick to fleshly commerce myself, were I to go bad."

"Badder than you currently are, you mean."

"Yes. Were you thinking of taking me up to bed?"

"In a minute," said Karp. "You asked for this and you're going to get it. To resume. Beemer is a major bad guy. We've had some killings we like him for, not directly thus far, but people he had beefs with have tended to end up dead more than pure probability would allow. His vics aren't taxpayers, of course, but my position is, it's bad for our image if guys get to commit murder with impunity. It's against the law."

"I love it when you say that. It makes little shivers run up and down my thighs."

"Ditto," said Karp. "Now, we don't have much hope of nailing Pennant for the heavy stuff, but we figured he might be vulnerable to an Al Capone move. We assume he's laundering his dirty money through Lenox, so we look. We subpoena their books and . . . surprise, surprise. Lenox is not all that profitable, although it's extemely generous to its employees in the form of bonuses. Pennant is drawing only a modest salary from Lenox, not nearly enough to support his lifestyle. And he pays his taxes on it to the penny. So if pimp money goes into Lenox, it doesn't seem to come out, or at least not into Pennant's wallet."

Marlene finished her drink, slipped down, and rested her head on Karp's lap. He was now able to use both hands on her head and did. She sighed and closed her eyes.

"I'm putting you to sleep with this, right?"

"Oh, not at all. This is divine: head rub and complex criminal procedure. I'm in heaven. Go on—so how does he launder his pimp money if not through Lenox?"

"Okay, so we're looking hard at young Beemer, his associates, their businesses, et cetera, and we find Danila Wilson. Ms. Wilson is very close to Pennant; you might say she's an intimate associate of his. She owns and operates a publicity agency, Wilson, Lowery, Jones."

"A front?"

"Not at all. A legitimate agency, that does legitimate publicity. They have rap stars, and straight businesses, and artists. This is a high-class operation. But a nice chunk of their business, it turns out, is managing the congressman's public image and his campaigns. They print up the posters and do the TV commercials. And it's kind of funny because even though the congressman is in his twelfth term and regularly wins by thirty-point margins, he pays them a very large amount of money. Inordinate, you might even say."

"Like how much?"

"Oh, for this campaign, four point three mil."

"Got it," said Marlene. "The pimp money goes in as fake contributions from Pennant's smurfs and comes back out to him as overpayments to his girlfriend's company."

"You're really smart, Marlene. Do you think it has anything to do with me massaging your head all these years?"

"Maybe, maybe not, but I think it would be prudent to keep doing it. I'm thinking a state case is going to be hard to make."

"Yes, that was Jack's point. Obviously, the way you handle something like this is you grab up the little guys, hit them with a blizzard of charges. We'd go with first-degree falsifying business records, because of the intent to conceal another felony, which in this case would be the pimping operations, and, of course, the 470.10 money-laundering second degree, nice felonies, and we'd hope that they'd deal, roll the big guys, right up to Pennant and Wilson, and Soames."

"Who is . . . ?"

"Sorry, Alonzo P. Soames, Soapy Soames—our congressman's campaign manager and main guy uptown. He actually writes the checks to Wilson and would obviously know the whole story."

"But . . . ?"

"We have some likely little guys, people making just over min wage, who got five-figure bonuses, and paid it all into the campaign war chest. Phony on the face of it, and enough to warrant a search of the relevant paper—the campaign records, and Wilson's, but I've been told that's a no-no. In writing. Basically Jack doesn't want to go up against that crowd right now. He thinks it would look like a vendetta against the people who supported his opponent. Especially with Ku Klux Karp as the lead agitator."

"They're still calling you that?"

"Not to my face, but it's well-known I'm this big racist," said Karp bitterly. "Jack adverts to it often in his subtle way. My own theory is that he wants me around mainly to keep the white vote in his pocket, one of the little ironies of my life. It goes to show you, once you're blackened, so to speak, in New York politics, that's all she wrote."

"So why don't you quit?"

"Marlene, don't start that again . . ."

She sat up abruptly and looked him in the face. "No, really. It's not like we need the money."

"What would I do? Conduct a practice devoted to defending us against dog-bite lawsuits?"

"That would be more fun than what you're doing now, although my dogs only bite people who deserve it. Besides, *I'm* a lawyer."

"You could've fooled me."

"Oh, don't get all spiky, again, for God's sake. We were just beginning to be cozy." She laid herself back again on his lap. "Okay, so then what are you going to do?"

"I don't know. Wait for something to turn up that Jack will have to move on. Leak to the press. Bluff. The usual, what I've been reduced to."

"What we should do is put the twins in boarding school and head for Europe."

He ignored this. "What irks me is that he really doesn't give a shit one way or the other about Pennant and the congressman. What he really wants is for me to admit that it's okay to screw around with cases for political advantage."

"So admit it," said Marlene sensibly. "It's true, isn't it?"

"Let's go to bed."

After a pause, she said, "Yes, let's. I assume you'll want to bother me with your disgusting lusts, as usual."

"Not at all. I got a very satisfying blow job from Big Albertine the transvestite on my way to Penn Station. I'm quite depleted."

"We'll see about that."

Karp was awakened just after dawn the next morning by gunfire. *Bang.* He jumped wildly out of bed. *Bang bang.*

And thumped his head against the narrow, sloping ceiling. Cursing and crouching, he went to the window, raised the roller shade, and peered down at the farmyard below, which was rose-gray and long-shadowed in the early light. He saw in extreme foreshortening a wiry, yellow-haired man in a white T-shirt and jeans: Ireland, the trainer. One of the mastiffs stood by his left side. The dog was wearing a training harness and a long lead. Ireland led the dog slowly toward the chicken house. As they reached about ten feet from it, its door flung open violently and a man Karp had never seen before leaped out. He was big, unshaven, wore a dirty raincoat and a black cowboy hat, and had a small black pistol in his hand. He yelled something incomprehensible and fired two shots into the air. The mastiff barked and heaved against the lead as the man vanished back into the building. Ireland said something to the dog and walked away with it. A minute later the man came out of the chicken house carrying his hat and coat. Karp saw Marlene come into view and walk off with him. Some kind of dog test, Karp imagined. He knew nothing about dog training and had no interest in learning anything about it. He thought the dog farm a dubious enterprise, rich in possibilities for torts and tax trouble.

He showered and dressed in cutoffs and an old, faded Hawaiian shirt, a member of a large collection he owned, as it was the family joke to give him one every birthday. This one showed big, tan pineapples and green palm fronds against black. He went down to the kitchen, where he found coffee in the Braun and a box of doughnuts open on the table, together with the *Times*. Karp poured, selected a cinnamon, and sat down to peruse. The house was quiet except for the thudding of the elderly refrigerator. From outside he could hear faint sounds of barking, a boy's call, the distant rumble of a large engine.

The back screen door popped open and the unshaven man came in. He stopped short when he saw Karp.

"Oh, sorry. I didn't know anyone was here. Marlene said I could get some coffee and . . . "

"Help yourself," said Karp. The man did, and Karp was not pleased to see that he intended to take his coffee break at the table. He was a younger man than Karp had first thought, midtwenties at most, big and athletic, with a round face that the stubble made look older. After a short silence, Karp said, "And you are . . . ?"

"Oh, sorry!" The man wiped powdered sugar off his hand and stuck it out. "Alex Russell. I'm the agitator."

"Excuse me?"

"The agitator. One of them."

"I caught your act from the window, with the pistol."

"Oh, yeah. That's the first test. If they won't stand up to an attack like that, you can forget training. Some of them pee and whine—I mean rotties, big Dobes. It's pathetic, really. But all of your dogs so far came through great."

"They're her dogs," said Karp in an undertone, and picked up his paper again in a way that suggested an end to the conversation. But

Russell, sensing the void in the dog-training part of Karp's brain, and wishing to fill it, resumed. "Yeah, I never worked with mastiffs before. Great dogs. Billy's a great trainer, too, but I'll tell you, and you can ask anybody in the business, the agitator makes the dog. You mess up, you don't drop the sleeve just right, you're a little too aggressive with a beginner, you're a little too slack with a varminty dog, hell, you can totally throw him off. It's all in the timing. And the acting. I mean, you got to act like a slimeball, you know? I mean really feel like you're up to bad shit. The dogs can tell if you're not sincere. Hi, Marjorie."

Karp looked up as the screen door banged open again. A pretty woman of about thirty with a big mop of dark curls walked directly to the coffeemaker and poured herself a cup. She sat down in an empty chair and poured in cream and sugar. "That Jeb is a handful," she said.

Russell said, "I know it. I got bruises up and down my arm."

The woman seemed to notice Karp for the first time. "You're the husband."

"I am. Who are you?"

"Marjorie Rolfe."

"Don't tell me. You're an agitator, too."

"You can tell, huh?"

"Uh-huh. My first clue was that you're wearing quilted bib overalls made out of leather. Unless that's a fashion statement."

"Oh, no," she said straight-faced, "that's part of the gear. The dogs are trained to go for the arm. We got sleeves, you know, to protect the arm. But some of them get excited, especially if you're down and they could bite you someplace else. See, that's why we have to wear these scratch pants."

"I think I'm following you," said Karp, putting down his paper. "So this is how you guys make a living, as dog agitators?"

They both laughed. Karp saw that the woman had a canine tooth missing. "Heck, no," said Russell. "I mean we get paid good money by the hour, but it ain't no living. No, I work down at the Safeway. Marjorie's a groomer."

"And, what? You answered an ad?"

"Oh, no," said Marjorie cheerfully. "We know Billy from the NA at St. Malachy's. We're all three junkies together. Recovering junkies."

The other two started talking about dogs and cars and the various afflictions that arose in the marginal life, and Karp finished his *Times* browse and his coffee and went outside. The sun was up over the barn now and already warming the air. Karp had been out to the dog farm a number of times since Marlene had purchased it, but never before when dog training was going full blast. He had always wanted a summer place on the Island; they had spoken of it often when they had both been struggling ADAs, but Karp had imagined a little cottage in Quogue, not this sprawling, crumbling spread at the end of the North Fork. Nor the felon, nor the huge dogs, nor the junkies in the kitchen, either. On the other hand, if you were married to Marlene Ciampi, you had to expect a little louche in your life. Marlene was not a Quogue-cottage person.

On the other other hand, this feeling was real, the one he had nearly all the time, of things out of control, of impending disaster, of entering the scratchy borderlands of the crazy country, and it was not good, he did not want to live the rest of his life feeling this way. If work had been going well—that was another thing, that remark about how he should quit and do something else. Guys worked and supported their families, they did an honest day's work and took what shit they had to and put something away to send the kids to college and to retire on, that was what guys were for. It had never occurred to Karp that he would be in a situation where no sacrifice would be necessary. He had made a bundle once himself, working as a private litigator, but he had not liked it much, suing faceless enterprises or defending them. What was the point? Whereas when you stood up for the People, there was something real behind it. Or not, as it seemed recently. And now he could no longer see himself as a . . . *martyr* was too strong, he would never have said that, although he was in fact the kind of man who would take a bullet for a short list of causes, his family one, his friends, and a certain vision of what the law was meant to be, a vision that apparently was not broadly shared in his profession, and hardly at all within his own office. It was not like it was on the TV. So why get out of bed and go to work? To feed the kids to keep the wolf from the door. But the kids had trusts now, the college taken care of, the little nest egg afterward, and the wolf was . . .

Circular thoughts, sliding into obsession. He told himself to stop it. It was the weekend, take a break, Butch. Take the kids to the beach. Lie down and hang out. He had one of those fat fact-filled history books he read for pleasure, no beach thrillers for Karp, no, usually something like

Norwich on Byzantium, or the rise of the Dutch Republic, or McPherson or Page Smith. Okay: book, beach, relax. Round up the gang, then.

He went into the barn, which was large, sagging, plank-built, painted crumbling white, and still smelled faintly of hay and its former tenants, with an added topnote of kibble and dog. It had a loft at one end, and at the other a flight of stairs leading to the trainer's apartment. Karp inspected the nursing Magog and her puppies. The bitch lifted her great head and gave him, the stranger, an unfriendly look and a coughing growl. Backing away, he heard a rustle from above and then a loud pop, followed by a cry from a boyish throat: "Got you!"

"Hello, who's up there?"

"Dad, I got another one!" In a moment Zak appeared at the edge of the loft high above, grinning and dangling a huge, dead rat by the tail. Karp took a step back to avoid a falling drop of rat gore.

"Do you want to go to the beach?"

"Maybe later. I want to hunt some more. This place is crawling with them." Zak dropped the dead animal, which fell with an unpleasant sound at Karp's feet.

"Do you have the safety on that thing?"

"It's automatic, Dad," said Zak, with a touch of patronage. "It goes on when you cock it." Zak placed the butt of the rifle against his knee and heaved the barrel down, then up with a smart click. He struck a Hemingway pose and pointed to the red tab sticking up from the foot of the breech. "See?"

Yet another thing to place in the worry file. The weapon was not, as Karp had once thought, a BB gun, but a Diana 34, a precision German weapon that could propel a .17-caliber pellet at a thousand feet per second and blow the brains out of a rat. Or child. The crazy wife had bought it for Zak's last birthday, and he loved it more than life.

"Well, just be careful," said Karp, and left the barn. He proceeded around the barn, where he found Marlene in consultation with a couple of contractors. Marlene gave him a friendly squeeze, but continued with her conversation, which was technical, boring, and presaged enormous expense.

After a few minutes of staring at the large rock that blocked the trench, he asked, "Where's Giancarlo?"

"In his garden."

Karp himself had never gardened, and as far as he knew, Marlene's vegetable expertise was limited to windowsill herbs and houseplants, but Giancarlo had decided to grow veggies on what seemed to his father an absurdly large scale. He had studied books on the subject and arranged for the rental of a rototiller and talked his brother into helping him break the soil for it. Then he had laid the garden out with mathematical precision, using stakes and strings, and had planted and watered and fertilized and weeded. Now the taut strings were nearly obscured by young growth. Karp had no idea what any of it was, although he thought he recognized young corn. They showed it a lot in the movies.

Giancarlo was in the field with a hoe. He was wearing bib overalls over bare skin, and on his head was a ragged straw hat, once Marlene's. When he saw Karp standing by the wire fence, he stopped, pulled off his hat, wiped his brow theatrically, looked up at the heavens, and said, "Paw, if it don't rain soon, we gonna lose the farm."

"Yes," said Karp, "we'll have to move to the city and live in miserable tenements, but someday your grandchildren will go to college. What're you doing?"

"Hoein'."

"I see you are. Why exactly does one hoe?"

"To rip out the weeds. You can use herbicides, too, but I don't like them. I like hoeing. It's hard work but it's also really like restful. You want to try it?"

"Sure, if you think I can."

"Well, I don't know, Dad, it's totally tricky." The boy grabbed up another hoe from a collection of tools lying by the fence. "You see, the metal part here, that goes down in the dirt, and the wood part, you hold in your hands."

"Met-al? Down?"

Giancarlo giggled. "Sorry, I guess I was going too fast for you there. See, you kind of chop down and then up and pull the weed out roots and all. You have to make sure you rotate your hips and always keep your eye on the weed. Follow *through* the weed." He demonstrated.

"Got it. Point me at some weeds."

It *was* restful, Karp found. After half an hour he had taken off his shirt and tied a bandanna around his head and was going down the row of feathery plants with a will, making the dirt fly. At first, his mind was

full of the office, and he took out his several frustrations on the dande-
lions and plantains. Later on, however, these thoughts faded, and he
became interested in the hoeing itself, how to lift the weed with a minimum of effort, how to keep a gentle rhythm going. At this stage it was
very much like shooting baskets, he was thinking, and he briefly speculated that athletic prowess largely depended on the constant repetition
of acts that were essentially as boring as pigshit. Both of the boys were
reasonable athletes, but neither was as yet outstanding. They didn't
seem impelled to practice in the way he had. Still, it was early for them.
He had not pushed them at all yet. Should he? He hated the men he had
observed who lived their athletic dreams out through their kids, and
though his own athletic dreams had been more or less blasted, he had
firmly resolved not to do this to them. He had himself been a high school
all-American and a standout in college until he had screwed up his knee.
The knee was an artificial one now, an emptiness there that worked well
enough when it worked, as now. Gradually even these thoughts faded,
replaced by mere sensation: the beat of the sun on his back, the shock of
impact in his hands, and the dull burning of friction where he gripped
the handle. Mindless work; what he needed.

After an unknowable interval, he stopped to stretch and saw that his
wife was standing by the fence, staring at him in wonder.

"I never thought I'd see the day."

"Bring me little water, Sylvie," sang Karp.

"How did he talk you into it?"

"He promised me a quarter of the crop and a peck o' salt. I thought
it was a pretty good deal."

"But now you're ready to go to the beach and have a picnic, which
your wife has lovingly prepared, despite the urgencies of running a vast
and complex enterprise. You look remarkably sexy as a peasant, by the
way."

"Mistress *like* Ivan?" said Karp, throwing down his hoe and advanc-
ing on her all sweaty and filthy, and she shrieked and they had a little
chase around the garden, while Giancarlo looked on with benign interest, like a faun.

At the beach, they found Rose Heeney and her daughter, and
Marlene set up her blanket and establishment adjoining and made the
introductions. The boys and Karp ran off to splash around. Marlene

looked sympathetically at Lizzie, who was making a good show of pretending that she did not care and rolled her eyes at Rose. "Men!"

Rose's smile in return was weak, and her face showed more strain than it had the previous day. She said, "Lizzie, go off and play with the boys. They have a raft."

"I'd rather stay here."

"No, go. Build a castle, swim. Go ahead."

Lizzie took the hint and wandered off.

"Something wrong?" Marlene inquired.

"Oh . . . yes, as a matter of fact. Red called late last night. He came back from a meeting and found someone had shot Lady, our dog. She was dead in the yard. A big stupid mutt, loved everybody. Completely useless as a guard, of course. Dan used to say she was a reverse watchdog. She barked continuously until a burglar arrived and then she'd shut up and go lick his hand." Rose pulled her sunglasses off and stared out to the water. Marlene saw that her eyes were wet. "Stupid dog. I don't know how I'm going to tell Lizzie. She practically grew up with her."

"Do they think it was a burglar?"

"No. It was some evil son of a bitch working for Weames. Escalating the threat."

"Weames is . . . ?"

"Lester Weames. Red's running against him for the union presidency. The Union of Mining Equipment Operators. Known as UMEO. It's a small outfit, basically covers strip mine operators in three or four states, very Appalachian and totally corrupt. Weames has been in there for eighteen years, screwing the workers and staying cozy with the mine operators."

"I thought they didn't allow that anymore. I thought the feds came in . . ."

"Well, you thought wrong," said Rose bitterly. "Southern West Virginia is not really that much a part of the US of A when you come down to it. Weames keeps the coal flowing, and the coal keeps the lights turned on and the Internet humming. Yeah, there've been investigations, but he's smart. He lives modestly and he's got a gang of loyalists around him who keep him clean. On the few occasions the feds picked up something, they threw them a couple of small fry and they went back inside the Beltway feeling they did a good day's work. The bottom line is nobody much cares, except Red."

"Will he win?"

"Oh, he might get the most votes. Red's real popular among the rank and file. But whether Weames will let him actually take office is a whole other story. His guys count the ballots. It would be better for Weames, though, if Red just forgot about it. That's been suggested in very strong terms."

"Threats?"

"Expressions of displeasure, yeah. Phone calls in the middle of the night. A dead skunk in the mailbox. Tires slashed. Now, Lady . . ." Rose sighed. "That's why I'm spending the summer here with Lizzie, instead of supporting him in McCullensburg, like a good wife. When they started to get rough, I discovered I was easily distinguishable from Mother Jones." A self-deprecating laugh here, but Marlene saw it was eating at her. "He's coming up here next weekend to try to talk me into coming back with him."

"Will he succeed?"

"Oh, I guess. I don't know. It's really confusing. A life of struggle and relative deprivation, that I can deal with. Dead dogs and death threats? I don't know if I can take it. It's a whole different thing, especially with kids."

"Uh-huh, I know what you mean."

Rose looked at her sharply. "Do you?"

"Oh, my, yes indeed," said Marlene fervently.

3

DANIEL HEENEY, RUNNING LATE, TOOK THE LAST OPEN SEAT IN THE CAR.
The westbound Amtrak out of Boston's South Station was full with a
weekend crowd. As he sat, he glanced at the girl sitting across the aisle
from him in the way most young men glance at girls on public trans-
portation, in quick appraisal, and the first thing he took in were the legs.
They were long, extremely long, too long for Amtrak's mingy accommo-
dations, and she had to park a dozen inches or so of them in the aisle.
They were well shaped, too, with slender ankles and bare, all the way
from her leather sandals right up to where they vanished into baggy
khaki shorts. When people moved past in the aisle, she hiked her knees
high, presenting him with an appealing glimpse into the shadowed
higher reaches. The rest of her was not so appealing, however. Homely,
was his first take. Very short hair, nearly a buzz cut, a big nose, too. She
was wearing a black T-shirt with some kind of red design on it, and it
hung loose in front. A shame, he thought, nice legs, no tits, and that face.
He pulled a physics text and a yellow highlighter out of his pack and
began to study.

When the train stopped at Providence, he became aware of a low
muttering coming from across the aisle and he looked up from his book.
The girl had equipped herself with a set of headphones, hooked into a
tape player sitting on the tray table. The phones were not the flimsy
kind that come with tape players, but big, padded Bose jobs with a tiny
red LED glowing on the side, which indicated to his experienced eye
that they had sound-damping electronics built in. At first he thought she

was voicing the words to a song, in the annoying way some people did while using earphones, but as he observed her, it became clear that something else was going on. She had a notebook out and she was writing rapidly in it, occasionally stopping to reverse the tape and repeat a section. Her mumbles seemed to be in a foreign language. Listening to a taped lecture, he thought. And a foreign student, too, probably. The train started again and her mumbling faded against the ambient sounds of the train.

When study at last paled, his gaze moved again from his text to the girl. She had a fat volume on the tray now; it looked like a dictionary. One of her legs was thrown up over the arm of her chair, her sandal hanging loosely on her toes, moving slowly with the motion, like a plumb bob. She seemed completely at ease, oblivious to her surroundings. There was something erotic about studying her he found, like spying through a dorm window. He liked the way the armrest dug into the meat of her thigh, exposing its tender inner skin. The shorts were so baggy, he could see almost up to her crotch. His eyelids twitched with the strain of peripheral visioning.

She looked up just then and he flicked his glance back to physics, to a page of equations whose meaning he had quite forgotten. He felt stared at, and his ears reddened. A minute or so later, he got up and went to the lavatory. His face in the spotted mirror looked even less attractive to him than it usually did. Dan Heeney owned the visage of a rococo cherub: milky skin, red-rose mouth, silky golden curls, the sort of face that was entirely out of fashion in an age that preferred the dangerous, hard-bitten, stubbled look. Although he had found that a certain kind of woman doted on such a face as his, he did not dote in return upon that kind. They reminded him of his mom. He had a taste for the crazy ladies, with the piercings and the spiked hair, but by and large they did not have a taste for him.

He finished, flung open the door, and almost walked right into her. She looked him full in the eye for an instant, made a polite noise, moved past and through to the next car. In the brief encounter, he had time to notice that the geometry of her face changed when seen full on, its strong planes snapping into a configuration that might with justice be called interesting or exotic rather than homely, more like the faces of the women who get to be stars in foreign films. Her mouth was wide, with full, slightly everted lips that seemed to balance the prow of the nose. Mainly he noticed the eyes. They were the palest possible brown, with yellow lights in them, just the color of cigarette tobacco.

These observations flashed through his mind in a moment and stimulated only the faintest curiosity, and little interest. She was, after all, just a face on the train, probably going to New York or D.C., probably a foreigner. He went back to his book and to the Fitzgerald contraction, its fascinating mathematics and its cosmological implications, none of which had to do with girls on trains, unless they were traveling at speeds approaching c.

But she was not going to the City, it turned out. She got off at New London as he did and took the shuttle to the ferry dock, boarding the *Sea Jet* along with him. He took a window seat, where he watched the shining Sound bounce along for forty-five minutes, his mind occupied with the various fears and hopes attendant on a family reunion in a family with some history of discord, and recent additional stress. Still, he was oddly aware of her presence on the craft, like an itching spot on his spine just beyond reach.

When the hydrofoil docked at Orient Point, Long Island, he found himself a few feet behind her, amid the crowd of debarking passengers, moving with their luggage to cabs and other vehicles jockeying into the curb. She had a soft cloth suitcase at her feet, and a military bag hung off one thin shoulder. The design on her shirt he now saw was Chinese calligraphy. He thought, I should ask her what it means, or make something up. You will meet a redheaded stranger who will change your life. The foreignness put him off, however. What if she spoke broken English, or none at all? No, she had a Boston College button on that bag, so a student there, so she had to speak English. Him being MIT would impress a BC girl. Or maybe not, given the nerdy rep. What was a foreign girl doing at the tail of Long Island on a summer weekend? An au pair, maybe, or an exchange student. He would never know, unless she happened to drop something and he picked it up. Maybe she would take the bus to Southold, in which case he would grab a seat next to her and say something. Maybe she was European, lonely, of casual European morals, looking for love. . . .

In the meantime he stared at the legs, at the way she stood on one of them and slowly rubbed the crown of her foot against the back of her calf. He rehearsed pickup lines. Come here often? What's your major? Are you Polish? French? I couldn't help noticing your . . . I couldn't help noticing your legs. Do you think you would ever let me chew on them, like you do on a spicy Buffalo wing?

Too late. A red pickup truck had honked from across the street. In the back of the truck were two boys waving and shouting, and also an immense, black, slavering dog. Two women were in the cab. The girl waved, grabbed her bag, ran across to the driver's side, spoke briefly to the driver, and then jumped up into the bed of the truck. Which oddly enough did not move away, but honked again. He looked up. The woman in the passenger seat was calling his name and waving. To his immense surprise (together with a little jolt of pleasure, which followed soon after) he recognized his mother. He crossed the street, where he observed that his sister, Lizzie, was also sitting in the front seat. A quick kiss, a brief explanation, and he found himself in the rear of the truck, being drooled on by the dog, with his knees within inches of hers. The boys stared at him shamelessly. Twins, he noted.

"Small world," he said.

She grinned, showing small, even white teeth. "That's what they say." She stuck out her hand. "Lucy Karp. These three are Zak, Giancarlo, and Gog."

"Gog is the dog," said Giancarlo. "You can tell him from Zak because Zak doesn't drool as much." A brief flurry of friendly punches and nuggies, to which Lucy put an authoritative, physical halt.

"They know they're not supposed to do that in the truck," she said, sitting again. "Who *are* you, by the way? I saw you on the train and the ferry."

"Did you think I was following you with evil intent?"

"No. You don't look like the following kind. Or evil."

This was said in a flat tone that did not invite banter. Deflated a little, Dan introduced himself, and they spent the rest of the short trip exchanging information. After the usual school and job stuff, he asked, "What were you doing with the headphones on the train?"

"Translating. A speech by the Polish finance minister into French."

"You can translate *Polish* into French?" he asked, not keeping amazement from his tone.

"Yes, and if you think that's impressive, I can also crack my toes." She demonstrated.

"No, really . . ."

"She can speak fifty-seven languages," said Giancarlo.

"My agent," she said. "And a lie." To the boy: "How's the garden coming?"

The boy told her, at length, interrupted from time to time by interjections from his brother on the subject of suppressing vermin.

From time to time she looked at Dan, to draw him into the family chatter, but not too far. A strange bird was his thought. Clearly some kind of genius but diffident about it, used to keeping it under wraps. He wondered what the real girl was like.

"Ah, the ancestral mansion," Dan exclaimed as they pulled into the drive. It was a large, two-story, brick house, painted white long ago, with the brick underneath showing pinkly through. The paint on the green shutters was peeling off in strips, and the lawn was high and ragged. Weeds thrust up from the gravel drive.

"Your ancestors need a lawn mower," Lucy said.

"My ancestors have gone to their ancestors, leaving debts and not much else. The place is in hock. My mom has the use of it for her lifetime, if she can pay the taxes and maintenance, which she can't, so it's up for sale."

Everyone left the truck and there were more introductions. Rose Heeney led them all around the side of the house and into a huge kitchen, where she served out sodas and iced tea to all. Rose announced that her husband and her elder son were coming in that Friday, and she invited the Karps to join them in a beach cookout.

"Why not," agreed Marlene. "Butch will be here, too. You'll get to meet him."

At this juncture, Giancarlo, who had wandered out, came back in and asked, "How come you have no furniture? Are you moving in?"

"Out, I'm afraid, dear," said Rose. "We have to entertain in the kitchen like the peasantry. It's the only inhabitable room in the house besides the bedrooms." The furnishings in the remainder, she explained, had all been sold off or taken by Rose and her brothers after their parents' death. "It's terribly Dickensian, or maybe Chekhovian, I don't know which. The decay of a distinguished old family. The Wickhams settled here in 1741." She added to Marlene, "I'm sure you'll want to hear *all* about them."

"You will even if you don't," said Dan.

"That's his father talking," Rose said. "I'm not allowed to be a bourgeois oppressor of the poor even for one tiny instant."

An uncomfortable pause here, which Marlene ended with a remark about how pretty the house was, after which Rose suggested a tour. Dan said to Lucy, "I'll show you around the grounds. It's included in the package. You also get a brochure printed on recycled paper and a handy souvenir key chain."

"Keep an eye on the children," said Marlene, "and take Gog," at which Lucy made a mumbled agreement and said, "Let's go, brats!"

Lucy and Dan left the house through the empty front rooms, preceded by the three children running with the dog, their footsteps echoing loud on the hardwood. They walked across the sketchy lawn to a low stone pumphouse. The boys and Lizzie ran into it and emerged with scraps of lath, pirate swords. Dueling and shouting, they ran off toward the dunes.

"Now this pumphouse is where George Washington and John Adams planned the American Revolution," said Dan.

"Really? Gosh, it doesn't look big enough."

"Yeah, it fooled the redcoats, too. This is the place. We used to have a plaque but the birds got to it. And I believe this"—here Dan kicked at a weathered butt—"is one of the cigarettes Jefferson smoked while he was writing the Declaration. Our home is indeed rich in history."

"I'll say! Why, compared to your ancientness, my family is just off the boat. And those dunes! Why they look just like the ones Columbus landed on . . . but . . . but, that's impossible."

"No, those are the very ones," said Dan in a plummy voice. "Let's explore among them. Who knows? Maybe we can find important artifacts of white imperialist hegemony."

They went up through the line of low dunes and sat down with their backs against the warm sand. Below, the three children raced in circles with the dog. Their screaming came back in snatches on the sea wind. They goofed some more about historical obsessions, about the scene in Boston, about their school life. Lucy mentioned that she had often been at MIT.

"Taking courses?" he asked.

"Oh, right—I can barely do fractions. No, I have sort of a job with the computational linguistics people. They pay me to inspect my brain."

"You're kidding."

She had an urge to say yes. She did not want to interrupt in any way this unexpected pleasure, sitting here on the dunes with a luscious boy who did not seem afraid of her—not of her height or of her face or of her other peculiarities. Of course, he did not know about those yet. For an instant, she was aware of an intense desire to be someone else, before she said, "No, I'm not. I'm a language prodigy. My brain is a national resource."

"Like the Arctic National Wildlife Refuge?"

"Except smaller. What kind of prodigy are you?"

"Oh, you know, the usual MIT crap—grades, boards, Intel Scholarship. Except I come from West Virginia and I'm not Asian." A little bitterness here, she thought. She didn't know anything about West Virginia. Coal? Hillbillies? That song. It must not have been fun growing up a nerdy, pretty boy in a rural high school.

"So . . . are you going back to Boston?" she asked.

"I don't know. I have a job up there if I want it, you know what I mean, just computer shit, but it pays. I kind of like the idea of kicking back here for a while. I mean I've been working my butt off this year."

That was interesting, she thought: his accent was drifting from middle American to something more regional. *This yee-a. Y'know whut a mean.* He's relaxing a hair.

She said, "So? Kick back."

"Can't do it. I need the money. And if I'm not working, he's going to want me to go back home. My father." Dan looked blankly out at the Sound. "We all have to support the struggles of the working folks."

"You sound doubtful."

"Do I? I was raised in the faith, but it's hard to keep on believing in it nowadays. Or anything. I guess I still do. Have you ever been in southern West Virginia? The Kanawha? No, nobody has. Everyone uses the stuff they make there, plastics and chemicals, and all kinds of toxic shit, and we all use electricity from the coal, and we don't think about the poor bastards who have to live there and make it and breathe it in and taste it in their water every day, and dig out the coal while their houses get slowly demolished around them from the blasting. It sucks, yeah, and we ought to do something to change it. But . . ."

More interesting, she thought. The accent reverts to mid-American when he goes into speech mode, plus something else. A little roll in the *r*. Irish?

They both listened to the wind for a long moment, and the calls of the children.

"But, what I *like* to do is to hang out with smart people in Boston, and do science."

"And feel guilty," she said.

He turned to look at her, frowning, and saw from her eyes that she was not needling him, or mocking him, but just reflecting what was in his own mind. It was faintly irritating nonetheless.

"Jesus, I don't know why I'm talking like this. I just met you. You don't need to hear all this crap."

"No, we could talk about celebrities, instead." She pitched her voice up and added a slight Valley drawl. "I think Jennifer Lopez is like totally cool. Or sports. How about those Sox!"

He laughed and she joined him. She had a throaty, full-belly laugh that he found surprising in a skinny girl, but pleasant.

"Okay, deep and serious—so what do *you* believe in?"

Oh, well, Lucy thought, here it comes. All things must end.

"I'm a Catholic."

He snorted. "Yeah, right. Luckily, I was spared all that crap. I think my mom is some kind of Episcopal, but of course Dad is a devout athe-ist. He used to sing 'Pie in the Sky When You Die,' whenever we drove past a church. That's another thing that endeared our family to the McCullensburgians."

He would have chattered on in this vein, but it dawned on him that the social smile had quite faded from her face, which now bore a curious expression of resignation, a slight tightening of the jaw, as if anticipating some attack.

"Wait, you mean you're *actually* Catholic?" A little frown creased his brow. "You believe all that God and the saints sh—business? And the pope?"

"Uh-huh. It's a package."

"Wow. Why?"

She shrugged. "Why is the sky blue? I don't know. I'm just a believer. Mom says I have the God gene."

"So . . . by the whole package you mean, um, virgin birth, raising the dead? Abortion? Birth control? Lourdes?"

"Well, it's a very big package. I'm not sure the *pope* buys the whole package. But pretty much, yeah."

"But you're *smart.*"

"And you're insulting," she snapped. She got to her feet, stuck two fingers into her mouth, and produced an amazingly loud whistle. The dog leaped from the shallows and started up the beach, followed by the twins and Lizzie.

"I'm frying. I'm going to take the kids for a swim." She turned and walked away.

After a moment, he followed, attracted, as was his pattern, by rejection, although this was a new, and actually a more interesting, variety.

Karp did not have to go to jail anymore. Although it had never been a place he liked to visit in the days when he had to go a lot, he still went from time to time. Usually, he went because he thought it was good for his soul to immerse himself in the literally stinking part of the system he administered. It was particularly stinking today because it was hot, stinking with the unmistakable penetrating stench produced when large numbers of male primates are kept confined. It had been hot for several weeks and was going to get hotter according to the smiling weatherpersons on the news. Karp would not have minded if they air-conditioned the jail, but he understood that his fellow citizens did not, by and large, agree. That would be coddling criminals, a practice now many years out of fashion, and it did not help to explain that the people in the Tombs were not criminals but the accused awaiting disposition, entitled to a presumption of innocence. But not to comfort.

His visit today was more than mere responsibility. Karp was visiting a prisoner named Woodrow P. Bailey, who was in the Tombs because he had beat up his girlfriend, using in the attack a forty-ounce beer bottle and a metal chair. Serious disfigurement had resulted, which put the alleged crime into the first-degree-assault category. Karp was visiting Bailey not because of this crime but because Karp had a little list, and Bailey was on it. The list contained the names of the employees of Lenox

Entertainment who had made significant contributions to the congressman's campaign. Karp sat down in the hard chair the interview room
supplied and dabbed his face with his handkerchief. Karp was not much
of a sweat hog, but the heat and humidity in the place could have drawn
moisture from a brick. The door opened and Bailey came in, accompanied by his lawyer. Karp kept his face from showing surprise. The man
with Bailey was not some kid Legal Aid assignee, but David Douglas
Root, a criminal lawyer who specialized in high-profile cases. If you were
a hip-hop artist and you got wasted and knocked down a nun with the
Navigator, Root would be your choice.

"Well, well, Butch Karp!" cried Root affably, pumping Karp's hand.
"A little shorthanded at the DA? Or are we just keeping our pencil
sharpened?"

Karp gave him a thin smile. Root was a big, medium-brown man in
a charcoal Zegna suit, a dazzling silk shirt, and round gold-rimmed
glasses. He was sweating, too, Karp was glad to see, but not as much as
his client, whose jail-orange jumpsuit was soaked dark under the arms
and around the collar. Bailey was heavy, dark-faced, with a dull, confused look. A drinker, Karp thought. He had a towel around his neck,
with which he dabbed nervously at his dripping face.

"Christ, it's like a fucking Turkish bath in here," said Root, taking his
seat. "I'm like to lose twelve pounds. So, Butch, what do we got?"

Karp looked at Bailey, not the lawyer, and said, "Mr. Bailey, as I'm
sure your lawyer has told you, you're charged with a very serious offense.
It's what we call a class B violent felony, and if convicted, it carries a sentence of from six to twenty-five years in prison."

"I was drunk," said Bailey in a low, resentful voice.

Karp ignored this. "How the case gets handled is really up to the
district attorney's office. We have a lot of discretion. Now, sometimes
when a person helps us out with an important prosecution, we're able
to cut him some slack on his own case. Helps us with information, or
testimony."

Karp saw the prisoner's brow knit with concentration. "I don't
know . . . I mean, what kind of case?"

Karp pulled out a notebook and read off a list of contributions Bailey
had made to the congressman's reelection war chest. A thousand dollars
in August directly to the candidate, and five thousand in September to

the Harlem United Political Action Committee, an organization the congressman controlled. The same in the previous year and in the three years before that.

"Where's this going, Butch?" asked Root. "What's this got to do with the case here?"

"I'm just curious how a man who works cleaning up theaters can afford to spare six grand a year on political contributions."

"It's no crime," said Root. "Besides, since when is the DA interested in federal election law?"

"We're not. We're always interested in money laundering, though." Karp spoke again to the prisoner: "Mr. Bailey, money laundering is a crime. It's when someone gives you cash they earned at a criminal activity and you help turn it over, convert it into honest money. So I have to ask you, did someone give you money to make political contributions?"

Bailey opened his mouth, but before he could say anything, Root said, "Don't answer that!" Bailey closed his mouth and wiped his dripping face.

Karp said, "You could do yourself some real good here, Mr. Bailey. You also might want to think about whether Mr. Root here is representing your best interests or somebody else's."

Root shot to his feet. "This interview is over. Come on, Woodrow, we're out of here."

Bailey looked back and forth between the two men and then got to his feet. Root signaled for the guard and then turned to Karp. "I intend to lodge a complaint with the bar."

"Oh? Gosh, what did I do?"

Root held up his hand and counted off on stubby, tan fingers. "One, you accuse my client of a crime out of the clear blue sky without a shred of evidence. Two, you impugn his political liberties, on the theory that a workingman of color can't possibly have enough interest in politics to contribute to a campaign. Three, you use the coercive power of the state to pressure him into assisting you in a political vendetta against a distinguished political leader. A distinguished *black* political leader, which is no accident coming from you." Root turned to Bailey. "This man is a well-known racist. I don't want you ever talking to him or anybody from his office if I'm not in the room."

"I'm a big fan of Harry Belafonte," said Karp.

The guard came. The door swung open. Root said, "And don't think I won't go public with this outrage."

"Who's picking up your fee, counselor? Pennant? Soames?" Karp asked as they left, but received no answer.

They had AC in the DA's office, but it was creaky and barely competent to deal with El Niño, or whatever was turning New York into Brazzaville. Little reciprocating fans hung in the corners of the larger offices, relics of the days before air-conditioning. Karp had his turned on. He had his feet up on the desk, his coat off, his collar open, and his shirtsleeves rolled up, none of which helped very much. Across the desk from him sat a small, dapper man in a beige linen suit, jacket and all, with his collar buttoned. His name was Murrow and he was Karp's special assistant.

"That line about Harry Belafonte was probably unwise," observed Murrow when Karp had finished telling him about the Bailey interview. "You'll read about it in the papers."

"Oh, fuck the papers! Besides, I do like Harry Belafonte. I used to have all his albums."

"Albums?"

"Yes, albums. Music used to come on shellac discs that had only one song on a side, and they sold them in books that looked like photo albums, and when LPs came out, they still called them albums."

"LPs?"

"Fuck you, Murrow. Young fart."

"So what are we going to do about the congressman?"

"Well, personally, I am going to leave the office right now and catch the early bird out to the Island. The congressman will keep, and since we've conquered crime, I don't think anything important is going to come up over the weekend. In fact, I might take a day or two off."

Murrow affected gaping wonderment. "You mean . . . you mean . . . not come into the office at all? On a workday?"

"Yeah, but I'll leave the key to the front door under the mat, in case anyone wants to try a malefactor in my absence." To the astonishment of all his colleagues, he actually left.

On the train, Karp dropped his tray and set out some files, more to assuage his conscience than because he intended to do any useful work. As chief assistant DA, he had general responsibility for the professional work of the office, which amounted to insuring, to the extent possible, that the four-hundred-odd attorneys employed there did not lose too many cases through incompetence or win too many through cheating. He also had a hand in recruiting and training, which he enjoyed, and in routine administration, which he loathed.

He picked up one of the case files and read. A murder case, this one, and typical: a couple of dumb kids in their early twenties had held up a convenience store and shot the owner. It was a good case. Ten years previously they might have gone with a plea in a case like this because they were so jammed with murders, and the bad guys knew it, and the DA's office had figured it was better to be sure the villains served eight for manslaughter than go for the expense of a felony murder trial and risk an acquittal. Now, with the drop in murders, they were set to try nearly everything. The People were in the catbird seat again. Karp should have been happy.

Karp was not. He knew he was a competent enough bureaucrat; he did his job with few complaints from either high or low. But he was not a great bureaucrat. He did not love bureaucracy. A thrill did not spring in his heart when he gained a 3 percent increase in the furniture budget. Political dealing bored him. He did not like manipulation, and he positively despised attempts to manipulate him, which were constant. He took his pen and made a notation on a pad. There was a flaw in the chain of evidence affecting the murder gun, which was the chief piece of physical evidence linking the defendants to the crime. It was not a case wrecker, but it had to be looked into, and the ADA in charge had missed it. Or maybe it wasn't that important; maybe he was just a pettifogging pain in the ass, which he knew was getting to be his rep among the younger ADAs. He wrote a stiff little note to the ADA and closed the file. Screw them, let them learn to do it right! He leaned back in the seat and closed his eyes. Coaching was fine if you were a coach. But Karp wanted to play. Suppressing this thought, and the desire, for the ten thousand and somethingth time, ever the good soldier, he opened his eyes, shoved the file back into the tattered cardboard wallet he used instead of a briefcase, and pulled out another one.

✿   ✿   ✿

"What's with Lucy?" Karp asked his wife. He had not seen his daughter since the Easter break. He had been at the farm for barely an hour, most of which time he had spent with the three children. Now they were alone together in the kitchen packing things for the cookout.

"What did you notice?"

"I don't know. She's more . . . um . . ."

"Normal?"

He laughed. "Yeah, now that you mention it. Lighter, maybe. More like a college girl, less like a nun. It must be the away-from-home effect."

"It's a boy," said Marlene. "Could you grab those beers?"

Karp heaved a stack of cold cases up to his waist and staggered out to the truck.

Returning, he said, "That's a lot of beer. How many people at this cookout?"

"Just us and the Heeneys. The Heeney men are beer people."

Then it hit him. "Did you say a boy?"

"Uh-huh. Rose's younger."

"*Lucy?*"

"Yes, Lucy. She's passed through puberty, although I think you had a trial that week, you might have missed it. Anyway, now she's eighteen, she's old enough to have a date, and she actually has one. Several." And here Marlene clasped her hands together and looked to heaven with a hearty "Thank you, Jesus!"

"Well, yeah," said Karp. "I'm glad. This is, this kid is like, you know, a regular kid, right?"

"Perfectly regular. Looks like an angel in fact, if angels are ever horny and eighteen. He's a freshman at MIT, so he can tie his shoes. I haven't run his sheet but I assume it's clear of major violent felonies, unlike you-know-who last year. STDs I would bet negative, too, a mom's prayer. Most of all, I think she's just barely beginning to understand that he's interested. That would be a first."

"Why? She's a great kid," said Karp defensively.

"Yes, and your daughter's primary belief, besides the one, holy, catholic, and apostolic Church, is that she's an ugly sack of shit and a freak. That tends to send the suitors running unless they have the prescience to whack her smartly with a ball-peen hammer."

"What suitors?"

"Any number. Warren Wang for one."

"The pudgy kid?"

"Him. Not that he'd be my first choice to look at over the turkey every Thanksgiving for the next forty years, but he was nuts about her. She wouldn't give him the time of day, and he was too chicken to try the hammer. Speaking of which, I told Rose we'd be there by seven-thirty. Get that box of meat."

When they were settled in the cab of the Dodge, Marlene cranked the engine, but did not immediately put the truck into gear. "I ought to warn you. I'd kind of hoped that we could make this a pleasant evening, for the kids' sake if nothing else, but there are tensions chez Heeney."

"He's a drunk," said Karp.

"Hmm, not really. He's a drinking man, and while I know you think it's the same thing, it's not." She paused to reflect. "Here's an example. This afternoon, we were in their kitchen making potato salad and coleslaw, all of us, chopping stuff, and we were having a good time. There was a little radio playing oldies, and Rose and I were singing along, and Dan and Lucy were making wisecracks. The boys and Lizzie were underfoot, trying to help. It was, you know—jolly. Everyone was getting along, it was real life. The old ladies were sucking on cheap Italian white, just enough to get a little buzz. Because of the radio we didn't hear the car pull up. So they just walked in and it was like a switch went off."

"Who 'they'?"

"Heeney. Red, they call him. And the son Emmett. A clone of Dad. The pair of them look like the guys the IRA sends by when you're getting too cozy with the Brits. It was amazing. I was facing the door when he walked in and he stood there for a second just looking. He had the weirdest expression on his face, like how could a bunch of people be having such a good time if he wasn't there, like it was a betrayal or something. Then Lizzie spotted him and they both mobbed him, Lizzie and Rose. Dan didn't move. Then Red kind of eased away from the females around him and said kind of in an aside, but clear enough, 'My other daughter,' meaning Dan. He has this big mop of curls and Red and the other kid are buzz cuts, like the Marines. So he goes over to him and gives him a hug and grabs him around the neck and yanks his hair. He yells something like 'Get the hedge clippers.' All jolly he-man fun. But Dan was mortified."

"I can't wait to meet this guy," said Karp. "I thought dads yelling about kids' hair went out in the sixties."

"Not apparently in southern West Virginia. Anyway, he sucked all the air out of the room."

"Sounds charming. I'm really looking forward to this now."

"No, he *is* charming. He's Irish after all. But besides that, the guy manages to combine the worst features of fascism and communism. It's quite a show. You'll see."

She pulled up on a sandy shoulder and honked. With shouts the Heeney men descended on the truck and unloaded. Karp appreciated the accuracy of Marlene's description. Emmett was a big, shambling kid with a football tackle's blocky build. Red Heeney was red in face and bristles, with the shape of a beer keg and a pair of bright blue eyes set to play continuously the message *I'm nobody's fool.* He clasped Karp's hand in a he-man grip and engaged him in conversation as they hauled stuff down to the beach. It was more of a monologue than a conversation. Heeney complimented Karp on the accomplishments and loveliness of his womenfolk, the excellent qualities of his sons, queried him about his former athletic prowess and his present profession. This was done with a certain amount of self-deprecating humor, but Karp, who was a skilled interrogator himself, understood that the man was laying charm.

Karp had no idea why, but he suspected that charming was instinctive in Heeney. The man was a natural politician. Like most of his type he had also to be the center of attention and the man in charge. He organized the picnic with somewhat more energy than picnics need to be organized, but with such good nature that no one except Daniel was offended. The fire was made, the burgers and hot dogs sizzled thereupon, games were organized and played aggressively, without sparing the feelings of the younger members of the party, whom Heeney encouraged not to be crybabies. Throughout, can after can of beer vanished into the mouths of the three Heeneys. They ate; Red Heeney presided. They all learned a great deal about his opinions, and about the union election he was contesting, the iniquity of the mining companies, the corruption of the administrations of Robbens County, of the state and federal governments, of politicians generally. Karp had to admit that the guy was at least an amusing blowhard. He found it oddly relaxing not to have to say anything. He often had to say a lot at work. Summer's blue dusk descended; some pale stars made their appearance through the humid overcast.

"Well, are you having fun?" Marlene asked Karp as they sat together on their blanket, replete.

"Yeah, it's like watching bears at the zoo. The boys are having a good time."

After supper, Heeney had organized a base-running game on the beach in which everyone had joined at some time, and the twins and all the Heeneys were still mad at it, the Heeneys now playing drunk and with increasing violence. As they watched, Dan Heeney slid into Emmett like Ty Cobb, knocking him over. A scuffle instantly sprang up, some shoving, some language, thrown blows. Red Heeney dived in and threw some blows of his own. Dan Heeney stalked off down the beach, like a ten-year-old, while the actual ten-year-olds watched openmouthed.

"He's not having a good time," observed Karp.

"Yeah, poor kid! Rose has been bending my ear. The sadness of her life: two men she loves and they can't get along."

"Why not? He seems like a nice enough kid."

"Oh, he's a doll. I offered him a job."

"What, shoveling dogshit?"

"You always say that, as if that was the only thing we do. No, I need someone to handle office drudgery and also do some basic training. Billy's up to his ears with all the outside dogs, and I want him to concentrate on the attack work. Lucy is also planning to stay. Needless to say."

"The plot thickens."

"Thicker than you think. I happened to mention the other day that I needed someone, and Rose practically sat on my lap until I agreed that Dan would be just right. They're going back home after the weekend and she doesn't want him there just now."

"Because he doesn't get on with Daddy and the bro?"

"Not exactly. She's terrified and he's her baby. Funny, because she's got Lizzie, but there it is."

"What's she frightened about?"

"Oh, this union business. Threats. Someone shot their dog. And the book in the Heeney family is that little Dan can't quite cope with the real world. That's part of the problem. He's really bright, of course, but school bright, which means that he's more or less stopped thinking that Red Heeney's opinions are the *Encyclopedia Britannica.* A guy like Red gets a kid like that and he has to project incompetence in worldly things onto him, just to balance things out and keep the kid subordinate. He's got book larnin' but he ain't doing no real man's work. Plus the lefty stuff: he's hanging out with the bourgeois exploiters, he's going to work for the capitalists in some way or another. Although, it's not articulated like that. It's a control thing. Heeney is a decent enough guy, but when he laughs, *everyone* laughs, and when he cries, *everyone* cries, or else. Oedipus in West Virginia, the usual."

"It seems kind of old-fashioned, doesn't it? Union violence. Working-stiff dad versus college kid. Like something from the thirties. Or a movie."

"Well, according to Rose, the thirties are still going on in Robbens County. And that family stuff—Christ, I got some of that crap from *my* folks. College girl, think you know everything . . ."

"Gosh, good thing we don't have anything like that in *our* family."

"Oh?" said Marlene. "What exactly do you mean by that remark?"

"Nothing, dear. There is absolutely nothing in common between the Red and Dan show and the Marlene and Lucy show. Not a thing."

"You're horrible." Marlene got up. "I'm getting another beer. Do you want anything?"

"Only your happiness," he said, so she kicked sand in his face as she departed.

Now real darkness fell. Heeney had, of course, brought all kinds of dangerous fireworks, which he and Emmett now set off, with drunken yells, while the twins vied with one another to see how close they could skip to exploding objects and white-hot missiles, Zak in the lead, Giancarlo following each dare, but in such a way as to constrain his brother from doing something really stupid.

Karp watched all this with a fair calm, suppressing his Jewish-mother instincts as he had learned to do during his many years of marriage to a shiksa desperado. Marlene was in charge of danger chez Karp. Karp was actually waiting for the Red Heeney finale and was not at all surprised at the form it took.

The fireworks ended, the exhausted boys and the little girl collapsed on the blankets with their mothers. Emmett and Red sat together, Lucy and Dan a little distance away. A Coleman lantern had been lit. By its light, Karp observed that Red Heeney had switched to sucking from a pint bottle. Emmett was still guzzling beer, and tossing the empties upon a large pile of the same, punctuating the night with tinny clangs at remarkably short, almost metronomic intervals. Heeney began to sing. He had a fine voice, a dramatic tenor, a whiskey tenor actually, but pleasant. He sang union songs, "Joe Hill" and "Dark as a Dungeon" and "Spring Hill Disaster," in which his family joined, and also, to Karp's surprise, Marlene and Lucy, and then Irish ballads and rebel songs, "Kevin Barry," "Four Green Fields," and others more obscure. Then Marlene and Lucy did "Rose of Tralee," like angels in harmony, which made Karp happy, but which took the center of attention away from Heeney, who replied with an angry "Come Out Ye Black and Tans," at the end of which he flung his empty pint arcing into the night.

"You're not singing, Karp," he declared.

"I can't sing. I can't carry a tune."

Heeney stuck out an accusing finger, a digit like a center punch. "Nah, you can't sing 'cause you're a fuckin' lawyer. Lawyers got no songs. You know why?" He thumped his chest. " 'Cause they got no hearts. No songs, no hearts. Isn't that right, Karp?"

"Maybe we have little small ones."

Rose said, "Red, it's late, maybe—"

"Shut up!" snarled Heeney. "I'm talking to my pal, the lawyer. Let me tell you what the law is. The law is nothing but the padding on the hammer the rich uses to bash in the heads of the working people. They don't care to see the blood and the brains, oh, no, they're too delicate for that, so they disguise it with lots of words, and they get a bunch of pimps and make them judges and lawyers to confuse the people so no one knows they been robbed. Property is theft, did you know that, Mr. Lawyer Man? That's what your lawyer is, a conveyancer of stolen property. But when some poor boy steals a crust of bread, oh, that's when the majesty of the law gets all riled up and grabs him and throws him in the dungeon, because property is sacred once it's legally stolen."

"Sneakers," said Karp.

"What?"

"Sneakers, is what they steal. Expensive sneakers. Or gold chains. Or designer jackets, those are big now. Now that you mention it, I have not once locked up a poor boy for stealing a crust of bread. I'd like to, of course, but in twenty years the opportunity has never come my way."

Heeney got up on his knees and leaned over the lantern. "Oh, smart guy. You wouldn't be so smart if I punched you in the nose, would you? Huh? Smart Jew lawyer. Huh?" He held up his fist to demonstrate the punching apparatus.

Karp didn't move. He said in a calm voice, "That would be an assault, Red. That would be against the law."

"Fuck the law and fuck you!"

"You're drunk, Heeney," said Karp in the same tone. "Settle down."

"And you're fuckin' yellow, Karp," Heeney said, staggering to his feet. "Get up, you fucker. Fuckin' Jew lawyer. I can take you, drunk or sober."

Heeney put up his fists and lunged forward, kicking over the lantern. Rose uttered a little scream and grabbed at her husband's arm. He flung her away with a curse. Instantly, his two sons were on him, Emmett tackling him to the ground, and Dan dropping onto his chest and securing his arms. Rose snatched the lantern out of harm's way, and the three Heeneys rolled and heaved on the ground, grunting and cursing. Marlene could see Rose was crying and, in a low voice, said to Karp, "I think the party's over. Let's scram."

Which they did, leaving all their gear to be gathered tomorrow. As they walked away, Karp noticed Lucy flip aside a bat-sized length of driftwood. She had been going to wade in with that if the bunch of them had jumped me, he thought with a shock. He didn't know whether to be ashamed or proud.

4

"WHAT'S WRONG WITH YOU, *NOW?*" ASKED MARLENE UNSYMPATHETI-cally. She was bustling around the kitchen, fully dressed, having already done an hour or so of work. He was elbowing at the table, robed, unshaven, grainy-eyed, head on fist, eyeing a bowl full of raisin bran and wondering whether to make the irrevocable commitment to pour milk in it.

"I'm crapulous without having been gloriously drunk," said Karp. "It's unfair. And if you want to know, I'm feeling unmanly."

"Oh, yeah, what a pussy! You didn't coldcock a helpless drunk. I've lost all my respect for you."

"Real men drink themselves into oblivion when they have a problem and take it out on bystanders."

"When life hands you a lemon, make lemonade," said Marlene, who was in fact making lemonade and handed him a lemon to demonstrate.

"Thank you," he said, and mimed an epiphany. "Gosh, I think . . . I *finally* understand that saying."

"Good. Now cheer up. It's a nice day, you're on vacation, so vacate!"

"Even though we have a dual system of criminal justice, one for the rich and one for the poor?"

She stopped her squeezing and turned to face him, hands on hips. "Oh, please! You're not telling me he got to you with that drunken ramble?"

"But it's *true.* I got up this morning and I was thinking obsessively about the congressman, how to get him, strategies, how to slowly weave the web, laws I could use, pressures I could put . . . and then it hit me—okay, let's say I do get him. Realistically, the best outcome is, he does eighteen months, most in a minimum security prison, and then a halfway house. Then he runs again as a victim of racism and takes 80 percent of the vote. I mean, what's the point?"

The answer (if she knew it) did not come then, for the screen door crashed open and Giancarlo burst in. He grabbed two doughnuts from a box on the table and announced, "Zak shot a crow. We're going to nail it to the barn."

"No, you are not," said the mother.

"Yes, Dan Heeney says that's what they do in West Virginia."

"Fine, if you're ever in West Virginia, you can nail all the crows you want, but not here."

Giancarlo snatched up a table knife and stabbed it into Karp's bowl several times, while laughing maniacally.

"What are you doing?" cried Karp. "Stop that!"

"Guess what I am, Dad."

"An idiot?"

"No, a cereal killer. Mom, can we *tape* the crow up?"

"Get out of my sight! Shoo!" Marlene yelled. The boy departed, hooting.

"He took the last two chocolate doughnuts," Karp said. "Two, not one."

"They always take two, for the other one. I think it's sweet."

"But if each one does it, then they have four, and there isn't any left for me. It's not fair."

"Could you pout more pathetically when you say that?"

Karp obligingly twisted his face.

"Charming," cooed his wife. "And incidentally, that answers your problem with the criminal justice system. Life is inherently not fair." Marlene emptied ice from a bag into the two-gallon thermos. "And another example is, I have to go to work in the hot sun while you gorge on doughnuts."

The sun was indeed hot. Marlene lugged her jug of lemonade into the shade cast by the barn and set it on a rough plywood table, on which there already stood a miscellany of tin and plastic cups. Then she strolled through her small kingdom to declare a break. Billy Ireland was behind the barn working a big shepherd named Lars on the spring lead with

Alex Russell. The dog was in a harness attached to a long lead fastened to a thick baby-carriage spring bolted into the wall. Russell was agitating. He came from hiding around the corner of the barn and snapped the dog in the face with a burlap sack. The dog leaped at the sack and grabbed it, at which Russell dropped it and retreated around the corner with every indication of extreme cowardice. The dog killed the sack, snarling and jerking it around. Marlene waited until the exercise was over before she approached. Ireland took the dog off the chain, snapped on a light lead, and sit-stayed him.

"How's he doing?" she asked.

"Coming along. A good dog. Nice and varminty with the sack." Ireland took in Marlene's tube top and cutoffs, adding, you are a fine-looking woman and I would boff you in a second were it not for the fact that there are lots of fine-looking women and not that many good training jobs for ex-felons and so I will wait until such time as you actually grab me by the dick before going further. But with his eyes, not aloud, which just suited Marlene, who got the message clear enough and thought (as she liked to do), I am *so* bad.

"There's lemonade," said Marlene, and walked away, feeling the eyes of both men on her. Past the greenhouse and the garden, through a wooden gate to what was once the pasture of the former dairy farm, a dozen flat acres of close-mowed grass. In a near corner of this field, her daughter was running their young mastiff Gringo on a fifteen-foot lead. She was giving the dog the most basic lesson, which was paying attention to the handler on the other end of the lead. As long as the dog trotted along at Lucy's left side, all was well. But when he turned to investigate some interesting object or scent, or stopped or lagged, Lucy did a sharp about-face and walked rapidly in the opposite direction, allowing the slack in the long lead to yank taut and digging the little spikes of the pinch collar into the dog's neck. Marlene watched this a few times, until Lucy spotted her and walked over, with Gringo showing his class by, for once, not having to be dragged along.

"Good dog!" said Marlene. "Good daughter! He's coming along, I see."

"Pretty well. He's a willing worker. I hope you made drinks, I'm dying of thirst out here." Lucy gestured to the far side of the field. "I'll go get Dan."

"Dan's here?"

"Yeah. You hired him and he showed up."

"I didn't expect him after last night. Besides, I hired him to train the goddamn computer, not the dogs. Wasn't he hungover?"

"He was. But he's noble. And responsible. He stumbled in at seven this morning while I was getting Gringo out, so I gave him Malo and showed him, so to speak, the ropes."

Marlene shrugged. "Well, tell him he can have a drink, too." She turned back to the barn. Lucy took a zigzag dog-training route across the field and watched Dan work his dog for a while. Malo was a stiff-necked bruiser, heavier than his brother, and Dan was doing a good deal of dragging. He was sweat-soaked; his face was an unhealthy yellowish gray.

"He's a toughie," observed Lucy.

Dan jerked his lead hard enough to pull the head off an Airedale. Malo gave him a hurt look and then ambled along in the new direction as if he had just decided that it was more interesting.

"That's it," she said. "The first principle of Kohler training: where the dog's head goes, the rest of him must follow."

"I'm used to it," Dan said. "He reminds me of my father."

They began walking side by side across the field. After an interval she asked, "Does that happen often? Last night, I mean."

Dan snorted. "Invariably. Emmett and I started jumping him when he was sixteen and I was twelve. Before that, he'd break things or knock Mom over." Dan paused and color came into his face. "I don't . . . it's not like he was mean or anything—just out of control. He never hit her or anything. Mom's always making excuses for him—he's under stress, he works hard, we have to be understanding."

"And are you? Understanding."

"Yeah, to an extent. It's traditional. A man gets drunk and starts fights. That's what men do. And all is forgiven afterwards. The cutoff line is does he beat the wife and kids and does he drink on the job, and I have to say Red Heeney's on the good side of that. And really, he's a great man. Words my mother taught me."

"So why does he act that way if he's so great?"

"Because he's angry at all the misery and injustice in the world that he can't get his hands on to beat up. So he beats up on anyone handy when he's got his load on. Maybe it's even true. My mom believes it, that's for sure."

"But?"

He smiled at her. "I guess there was a but in there. Smart of you to pick it up."

"Language is my game," she said coolly.

"Right, I'll have to watch myself. Anyway, the but is, I'm tired of it. I'm tired of all that like last night. And what causes it. Because it's . . . I don't know . . . finished, all that old working-class stuff. He wants it to be like that again and it can't, not like the twenties and thirties, with the union songs and the struggle. All his guys, this pathetic little union he's got there, all they want is a satellite dish and a Camaro and enough booze or weed to get shit-faced. When you come right down to it, it's a company union. Always has been up there in Robbens County. They killed all the real union guys back in '23, and since then the company's had this cozy relationship, first with the underground miners and now with the pit mine equipment operators. The UMW couldn't get in there and neither can the clean unions like the Operating Engineers. He wants class-consciousness, but the only thing they care about is if you're from here or from away, which is the whole planet that isn't Robbens County. And your family, they care about that. Are you a Jonson or a Cade boy? Or a Weames. I got to hand it to him, it's amazing he's gone as far as he has. He actually has a shot at making Weames have to steal the election."

"Isn't that, like, illegal?"

"Oh, right, legal! This is Robbens County we're talking about, not the United States. And, yeah, I should support him and all, because he's right, and sacrifice myself like he did, and like he made my mom do, and Emmett. But—okay, here's the big but—I want to just have . . . I don't know, like a normal life. A family you can bring somebody home to without them getting a quiz on their place in the class structure and a lecture about what went on in the mines in 1919 and how unjust and cruel." He laughed. "Right, poor me . . . it's so boring it makes me puke."

"I know what you mean," she said.

"Not really," he said, a little bitterness creeping into his voice for the first time. "I mean, you have this nice normal family. . . . What's so funny?"

"Oh, nothing," she said when she had brought herself under control.

"My normal family life." To his confused look she said, "Oh, forget it. Come on, I could drink a quart," and she trotted away with her dog.

That afternoon, Karp was standing in the shade of the barn, watching Ireland and Russell work another dog, a Doberman, on the spring lead. They were using a sleeve, a thickly padded device that Russell wore on his right arm. He was annoying the animal with a switch, and when the dog leaped at him, he allowed it to grab the sleeve and tear it off him. Russell then retreated out of sight and allowed the dog to chew up the sleeve for a while. The agitator had, of necessity, a sure sense of exactly how far the dog could lunge against the spring. Karp, watching, felt sorry for the dog, with whom he identified. He had been trained in very much the same way and was currently in a situation not unlike that of the plunging, snarling Doberman. After a number of such sessions, Ireland took the dog back to its cage and Russell walked over to Karp, sat down with his back against the barn, and lit a cigarette.

"So that's how it's done," Karp said. "Do you ever get bitten?"

"Me? Hell, no. Guys *have* been tore up pretty bad, if they don't know what they're doing. I seen a dog rip a guy's face off, once. Grabbed him on the cheek and *whang!* The whole thing, the whole half of his face, just come off like a fuckin' glove." He gestured with his cigarette. "You got company."

The dogs broke out their chorus as a battered, dark blue Jimmy with West Virginia plates rolled into the yard. Its left fender was pink with Bondo and its chrome was dented. A working stiff's car, Karp thought, and wondered if it was that way by design. Emmett Heeney was driving and looked uncomfortable, almost grim. The passengers were Rose Heeney and her daughter. They got out and Rose walked over to Karp.

"I realize you probably never wanted to see me again," she said, "but I had to come over and apologize."

Karp shrugged and put on a smile. "No problem. It happens."

"He doesn't know what he's saying," she added. "He's under a lot of stress."

"It's fine, Rose," Karp said, now becoming a little embarrassed himself. "You want to see Marlene? I think she was in the barn." Rose turned to go. "And I was just going to take the boys to the beach. If Lizzie wants to come . . . ?"

Rose smiled a grateful assent. She entered the barn, with Lizzie running ahead, and stumbled on something. She paused to let her eyes adjust to the dimness. She was thinking, I am so good at this, and reflected on what a shame it was that pride could not really be taken in what was her one real skill: pretending not to be mortified, the kind of charm she had learned at her mommy's knee early, learning to lie about Mom and Dad not being available and charming the men who came about the bills one has when one is trying to keep up appearances without quite enough liquidity. She had thought that marrying a dragline operator from West Virginia, a man dedicated to the fight for justice, would have excused her permanently from mortification, but it had not proved to be the case. She had nearly stopped feeling sorry for herself— it was by now a routine, the famous Wickham shit-eating grin, a little la-di-da toss of the head, crude to be angry with such a one, right? And by extension with the one who had done the damage, broken the window or the jaw—although she still felt for the children, not Emmett so much, but for Dan; Lizzie was starting to be old enough to understand, too.

The dogs were barking and she had to call out. Marlene appeared out of the gloom, wiping her hands on a towel. She shouted at the dogs to shut up, which they did. Rose went into her cringe. Marlene ignored it and said, "Want a beer? I'm having one."

They went into the kitchen. Rose declined the beer, accepted an iced tea. Marlene said, "Well, that wasn't the worst party I ever went to. No one got shot and we didn't even have to call the cops. Or an ambulance. I expect you've been in situations where there were both."

Rose felt herself blush. She nodded. "Yes. He's famous in McCullensburg for it. I'm sorry. I thought, well, away from home . . . a civilized little gathering." She looked up at Marlene and found a colder face than she had expected.

"You're not angry at me, are you?"

"I don't know yet. Let me ask you straight: Do you *know* me?"

"Know you . . . ?"

"Yeah. Do you know who I am? What I used to do? I mean, is this hanging around me you've been doing, cultivating me and so on, connected with what went on last night? You're not looking for a little help, are you? In your domestic situation, I mean."

As soon as Marlene said this, she saw from the confused and shocked expression on Rose Heeney's face that she had been off base and felt a flash of shame.

"I don't know what you're talking about," Rose exclaimed. "You think I need a . . . whatever you are, a private detective?"

"Not as such . . . calm down, Rose. Sit down and finish your tea. Okay, I was out of line and I apologize. It's just that I used to have a business—actually according to my husband, it was more of a crusade—in which I . . . um . . . discouraged guys from beating up on their wives."

"Discouraged? You mean like counseling?"

"In a manner of speaking. It was an extremely firm kind of counseling. Tough love on steroids." A blank look. "Not to put too fine a point on it, along with several accomplices, I beat them up. On several occasions I had to shoot them, or trained the women in question to shoot them, and they did."

"You mean . . . dead?"

"On several occasions. The point of which is that I have a rep that's still alive in the City, and of course I forgot you don't come from the City. But anyhow, from time to time, a woman drifts into my life and inveigles me into an acquaintance in the hopes that I will fix her domestic situation."

"And you thought . . . I mean, that I wanted you to *fix* Red?"

"Yeah. So sue me, I'm a little paranoid."

Rose was staring at her, wide-eyed. Then she made a couple of preparatory snorting noises and burst into laughter. After a startled moment, Marlene joined in.

"They don't," Rose got out amid the guffaws, "they don't *have* that kind of service in McCullensburg, but if you ever wanted to open a branch office . . . oh, my!"

"Yes, well, easy for you to laugh," said Marlene after they had descended to chuckles. "It's no fun turning off the desperate. But you can see where . . ."

"Oh, sure, I understand. But the fact is, even though he acts like a big redneck bully, he loves me and the kids and there's never been anything remotely violent between us, with the exception of subduing him when he gets out of hand, like you saw. Do I wish he didn't do it? Yes, of course, but we have a good marriage and there are worse things, which

I probably don't have to tell you. As a matter of fact, by McCullensburg standards, he's a sensitive New Age man."

"What's so funny?" said Dan Heeney, coming in from the next room. Marlene had started him on the farm accounts, which were in a fearful mess, and he had fallen into the concentration stupor of the computer jockey, tweaking files and exploring the old Macintosh, until the noise of the two women brought him back to earth.

"Oh, Dan, you're here," said his mother, arranging her face from hysterical back into the familiar lineaments of Mom. "Can you spare a minute? We need to discuss something."

"The answer is no," he replied, his face sullen.

Rose said sharply, "Dan!" and then got up and said to Marlene, "Oh, God, I'm sorry, you've had enough of the Heeney family business. We'll talk outside." She went through the screen door, and after a moment's hesitation, Dan said something nasty under his breath and followed her out.

Marlene sat there, quite happy not to be involved. A little guilty, but she could live with it. She stood, intending a little discreet eavesdropping, but sat again and took a swallow of beer. She rubbed the cold can against her forehead and listened to the refrigerator clunk.

From the doorway of the barn, Lucy could see Dan and his mother on the other side of their car, just the tops of their bodies over the hood of the Jimmy. She couldn't hear what they were saying, but she could read the body language. Rose was arguing with him, her body stiff and bent a little toward him; he was turned slightly away with his face averted. Suddenly he broke away with a shake of his head and started back toward the house. His mother went after him and clutched at his sleeve, but he pulled away. Then Emmett leaped from the cab, caught up with Dan, grabbed him, and spun him around. Lucy heard their voices raised. Both their faces had gone red. Emmett shoved Dan toward the truck, Dan shoved him back, and when his brother snatched at the front of his shirt, Dan popped him one in the mouth, a short left. Emmett stepped back and felt his mouth. He looked at the blood on his hand and went at Dan.

Lucy knew a thing or two about boxing, and she could see that neither of them was a skilled boxer, just fairly decent bar fighters. Half a dozen blows traded, and a little wrestling, and then they were down on the ground, each trying to choke and pummel the other into submission. Emmett, bigger and heavier, soon got astride his brother and rained blows on his face. Their mother was screaming, now, "Stop it, oh, stop it," Lucy could hear that much. Rose bent over and tried to separate them, pulling at their clothes, their hair. A random elbow or knee clipped her in the jaw and she sat down hard. She put her face in her hands and wailed, a high, hopeless sound, like a small child. The twins and Lizzie, who had been playing with the puppies in the barn, came running out to stand next to Lucy. The boys watched in fascination. Lizzie bit her lip and was very still.

Lucy started toward the fight, not really thinking about what she would do when she arrived, but here she was forestalled by the arrival of her father and the agitator Russell. Russell yanked Emmett off Dan. Lucy could see blood all over Dan's face, and before she quite knew it, she was running toward him. She saw Emmett throw a clumsy punch at Russell, who ducked it and countered with a short, solid blow to the solar plexus. To Lucy's vast surprise, she saw her father slip behind Emmett and put him in a competent-looking half nelson. The young man bucked and yelled, but Karp was able to jam his face up against the truck and held him there, talking calmly, until, by a nod of his head, Emmett indicated he was through fighting.

Daniel had vanished. As soon as his brother was off him, he had taken off running. Lucy called out to him, but he ignored her and ducked between the house and the greenhouse, heading toward the big field, the dunes, and the beach. Lucy looked in the direction he had gone for a moment and then went to see if she could help Mrs. Heeney. Marlene was already on the job, however.

"What the hell, Rose! What was going on here?" Marlene helped Rose to her feet and examined her face. "Christ, you're going to have a fat mouse there. What happened?"

"Marlene, I don't want to talk about it," said Rose, pulling away and brushing the dirt from her blouse. "I'm fine. Just let me go home."

Emmett said, "I'm sorry, Mom." He actually hung his head. Lucy noted that he had turned from a somewhat frightening man to a sheepish, overgrown boy.

"Oh, just get in the truck, Emmett!" Rose snapped. "Lizzie! Come on, we're going."

They departed without another word. Karp and Marlene exchanged a look and a shrug. "Well! Who wants to go to the beach?" he said cheerily, got a yell of assent from his sons, and took them into the house.

"What happened?" Lucy asked her mother.

"Damned if I know. She wanted Dan to do something he didn't want to do but his Dad wanted him to, and Emmett apparently tried to muscle him."

"He wants to stay here and not go home to West Virginia. I'm going to go after him."

Lucy ran into the house and emerged a minute later with a bulging plastic freezer bag. She whistled up Gog, who emerged from the barn drinking and drooling but, as ever, game for a walk.

She followed the dog past the field and across the road and into the dunes and found Dan sitting near the place they had gone the first day.

"Are they gone?" he asked.

"Yes." She knelt in front of him and took a damp washcloth out of the bag.

"How did you find me?"

"I have an expensive tracking dog. Hold still, I'll get the blood and dirt off you."

She did so, gently and carefully. He closed his eyes and let her do it. He thought of his mother doing the same service, innumerable times, and considered in his analytic way just why this was different. He closed his eyes and let her work; he could smell the soap on her skin as she leaned close.

"There." She affixed a Band-Aid to a cut on his eyebrow. "You still look like you lost a fight, but you won't scare the children."

"Thank you. Are we playing doctor now?"

She ignored this. "What was he trying to do, your brother? Take you back by force?"

"Something like that. Emmett isn't really stupid, he just acts like it sometimes. Dad is God Almighty and I'm his play-pretty, and—"

"His what?"

She saw a blush creep up his battered cheek, which she thought charming. "Toy, I mean. When we were growing up, he was the enforcer. 'Emmett, go get your brother and make him fix his room.' He's still doing it. I used to daydream about sending away for one of those karate courses and studying in secret, and one day when he tried to beat on me . . . boom! But, needless to say . . ."

"You got him a few good ones," said Lucy encouragingly. "He's pretty tough."

"Yeah, he is. The only good part about being Emmett Heeney's brother was that he was the only one allowed to beat on me. I never had a hard look from another kid all through school." Dan paused, took a breath. "I'm not going back there. I hate it there."

"I figured that's what the fight was about. Why didn't your dad come over and yell at you himself?"

"Because he knew I'd say no, and he'd lose a point. He can't make me do anything. I'm eighteen, I have a full scholarship, and I can make enough money doing programming to pay my own way. Dad's a negotiator, and the first rule of negotiations is never put yourself in a position where you're going to lose. So he sent Mom and Emmett. That way he can throw up his hands and blame them. But the fight . . . it wasn't really about that. Mainly it was he made a really nasty remark about you. He made out . . . you know. That you were why I didn't wanted to go home and pass leaflets to the working class." Dan was starting to blush again.

"And you slugged him to defend my *honor?*" Before she could help it, a giggle burst from her mouth and she felt herself joining him in shameful red.

"I guess, in a way." The unfamiliar idea made Dan uncomfortable at first, but after a short while it seemed right. It was not impossible to think of this girl in those terms. Whether in fact Emmett had been correct in his surmise did not get discussed at this point.

"Well, thank you," she said. "No one has ever done that for me before. Of course, it's so rarely threatened in any way. My honor, I mean. I'm sorry you got so banged up."

"I've been beat worse." He picked a grass stem and started to chew it, then flung it away with the thought, oh, great, the perfect hick look, a big shiner and a grass stem in the mouth.

"So," said Lucy, "what now? You'll stay here? At your house?"

"No, they're all leaving after this weekend. People are coming to fix the place up and get it ready for sale. Maybe I'll get a tent and just live on the beach."

"Don't be silly! We can put you up, if you can stand us. I'm sure my mom won't mind. She likes a medieval ménage—dogs, servants, retainers, children, all banging against one another and having to be straightened out. It's her fun."

They walked back toward the house by a shortcut, a sandy path that wound around the kind of slight rise that passed for a hill in eastern Long Island, and through a shady copse of pines. At the base of this hill there was a seep under some boulders where Lucy had once found dog violets, and she wanted to see whether there were any now. Suddenly the sound of machine-gun fire burst out, as imitated by a ten-year-old boy. Lucy flung up her hands, screamed, and collapsed on the path. There was more machine-gunning.

"Die dramatically," Lucy advised from the ground. Dan did an *ahrrrg*, staggered, and fell in a heap.

"I got you!" crowed Zak from among the boulders. They rose and inspected the machine-gun nest, a sandy notch dug out and camouflaged with branches. The machine gun was a length of three-inch plastic drainpipe.

"I thought you guys were at the beach," said Lucy.

"We were but it was boring. I was being imaginary until you guys came along. You didn't see me until I got you."

"Yes, but we weren't looking for an ambush. Next time you want to be lower down, so you're not silhouetted against the sky. They call it the military crest. Where are the rest of your men?"

Zak pointed out a few places nearby. "Uh-uh," she said, and knelt to scratch a plan in the dirt. "Okay, let's say an eight-man squad. Your machine gun is here. Automatic rifles here, here, here, and here. You wait until their point man gets here, and you open up with your automatic rifles from both ends. The enemy forms a perimeter right here, where the trail dips a little, and that should be right in the beaten ground of your machine gun. They call it a kill sack. See?"

"What if they run into the woods?"

"Well, you already mined the woods, and if you have mortars, they'd be preregistered right there. The point of an ambush is to get everyone down in the first minute. So they can't call for support."

Zak nodded, taking it in. Dan gaped. Zak said, "You learned that from that guy, right?"

"His name is Tran."

"Yeah. Dad really doesn't like him, does he?"

"No, he doesn't."

"But Mom likes him. And you like him."

"I don't like him. I love him."

Zak looked puzzled. "You can't do that. Love is like like but more."

"Actually, it's not. Like is from here"—she touched his head—"love is from here." She poked him in the center of his chest so that he squirmed away. *"La coeur a ses raisons que la raison ne connais pas."*

"That's French," said Zak.

"That's right. You should go back to the beach before Dad thinks you're drowned and calls the police."

Zak laughed and trotted off with his drainpipe, spraying the woods with deadly blasts. They walked on.

"Wow, what was that all about?" Dan said after a minute. "Who's Tran?"

"Tran is an elderly Vietnamese gentleman. He was sort of my governess when I was growing up. He also worked with my mom."

"And he taught you military stuff? Was that all on the level?"

"Oh, yes. And from a distinguished practitioner. We did small-unit problems all afternoon in Central Park. I also know how to tail someone, shake a tail, and clear a building of defenders. And shoot."

"Why?"

"Oh, partly it was practical. My mom had a lot of enemies at the time and he wanted to protect me. The other stuff . . . he was of the opinion that you never could tell what was going to happen in your life. He was planning to teach literature and ended up guerrilla fighting almost his whole life. So he wanted me to be prepared. Weird, but there it is. Yet more useless knowledge in my head."

"What happened to him?"

"Oh, he's a small-time gangster now. He's a pretty awful person, I guess, but he's *our* awful person. He and my mom get along fine."

Marlene had no problem putting another plate on the table, after having first called Rose Heeney to tell her these plans. They had a polite conversation, like two school mothers arranging an overnight for a fifth-grader, as if Heeney violence had not occurred on Marlene's doorstep. The weekend oozed along peacefully. Sunday, Lucy whipped the twins out of bed with the cry "Pagan babies! Up! Up! Prayer is better than sleep!" and drove them off to mass at St. Perpetua's in Southold. Just after one, the Heeneys came by, with their car packed for the trip. Marlene gave them a civilized lunch at which no alcohol was served, nor were the fights mentioned. Heeney discussed dogs he had known and trained for hunting, to all appearances an affable good old boy. It was perfectly artificial, but not at all unpleasant. Giancarlo gave Lizzie an origami crane, but secretly. Dan and Lucy allowed their eyes to meet for tiny instants, but otherwise kept away from one another. When the clan left, something heavy seemed to go out of the air. Dan Heeney felt a pang of disloyalty, for he felt this, too, but it did not prevent him from enjoying the rest of the day.

That evening, Marlene put Dan in a tiny room at the end of the upstairs hall, originally the hired girl's room, as Marlene explained, and more recently used for sewing. It held a narrow iron cot, a dresser, an old Singer, and a dressmaker's dummy.

"You won't mind sharing a room with Ermentrude, will you?" Marlene asked, indicating this object.

"No, ma'am."

"Feel free to run up a party dress, if you want."

He blushed and showed an uncomfortable smile. Oh, now I've impugned his manhood, Marlene thought. Should I watch the badinage henceforth? Maybe not; the boy needs a thicker skin, and this family is the place to get it.

While Dan was thus engaged, Lucy was on the phone with her best (and nearly only) friend, Mary Ma in New York. After the usual exchange of the latest, Lucy asked, "Listen, Ma, do you know Dan Heeney? He's in your class."

"Dan Heeney the Lollipop?"

"The what?"

"If it's the same guy. Tall, golden curls, big blues, looks like an angel on a Christmas card."

"That's him. Why do they call him that?"

"Because everyone's dying for a lick. It takes something to draw us MIT girls from our studies, but he's a something in that class. How do you know him?"

"He's living in our house out here."

"Lucy! You sneaky bitch! How did you arrange *that?*"

"I didn't; it just happened. Anyway, what's he like?"

"Smart enough to stay in Cambridge. Manners. Eats with his mouth closed, which is not universal among the elite here at MIT, I'm sad to say. Oh, the tragic flaw. He's in love with Olivia Hampton; she's sort of a skanky, depraved SoHo wanna-be type, works in a coffee shop near here. The Human Bean? She's a singer, ha ha. Anyway, he worships her, apparently, and of course, she thinks he's appalling. What a waste!"

Lucy was not exactly let down by this news, as she had not allowed herself to rise very high up. If Dan Heeney noticed a certain cooling of her attentions, he did not show it. He was in any case used to being held in low esteem by girls he was interested in.

Karp left for the City on Tuesday, and life at the dog farm settled into a pleasant, disorderly routine. Dan often recalled during this period Lucy's remark about her mother's medieval aspect. The farmhouse often did resemble a lesser court of that period: the cooking of huge, spicy meals for many noisy people; enormous black dogs underfoot, snapping at scraps and being cuffed away from the plates; strangers arriving at the last moment, always fairly interesting ones, cops and dog breeders, relatives and priests; the dog handlers, louche, profane, and voluble, always in and out of the house, with their half-fabulous animal tales; the children raucous and filthy, bringing unwholesome objects in for inspection; oldies blaring from the greasy radio above the sink; the silence that fell in the midst of all this when Lucy bowed her head and said grace. It was as different as possible from his own family's mealtimes, which were nuclear and short, Red always having to dash for meetings, Emmett stuffing it in and jumping up to go play ball or see his girl. After that and after the intense year at school, monastic despite his best efforts, it was like living in a dream, the colors brighter, the scents more heady than in real life.

Lucy and Dan became friends. Aside from a minimal spell Dan spent at the farm office, they were together all day, working the dogs, corralling the twins, doing the necessary chores, and all the while talking. They discovered that they were both serious people, more serious than the average person their age, far more serious than the type of youth the media held up for emulation. He told her about superstrings and explained relativity to her so that she almost got it. She taught him how to say ridiculous things in foreign tongues—*Help, a dwarf has bur-gled my kaleidoscope*—in Urdu, in Yoruba, in Gaelic, and showed him Chinese poetry in calligraphy, and what the calligraphy meant and the poetry, how that whole ancient culture danced in the sounds and in the lines. They told stories about their parents. Almost all of his were about his father; almost all of hers were about her mother. They agreed that neither of them was from a normal family.

"What if my father had married your mother," Lucy proposed.

"A perfect family," he said. "Meals on time. No craziness. The most exciting thing would be waiting for SAT scores to come. And the reverse—your mom with Big Red Heeney?"

They both laughed. "Homicide," she said. "Two weeks after the wedding, tops." About religion they did not speak seriously, only in the half-joking way that friends do when one is devout and the other is not. She took him to mass once because he was curious, but she didn't ask him what he thought and he didn't volunteer anything beyond the polite. He didn't ask to go again.

This life went on for some weeks. On the Fourth of July, Karp came out and stayed for four days, and when he returned, Lucy and Dan went with him. A year in Cambridge had not turned him into a city boy. He frankly gawked: at the loft on Crosby where the Karps dwelt over the Chinese grocery store; at the continuous circus of SoHo and Chinatown; at the sort of people Lucy seemed to know—beggars, street Arabs, elderly Chinese, nuns. She would fly across a crowded street to have a long conversation in Spanish with a bundle of rags.

They went to dinner at a Chinese restaurant owned, it seemed, by the parents of a girl he recognized vaguely from MIT, and in a private room they all ate a large meal, no single item of which was recognizable to him, after which they went uptown to the ballet. She had tickets. He paid for the cab. She never had any cash; she was always giving bills to people on the street. He had never seen a ballet before and did not think he would ever make a habit of it, but the prima was certainly the most beautiful and graceful being he had ever seen in his life. Who turned out to be a dear friend of his little guide. They went backstage afterward, and the goddess flung herself on Lucy's neck and insisted that they all go out to Balthazar and have drinks. This they did, together with several of the company and assorted balletomanes. They drank a good deal, Dan being heavily vamped by beautiful people of both sexes, which he was not used to, but which he handled fairly well. He knew he would definitely not have handled it well had Lucy not been sitting there, speaking Russian to some blonde and occasionally giving him a friendly eye-roll.

After a night spent in the loft, they went back to Southold on the early train. Marlene had a worried look on her face when she picked them up.

"You need to call your brother," she said to Dan. "He called early this morning and I gave him the loft number, but you'd already left, because he called again. He sounded upset."

"Oh, it's probably nothing. Emmett spends a good deal of time upset. He probably can't find his fishing rod and thinks I know where it is."

Dan called from the phone in the office. Lucy was in the yard when she heard him cry out, "What! Oh my God!" She ran into the house. He was slumped on the old couch, his face paper white, the dead phone clutched in his hand.

"Dan! What is it?" she cried.

"I have to go home," he said in a horrible, creaky voice. "They're all dead. Somebody killed them. They even killed Lizzie."

5

MARLENE DROVE HIM TO LA GUARDIA AIRPORT IN HER TRUCK, WITH HIS few belongings in a nylon bag that sat on his lap. He said nothing during the trip. Several times he passed the back of his hands across his eyes and sniffled. Twice he uttered a sigh, or groan. She did not try to initiate a conversation or to comfort him. Comfort was not notable among her talents. Vengeance was, but he did not ask for that, nor did she offer. When she let him off at the US Air terminal, he turned his face and said, thank you, ma'am, you've been very kind. She said, I'm sorry for your loss, if there's anything I can do . . .

Then he was gone through the glass door. She brought Gog into the front seat and drove off.

What she felt most was embarrassment, tinged a little with shame. Murder was like that, the instinct of the pack to turn away from the injured one. Marlene had never sympathized with the whole yellow-ribbon shtick, the little mounds of toys and notes and candles people placed nowadays at the scenes of killings. What possible good could it do to place a teddy bear? Selfish juju, stupid and sentimental. It said, hoo, boy! God, don't let it happen to *me!* This family had barged into her life, unasked, with their burden of violence. Now it had claimed them and they were gone, and she felt relief. That was part of the shame, but there it was, she had to be honest. Of course, she felt sorry for them, too—she had genuinely liked Rose, and the little girl, that was unspeakable, but there were so very many unspeakable things going on around the world. Sorry was such a pathetic little emotion. And the other part, the thrill of terror that violence brings when we think of our own loved ones, well, she had that covered. No one was going to take her babies, not unless they could get past a brace of ferocious, highly trained dogs, and her well-armed self, and her ferocious, highly trained friends. Still, a little uneasiness there, the old instinct still present, half-asleep. No, not anymore. She couldn't take it. Don't get involved, tattoo it on your forehead, Ciampi!

Suddenly, she swerved across four lanes of traffic and left the highway, occasioning a chorus of horns and a grand display of flip-offs.

"What we should do is go see Butch," she informed the dog. "How would you like that, honey? See the old neighborhood?" The dog shook himself, flipping drool. Marlene steered the truck onto the westbound highway and turned the radio on to WQXR. Some kind of motet, Monteverdi. Up with the volume, music from another time of rampant murder, soothing. It still worked. She picked up her cell phone and dialed.

The twins asked Lucy why she was crying, or Giancarlo did, his brother standing silent by his side. She told them, and Giancarlo burst instantly into tears. She was like him in this, she thought, crying easily. She cried often in church, at mass; a leaf falling, a certain cast of light, a poem by Li Po or Hopkins, would all start the faucets, although on the several occasions when she had faced real and mortal danger, she had not shed a tear. Since Dan's awful phone call, she had been dripping shamefully, off and on. Immediately after the call, she had embraced him, spontaneously, their first (and clearly to be last) fleshly contact, but he stiffened and did not want to talk or be comforted, at least not by her. Her mother had whisked him away so quickly, there had been no time to . . . what? Have a relationship? She could see he blamed himself, for not being there, for not dying with them, and she wanted to explain to him, to make him understand that this was not a wise thing to do.

So she and Giancarlo cried together, but Zak didn't cry. His face went white and pinched-looking and he slipped away, slamming the door.

"Why?" wailed GC, the eternally unanswerable question.

"Some gangsters wanted to kill her dad," she said, "and they wanted to make sure no one could identify them. So they killed everyone in the house. Anyway, that's what Emmett thinks. Emmett was out that night, so he escaped."

"I didn't mean that."

"I know. Here, wipe your face." She handed him her bandanna, already quite damp. "You meant, why do bad things happen to nice people like Lizzie and her parents. Because only God is good, and God is far away. Evil is in charge down here."

"But *we're* good."

"Only by reflection of God. We see the sun shining out of a puddle, but it's not the sun. We can't be good, really, but we're obliged to try. Meanwhile, the rain falls equally on the just and the unjust."

"It still makes me sad."

"Yes, me, too. Man is born to sorrow as the sparks fly upward, but we feel better after a good weep. We're a pair of weepers, aren't we?"

"Uh-huh. We take after Mom. Dad doesn't cry much. I don't think I'll cry as much when I'm grown up, though. Zak doesn't cry either, and he doesn't like to watch it. That's why he left."

"Where did he go?"

"Probably to shoot something," answered Giancarlo equably. "That's what he does instead."

Karp listened to Marlene's news in silence, made the conventional noises, asked, "You think it was a hit?"

"The whole family? I doubt it, unless the Colombians are diversifying into coal. That poor child!"

He waited.

"I know what you're thinking. But I'm in the dog business now."

"That's good, Marlene," he observed neutrally. "You going back to the place?"

"No, I thought I'd come into town and stay over. I'm on the Van Wyck. I thought we could spend the evening together, go out, see a movie. I need distracting."

Karp hung up the phone and let the camera of his mind pan over the innumerable murder-scene photographs he had looked at during the twenty years he had been prosecuting murders. He had not, of course, viewed the ones of the Heeney murders, but he could slot in the faces well enough. They all looked like life-size dolls, the fresh ones did, instantly distinguishable, even without the visible blood and damage, from a sleeping person. You always passed them around to the jury, the defense always objected to this, and the judge always let them pass. A cheap trick; the jury wanted vengeance for the horror on the glossy eight-by-tens and the poor schmuck in the box was the closest they could get to it. But Karp always did it anyway. He had never known a murder victim personally. One "knew" lowlifes who got whacked, but that was not the same thing. He had come close from time to time, Marlene being what she was, or had been (he hoped), but it had never actually come to him.

The phone buzzed its intercom tone. The DA wanted to see him right away. Karp grabbed a pad and walked across the hall to his boss's office. Keegan was behind his desk, a burly, fleshy, florid Irishman with a still intact white mane, although there was a rumor that he weaved. He was taking a Bering corona from its metal tube as Karp walked in. This was a bad sign. It meant that something had happened to the prop cigar he always had at hand or in mouth, which never got wet or smoked, but which sometimes, in moments of anger or stress, got chomped on or flung across the room. As now, obviously.

Karp took a seat without being asked and sat erect, pad on lap, miming the loyal retainer.

"I had a call from the congressman just now," Keegan began. New York boasts a number of congressmen, being so very populous, but Karp knew which one had called.

"Oh? I hope you conveyed to him my very best regards."

"Don't be cute. What are you doing with this mutt, Bailey?"

"Prosecuting him for first-degree assault."

One of Keegan's bushy eyebrows elevated itself. "Personally?"

"No, of course not. But I'm taking a personal interest in the case."

"So I gather. My man was telling me all about it. He said you threatened to shove Bailey under the jail forever and a day unless Bailey told you a pack of lies about how the congressman paid for his last campaign."

"That's true," agreed Karp, "except for the lies part. Bailey is a smurf for Beemer Pennant, and Pennant, we know, is laundering pimp money through political action committees run by your pal. I thought it was worth a shot."

"I see. Even though I told you that there isn't remotely enough evidence of alleged laundering to justify pissing off my one political ally north of the park."

"I thought he was all for the other guy last year."

"He had to be for the other guy, but he wasn't for the other guy hard enough for him to win. And there are other elections."

Karp knotted his brow dramatically. "Okay, let's see if I got this. You don't want to annoy your guy uptown, since we don't have enough evidence to move forward, but you don't want me to put the squeeze on this mutt, which might result in us getting the evidence. So . . . um . . . how will we ever get your guy uptown?" Karp snapped his fingers. "Oh, *now* I understand. You think it's *okay* for the congressman to launder money for a pimp and a murderer, so we'll kind of give him a walk on it."

"Oh, for Christ's sake. Forget I said anything. I'll take care of it myself."

"Fine. What about Mr. Bailey?"

"I *said*, I'll take care of it." The DA's face was closing in on the color of fresh hamburger, and the prop cigar was directed at Karp like a weapon. Karp wondered if the DA was going to sacrifice this one so soon after breaking it out. Again he reflected upon how stupid it was, this silly duel between him and Keegan. Keegan would never change, would never quite get it. While in many respects his instincts as a DA were perfectly fine—he knew the law, knew procedure, was essentially honest— he remained capable of identifying his own political survival with the Good and the True. *Casuistry* was the technical term; maybe it had something to do with the twenty years Keegan had spent in Jesuit institutions. Lucy would know.

"Out of curiosity," said Karp, "what are you going to let him cop to? Community service?"

"If I want, gaddamn it." the DA said, his voice rising.

"Okay, but just so you're aware: he sliced his girlfriend's nose off. She took a hundred and eight stitches. I thought we frowned on that kind of stuff. In any case, the poor woman is attracting some press interest. A big-time plastic surgeon from Downstate is volunteering to fix her up."

A little lie there. In the old days, before he became corrupt, Karp would never have told it, nor would he ever have used the press as a shillelagh. On Keegan's face he observed the frustrated anger turn into a more calculating sort. That was one thing Jack Keegan would never do, place himself in the position of seeming soft on a heinous offense in the light of publicity; no, not for a wilderness of congressmen.

"Ah, you can do what the hell you like," Keegan snapped. "One thing though—I want to see any deal you make on this whole issue, and I want to see it *before* it's made. Is that clear?"

Karp rose. "Perfectly clear, boss."

Back in his office, Karp made a call to Bill Ricci, who was the ADA officially in charge of the People's case against Bailey, and instructed him to make no deals whatever with Bailey, to go for the highest penalty allowed by law, and to prepare for a trial. Then, after an uncomfortable interval of self-contempt, he dialed the number of the *Post* and spoke to a woman he knew who specialized in human-interest crime stories and gave her the details of the situation of Ms. Carolyn Watson, the former (he surmised) love interest of Mr. Bailey. After that, inured to perfidy, he had no trouble in calling a famous plastic surgeon for whom he had once done an enormous legal favor. This favor was called in. The man seemed relieved to be off the hook. Having thus arranged reality to comport with his recent spontaneous fiction, Karp signed out of the office and had his driver take him to the Sloan-Kettering Center at Sixty-seventh and First.

The call to Downstate, which was just across the street, had reminded him of a neglected duty. Neglected because Karp hated hospitals. He was ashamed of this, but he could not help it. The smell got to him, the disinfectant, the sweetish floor wax, the sharp tang of alcohol, and the darker odors against which the cleaner ones fought; and lost to a large extent. His mother had died in a place like this when he was fourteen; Marlene had spent considerable time in hospitals, too, and each time he had to go was like a small death.

Raymond Guma was sitting up in bed talking to Eddie Bent. Guma was a very old friend of Karp's. He had been a veteran at the DA's when Karp arrived, and although not strictly speaking a mentor, since his reputation was not the best and everything he had to teach was barely legal, Karp treasured him as a reminder of the dear old days at the DA, when guys in fedoras and three-piece suits with watch chains had fought the Mob in its power, and neither Miranda nor Escobedo had yet been heard from. Guma knew more about the Mafia than anyone else in

New York, not excluding the heads of the traditional Five Families.

"Butch Karp!" exclaimed Guma when Karp walked in. "For a minute there I thought you were the priest. Got a little worried."

"You don't look like you need a priest, Guma," said Karp. "A girl maybe."

Guma brought up a hoarse laughlike noise. He actually did not look as bad as Karp had expected and feared. He looked like a shriveled, old monkey, true, but he had always looked a little like one. The cancer had made him into a 7/10 scale model of himself. He wore a blue stocking cap with a Mets emblem on it over his hairless head, which did not detract from the simian appearance at all.

"You know Eddie, Butch," said Guma.

"Sure. Long time, Eddie."

Eddie Bent nodded gravely to acknowledge it had been. Edigio Frascatti, a turtlish man of past seventy, was a retired *caporegime* of the Genovese. Guma had once put him away for a decent interval, but Eddie Bent had no hard feelings. It was never personal with those guys.

"We were just talking about great unsolved hits of the past," said Guma as Karp pulled up a straight chair. "You'll recall Sam Riccardi."

"Oh, yeah, Sam," said Butch. "Fat Sam Riccardi. We never found the body, and I always entertained the hope that Fat Sam slipped away to South America. I kind of fancied him in a flowered shirt and a big straw hat drinking margaritas with some senoritas. You're telling me no?"

"He's in Shea," said Eddie Bent, pointing Queens-ward with the corkscrew index finger from which he derived his sobriquet.

"But not taking in a game?"

A barely audible chuckle from the mobster, and the finger pointed downward. Meaning, in the concrete.

"Any idea who did it?" asked Karp, feigning an innocent grin. They both grinned, too, but wolfishly, showing a good deal of gold.

"It was an open contract," said Eddie Bent, a generous admission. "It's better to do it like that, you know? Sam was . . ." Here he looked pained and touched his chest.

"A friend?" Karp inquired.

"Yeah. Sam was good people. Not, you know, *una bagascia.*"

"That's a cheap cunt to you, white man," Guma interjected.

"But he was skimming," said Karp.

Eddie Bent nodded sadly. "He was comfortable, you know? No fuckin' reason for it at all. He was warned. He was slapped around. Fuck, I slapped him around myself. What can you do, the guy won't listen to reason. What it was—I'll tell you what it was, and this is the sad part. Sam was a soft touch, you know? Guy walks in with a hard story, Sam liked to peel off from his roll. Which is fine, God bless him. But he was peeling off from our roll, too. He liked to be liked, Sam. Anyway, there's a guy you call in cases like this, been around for years. Everybody uses him. There's maybe a couple three guys in the business like that in the country, it's like a—what d'ya call it, like Con Ed?

"A public utility?" suggested Karp.

"That's right," said Eddie Bent, smiling. "A public utility. No fuss, no muss. The guy walked in here right now, I wouldn't fuckin' know him from Adam."

Karp did not actually believe this, but did not object. Instead he said, "Funny you should be talking about this stuff. I just talked to Marlene. She said a guy she knew, actually I knew him, too, a union guy, just got whacked the other night. We had dinner with them a little while ago. They killed the whole family: him, his wife, and their little girl, ten or so."

"Ah, shit, that's terrible!" said the mafioso. "That's fuckin' awful."

"Not a professional hit, would you say?"

"Oh, no. No fuckin' way. A pro, the target just vanishes, he's gone. Unless you're talkin' animals, Colombians, or the Chinks. They do shit like that. A union guy, you say?"

"Yeah. In West Virginia."

"Oh, well, West fuckin' Virginia, you're talkin' amateur hour there. That would definitely be a local thing. I would also say definitely it wasn't us. We're more or less out of that shit now, is what I hear."

"And the perp probably not one of those guys you were just talking about, either?"

Eddie Bent gave a contemptuous snort. "Nah, them're class guys. And never with a kid, like you was telling us, not a chance. Hey, expensive? *Mamma mia!* But, like they say, you get what you pay for."

Karp couldn't argue with this. Guma told a few stories about what was being done to him cost, and they all speculated about what he could've bought for the money, had Medicare been into fun stuff. A nurse came in and told them they had to leave in five minutes.

"Yeah," said Guma, "for what these last two months cost, I could have had myself whacked out, what, twice?"

"About there," Eddie Bent agreed. "Fifty grand, a hundred. It depends."

Karp asked, "What did Hoffa go for? Back in the days when you still did unions."

Eddie looked up at the ceiling and smiled. "I'll have to check my tax returns, see what I paid."

"But a guy like you were telling us about, that would be the kind of thing you'd call them in for. An open contract."

"That kind of thing. This one guy I'm thinking of, I mean, they don't give those, what the fuck, résumés, we did this one, we did that one. No advertising. But if you told me for sure he did Hoffa, I wouldn't fuckin' fall off my chair. You know what I'm saying?"

After her daily cry session, Lucy washed her face and spent the afternoon running dogs, first Malo and then Gringo, until her body was covered in sweat and dust. The sky was nacreous and seemed to press down heavily on land and sea. She took the twins swimming. Neither of them seemed affected now by what had befallen their late playmate. She tried to keep from resenting the easy amnesia of childhood. She could not shoo from her mind the image of Dan Heeney's face as he held the telephone tightly clenched in his hand.

Back at the farm, the Damicos had arrived with blasting gear, to remove the boulder that blocked the new water line. Assured by this event that the boys would be fixed and fascinated and out of trouble for at least a few hours, Lucy went into the house with the intent of retiring to her room for reading and a nap. Perhaps she might pray, although this had been dry for her recently. At one time, prayer had been able to move her into an alternative state of being, and this had taken the place of much that girls her age considered indispensable to life. The saints, however, had withdrawn. Perhaps that part of her life was closing down; perhaps she would become more like her mother. Thinking this, she shuddered slightly.

As she passed through, she noticed that there were messages on the

answering machine and played them: her mother, from the City, inform-
ing her that she would be staying in town that evening, and issuing
instructions for feeding children and animals. Next, several for her: Dr.
McGinnis, from MIT, wondering when she would return to Boston, and
trying to schedule something for next week; ditto, Drs. Sykes, Omura,
Dunn, Salmonson. Lucy was popular in the research community, which
held, not without reason, that somewhere between her ears was a clue to
one of the major unsolved problems of science—how natural languages
are acquired and processed. These demands tended to depress her. She
understood that her gift came with responsibilities, but lately these had
become more onerous, the demands of the scientists more irritating.
Resentfully, she considered transferring to a school far from the centers
of science, someplace isolated, West Virginia maybe, ha ha. In any case,
she was too tired to return the calls just then, or not exactly tired, but
drained. There was no call from Dan Heeney, not that she had really
expected one, but that added to the draining.

She went upstairs, removed everything but a halter top and underpants, turned the fan on high, and took up Lockwood's *Indo-European
Philology,* of which she got through two pages before sleep claimed her.
From this she was awakened by a dull thump, which shook the bed and
raised puffs of dust from the chalky walls. She pulled on shorts and sandals and went outside. Phil Damico was up in the backhoe, using its grab
to lift thick steel-mesh mats out of the trench and deposit them neatly in
the bed of their truck. She watched the operation for a while and did not
object when Phil allowed Zak, delirious with joy, to sit on his lap and
tweak the controls.

Later, she prepared supper, a cookout, and invited Billy Ireland to
join them, thinking it was unfair to let the scent of grilling meat float
around the place without so doing. It was a pleasant meal. She liked
Ireland. She thought her mother a fool for flirting with him the way
she did and felt no urge to do so herself, although she had to admit that
she shared her mother's taste for the bad boys. After eating, they sat at
the redwood table in the yard, drinking beer and watching the boys
chase fireflies. Ireland told her a long and involved story about his hard
life on the wrong side of the law. Meth had been his downfall. He had
got hooked and had done some stickups under the influence. Lucy had
spent considerable time among the addicted and the down-and-out

and knew they loved to retell their former degradation. She listened companionably and was not shocked. Somewhere during this conversation she decided that she would not return to Boston, but spend the summer at the farm. She did not pursue the reasons for this, beyond telling herself that she needed a break from being a lab rat. She did not mind the linguists so much, but the neuro guys were starting to get to her. She knew that in their secret materialist hearts they were dying to dissect.

Marlene drove back to the Island the next day, full of good food and drink, having spent also a night of lust that made both her and her husband ask themselves why they did not get away together more often. Against her always upwelling feelings of discontent she counted her blessings: money, a loving husband, health, one eye, money, a body in the early stages of decrepitude—up a whole size since college—a large number of ugly, fierce dogs, three lovely mutant, peculiar kids not as ruined as they might have been by exposure to violence when young, but who knew?; an amusing and distracting business, but distracting her from what? Yes, that was sort of the problem now, wasn't it? Marlene had reached the age where she no longer thought either love or friendship would save her, that the decades of her career would not make her mark on the world. The children, of course—the children still needed her, the twins anyhow, Lucy hadn't needed her since age seven, what with her constant commerce with God and all the saints, but even the twins wouldn't need her for long. Already Zak was squirming away when she hugged him and tried to sniff his hair. Giancarlo was more patient, of course, but she could feel that he was suffering her intimacies as a favor, not because he needed them anymore. Empty-nest syndrome? Not likely, as she had never been much of a nester when it had been chock-full. So what was it, this niggling feeling, this tendency to snap, to be bored with the stuff of daily life?

"What is it, dog? Analyze me. What should I do with the pathetic tag end of my life? Do I want to run a corporation? Tried that. Private eye? Tried that. Lawyer? Yeah, but only certain kinds of cases, and even then, do I really want to get into that dusty pit with Butch? Doing good? I gave all my money to the Church. Should I also make soup and visit smelly old people, in competition with my daughter? No, thank you. So what?" She nudged the dog. "So? Give me some advice—are you my best friend or not?"

The dog raised its great head and stared at her. It said, maybe it's been too long since you felt the bones of your enemies crunch between your jaws and tasted the rich tang of their blood.

"Oh, right," she snapped, "that's what you *always* say."

"Really?" said Marlene when Lucy told her the changed plans. "I thought you had all kinds of stuff they wanted you to do in Boston."

Lucy made a sour face. "Yes, but I don't want to do it. I decided to play hooky. Let there be wailing and gnashing of teeth up and down the river Charles!"

Marlene registered mock surprise. "Lucy! You're being *bad?* Oh, come to my arms! You *are* my little girl after all!"

"Cut it out, Mom," Lucy said as her mother enveloped her in a theatrical hug. "So, is it all right? I mean, I could work. I could finish Malo and Gringo."

"No, don't be silly—I mean, you *live* here, just as much as the twins do. I'm delighted, to tell the truth. If you're here with the boys, it'll free me up to do some things. We'll have a nice time."

"We won't snap and snarl at each other, will we?"

"Of *course* not, darling," said Marlene in a sugary voice. "As long as you don't oppose me in any way and anticipate my every need, we'll get along fine."

"I mean seriously."

"Seriously? What can I say, baby? I love you. I realize I get on your nerves sometimes, and I accept that most of it's my fault. I'm not an easy person to get along with."

"Well, you're not boring anyway," said Lucy, not wanting just at the moment to pursue the subject of why Marlene was hard to like. "What things?"

"Excuse me?"

"The things you said me being here to watch the boys would free you up for."

"Oh, you know . . . things," said Marlene airily, and then Billy Ireland had to see her about something and the moment passed.

As did the next ten days, amid the welter of ordinary life. The water line was completed, hose was laid, the vegetables therefore flourished in the face of unrelenting heat, and those parts of kennel life that depend on plentiful water became easier. The bitch Magog emerged from her confinement stiff and blinking and coursed around the exercise field with her mate and with Lucy, whose special dog she had always been. The puppies, remarkable for sturdiness, curiosity, and hideousness, were everywhere underfoot. Ads were placed; people came in expensive vehicles to look them over. On these occasions, Marlene demonstrated with Gog what a 210-pound Kohler-method guard dog looks like in action. She had added a few personal fillips to the standard training, in one of which Gog knocked his agitator to the ground and, on command, ripped his balls off, in fact, a brace of handballs sewn into a leather bag and attached with Velcro to the crotch of Russell's padded overalls. This always drew gasps of amazement and a pattering of applause from the ladies attending. Magog, who was actually a bit brighter than her old man, also demonstrated the location of personal objects, her forte.

Lucy got her trainees to float on the end of a lead with hardly a tug, to sit, to lie down, to stay. With the aid of a live wire from a fence charger, she taught them what every guard dog must learn: not to eat food except from their bowls. (*Zzzzzt!* Howl!) Lucy did not mind doing this in the least. She was tenderhearted, but not sentimental. GC harvested early tomatoes and young, tender lettuces. Zak shot three rats and a particularly stupid crow.

Lucy happened to be in the office when the phone call that ended all this arrived. It was Dan Heeney on the line. She felt her heart unexpectedly lift when she heard his voice and cruelly fall when he asked bluntly, "Is your mom there?"

"Sure, she's around. How *are* you?"

"Fine. Okay, I guess. Getting along."

"Wow, that's vivid. It really gives a precise word-picture of your mental and emotional state."

"Lucy, I really have to talk to your mom." Now she heard the tension in his voice and said sure, she'd go get her, and did.

When Marlene came on the line, he did not pause for pleasantries with her, either.

"Why I'm calling, ma'am, I mean bothering you, is you said, if there was anything you could do . . ."

"Sure. If you call me Marlene instead of ma'am, I'm at your service. What's up?"

"Okay. Well, Emmett doesn't know I'm calling. I mean maybe this is crazy."

"What is?"

"I mean . . . okay, they arrested this guy for the murders?"

"Good. I'm glad. Who was it?"

"A guy named Moses Welch. He lives down in Fairless Holler, about three miles from our place. Mom used to give him odd jobs, like hauling stuff, digging the garden, like that. He's about Emmett's age, a couple of years older."

"How did they find him?"

"From his shoes. He had blood all over these yellow boots he was wearing, spatters and along the sole. He was in town and someone noticed and told the cops, and they went and picked him up. It was human blood and the right kind. When the tests came back from the state lab in Charleston, they charged him."

"And . . . ?"

"Well, it's crazy. Moses Welch didn't kill my family. Moses Welch can hardly drive a car. He's got an IQ of about twenty. He wouldn't know which end of a gun to point."

"So how did he get their blood on his shoes?"

"They weren't his shoes. He said he found them under the bridge over the Guyandotte. Almost new shoes. He thought it was paint on them."

"And you believe him?"

"Well, yeah! The guys who really did it tossed them over the bridge and he found them."

"And the cops don't buy that?"

"Oh, hell, ma'am . . . I mean Marlene—we don't *have* any real cops here. We got J. J. Swett. He's been the sheriff for about a hundred years and he's got a total of six officers, and none of them can tell their sorry butts from a hole in the ground. Besides, all of them are in with Weames or the coal company."

"Weames is the man your father was running against."

"And he beat him, too. Emmett did an exit poll after the election; Dad won by ten points. Then Weames announces the results, and of course he said he won. Dad was going to bring DOL into the election to investigate. That's why Weames killed him. Or had it done."

"You sound pretty sure about this."

"Well, hell, I didn't need to go to damn MIT to figure *that* out," said Dan, his voice grating and loud over the phone. "One—he threatened Dad; two—he knew he was going to go down if there was an investigation of the election; and three—it wasn't some damn *retard* that did this."

"Is that what Emmett thinks?"

"Oh, yeah. Except he thinks he's going to find out who did it and kill them himself. That's why I need your help. Could you come here? My mom told me . . . I mean about what you used to do, and you're a lawyer, too. Moses got a lawyer, but he's a joke, the courthouse drunk. He can't defend anyone on a murder charge. We've got some money from the insurance. We could pay you . . ."

"Hold on a second. You want *me* to defend this man, this suspect in your family's murders?"

"Well, yeah, to start with. If they convict him, hell, it's all over. No one will ever look at the thing again, not in Robbens County, anyway. And then after you get him off . . . well, you know, find out who did it."

"Find out . . . ?" exclaimed Marlene incredulously. "Okay, look, Dan—I appreciate that you have a problem there, but first of all, I am not licensed to practice law in West Virginia. Second—"

"You went to Delaware. My mom told me about that girl who killed her baby."

"She didn't kill her baby. And that was different. I had a local co-counsel and—"

"Well, you'd have Ernie Poole, wouldn't you?"

"Who?"

"The fella who's defending Moses now."

"The drunk? Oh, thank you very much! Second, as I was saying, in the real world, as opposed to books and movies, crimes are solved by the cops, not by private investigators. I can't just drop into a strange part of the country, ask a few pointed questions, beat up some villains, and come out with the answer. It don't work that way. A triple-murder investigation is a big, big operation."

"You *have* to come," cried Dan, his voice breaking. "I haven't got anybody else. Everyone around here is too scared now, or bought out by the company or Weames. And Emmett is drinking and talking big about going over to Weames or one of his people and beating the truth out of them, and he's going to get killed, too, and he's all I've got left in the world." Heavy breathing, then stifled sobs.

Marlene sighed and rolled her eyes upward. Lucy, who had not gone far, asked, "What's wrong?"

Marlene put her hand over the mouthpiece and said, "He wants me to go down there and . . . Okay, Dan, calm down. Get hold of yourself! Look, here's what I think you should do." She paused there. What *should* he do? She had no idea, except maybe not to have called, not to have had a mother who struck up a conversation on a Long Island beach with a woman who should have known better than to blather on about her colorful past, and then gotten herself killed in some godforsaken hole in West . . . No, that was the wrong line of thought. The question was, what should *she* do? Marlene felt Lucy's eyes on her.

"What I think you should do," Marlene resumed, "is get your drunk lawyer friend to hand you copies of all the paper he's got on the case, as complete a record as he can—arrest reports, evidence reports, whatever. I'll need to look at all that. Where are you guys staying now?"

"At our house . . . Wait, does that mean you're coming?"

"At your house?" cried Marlene. "You're living in the *crime scene?*"

"Uh-huh. It's our house. They took all the, you know, the murder evidence out. And we hired a couple of women to clean it up and paint and all."

"Oh, great!"

"What's wrong? Did we make a mistake?"

"Oh, no, it's not your fault—but just so you know, in the regular world, crime scenes are usually sealed for a considerable time. Sometimes even until the trial. I've known defense lawyers and prosecutors to actually tour a jury through a preserved crime scene. Well, it doesn't matter now."

"But you're coming, right?"

She blew out a long breath. "Yeah, I guess. Hang in there, kid. And try to keep your brother from doing something stupid." After a few more similar encouraging banalities and a brief logistical discussion, she hung up.

"Speaking of stupid," she said to the air.

Lucy was almost trembling with frustration. *"Mah-umm!* What is going *on?"*

Marlene explained the situation. "I want to come, too," was the response.

"Idiot child, you can't come. I couldn't go at *all* if you weren't here. The boys . . . ?"

"They could go to summer camp. And you might need help down there."

"Yes, and if they held court in Estonian, you would be invaluable."

"That is really nasty."

Marlene hung her head and controlled her temper. "Yes. I'm sorry. Look, here's what's going to happen. What we have here is a case of panic. It's a delayed reaction to the shock, and God knows those poor kids have a right to be a little weird. I will go there, take a look around, calm them both down, find them a decent *West Virginia* lawyer, and depart. It should take a week, two tops."

"You going to take your gun?"

"No, but I am going to take a lot of Kleenex." Marlene held her hands palms up and pirouetted once. "Look, this is the new nonviolent mom, just like you always wanted. It's a mission of mercy."

"Uh-huh. Are you taking the dog?"

"Well, yeah," said Marlene, startled a little by the question. Of course she was taking Gog. She would take her shoes, her toothbrush, and a change of undies, too.

Lucy raised an eyebrow over a baleful look, then left the room.

This is ridiculous, thought Marlene—why am I trying to impress my daughter with my benevolent intentions? Feeling annoyed at herself, at the Heeneys, and at Lucy, she decided to call her husband and vent.

"Well, any comments?" she demanded after she had apprised him of the situation and her plans.

"I'm jealous," he replied. "You get to go flitting off to fight evil, and I have to stay here and *be* evil."

"I thought you were the good guys."

"Oh, yeah, maybe once a week. Meanwhile, 75 percent of the cases we handle involve putting black and Latino kids in jail forever for selling dope. The really evil still flourish, as you may have noticed. And my youth and beauty are fading and every day is like every other day, and it's hot as a bitch in here, and you're wandering away to the cool mountains to wipe noses. It's not fair."

"You're right. Are you going to whine any more?"

"Yes. I might even get all red and sweaty and snotty-nosed."

"Seriously, what do you think?"

Karp paused before answering, detecting one of the numerous no-win queries (Am I too fat? Does this look good on me?) that husbands are so often called upon to answer.

He said, "It seems like a charitable act as long as you don't get involved. I assume Lucy is going to watch the boys. You have no problems with that?"

"Of course not—for a couple of days? She's the most responsible creature on God's earth. They'll be prepping for seminary by the time I get back."

"Maybe I'll take some leave anyway."

"Do that. What did you mean about getting involved?"

"I meant *involved.* Legally, emotionally—it's not your problem, it's a complex situation in a part of the world you don't know diddly-squat about, and where you're liable to make things worse." In your inimitable fashion, Karp thought, but declined to say.

"Make things worse? Gosh, this is just fucking great. I volunteer to upset my life and go help out a couple of kids I barely know, and all the support I get from my family is a kind of insinuating suspicion. For crying out loud, don't you trust me?"

No, thought Karp. "Of course," he said.

6

SHE DECIDED TO LEAVE JUST BEFORE DAWN, TO GET FREE OF THE CITY-
bound traffic and be out on the great American road at sunup. Having
committed herself, having spent the whole of the previous evening gen-
erating quality time with her sons (Monopoly, casino, hours of Tolkien)
and explaining what she was doing, having overinstructed her daughter
and her manager, she felt for the first time in a long time like the old
Marlene, or at least like the nostalgic memory thereof. As she loaded her
bag and dog into the Dodge, she discovered she was humming the Pirate
Jenny song from *Threepenny Opera*.

She stopped when she saw that her daughter, dressed in an old flan-
nel bathrobe, was watching her from the doorway, smiling.

"Off on an adventure," Lucy observed. "You're as happy as a puppy."

"It's not an *adventure*," answered Marlene a little testily. "It's a very
dull mission of mercy. I should be back in a week, tops."

Lucy shook her head pityingly. "Oh, Mom . . ."

"What? What's with this 'Oh, Mom'? I fail to understand why everyone is making such a big deal out of this. Could you please explain that?"

Lucy walked over and embraced her mother and kissed her cheek.
"Take care of yourself, okay? Call me when you get there, and give my
regards to the Heeneys."

Marlene made agreeable noises and hugged her back, thinking at
the same time that their natural positions had somehow been reversed,
that Lucy was being understandingly parental and she childish. This
thought occupied her mind for the two minutes it took her to get off the

property and out onto the dark road. She punched up the radio: AM, oldies. Marlene had a tape player in her console but rarely used it. She liked the local stations, liked the way they waxed and waned as the miles vanished under the wheels, little driblets of what remained of regional culture in America. The station took her into the City, around the fat underbelly of Brooklyn and over the Verrazano to Staten Island and Jersey. The sun was well up when she drove onto Interstate 78 in the middle of the Garden State, which, to her surprise, was quite gardenlike in these parts, and took it west into Pennsylvania.

By noon, she was in Youngwood, Pennsylvania, and hungry. She drove off the turnpike, ate at a Hardee's, walked and fed the dog. Full of unhealthy greases and sugars, she continued onto the 70 cutoff and then south on 79 to Charleston. South of Charleston, the land rose, the divided highway petered out at Logan, and she found herself on winding, two-lane blacktop running along mountainsides covered with dark second-growth timber. The radio was all country and western and static now, the little stations fading in the valleys and bursting out again on the ridges. As she drove deeper into the southwestern part of the state, she began to see the marks coal had made on the country. Scrapes of blackness against hillsides, with huge gallowslike structures rising above the hills, and factories with brick smokestacks and square yards of smashed windows. Once she crossed on a narrow bridge and saw a newer industrial complex of some sort tucked into the curve of the river below, lines of ocher buildings, shooting out white smoke and yellow, and a smoky flame like a badly trimmed candle twisting above a tall pipe. The river was a bright medicinal green. By three she was in Robbens County, climbing a steep grade and then descending past several roadside crosses and an escape road for runaway trucks. McCullensburg was at the bottom of a fourteen-mile-long, seven-degree grade, built on what looked like the only halfway flat patch in the county.

It was not a pretty town. The usual strip development hung on its outskirts, gas stations and fast food and little, sad, hopeful businesses in concrete-block structures, a beauty shoppe, an upholsterer, a lawn-mower guy. She turned left on Market as directed and passed through the business district. Like many towns in this part of the world, it had peaked around the late nineteenth century when coal was king. The two-story brick and stone buildings were of that era, and the courthouse square had a courthouse in it, this a handsome Federal-style building flanked by old trees, complete with white columns, a portico, and a tall cupola. Six streets and the town was gone. She proceeded along Route 199 into the scant suburbs, small bungalows with aluminum siding mainly, and squat, ugly, manufactured housing, with the occasional faded wooden carpenter-Gothic Victorian. She took a turnoff marked 3112, whose blacktop soon became rutted gravel hairpinning back and forth across the steep face of a mountain.

The large mailbox that said HEENEY had been shot full of holes. The house itself was set in a grassy field surrounded by a neat white fence, and hanging over it loomed a group of large, dark oaks. The renovated farmhouse had a cedar shake roof, two cobble chimneys, and a field-stone foundation, obviously of considerable age, but well maintained; two stories, painted buff with dark red shutters and trim. The original barn of the place stood broken-backed and sagging, covered with creeper, but a weathered shed near the house served as a garage. She saw the Heeneys' GMC there and a very old and dusty Ford next to it. She parked and got out, groaning and stretching. She let the dog out, who did the same.

The front door of the house popped open and there was Dan Heeney, looking worn and even younger than he had on Long Island.

"You got here."

"I did," she said. "Here I am to save the day, just like Mighty Mouse. But first I need to pee."

"Uh, sure, right," he said, as if unsure, and led her (and she her dog) into the house. It was spacious and well furnished with local stuff, hooked rugs and country chests, set off nicely by a few pieces of the kind of fine old cherry and mahogany accumulated by families that were well-off in the late 1800s. Marlene thought of Rose decorating this place on a fairly tight budget, out of trips to swap meets and castoffs from her family, and felt a pang of loss deeper than expected for a woman she had scarcely known.

In the bathroom (which showed the grungy effects of two young bachelors living there alone) she heard voices raised. She finished and followed these into the kitchen. Dan and his brother were standing across the room from one another, glaring and calling each other unpleasant names.

"What's up, boys?" she said cheerfully.

Both young men had red faces. Marlene didn't know whether it was from anger or embarrassment, nor did she care.

Emmett actually stamped his foot and yelled at his brother, "Goddamnit, what the hell did you think you were doing?"

"We need help, Em, and you're too damn boneheaded to see it."

Emmett cursed and got redder and made a move toward his brother, from which he was brought up short by a rumbling growl from Gog.

Marlene said, "Emmett, you're upsetting my dog, and you're upsetting me. We both prefer peaceful discourse to yelling. I have just driven twelve hours straight to help you all out, and whether or not you are personally willing to accept my help is beside the point. Right now, I'm a guest of your brother in his home. I'm sure your folks taught you better manners than what you've been showing." She indicated the enameled kitchen table. "Let us sit down and take counsel with one another and see where we are."

All three sat. After a brief silence, Marlene said, "Welcome to McCullensburg, Marlene. Did you have a pleasant trip? Would you care for some refreshment? A frosty glass of beer, perhaps? A mint julep?"

Dan looked startled for an instant and then broke into a sputtering laugh.

Emmett tried to keep his face grim and failed. "Dickhead."

"Shit for brains," said Dan kindly. "I think I can offer you a beer," he added, rising to open the refrigerator. The bottom two shelves were completely packed with cans of Iron City.

They popped, they drank. "How was your drive?" Dan asked.

"Pretty good," she said. "Your state seems extremely mountainous, however. I guess you noticed that already."

They laughed and told several mountaineer jokes, mainly hinging on people or animals having legs on one side shorter to compensate for the slope. Judging the ice to have been sufficiently broken, Marlene said to Emmett, "I couldn't help overhearing—I take it you don't approve of what Dan did. Calling me, I mean. Would you mind telling me why?"

Emmett looked uneasy as he replied, "Oh, you know, nothing personal, but Dad always told us to handle things ourselves. There's no need to have you all bothered about our troubles."

"That's good advice, generally," she agreed. "But if it'll make you feel any better, I don't intend to do very much. Dan said that the police had a man . . ."

"Moses Welch," Dan put in.

"Right. Who Dan thinks is a frame-up. What do *you* think?"

Emmett dropped his head for a moment, considering. "Yeah, I guess. I mean we all know who really done it. Or hired it done. Mose, all they got on him is the boots. And him being . . ." He tapped his temple.

"Okay," she said, "so the first thing is to look into his case. If, in fact, he's innocent, we want to get the charges dismissed so that the cops will keep looking for whoever really did the murders." She saw them nod in agreement. "Okay, Emmett, tell me about the night of."

"It was about a week after they stole the election. A Friday. We had a meeting here, about twenty guys from the union. Dad was telling them about him going to Washington and his meeting at the Department of Labor. They were real depressed at first, but he got them up again. He thought DOL would throw out the results and call another election and supervise it and then we'd win. The meeting went on till about ten, ten-thirty. Then everyone left. I went over to Kathy's house—that's my girl-friend—and stayed over. I usually do on weekends. The next morning, we slept in and then I came back here. I came around back and saw that somebody'd taken off the storm door in the back and tossed it down next to the stairs, and the back door into the kitchen was all ripped up around the lock, like with a wrecking bar." Emmett paused, swallowed.

"I found them inside. Mom and Dad in their bedroom. Lizzie in her bed." He paused and took several breaths. "It was pretty bad. Do you want to see where it happened?"

"Later. What did you do?"

"Well, they were dead. Anyone could see that. They used a shotgun on Dad and Mom. He must have known they were coming because he was out of bed and he had his pistol. He had a .38 he kept under the mat-tress. Lizzie was in her bed. They shot her sleeping. In the head."

"You said, 'they.' What makes you think there was more than one of them?"

"Had to be. Lizzie was a light sleeper. Her room was right next door to theirs. No way she wouldn't have got up to a couple of shotgun blasts. But she was shot in her bed, sleeping like I said. You could tell that."

"I take it she wasn't killed with a shotgun."

"No, a pistol. Which they didn't find on Mose or anywhere around his place. They said he must've tossed it."

"I guess they probably didn't look all that hard," she said. "Blame the lame; it's a famous stupid cop trick. He's confessed to it, naturally."

"Sure," said Dan. "They promised him a dish of chocolate ice cream is what I heard."

"And what was his lawyer, what's-his-face, doing while all this was going on?"

"Ernie Poole," said Emmett. "Sleeping, probably. That's what he mostly does. He stands up to be counted in the court and then takes a nap. It's a joke."

"Good. I love a joke. So after you found them, you called the cops."

"Right. Swett came over with a couple of his guys. They found Dad's wallet was missing. He always carried a bunch of cash on him, so they said that was probably it, a random robbery. They said the killer came on foot."

"Because . . . ?"

"Well, that part made sense," Emmett admitted. "After they shot our dog, Dad rigged up one of those sensors like they have in gas stations, across the drive. At night it turned on the floodlights and rang a little bell in the house. They said that would've got him up, and it would have."

"I see. Did they do any crime-scene work? Take prints, vacuum for fibers, like that?"

Emmett let out a bitter laugh. "Hell, no! Those jerks don't do any of that stuff. They just about good enough to grab drunks and kids smoking weed in the bushes. The state cops do all that kind of thing."

"And did they call the state cops?"

"Yeah, they sent a team of guys out from the barracks in Logan. They took up the carpets and all and sprayed a lot of black powder around. They said they would be back and not to touch anything. I stayed with Kathy that night. Then the next day, Mose Welch came to town to show off his new boots, and they arrested him. It went with what they said about the car. Mose can't drive."

"I see. How convenient. And then . . . ?"

"Nothing. I called the sheriff and he said the case is over, you can move back in, so we did. I got some people in to help clean up and fix the back-door locks. I still haven't put the storm door back on. Not that we need it any with this weather. We've been here since."

Marlene made some notes on her pad. "Tell me, does this Moses Welch have any relatives, a guardian of some kind?"

"I don't know about a guardian," said Emmett, "but Fairless Holler got a load of Welches. It's their home place."

"And of these Welches, which do you think would care the most about old Mose?"

The two Heeneys considered this for a moment. Then Emmett said, "I guess that would be Betty Washburn. She's his sister. He used to live in a busted-up trailer back of their place, and I guess she kept him fed and dressed, more or less."

"Good, we'll go see Mrs. Washburn," said Marlene briskly. She turned to Dan. "Meanwhile, did you get any paperwork from Poole?"

"No, sorry. He wouldn't give me any. He said it was none of my concern."

"Technically, he's right. Well, we'll have to change that. Starting with me. Show me a place I can get cleaned up and changed, will you?"

Neither of the Heeneys had ever seen Marlene in any apparel but the sort of rags she wore around her farm. She now emerged in a gray Anne Klein silk and linen suit over a pearly, loose-necked blouse, dark nylons, and Blahnik sandals. Her face was made up and her expensive haircut had been arranged the way her hairdresser had intended. A whiff of L'Aire du Temps hit them; their eyes widened; she grinned back at them.

"What do you think? Good enough for Robbens County?"

"I guess," said Emmett. "What are you going to do?"

"A couple of things. One is I have to get up to speed on local criminal statutes and procedure. I don't suppose you have anything around town like a library with a computer connected to the Internet?"

They both laughed. Dan said, "Uh, I think so. We got electricity and indoor plumbing, too. Follow me, lady."

He led her to a bedroom, a teenager's den, posters on the wall, dirty clothes strewn about, an unmade bed decorated with books and magazines, and on a table, a squat, black IBM tower, a large monitor, and a DeskJet printer.

"Oops," she said. "I forgot MIT. Sorry."

"No problem. What do you want? I got a satellite hookup."

"Great. Get me the state criminal code and the rules of criminal procedure for a start. While you're doing that, I'll take a ride with Emmett."

She went to leave and then stopped. "No, wait. Could you bring up a word-processing program?"

He did. She sat and typed out a short document and printed it. "Emmett! Let's go see Mrs. Washburn."

They drove back through town, north on 130, and off the blacktop onto a rutted gravel road that wound back and forth across a narrow stream on timber bridges. Through gaps in the trees Marlene could see little groups of structures—small, rickety houses with washing flapping on lines in their yards, some newer mobile homes, and weathered gray sheds falling back into nature. Every dwelling had several elderly vehicles in front, in various stages of demolishment or repair. From time to time a glint of metal indicated a dump in the woods. The GMC jumped and shook; a rooster tail of tan dust rose behind it.

"This is Belo Knob," Emmett told her. "I mean the mountain we're on. The town's on a flat place where five mountains come together, like in the middle of a flower. Belo's on the north side, say twelve o'clock. Then Hampden's at three, where our place is, Hogue is at six, down south of town, then Filbert Ridge, that's the highest one, at seven through nine o'clock. And then Burnt Peak's up at ten or eleven."

"And the hollows are on the mountains?"

"Up in there. The hills are all cut up by streams and those make the hollers. This is Peck Creek we've been going over, and Fairless comes into it, just up here a piece."

They turned off the gravel onto an oiled dirt road and off that onto a driveway marked by a white-painted truck tire. The Washburn home was a one-story affair with pale green siding and a narrow porch in front, on which stood an ancient round washing machine and a rocking chair. An old-fashioned "streamlined" aluminum house trailer with no wheels squatted on concrete blocks just to the rear of the house. In the front yard were a rust-red, twenty-year-old Ford pickup and an El Camino with the hood gaping. Among these stigmata of rural poverty stood, jarringly, a satellite dish eight feet in diameter, round and white as the moon. When they pulled up, two yellow dogs ran out from beneath the house and ran around their truck, barking and snarling.

The woman sitting in the rocker yelled at the dogs, to which they responded not at all. She rose heavily, picked up a baseball bat, and started toward the GMC. The dogs retreated. Emmett and Marlene left the car and walked up to the woman. Marlene thought she must have weighed 250 pounds; her upper arms looked the same size as Marlene's thighs. Her hair made a long, dirty-blond braid down her back; her eyes were small, almost colorless, and wary. She wore denim cutoffs and a pink, sleeveless sweatshirt with a picture of Tweety bird on it.

"How're y'doing, Betty," said Emmett.

"Fair," said the woman. Marlene noted she continued to grip the ball bat. "I'm sorry about your loss, Emmett, but you know my brother didn't have nothin' at all to do with that."

"I know that. That's why we're here. This here's Marlene Ciampi from New York City. She's a lawyer. She wants to help get Mose out of jail."

The woman stared at Marlene unbelievingly. "We can't pay nothing."

"There's no need to pay, Mrs. Washburn," Marlene said. "I'm taking your brother's case pro bono."

"Who?"

"It means I'm working for free."

The woman's eyes narrowed. "Why'd you want to do that?"

"Because Rose Heeney was a friend of mine. Lizzie played with my kids. I have two boys her age. Someone killed them and I want them to pay for it, and the first thing we need to do to make that happen is getting your brother free of the false charge that *he* killed them."

Betty Washburn flicked her eyes rapidly between Marlene and Emmett, and Marlene could see how difficult it was for her to accept anything a stranger said at face value. Finally, her features relaxed a trifle, as did her grip on the ball bat. "Well, you all better come on in, then."

The house was cooler than the yard, but musty. The ceilings were low and made of pressboard. Everything in the house was old and worn. It was clean, though, the furniture and floors rubbed down past the finish so that their substance was slightly ground away. They sat in the kitchen around a wooden table covered by sticky lace-pattern plastic. Betty Washburn served them thin, oversweet iced tea in jelly glasses. Marlene explained that before she could do anything for Mose, she had to be named formally as his attorney. She asked whether Betty was his official guardian.

"No'm. He don't need no guardian. Mose, he kept to hisself and never hurt nor bothered no one. He got his playthings and his animals. He's real gentle with my kids. Sometimes he takes him long walks in the woods. Tell you the truth, I'm more scared of what other folks might do to him than what he might do."

"I understand. Tell me, has Mose ever been examined by a psychologist?'"

"Yeah, way back, when Maw first noticed he wasn't right. We took him upstate to this school? You know, for slows. They said he wasn't going to ever get much more'n five years old."

"Do you have any papers relating to that?"

"There was some in a box. I took it in when Maw passed. I guess they's somewheres around."

A search was organized, a dusty cardboard box appeared, and after rummaging, Marlene came up with a brown envelope containing a paper with several paragraphs of psychological bureaucratese pertaining to Moses Welch's mental abilities. She stuck it in her bag.

"Okay, the next thing is, we'll have to go down to the jail and get him to sign a paper. Have you talked with his lawyer at all?"

Mrs. Washburn sniffed. "Him? Ernie Poole ain't no more use'n tits on a boar hog."

"So I hear. Maybe I can persuade him to be more useful. Anyway, we need to go see your brother."

"What, now?"

"Unless you like having him sit in jail."

Mrs. Washburn seemed to think about that for a slow minute. Then she said, "Well, let's go do it."

She rose up, she grabbed a white patent leather handbag, and strode out of the kitchen. They followed her into the house's main room. In it were a sagging couch covered by a tan chenille bedspread, a green La-Z-Boy, a couple of rickety tables, a standard lamp with a paper shade, a wooden chest covered by a plastic doily, and a shining thirty-two-inch color television set. Two little girls were sitting on the couch watching cartoon people fight each other. They were dressed in worn tops and shorts, and each had her blond hair in a bowl cut, which Marlene was sure had been done in the kitchen with an actual bowl. Mrs. Washburn barked, "Girls, get on your shoes. We're goin' to town to see Uncle Mose."

The elder of the two said, "Do we hafta, Maw?"

"Don't pert off, child. Do as you're told."

In short order they had a convoy of two started, Mrs. Washburn following in the red pickup.

"The Welches are good folks," said Emmett over the roar. "They just have a lot of troubles."

"Are they very poor?"

"No, really about average for Robbens County, I guess. Burt—that's the husband—he's got a mechanic's job at the mine. They got a sick kid, and Burt was laid up most of last year."

"Anyway they've got satellite TV," Marlene observed.

"Oh, yeah. Folks around here'll live on lard and flour to pay their satellite bills, thems as don't outright pirate the signal. My dad used to say that satellite destroyed the working class worse than the mine owners did. Sports and porno for the boys, soap opera for the ladies, and cartoons for the younguns. There wasn't any TV at all up here, and hardly any radio, before the dishes came in. The hollers had their own way of life. Now they're getting just like everyone else."

"Is that bad?"

"It is if they become dogs and don't mind feeding off whatever scraps the big boys toss at them. My dad reminded them of what they used to be, fighting men, union men, and all that. Now . . . hell, I don't know what's gonna happen to them."

Marlene did not know either. She was from a union family herself, but had never been particularly interested in working-class politics, beyond the usual guilt at worldly success and a tendency to vote the straight Democratic ticket. Lefty posturing had bored her in college, especially as pitched by the upper-middle-class kids who typically espoused it. A vague social responsibility stirred in her breast; she suppressed it. She said, "Well, let's see what we can do about getting this guy out of the can and the investigation started up again."

The jail was in the basement of a two-floor, brown-brick structure adjacent to the handsome courthouse. Marlene and Mrs. Washburn went in, while Emmett took the Washburn girls for an ice cream. The deputy in charge was a scrawny man in a tan uniform and clear-framed glasses, with thinning hair combed across his scalp. He was not pleased to be taken away from his television set. He nodded to Mrs. Washburn and stared at Marlene. "Only family allowed to visit," he warned.

"I *am* family," said Marlene. "I'm Cousin Marlene. From Ashtabula?" The stare increased, became incredulous; Marlene met it with her own more powerful one. The man grumpily relented and led them down a sewer-smelling iron staircase to the basement.

The jail had four cells. Moses Welch was in the only occupied one. He was a large man, fleshy like his sister, with the sweet, confused expression of the dim in his pale eyes. His hair was startlingly blond, almost white, and hung lanky over his ears.

"Hey, Betty," he cried when they appeared. "Hey, Betty, did you bring ice cream?"

Marlene was surprised and touched by the way brother and sister hugged. Betty sat on the bunk next to him and brushed the hair back from his forehead. "We'll see about ice cream later, honey. I want you to say hello to Marlene here. Marlene says she's gonna get you out of this jail. "

Marlene said, "Hello, Mose."

"I saw a mouse, Marlene. It was just there."

"That's nice," said Marlene. "Mose, tell me: Do you know why you're in here?"

"Yes'm. On account of I kilt those folks."

"Yes, but you really didn't kill them, did you?"

"Sheriff says I did. On account of those boots."

"Yes, but you didn't really."

"Those boots is too tight anyways. They was real new so I thought they would fit me. I never had no real new boots."

"Uh-huh. But you found those boots, right?"

"Yes'm. 'Neath the green bridge where they's frogs and all."

Mrs. Washburn said, "He means the bridge on 130 over the Guyandotte. He's always playing down there."

"Right. You found the boots, but you didn't kill anyone," said Marlene. "That's what you have to say from now on."

"Will I get in trouble?" the man asked, worry appearing in his mild eyes.

"No, you won't, because I'm going to be your lawyer now. Do you know what a lawyer is?"

A confused shake of his head.

"A lawyer is for when you get in big trouble. She tells the sheriff you didn't really do it. Do you want me to be your lawyer?"

The man looked at his sister, who nodded. He nodded, too.

"Okay, great!" Marlene took a paper out of her bag. "Can you write your name?"

"Yes'm. Betty learned me how."

"Good. Then I want you to write it on this line here." Marlene gave him a felt-tip and he did so, slowly, his tongue protruding in concentration.

"Can I have my ice cream now?" he asked brightly.

Marlene watched Mrs. Washburn drive off with her two chocolate-smeared kids. "Emmett, where's this Poole hang out?"

He pointed across the square. "That's his office there. Unless he's drinking at the VFW."

"I might be a while, then."

"I'll be here. Take your time."

She took her dog and entered the building, a three-story brick structure with a lunchroom on the ground floor. The directory inside the door displayed the names of the tenants, mainly lawyers and bail bondsmen, court reporters, and a couple of real estate firms. Ernest J. Poole occupied 3-E. She climbed the stairs and knocked on the door. Nothing. She pounded. Silence. The door was unlocked. Inside she found an anteroom with a secretary's desk and a shrouded typewriter, both covered with dust. A philodendron had died in a pot in the corner. She saw a frosted-glass door with the lawyer's name on it in gold letters, tapped on it, and called out, "Mr. Poole?"

She heard an indistinct human noise that she accepted as an invitation and entered. The lights were out, the venetian blinds shut. The smell was of unwashed clothes, sour-mash bourbon, and the underlying ketone stink of a drunk. The drunk was lying sprawled on a brown leather couch, drunk. Marlene nudged him. No response, except a groan and an effort to bury his face in the corner of the couch. She found the light switch, flipped it on, made a tour. The desk, a heavy mahogany structure, was covered with a scant drift of papers and unopened junk mail, a large, butt-choked ashtray, a half-empty fifth of low-end bourbon, crumpled take-out food bags, filthy paper plates and cups. These also stuffed to overflowing the nearby wastebasket. Black flies buzzed heavily through the fetid air. One wall held diplomas (UWV and Vanderbilt law school) and the sort of award plaques small-town lawyers accumulate, together with group photographs of the occupant with local notables. The newest looked about twelve years old. In the photographs, Poole was in his forties sporting a sharp Chamber of Commerce optimistic look. He wore his thick, dark hair fashionably long. A square jaw with a dimple in the chin, a broad forehead, a manly nose, and a wide mouth completed a face that might once not have been out of place on a campaign poster. Marlene yanked up the blinds. A whimper sounded from the couch. She found a coffeemaker, filled the pot with cold water from a cooler, and poured it over Ernest J. Poole's head.

He sat up, sputtering. The candidate's face, she saw, had been considerably eroded by the bad living, the features softened and gullied, the skin coarsened. The head of hair was, however, still intact, although not as neatly barbered as it had been in the photos.

"Wha . . . wha . . . who . . . who the hell are you? Goddamnit, I'm all wet."

"My name is Marlene Ciampi, Mr. Poole. I'm Moses Welch's new lawyer."

"Whose what?"

"Moses Welch. He's been indicted for murdering the Heeney family. You're his court-appointed attorney. Now you're my local co-counsel." She held out the paper the defendant had signed for him to read. He glanced at it without interest; all of that was reserved for the bottle on the desk. He rose, wobbled, stepped, reached for it. She was quicker.

"Give me that! That's mine," he snarled. He made to grab it from her, but was arrested by a noise like a cold engine cranking. Gog bounded between man and mistress and exhibited his famous smile of destruction. Poole shied away and fell back on the couch.

"Get that animal away from me!" he demanded weakly. "If it touches me, I'll sue."

"If he touches you, you won't be in any condition to sue." Wiggling the bottle before his eyes, she said, "I know you need a drink, but you can't have one now. You need to do some work first. I'm going to make you a pot of strong black coffee, which you will consume until you are as sober as you ever get. Then we will have a professional conversation about our client and decide what to do next."

He gaped at her and wiped at his reddened eyes. "Who the hell *are* you?"

"I told you. I'm Marlene Ciampi, I'm Moses Welch's—"

"Yeah, I got that. What're you doing in McCullensburg?"

"I was a friend of Rose Heeney." Marlene put the coffee on. "Her sons engaged me to get Moses Welch out of this stupid situation and get the police back onto looking for the real killers."

"That's your plan, is it?" he asked, his voice tired and hollow. He rubbed his face vigorously with both hands. "You don't know much about Robbens County, that's for sure."

"No, I don't. That's another reason I need your help."

He snorted a sort of laugh. "Well, if you need *my* help, lady, you're in a sorry state. I tell you what I will do though. If you put a shot in my coffee, I will enlighten you as to how things are done around here. After which, you will kindly get the hell out of my office."

Marlene had nothing to say to this. She poured out a mug of coffee, added a splash of the bourbon. His eyes were fixed on the bottle's lip. With body English he urged a more generous pour, but was passive when he saw it would be minimal. He drank and talked. She sat on the edge of his desk and listened.

"Well, let's start with Moses Welch. Moses Welch is an idiot. He should have been put away a long time ago, but the Welches, of course, wouldn't hear of it. It's only a matter of time before he walks in front of a train or a coal truck or decides to grab some little girl and play doctor. He came to town in shoes soaked in the Heeneys' blood. He was duly arrested. At the arraignment, I pleaded him non compos, which he is. That plea was rejected by Judge Murdoch, and Mose was deemed fit to aid in his own defense."

"That's nonsense."

"I know. Don't interrupt. I have petitioned the court for a psychiatric examination, which will demonstrate that Moses Welch is, in fact, incapable of telling right from wrong. After he's convicted, he'll be remanded to the state institution at Morgantown indefinitely, which is probably the best place for him, all told. I want some aspirin."

This was found, a bottle of two hundred in a desk drawer. He downed four with the coffee. "There. That's the sad story of Moses Welch. Case closed. Now, please go away and leave me alone."

"But he didn't do it."

"He confessed to it."

"Yes, and you were probably right there with the ice cream. Oh, hell, just look at the poor sap! He wouldn't hurt a fly. Besides, the Heeneys were killed by at least two men."

"How do you know that?" Poole's hands shook when he said it, slopping the coffee.

"Because the Heeney boys figured it out. Lizzie was killed with a pistol shot to the head. Do you actually believe that our retard walked into the Heeney home, outshot an armed man, killed him and his wife, and then calmly pranced into a little girl's bedroom and shot her while she was still sleeping peacefully? Have you ever heard a twelve-gauge go off in a confined space?"

"He could've shot her first."

"Oh, please! And then put away his pistol, grabbed his shotgun, and dispatched the Heeneys? With Red Heeney alerted and a .38 in his fist? Who're we talking about here, John Wesley Hardin? Whose side are you on anyway?"

"You don't understand."

"Okay, enlighten me. Explain why you're selling out your client."

"I'm not selling out my client. I'm doing what I have to do to keep more people from being hurt. Look, miss, whatever your . . ."

"Marlene."

"Marlene. Let me ask you this—what do you think is going to happen when you mount your spirited defense of Moses Welch's innocence? You think everyone in town's going to say, oh, jeez, we made a mistake, thank you so much? Do you think the sheriff is actually going to look for someone else? They will not, and he will not. What they will do is look for the source of the upsetting reversal of a very nice arrangement. They will find it in you, and in me, and in the Heeney boys, who called in a fancy out-of-town lady lawyer. And they will expunge the persons responsible."

"Who is this *they?*"

"The *they* who run our little town. They didn't like Red Heeney unsettling things, with the results you know. It will be the same with you and me and the Heeney boys. What I'm trying to say is, you can't bring Rose back. Do you really want to be responsible for wiping out the rest of her family? Can I have a little more?" He held out his cup like a beggar, eyeing the bottle.

"No. Are you talking about Weames and the union?"

"Oh, he's part of it."

"And what's the whole thing look like?"

He laughed, a short pair of dry syllables, like a curse. "Have you got a year? A decade? I don't. I'm tired, lady. Why don't you go off and do good in some other nice county? Oh, my head!"

He lay back on the couch and groaned.

"Where's your file on Welch?"

He gestured vaguely at an oak filing cabinet. She rummaged. The file was thin, consisting only of the indictment, the arrest record, the three autopsy reports, a copy of the letter requesting a psych consult, and some technical data from the state lab regarding the blood on the defendant's boots. Or alleged boots. She noted where the report said they were a size nine, a small man's size. Mose was a moose; he'd said they were too tight.

"Didn't you file any motions to dismiss or to suppress?"

Poole groaned. "Dear lady, you're thinking like a lawyer. There's no law in Robbens County."

"We'll see about that." Marlene searched Poole's law library, found a form book and a criminal procedure volume. She had not typed mechanically for some years, and it was tedious doing it with two fingers truncated, but she soon had the standard motions completed. She brought these over to Poole; included were her "Notice of Appearance" form, which let the court and all interested parties know that she was now representing Welch, and the substitution of lead attorney declaration.

"Sign these," she ordered.

"You're crazy."

"I've been told. Sign!"

He signed. She took the papers and said, "Get cleaned up. I expect you to be respectable and sober in court first thing tomorrow. They do have court here, don't they? Or do they just meet in a cellar and decide who lives and who dies?"

"Both."

She left Poole's office and walked across the square, attracting some attention. People came out of shops to look and traffic slowed. She noticed this and remarked to the dog, "They probably don't see many Manolo Blahniks in this town. Maybe I should have gone with something less stylish." The dog said, they tremble at my size and ferocious aspect. "I was joking," she said. "Stay, and don't bite anyone." The courthouse proved to contain, as in many small-county towns, the entire county government and was busy without seeming hectic. Finding the court clerk's office, she handed her documents in to an angular, middle-aged woman with thick, harlequin-framed glasses on a chain and a head of peculiar, tiny champagne curls. This person looked at the documents, studied them in fact, while also studying Marlene out of the corner of her eye. Marlene took her receipt and left, but noted without surprise that the clerk was on the phone before the glass door had swung shut.

Emmett was sitting in the Jimmy in the same place. "How'd it go?" he asked.

"Like clockwork. Let's go home. I need to make some calls."

The first one was to her husband. She described her day, to which he replied, "He actually said, 'There's no law in Robbens County'?"

"Words to that effect."

"So I reckon you're gonna have to tame that town with your blazing six-gun, clean up the bad guys, and save the farmers."

"Oh, stuff it! And it's miners in any case, and I'm not going to clean up anything. I just want to get this poor schmuck out of jail and get the cops to do their job. That might be a problem, if Poole is right about the state of local justice. He seemed like he still has enough brain cells left to convey actual facts. We shall see. What's happening in the real world?"

"You didn't hear? Probably the stagecoach with the paper didn't get there yet."

"Hey, half the people around here are watching CNN on satellite as we speak. What happened?"

"Oh, some hyped Latino kid tried to stick up a grocery over in Alphabet City with a cheap .22. The guy who ran it was one of our fine recent immigrants from East Asia. When he understood what the kid was doing, he hauls out this native blade and goes for him. The kid shoots him, the guy takes the bullet and keeps chopping. End of story? Our storekeeper cuts the kid's head off and places it in his window. The body gets tossed in the Dumpster. Apparently that's what they do in the colorful markets of his native land. It discourages thievery, he says."

"I bet it does. He speaks English?"

"He barely speaks Chinese. No, we had to get a guy down from Columbia to translate. Where is my daughter when I need her? Anyway, he's a Karen, apparently, from Burma or Myanmar or whatever the hell they're calling it today. Totally illegal, of course, and we don't have relations with his country of origin. I love this town."

"Is self-defensive decapitation an offense?"

"Not as such. Probably get him on failure to properly dispose of a corpse, a D-class misdemeanor, and failure to report a crime. I'd love to bring that one into the criminal courts with the litterers and fare jumpers. Meanwhile the Latino community is up in arms and the Asians want to give him a medal. The poor little shit!"

"Who, the kid or the Karen?"

"Both. Once again we are reminded that the law is a cultural construct."

"Which also reminds me: Do you know anyone at the Department of Labor?"

"Not really. Why?"

"Because if this place *is* as corrupt as Poole says it is, we may need some federal muscle. Isn't killing a union leader a federal case?"

"It might be," said Karp after a moment's consideration. "I know someone who would know for sure, though."

"Who? Oh, right, your guy Sterner."

"Uh-huh. Saul would be the one to call. Strangely enough, I have a message slip from him right here. I was just about to call him when you called."

"Well, see what he has to say and let me know. If I can pass this stinker off to someone real, I'll be a happy Girl Scout."

7

KARP DIALED THE NUMBER ON THE MESSAGE SLIP, AREA CODE 202, A Washington number. Saul Sterner was a *macher* in that town, or had been. Karp tried to figure out how old he was. He'd been general counsel at Labor in the Johnson administration and then done labor law for a while at the highest levels, chief counsel for the mine workers and then for the AFL-CIO. Somewhere in between all that, he had taught for a half dozen years at Boalt Hall, the University of California Law School, which was where Karp had met him. They had kept in touch on and off over the years. He must be eighty, at least, Karp thought.

But the voice over the phone was vigorous, the old New York accent softened neither by the years nor by dwelling among the mighty.

"Butch, you *momzer,* how the hell are you?"

"Can't complain. How about you?"

"I can complain, and I do, but no one listens. How's Keegan treating you?"

"Oh, you know Jack. He has his little ways."

Sterner chuckled. "That's what I hear. Listen, let's get together. I need your counsel on an issue."

Karp doubted this; Sterner famously had as much use for counsel as a guided missile. "I'm flattered. What kind of counsel?"

"Ehhh . . . a little something out in the country, a union thing."

"You don't want to talk about it on the phone."

"Not particularly. Let's have lunch tomorrow. I haven't seen you in a million years."

"You want me to come down there?"

"Nah, I'll come up. I got some things at the federal courthouse in the morning. We'll sit, we'll eat pastrami, we'll talk."

"Sam's on Canal?"

"Perfect!"

"I'll be there. Listen, Saul . . . it's funny, because I was just about to call you. It's something you'd probably know about. Marlene's down in West Virginia working for some friends, a couple of young men. Their dad was killed, actually the whole family, father, mother, and sister, all shot in their home. Marlene thinks it could be related to a labor problem. There's a possibility that the murders came out of a disputed union election. What'd be the federal interest there, if any?" There was silence on the line for so long that Karp thought they might have been cut off. "Saul? Hello?"

"Yeah. What's she doing there, Marlene? I thought she was out of the PI business."

"Well, yeah, she is. This was a favor. The woman who was killed was a friend of hers, from the Island, and her kids think there's something fishy going on with the investigation. From her first pass at it, so does she. They picked up a retarded guy and tried to stick him with it, but she says it's a frame, and clumsy, too."

"Well, that's very interesting, Butch. I should say, small world. That was just what I wanted to talk to you about as a matter of fact."

"The Heeney murders?"

"Them. Let's say twelve-thirty at Sam's on Canal." Click.

Karp recalled that Saul Sterner had a thing about punctuality. Teaching, he would ceremoniously lock the doors of his classroom at the stroke of the hour. After a couple of weeks, everyone was on time or had dropped the course, and at that point he gave a little lecture on the subject: Ladies and gentlemen, the legal profession begins with the ability to show up at a certain place, a courtroom, at a time certain. If you can't do that, I don't care to waste my time talking to you.

Karp was, accordingly, there at the minute and found Sterner waiting for him in the bright and noisy dining room, dressed, as always, in a brown suit off the rack and 100 percent made by union labor in the United States. No pinstripes for him, the uniform of the enemy, no foreign-sweated stitchery. In the old days, it would have been covered with cigarette ash, but no more. As Karp approached the table, Sterner was reading the menu through bifocals, reading it suspiciously, as if it were a defective opinion, his chin down on his chest, his pugnacious jaw and the thick lower lip thrust out in concentration. His head was large for his stocky body, his nose was large, too, the forehead over it wide, freckled, and fringed by white, curly hair. His hand delivered a crushing grip still. Karp thought he looked good for a man as old as he was and said, as he sat down, "You're looking good, Saul."

"Ahhh, you don't know. It's no fun getting old. Every time I forget my keys nowadays, it's *oy vay,* Alzheimer's."

"Never."

"Hey, everything passes. I'm happy, I had a good life, I knocked some heads, I kicked some heinie. What more can you ask?"

"That's the secret of life? Knocking heads?"

"You mean it's not?" said Sterner, miming wonder, and laughed. "Meanwhile, I'm having the corned beef. The waiter says the pastrami is dry. This I take as a symbol of the end of the world as I knew it. That there should be dry pastrami at Sam's on Canal Street. A *shandah!* Also, the waiter was a Lebanese kid instead of an old Yid who would tell me I was lucky to get pastrami at all." Sterner laughed again. "Tell me, do I sound enough like an old fart yet, or should I mention my bladder?"

The waiter arrived and took their order without insult or badinage. The two men exchanged small talk for a while, until Sterner leaned closer and peered at Karp over the tops of his lenses. "So. Tell me what you know about Red Heeney."

"Next to nothing. His wife's family happened to own the place next to the one Marlene bought out by Southold. They became friendly on the beach. Their youngest is . . . was, I mean, the same age as our twins. I met Heeney once at a cookout."

"What did you think?"

Karp hesitated. "Frankly? Not to speak ill, but he wasn't my type. He jumped me as a matter of fact. Wanted to punch my face."

"You probably deserved it."

"I usually do. But I take it you were a fan of his."

"Well, he wasn't a friend, if that's what you mean, but, yeah, I guess you could say a fan. What I liked about him, he was a fighter. My God, twenty-five years of organizing, and in that hellhole, too, first with the

chemical workers and the operating engineers, and then with this cocka-
mamy union they got, the Mining Equipment Operators."

"What's wrong with it?"

"Oh, it's a company union," Sterner answered with a sneer. "A piece
of shit. It belongs to the Majestic Coal Company, has since the year one.
Red thought he could get in there and turn it around from the inside.
And they killed him for it. Something like this hasn't happened since
Jock Yablonski back in '69. You remember that, don't you?"

"Vaguely. They killed the whole family there, too, didn't they?"

"Yeah, in Clarksville, Pennsylvania. Jock was fighting for the presidency of the UMW. Tony Boyle was president, a corrupt dirtbag, and
they had an election and Tony stole it. Tough Tony Boyle. He had some
local hillbillies do it, and we were able to trace it back to him, through
the payoffs. He died in jail."

"And you're assuming it's the same deal here?"

"Absolutely. They never learn anything, these bastards. I'll tell you
one thing about Red Heeney. He was the real stuff. You know, the goddamn pathetic labor movement we got in this great land of ours, they're
all waiting for the one, like the Jews waited for Moses. They don't expect
the revolution anymore, they're not that stupid. They just want a labor
leader who won't make them sick, who won't be found with his hand in
the pensions or in bed with the Mob. A mensch—a Gene Debs, a Walter
Reuther. A working-class leader, with arms on him." Here he made a fist
and pushed back his sleeve to demonstrate what an arm was. His was still
impressive; he had acquired it humping sides of beef at a meatpacker's
while working his way through college and law school. "Not one of these
shifty-eyed bozos in sharp suits they got in there now. And not one of you
middle-class well-meaning types either."

"I thought that was the point. The workers get rich, send their kids
to college, and give them a social conscience."

"Forget it. We live in a classless society, remember? Social mobility.
The ruling class lets a couple of workers' kids win the lottery and this lets
them grind the faces of the poor with impunity. 'Hey, they had *their*
chance at the gold ring and they muffed it, so fuck 'em.' Some chance!
So the kids go to college, and start working, and they get some money,
and have some nice things, they learn how to dress, and talk nice, and
before you know it, they're voting Republican."

"That's progress," said Karp with a smile.

"Pish on progress, then! Yeah, it's progress *if* you win the lottery; everyone else can rot in trailer parks on a minimum wage that wouldn't support a family even if both parents work full-time."

Their food arrived, sandwiches thick as dictionaries, and Dr. Brown's Cel-Ray, in cans, instead of the beautiful brown bottles it used to come in. Sterner took a big bite of his and continued to talk around the wad. "And so everything is fine and dandy, we say. Better than Russia, yeah, but that's some better! The problem is the public is too insulated now."

"How do you mean, insulated?"

"From the concrete realities. Think about it. Take a look around this place." Sterner made a broad gesture. "Every single object you see except the human bodies—all the clothes, the shoes, the tables, the plates, the silverware, the floor tiles, this corned beef sandwich, which by the way is cold in the middle, the patzers used a microwave, and this is not real Jewish rye either—*ev-er-y-thing*, was made at some stage by a worker using his body, and not only using his body, using *up* his body. And probably none of the people in this restaurant have a single friend who does that. See, that's the difference between us and them. They consume themselves making the world we live in; they're less every year, just like piles of coal. And they deserve better than what we give them, which by and large is *bubkes*." He put the sandwich down and examined Karp closely. "What, you're not impressed by my argument?"

"I'm always impressed by your argument. But what's the alternative to what we got now? Socialism? Great idea, doesn't work."

Sterner frowned and extended his jaw like the ram on a trireme. "Listen, do me a favor and don't talk to me about socialism, because you don't know what you're talking about. When anyone says the S-word, you've been trained to think, 'Ugh, Stalin!' You think I'm talking that shit? I spent years fighting Stalinists, and I mean literally sometimes, with *this*"—again the fist held up—"but I will say one thing for that shithead, for the Soviet Union, their one good deed: They scared the bejesus out of the plutocrats, which was why they let Roosevelt save capitalism, and why they finally legalized unions. Unfortunately, the Reds were too far away to scare our plutocrats enough, which is why we're the only industrial democracy with no real social democratic party. I except the Japanese; who the hell can figure them out? And when the Cold War started, our marvelous union leaders kicked out everyone who had any tinge of socialist leanings, leaving what? Gangsters and turtles. Ostriches! The result? Unions are down to, I don't know, 11 percent of the labor force? The Chinese make half our consumer goods in their sweatshops and two-thirds of our country has no unions at all. That's why Red Heeney was important."

"I was wondering when you'd get back to him," Karp said. "I take it he wasn't called Red just because of his hair."

"No, like I said, he was a true believer. And I'm not going to let them get away with it."

"What's your involvement?"

A sly smile here, a waggle of the hand. "Eh, you know, some phone calls. I'm a kibitzer now. I make suggestions."

"I thought you were a mover and shaker."

"Please. That was years ago. You want some cheesecake? On second thought, they probably ship it in from Korea. What I did do was, I called Roy Orne. A good guy. I knew his dad from the CIO days, a coal union man. So we talked, and he wants to handle it on the state level, but quick and quiet. I said I'd get back to him with some names."

"Wait a second, Saul, slow down. Who's Roy Orne?"

"What, you still don't read anything but the sports pages?"

"And the crimes," said Karp. "Who is he?"

"Dumbbell! He's the governor of West Virginia, that's who! Look, here's the situation. Robbens County, where the murders took place, is a wholly owned subsidiary of the Majestic Coal Company. Not only does the company own the union, it owns the district judge, the sheriff, most of the land, all the mineral rights, the congressman, and at least one U.S. senator. This has been going on for eighty years. Clarkesville, PA, was a rough and dirty town, but Clarkesville is Scarsdale compared to Robbens County. It's in a class by itself. You know anything about the history?"

"Not a thing, except what I gathered from Heeney and his wife. Union troubles?"

"More like a war. The first thing you have to know is that when coal got big, back in the 1880s, all the way through to the 1920s, West Virginia had the worst mine safety record of any state. They were able to keep the UMW out of the state until 1902, and even after that, there were whole chunks of it that organizers just couldn't get to. Organizers were arrested as a matter of course, and beaten, all over the state, but in Robbens they were just shot, bang, and sometimes their families, too. Okay, World War One there was a boom in coal, and after the war the operators laid off the miners they'd hired and cut wages. The UMW targeted three counties in southern West Virginia as its top priority—Mingo, Logan, and Robbens. There was a full-scale war in Mingo County. The operators brought in thugs, the so-called detective agencies, the miners armed themselves, dozens of people got shot. Then a couple of miners going to a trial on trumped-up murder charges were assassinated on the steps of the courthouse by company dicks. The miners went crazy. They took hostages. The mine owners and their political allies called in the National Guard— machine guns, tanks. Airplanes dropped bombs on the miners' camps. This is in America, remember. Finally, President Harding, the old fascist, sent in federal troops and the miners surrendered. That was the end of the war and the organizing drive. The coalfields didn't get unions until the New Deal came in. You knew any of this?"

"Some. And I assume the same thing happened in Robbens."

"You would assume wrong. Majestic had two advantages in Robbens: one, they owned the whole thing, all the coal patches. Two, they didn't bring in outside detectives. They used locals, and the locals were a lot worse than the goons. What they did was they fomented a civil war, based on existing feuds. Everyone in those parts has a connection to one of two families. You're either a Cade or a Jonson. Majestic hired Cades to kill Jonsons and Jonsons to kill Cades, and of course, anyone came in from outside got killed just on general principles. They set up a phony union, the Independent Mine Workers, so that by the time the feds got around to investigating, they had everything nailed down. There's no local law enforcement to speak of. This is like Latin America, no difference."

"I don't understand," said Karp. "No one did anything? The state? The feds?"

"No one complained. They were afraid to. Finally, underground mining became unprofitable and they switched to surface mining. The same kind of union, of course. They junked all the underground miners, put a bunch of mostly sick, busted men out to pasture on miserly pensions. But their stock does very well. Majestic's part of AGAM, a multinational commodity operation. Believe me, their corporate officers don't eat at Sam's on Canal. So into this mess walks Red Heeney. He's got two strikes against him—one, he's an outsider. They don't care much for outsiders in Robbens. The other thing is, everyone's scared there. They're used to taking what the company cares to give them, or else. So he performs a little miracle. He goes in there, gets a job driving some kind of big tractor, a bulldozer, whatever. And he starts organizing, finding men he can trust. All this is done secretly, just like in the bad old days, which, by the way, are still going on down there. And not just down there, either. He joins the company union, plays it cagey; for years this is, he's quietly building trust. He's waiting for his chance."

Here Sterner paused and took a sip of his drink, the ice clashing noisily in the glass. His eyes were glittering; he loved to tell a story, as Karp remembered from law school. It was part of what made him such a good teacher.

"So, one day he gets his chance: there's a disaster. The company has all these old impoundments, big ponds, where they keep the water they pumped out of their underground mines. They're supposed to maintain them in perpetuity, but, needless to say, they don't. Also, they're blasting at the strip mines. They're supposed to be limited as to when and where they blast, and how heavy the blast can be, but again, they cut corners. What happens is, they set off a charge and a dam gives way and a wall of water rushes down one of those little valleys, and twelve people die, five of them kids. A whole family's wiped out. Red organizes a meeting at a church, he gives a speech, and believe me, that man could talk! Holy Moses, what a mouth on him! He gets them all stirred up, he mobilizes his shadow organization, and the next day the whole workforce goes out, a wildcat strike, the first strike in Robbens County since 1921. And, *alevai!* The company backs down. It's finally dawned on them it's not 1921 anymore. Red's a hero. At first they figure they can coopt him. He plays along, acts nice. Then, this year, he challenges this dirtbag Weames for the presidency of the union. Of course, they steal the election. But Red comes to me, I go to Labor. I still have some clout there, not much, but I use what I have. They're going to contest the election, send in investigators."

Sterner stopped, shook his head. Suddenly, but just for a passing instant, he looked his age. "What a waste! And I consider it partially my fault. I encouraged him. I honestly, so help me, did not think they would stoop to this."

"You're pretty sure it was them?" Karp asked. "The union?"

"No question," said Sterner with finality. "All right, Governor Orne's got a problem. He's a decent guy, but if you're the governor of West Virginia, you can't just spit in the face of Big Coal. On the other hand, he needs to show the state he's not a coal company patsy either. He needs a victory where the bad guys are really, undeniably shits. But if the feds come in on this, if it's a big national story, he's essentially out of the picture. He's got political assassinations happening and he can't cope by himself? He looks like a patzer. Not to mention, we got a U.S. AG in there now who's not exactly a friend of the working man. So let's say Orne does it himself. He's still got a problem. His own legal apparatus has been lying down for Big Coal for years. It's his first term, he's not sure who he can trust. Also the state's attorney in Robbens is a kid. Orne put him in there, true, but he's not up to this kind of case, this kind of pressure. The governor wants to send in a special prosecutor."

Karp nodded. "That seems like a good idea."

"It *is* a good idea. *My* good idea, as a matter of fact." Sterner looked at Karp expectantly. "Well? What do you think?"

"I told you. I think it's a good idea."

Sterner wrinkled his nose and looked upward. "No, no! I mean *doing* it. *You* doing it. You think I'm buying corned beef sandwiches—even mediocre corned beef sandwiches—just so a fella can tell me I got a good idea?"

"You're serious?"

"Of course, I'm serious. I told Roy about you. He thinks you'd be perfect. Superb reputation, all the right skills, no local interests . . ."

"No license to practice law in West Virginia," added Karp, "no knowledge of the laws and procedures thereof, no interest in doing it. Plus I have a job."

Sterner's eyes seemed to drift away from Karp's for a moment. Could that be a tinge of embarrassment?

"Well, as to that," said Sterner, "I talked to Jack. He's all for it."

"You talked to *Jack?*" Karp asked coldly. "*Before* you talked to me?"

"It came out. We were at a party thing the other night, meet and greet with some little Kennedy. Your name came up and I mentioned this thing and . . . you know how people discuss."

"Actually, I don't. I never go to meet and greets. But I'm not surprised that Jack is less than reluctant to let me go for a long stroll through the woods. I put him in a situation he'd like to slide out of, and he can do it a lot easier if he doesn't have to look me in the face every day." Here Karp summarized for Sterner the business with the congressman, the pimp, the pimp's girlfriend, and the hapless Bailey.

To Karp's surprise, "So what?" was Sterner's reply. "You want this fella, you'll get him on the next round. He's not going to go away. Although you force me to say that your target has a first-class voting record on labor issues."

"Saul, he fucking takes money from a pimp and a murderer," said Karp, loud enough to draw glances from the surrounding tables.

"Yeah, and pimping is bad and murdering is bad and bribery is bad, and worst of all are infractions of an election statute that nobody understands in the first place. And you know what? Pimping and murdering and bribery went on before you got there, and believe you me, they'll be there a long time after you go."

"Saul, stop it . . ."

"No, listen to me! Every year, I used to look out into the lecture hall on the first day of my litigation class and I would think to myself, another bunch of embryo shyster assholes. Ninety-five percent of them were going to end up with the three-car garage and the Jags and the Guccis. I wasn't interested in them; I was looking for the few that had a real passion for the law, a real understanding for what it meant to the human race. I didn't find all that many, sad to say, but you were one of them. I kind of hoped you still were."

"Sorry, I'm a shyster asshole, too, now, and I don't even have a Jag."

Sterner did not return Karp's smile. "Butch, be serious! This is a major thing here. This is epic. It's bringing the relief of law to a bunch of people who have hardly known what law is. It's freeing the serfs, for crying out loud. Are you telling me you can't do it because you're more concerned with pinching a guy who took a little dirty money?"

Karp raised other objections; Sterner countered them. Karp felt himself rolling. He was no mean arguer himself, but he understood that he was up against one of the great negotiators of the twentieth century, a man who had reportedly wrestled Lyndon Baines Johnson to the mat more than once. It was like batting against Nolan Ryan, almost an honor to be struck out.

❖ ❖ ❖

Why am I sleeping in bloody sheets? Marlene asked herself, and immediately the answer came: because I am in the bed where Lizzie was murdered. She tried to move and found she couldn't; something was holding
her down. The killers. She felt a thrill of terror and struggled to move. A
heavy weight was resting on all her limbs; she screamed. The weight
diminished. She was in a dim room. There was a shape there, a man. She
let out a little shriek and felt on the bedside table for her key ring.

She lit the little Maglite attached to her keys. Dan Heeney, dressed
in a faded bathrobe, blinked in its beam.

"Marlene, are you all right?"

She dropped the beam. "Yeah, I'm fine." She was in fact in Lizzie's
room, but on a new bed with fresh bedclothes.

"You were screaming. I thought . . ." He hefted the pistol in his hand.

"No, just a nightmare. What time is it?"

"Around four."

"Oh, great! I must have woken you up. Sorry."

"No, I haven't been sleeping much lately."

"I bet. Why don't you put that thing down?"

He dropped the pistol into the pocket of his bathrobe. Its weight
pulled the robe ludicrously down on one side. He made no move to
depart, and he looked so woebegone that she said, "Pull up a bed. I'll
never get back to sleep now." She yawned and stretched. He sat gingerly
on the corner of the bed.

"So, what do you do when you're not sleeping?"

"Oh, I'm on the Net mainly. Talking to people, insomniacs and people in other time zones. Reading physics. Trying to find answers."

"To physics?"

"No. Just stuff." A self-deprecating laugh. "Religion. Life after death.
I can't believe they're just, you know, *gone.*" It was dim in the room, the
only illumination coming from a baseboard night-light, a white plastic
duck. His face was a blur, but she could feel his eyes on her. "Do you . . .
I mean, are you like Lucy? You know, heaven and hell and all that?"

"And purgatory. I guess I'm what they call a recovering Catholic.
You are not religious at all, I presume?"

"No. The opiate of the people. My mom was. I caught her a couple
of times in their bedroom, with her eyes closed and her hands clasped,

like in those pictures. Praying, I guess. But she kept it to herself. He was so down on it and there were enough things that got him pissed off, she probably figured she didn't need one more." He let out a long breath. "So, the deal is what? They're all in hell according to you?"

"Actually not. The Church teaches that we can't tell for certain anyone's in hell who doesn't really want to be there. We think it's presumptuous to try to second-guess the mercy of God. What we have is the assurance of heaven if we live a certain kind of life. That's not the same thing as saying people who don't live that kind of life are going to end up frying."

"Why would anyone want to be in hell?"

"The same reason lots of people manufacture a hell on earth. Sin. Evil. Why would you think they'd stop just because they're dead? They might not even know they were in hell."

"But you think that, assuming heaven exists, we'll, like, be reunited with our loved ones when we die? Like in the gospel songs on the radio?"

"You know, I am absolutely the wrong person to talk to about this," said Marlene, a little more sharply than she meant to. "Lucy could give you chapter and verse. My take is, it's either nothing—in which case, who cares? We experience nothingness every night of our lives and it doesn't bother us. Or it's an indescribable adventure, full of the ineffable pleasures of the beatific vision, in which case, whoopee!" This last was delivered in a light tone, to which he did not respond.

He shook his head, as if to clear it of something sticky. "I just feel this pain; not all the time, but sometimes I'll just be going along and it hits me. They're dead! It's like taking a shot to the belly. I have to sit down and catch my breath. Is that ever going to go away?"

The line "blessed are they that mourn, for they shall be comforted" floated for an instant through Marlene's mind, but she banished it. She feared being hypocritical more than nearly anything, and so she said, "I don't know, but I think finding who did it and nailing them would be a good first step." Did she really believe this? That was the problem: What did she believe anymore? She sat up in bed. "And, as long as we're up, why don't you let me get dressed and I'll get started on the laws of your fine state."

He shot to his feet. "Um, sorry." He went to the door. At which he paused and asked, "You think I should call Lucy? I mean, would she mind? I don't feel like talking to anyone from around here. They're all, I don't know, *involved*. Do you know what I mean?"

"Yes, I think calling Lucy would be a good idea. Making a gigantic pot of coffee would be another one. Also, you can find me the number of the nearest television station."

By eight, Marlene was washed, combed, dressed, caffeine-wired to the gills, and pounding on the door of a frame house on Maple Street, McCullensburg. The house belonged to Ernest Poole and needed a coat of paint. And a mowing out front. No answer, front door locked, so she went around the back, jiggled open the cheap lock, and went in with her dog. A smell of garbage in the kitchen, and the remains of a Colonel Sanders on the greasy table. Poole himself had not made it up the stairs last night. She found him in a club chair in the dusty living room, a neat pool of vomit between his feet and an empty bottle of Harper stuck upright between his thighs, like a transparent erection. After making a quick recon of the ground floor, she found a carpet runner in the hall and tipped the man out of his chair onto it. He groaned and twitched, but did not shed his stupor. The floors were hardwood, worn and smooth, so she had little trouble dragging him down the hall to a bathroom. She got him into the tub in sections, upper body first and then the legs. The mastiff looked on with interest, having licked up the vomit while Marlene was thus engaged, and hoping for more.

Poole writhed like a bug on a grill when the cold water hit him and sat up, banging his head on the tap. It took a moment for his eyes to focus. When they did, they fixed on Marlene, at first in stunned amazement and then in fury. He clambered to his knees and shut off the water.

"You! What the hell are you doing in my home?"

"I'm helping you get ready for court this morning, counselor," she said brightly.

"You're trespassing. Get out!"

"Gosh, and here you invited me in. That's not trespass."

"I did not invite you."

"Yes, you did, the other day. Don't you remember? I thought we had a good understanding. Oh, no! Don't tell me you forget *everything* that went on."

His eyes shifted. His brow wrinkled with the effort to recall.

"Why don't you take off your clothes and have a nice, soothing shower, and shave. I'll make you some breakfast. We have plenty of time to be in court at nine-thirty." She flounced out.

She found coffee, but the milk was sour. The bread was stale. Butter had he none, but she found a jar of strawberry jam in the back of the nearly bare refrigerator, which, when scraped of its interesting fungal cultures, did for smearing across the toast. She produced a tall pile of this, perked the coffee, and set the table. In the cabinet above the stove she located the inevitable reserve bottle and poured a shot into a mug of coffee. Next, a quick dump and wipe in the kitchen; not for nothing had she raised three children and a husband of more than usual sluttishness.

He came in dressed and clean-shaven, if red-eyed, smelling of Listerine and some old-fashioned lilac cologne. He looked around the kitchen suspiciously. His glance drifted to the cabinet above the stove.

Observing this, she said, "It's in the coffee. That's all you get until after court."

He sat down. He took a long swallow of the spiked coffee, closed his eyes, sighed. "Would you mind telling me why you're doing this?"

"I need you. Isn't it nice to be needed? I'm converting you temporarily from a dysfunctional drunk to a functional one, like half the people in the country. After this business is resolved, I'm out of here, and you can finish converting your liver into Silly Putty and die. It's nothing personal. Eat some toast while it's warm."

"I'm not hungry."

"Eat some anyway. Your body needs calories and carbs. You should take some B vitamins, too."

He took a piece, nibbled it. Finishing one, he took another, and another. She sipped coffee and watched him. "See? Advice from one who knows."

He regarded her balefully over his cup. "A functional drunk?"

"Extremely. Why do you drink, by the way?"

"Why do *you?*"

"To quell my rage and my sympathies," she said. "I see cruel, malevolent people getting away with murder all around me and I want to stop them. Not to put too fine a point on it, I want to kill them, and I'm good at it. My options are being either a sober and happy murderess or a slightly stoned mom and businesswoman. I raise and train dogs, and I have three lovely children and a husband. I wish to retain them and their affection, which I can't do if I'm my real self. Now you."

After a silence he said, "I killed my wife."

"On purpose?"

He stared at her, his mouth a little open. "Of course not! It was a car accident. We were driving home from a Christmas party in Charleston. The roads were slick and it was foggy. I ran right into the rear of a truck carrying pipe. The pipe came through the window and hit Sheila. She was decapitated. I didn't have a scratch. She was six months pregnant and happy as a horse in clover. It was a really great and loving marriage. That sad enough for you?"

"Yup, that's pretty sad."

"Can I have another drink?"

"Not until after court, counselor. It's not *that* sad."

"Tell me something," he said after his eyes dropped. "How did you get to be such a colossal bitch? Was it heredity, or did you work on it over the years?"

"It took a lot of work. When I started out, butter wouldn't melt in my mouth," she replied without rancor. "You finished with that? Excellent! Let's go." This was good, she thought. If he hated her, it might move his mind off its dead center. He might even get mad enough to kick some butt in a courtroom.

It was wide and high, paneled dark and painted white. Its Georgian-glass windows were open to catch any breeze, and through them, besides an actual grassy breeze, there came the sounds of light traffic, a lawn mower, and farther off, someone practicing scales on a trombone. Small town, thought Marlene, this is what it would be like practicing law in a small town. The only discordant note was a television crew—a cameraman, a sound technician, and a reporter with spray-fixed hair and tan blazer. Every seat in the courtroom was occupied, in the main by the sort of people who occupy seats in courtrooms the world over—retirees and idlers of a certain stripe—but there was also a contingent of hard-looking younger men in one of the back rows. Unlike the people in New York courtrooms, she observed, all of these were white. Moses Welch was there, at the defense table, blinking amiably, his moon face untroubled by complex thought or obvious fear. At the prosecution table was a burly man in his late twenties wearing a blond crew cut and a cheap blue suit. On his face was the overly serious expression of a young man who wishes thereby to acquire gravitas. This was, Poole informed Marlene, the state's attorney, Stanley Hawes. Marlene nodded politely to him. He seemed surprised at this, but, after an awkward pause, nodded back. The judge entered. As she rose with the others, Marlene had to stifle a giggle. Judge Bill Y. Murdoch was practically a caricature of a corrupt judge; he could have walked out of a Daumier, lacking only the little round cap that French judges wear. He was pink, plump, beautifully barbered, with a boar's snout, a carnivorous slash of a mouth, and small avid eyes set off by dark eyebrows pointed like chevrons.

The judge spent a few moments speaking with some court officials and a very fat man in a tan uniform, pointed out to Marlene as J. J. Swett, the county sheriff. Murdoch kept looking up at the TV crew. He did not look pleased to see them. After the sheriff and the others had dispersed, Murdoch stared down at Poole and rattled some papers in his hand.

"Ernie, you mind telling me what this is all about."

"They're motions, Judge," said Poole, getting to his feet.

"I know they're motions, Ernie. I can read. I mean why are they being filed at this date? I thought we had agreed to a disposition of this case. And you're changing your plea to not guilty?"

"Yes, Judge. What's happened is the defendant has a new counsel, a co-counsel, actually, who has a different idea as to how the defense should proceed."

Murdoch inspected the papers again. "That's this Kee-ampi fella?"

Marlene rose. "That's Ciampi, Your Honor. That's me and I'm not a fella."

A rustle of titters in the courtroom. Murdoch banged his gavel and glared them down and glared particularly at the cameraman, who had switched on his lights.

Murdoch turned his glare onto Marlene. "And what exactly are you doing here, Miss *Ciampi?*"

"I'm representing the defendant, Your Honor."

"He already has counsel."

"Yes, and he decided to retain additional counsel."

The dark eyebrows compressed in a scowl. The judge made a summoning motion. Poole, Marlene, and Hawes approached the bench.

The judge said, "All right, what's going on here? Ernie, you know Mose Welch can't hardly decide which flavor of ice cream he likes. How the hell can he opt for new counsel?"

"You declared him competent to stand trial, Your Honor," said Poole. "He can aid in his own defense, and choice of counsel runs along with that competence."

Murdoch's color rose. "Ernie, damnit, whose side . . ." He stopped short; no, he couldn't really say *that*. He turned his attention to Marlene. "And what's your interest in this case? A do-gooder, are you?"

"Not at all, Judge. I am an attorney licensed in the state of New York, and I was a friend of one of the victims, Rose Heeney. Her sons called me and asked me to defend Moses Welch."

"The *victim's* sons called you? *They're* paying for this?"

"No pay is involved, Your Honor, but, yes."

"Would you mind telling me why the victims want to get the murderer off?"

"Because he's not the murderer," said Marlene.

"He confessed to it," said Hawes.

"Yes," said Marlene, giving the prosecutor a mild look, such as elementary-school teachers give pupils who are trying very hard. "And as you see, we're moving to suppress the confession. My client was kept incommunicado for fourteen hours, his family was kept from him, and he was coerced into signing a document he could not read by the promise of ice cream. He now repudiates his confession."

"There was no coercion," said Hawes, "and I resent the implication that the confession was obtained through force of any kind."

"Force isn't necessary," said Marlene. "We're not arguing from *Brown*. We would argue from *Spano* that the offer of any substantive good desired by the person in custody, whether food, or reading materials, clothing, or any ordinary or extraordinary privilege, as a quid pro quo for confession, is coercive per se, especially after an all-night interrogation, as was the case here. Also, given the defendant's mental abilities, his waiver of his right to counsel is highly suspect under *Tague.*"

Hawes stared at her, perhaps trying to remember who Tague was.

Judge Murdoch frowned again and looked up at the TV camera. "All right, all right. I'll hear arguments now." He waved them back to their places.

Marlene began. Her essential argument was from *Tague v. Louisiana,* a U.S. Supreme Court case that held that the burden was on the state to demonstrate that the defendant understood his waiver of the right to counsel. Moses Welch had the mind of a five-year-old, which any reasonable person observing him could see. He should have been treated like a five-year-old therefore, and no confession should have been elicited from him without the presence of his family and legal counsel. The bribery of the ice cream was in violation of the Supreme Court decision in *Spano v. New York,* in that the combination of the all-night session, the denial of contact between a childlike prisoner and his family, and the bribe combine to produce an inherent untrustworthiness.

In his rebuttal, Hawes cited *Connelly,* in which the Supreme Court ruled that even if the mental incapacity of the defendant is the cause of the confession, due process is not violated absent police conduct causally related to the confession. He called J. J. Swett as a witness. Swett, a moonfaced porker with beetle-black eyes, long silver locks, and lobe-long sideburns, took the stand and lied that there had been no bribe of ice cream. Marlene did not bother to cross-examine. Murdoch denied the motion with obvious relish.

Marlene argued the next motion, to suppress the key evidence in the case, the bloodstained boots. She had not expected much from this and was not surprised when it was denied. She also applied for reduced bail, on the grounds that Mose Welch could not drive, had no money, and was hardly a flight risk. This was also denied. Swift justice in Robbens County, Marlene thought as she gathered her papers. In the real world, sometimes judges took a couple of days to reach a literally judicious decision on motions of these types, but not here apparently.

Three strikes, then, but Marlene still felt some satisfaction, and this increased after her interview with the young man in the tan blazer. She figured that justice in Robbens County was not used to the glare, its usual habit being to crawl around under damp rocks, and she had no compunction about accusing the county of trying to railroad a helpless mentally handicapped man because they were too stupid or too lazy or too corrupt to search for the real killers. She hoped that at least five seconds of that would that evening bounce out of space down through every dish in the county.

She walked out of the courthouse with Poole.

"See what I mean?" said Poole.

"Oh, I thought we did okay. They're on notice that we intend a real defense. In my experience with small-town cozy corruption, that tends to shake them up. They'll make mistakes, which we will capitalize on. You didn't doze off at any rate."

"No, but I intend to shortly. I intend to sink into my accustomed alcoholic stupor. Care to join me?"

"No, thank you. Before you collapse, I'd appreciate it if you'd assemble all the discovery material we asked for. I'm particularly interested in any crime-scene photos and a sense of where these bozos looked before old Mose dropped into their laps."

Poole was shaking his head. "You still don't get it, do you? Motions? Discovery? The bottom line is still, *they get what they want*. They like to get it with all the legal niceties if they can, but if they can't, if you block them there, they'll get it anyway. You see those cars?"

He pointed to a Mercedes sedan and a Land Rover parked in the stalls nearest to the courthouse curb. "The Merc belongs to Judge Murdoch. The Rover is Swett's. Both vehicles each cost more than the annual salaries of their owners. We are not subtle about corruption in Robbens County. Unsubtlety is in fact the point. The message is, play along and you get taken care of. Don't play along and you also get taken care of, which is the message of what happened to Red Heeney and his family. The Heeney murders are not going to be investigated and the murderers are not going to be caught, tried, and convicted."

"We'll see about that." Marlene reflected that she had used that line rather too much lately.

Poole flapped his hand weakly at her and turned away. "Go home, Ciampi," he said over his shoulder. "Go back to America."

8

"So, ARE YOU GOING TO DO IT?" ASKED MURROW.

"I might," answered Karp. "I practically said I would just to keep him from *hoching* me. He's the kind of guy who, if he thinks faking a heart attack will roll you, will turn gray and collapse."

"Can I come, too? I kind of like the idea of fighting real bad guys, like in the movies, instead of the pathetic characters we usually put away."

"No, you have to stay here and watch the store while I have all the fun."

Murrow slumped in his chair, clutching his chest and producing a good imitation of Cheyne-Stokes respiration.

Karp laughed briefly. "I better stay here. You need supervision."

"You'll do it," said Murrow confidently. "I can see it in your eyes. I'd do it in a minute, in the unlikely event that anyone ever asked me to."

"Yeah, but you're a young squirt without responsibilities, and you don't have a wife working the very same operation unofficially."

"Would that be a problem?"

"Oh, Marlene? Investigating a sensitive and complex case on her own? A problem? No, why would you think that? Fortunately, I have reason to believe she's unarmed at the present time." Karp leaned back in his chair, swiveled to face the window, chewed on a pencil. Murrow, seeing this, left quietly, closing the office door behind him. He knew these were the signs that Karp was entering Karpland, as all the office called it, and was therefore not to be disturbed until he reentered the terrestrial sphere, usually with the solution to some intricate problem.

Being manipulated stood high on the list of all the things Karp didn't like. Why should he disturb his life and dash off to some godforsaken province because it was important to Saul Sterner? Let them handle it themselves. Let them all shoot each other. Red Heeney was an idiot who'd gotten his wife and daughter killed along with himself because he was stupid and full of bravado and a drunk besides, unlike himself, who was cautious and smart and free of alcoholic fumes in the brain, and unlike also his wife, who was rattling around in the same hellhole that had killed the Heeneys, New York not being dangerous enough for her anymore. Marlene, he knew, was in a familiar phase of her cycle. A set-tled life afflicted her like a slow toxin, building up in her soul until it flipped a switch, at which point she had to do something grotesque and outrageous, usually involving gunshots and financial ruin. The woman had given away something like $40 million because the money had a smell of deceit and death on it. Nice that she could afford such scruples, whereas he had to punch the clock at the DA every day until forever, until he retired a desiccated husk and corrupt to the eyes, waiting for the cancer to get him, like Guma.

He wondered what she was doing this minute. Should he call? Did he have the Heeney phone number? Somewhere around here. Probably something quasi-legal, if not an actual felony. And naturally he was going to have to go in there and fix things, smooth things over, paste a legal fig leaf over whatever mess she made. And she would make a mess, she always made a mess. Whereas he had a safe, re-spectable, boring, tedious, stupid job, supervising the installation of impoverished morons in state penal institutions. Meanwhile, he couldn't just take off and ditch Lucy with the boys and that goddamn dog farm. What he should do is take three weeks of leave and just go out there and lie on the beach until he got sunstroke. Keegan wanted to get rid of him anyway. The office could run itself. It was summer-time. The living was easy. Prosecution was easy, too, since they'd cut the budget of the Legal Aid Society practically in half and the courts were hiring barely conscious hacks at $40 an hour to defend indigents, meaning the vast majority of persons brought before the New York DA. It was even more of a joke than it had been when crime was ram-pant, except, of course, when crime had been rampant, you could kid

yourself with the illusion that you were defending something worth-
while. The staff had grown slack, he had grown slack, slack and stupid
and old.

He took the pencil out of his mouth and examined it with distaste. It
looked like a dog had been at it. He tossed it at the wastebasket; it
bounced off the rim and fell on the floor. He couldn't even sink shots
anymore. The phone rang: Dick Sullivan, the new homicide bureau
chief, with the latest on Lok the Decapitator, as the tabloids had named
him. The ME report had come back on Emilio Solano, the seventeen-
year-old deceased in the case. Apparently Lok had hacked the robber
heavily enough to render him quite helpless before delivering the fatal
chop. Therefore the decapitation was a homicide and not strictly self-
defense. Sullivan was going to charge him with manslaughter one.

"Sounds right," said Karp. "Will he plead?"

"Not likely. The Asian community's got a huge defense fund already.
They've retained Morrie Silver on it."

"I hope you gave him my regards, the sly fucker."

"He sends his, likewise," said Sullivan. "He was dickering for man
two, minimum sentence, minimum security, the usual."

"I hope you told him to blow it out his ass."

"Not in so many words. Anyway, I guess maybe we're going to have
to try this beauty, in the full glare of the media, editorials, ethnic cleans-
ing, et cetera." There was a question in his voice. Sullivan had not been
Karp's first pick for homicide. He came from the Queens DA, and Karp
liked promoting people from within. Besides, Queens? Karp suspected
that there had been some political juice for Keegan in the appointment.
The man seemed competent enough, however.

"Well, try him and win it, Dick. That's what we used to do around
here all the time."

"I assume it's okay with the chief."

"It's the right thing to do," said Karp blandly. "The district attorney
always does the right thing, as you know."

Karp hung up, cursed, paced, kicked a steel filing cabinet. Sullivan
would not take his word for it and would call Keegan, and *of course*
Keegan would not stay the hell away from meddling in a case that
involved two important electoral communities and was getting major
press. Karp sat down and jabbed at a speed-dial button.

A treble voice answered, "Wingfield Farm, registered mastiffs, GC Karp speaking."

"Hello, this is Madonna. I'd like a dozen registered mastiffs in assorted colors, please."

"Hi, Dad."

"What are you doing in the office?"

"Answering the phone."

"I know that, dummy. Why aren't you playing and generally having a carefree little-boy childhood?"

"Lucy made me. She's being Cruella."

"You poor thing. I'm thinking of coming out there for a couple, three weeks. Maybe Lucy would let me answer the phone sometimes."

"We can use the help," said his son with a disappointing lack of boyish enthusiasm for merry hours spent with Daddy. "Actually, I like being inside. It's too hot out and I can play on the computer. Do you want to talk to the Luce?"

Karp said he did and heard the phone drop with a clunk. Minutes passed.

"Dad? What's up?" asked the Luce.

"You're being Cruella."

"Did that little rat call you and complain?"

"No, I called. Do you really need someone manning the phone?"

"*Boying* it, technically. Yeah, until we move the pups. The phone's ringing off the hook since we placed ads."

"Everything okay? The felons all in good order?"

"Yeah, they don't mess with Cruella. How's your lonely grandeur?"

"Hm. That's what I wanted to talk to you about. I'm on the horns of a dilemma."

He explained briefly what Saul Sterner wanted him to do, adding, "So the good part of the deal, besides its inherent virtue, is that I'd get to be with Mom for however long, the summer at least, until we saw how things lay, sort of a vacation in the mountains."

"Meaning you could keep an eye on her."

"That, too," said Karp, glad once again that another person in the world shared his view of his wife. "On the other hand, I'm uncomfortable with both of us being out of town and you stuck here in charge."

"We could all come down there," said Lucy brightly.

"What about the farm?"

"Oh, we'd bring Magog. Billy can handle the place after the puppies are sold, and if not, he can hire a teenager from town."

"I don't think so. That's all we need is to have to worry about you all. Apparently it's a pretty violent part of the country."

"Violence! Heavens to Betsy! What a sharp contrast that would be to my entire childhood! Well, you've succeeded in terrifying me out of that idea."

"I was actually thinking of the boys," said Karp, a little more sharply than he had intended.

"Oh, right—sorry," she said, and actually was, because she had not thought for a second about her brothers. What had immediately occupied the center of her thoughts when her father had proposed going to West Virginia was the prospect of seeing Dan Heeney again. "Okay, if you decide to go, I can hold the fort here. Don't worry."

"Are you sure? I mean, they can get someone else."

"But you're dying to go, right?"

Karp hesitated before replying to this. "I'm not sure . . . the main thing is I'm concerned about you. You have all that scientific stuff to do up in Boston. It doesn't seem fair to tie up your summer with baby-sitting."

"It's starting to sound like you're using us as an excuse. You're the responsible parent and Mom is the cuckoo."

"Not really . . ."

"Really. Look, the way it sounds is that they want you and you can do it better than anyone. And it's important—getting the rats who killed them. It's just your kind of thing. As far as the Boston guys are concerned, I already blew them off. It's not like they can find another me by placing an ad in the *Globe*. It's a seller's market in the prodigy biz."

"You actually are irreplaceable," said Karp fervently. "And I don't just mean all the Swahili."

"And you likewise. Since you're all guilted up, this would be a good time to ask you if I can get the Toyota fixed. It would be great to have."

"Is it fixable?" asked Karp, who knew little about vehicles.

"Russell says yes, and apparently he's a car maven as well as a dog agitator, kind of a Renaissance man. I'll pay for the fixing if you'll handle all the plates and insurance crap."

"A done deal. Are you absolutely sure . . . ?"

"Of course. Go. Don't worry about us. And keep in touch, okay?"

After hanging up, Karp sat back in his chair. He had a peculiar feeling, hauntingly familiar, but it took him some little time to identify it. The last day of school? Winning a big case? Oh, right, he thought: happiness. He kicked off and spun his chair around half a dozen times. Swiveling around to the desk again, he dialed Saul Sterner's number.

Marlene was swinging in a hammock strung in the Heeneys' backyard, using a finger against the skull of her dog to push herself in a gentle rocking motion, and at the same time scratching him in the place he liked behind his ear. The dog was happy with this arrangement; Marlene less so. She did not like being stymied. She finished her beer and tossed it in a graceful arc, which did not quite reach the lip of the rubber trash can. Dan Heeney stirred himself from the lounge chair where he was drinking, reached out an arm, and flipped the can in. It was hot under a milk-glass sky. Only vagrant zephyrs stirred the dusty leaves of the maples. She was officially thinking about their next move, but productive thoughts were slow in coming. Had this been a real case, she would have been working with a private detective, doing the investigation that the cops had fluffed, maybe establishing an alibi for the defendant, maybe collecting new evidence. In this particular abortion, however, this was not going to do much good, because the cops and the criminal justice system would take anything she discovered and lose it, or phony up something that undermined it.

Stan Hawes might be interested. She didn't think he was really dirty yet, but it would take an extremely pure-minded state's attorney to actively cooperate in wrecking the biggest case he was likely to see in a decade. She needed something new and major then, the murder weapon maybe, or a signed confession from the real guys, one about as likely to turn up as the other. There was no crime-scene forensic evidence that did her any good. There were prints in the house from dozens of people, but distinguishing among these, separating the killers' from those of the Heeneys' many guests, was a job beyond her resources. If she had been there from the beginning, in charge of the investigation, or even on defense from the get-go . . . no, useless thoughts: if your grandma had wheels, she'd be a garbage truck. Still, if the cops had done a half-assed job, there might be areas still worth investigating. Where, though? She rolled out of the hammock, went to the cooler, and cracked another Iron City, feeling Dan's eyes on her as she did so. He was waiting for her to pull out rabbits, but she was all out of rabbits today.

She walked across the lawn, the grass cool on the soles of her feet, the can icy when she pressed it against the back of her neck. Go back into the house, look at her notes, maybe something would pop up. She closed her eyes, her mind blank. When she opened them, she was staring at a mountain. This was not unusual, as there were mountains everywhere one stared around here. This one, she recalled, was known as Belo Knob. There was a flash of light from the mountainside and then another. She heard, above the buzzing of the insect life, the distant grind of a truck in low gear, climbing. She looked up at the mountain again. The truck had disappeared. A road on a hillside: Why was that of interest? She didn't know yet, but it was, something about the night of the crime. She wandered back to the hammock and sat on its edge.

"Dan, the night of the murders," she said tentatively, "there were people at the house—Emmett said . . . ?"

"Yeah, there was a dissident-faction meeting, maybe about twenty guys. It lasted until ten, maybe ten-thirty."

"Right, and then the killers came. But, what I'm wondering is, how did they know the house was empty except for your family?"

Dan twitched his shoulders. "I don't know. They were watching the house?"

"Uh-huh. But from where? Where was their car while they were watching? It couldn't have been in your driveway or on 119 or on that little access road. Someone would've spotted them. A bunch of dissidents, all paranoid as hell, probably armed . . . the killers wouldn't have wanted to take that chance. Come here a minute."

They walked around the house. Marlene pointed to Belo Knob. "There's a road across that mountain."

"Uh-huh. Belo Road. It hooks up Route 10 on the east side of the knob to 130 on the west, and it picks up a bunch of no-name dirt roads that go to where folks live up there. What about it?"

"I was just thinking that if someone parked their car on that road, they'd have a pretty good view of your yard. They could see when the last guest left. Have you got a large-scale map of the county?"

"Sure. It's on the computer."

A few minutes later, Marlene was looking over Dan's shoulder at a bird's-eye view of the house they were standing in. He punched a key twice and the view expanded to take in the south flank of Belo Knob. "We have fifty-meter resolution on this. The whole county, and we have the subsurface, too, down to three thousand meters."

"Where did you get this?" she asked. "It's fantastic."

"My mom. There's a state law that says the coal companies have to map all their abandoned shafts, mines, and impoundments and share the information with the community. The state makes them do the mapping, and they also do their own mapping and subsurface exploration, to plan where they're going to cut next. They use sonar to find what the rock's like under the mountains. My mom's little enviro group sued Majestic to release this data."

"And won?"

"Amazingly, yes. It was a federal court decision. That's how we knew that Gillis Holler was going to happen before it did." He saw her puzzlement. "A local disaster." He hit some other keys. The view on the monitor changed to what looked like a cutaway of a layer cake prepared by a drunken pastry cook.

"This is Hampden, to our east. The coal-bearing strata show up in gray, and those red lines are old shafts and adits. Where the coal strata are exposed, that's Majestic Number Two, the main surface mine in the county. They're taking the whole top off Hampden." His finger tapped the screen. "This blue blob is an impoundment, or was, Impoundment Fifty-three A. They set off a charge at Number Two and the shock waves whipped along this boundary layer, under the limestone stratum, see? And focused right here. It cracked open the rock between the bottom of the impoundment and an old shaft. Half a million cubic feet of water came out of that shaft like a steel rod and blasted half a dozen houses and trailers into toothpicks."

He told her about what had happened after that, the wildcat strike, the election. He spoke with regret mixed with cynicism, a young man's approach to corruption and horror. She'd heard some of this from Rose, but she let him talk until he was through and then steered him back to the matter at hand. The south flank of Belo appeared once again. His fingers on the mouse made the vegetation details vanish, leaving only landforms, roads, and structures.

"Can we go there?" she asked.

"Sure. You mean now?"

"I almost always do." She ran off to gather some items.

Belo Road was rutted and ran narrowly through hemlocks and laurels, two lanes of thin blacktop chopped into the mountainside. Marlene drove, flicking her gaze between the road ahead and the steep slope to her left, a wall of vegetation. Which vanished briefly and then reappeared. Marlene hit the brakes and threw the truck into reverse. There was a wide place in the road, a sandy area just big enough for one vehicle, under a big slate outcrop, dripping with seepage. She jumped out and crossed the road. Dan came up beside her.

"This has to be the place," she said. "You can see everything from here—the house, the yard. Christ, what a waste! If they'd brought a crime-scene unit up here the morning after the crime, they would've got tire tracks and footprints and God knows what else. Well, let's look around anyway."

"What are we looking for?"

"Oh, you know, the usual. A matchbook with the name of a nightclub on it. The murderer's diary . . ."

"A lot of broken beer bottles," said Dan, standing at the base of the slate outcrop. Marlene looked and saw the remains of at least two dozen brown beer bottles and two white-glass Jim Beam pints lying in the shallow declivity below the rock wall. Marks on the wall showed that they had been thrown against it. Marlene returned to her truck and brought out a sheaf of plastic supermarket bags. She stuck her hand in one of them and selected several of the more intact bottles.

"What're you doing that for?"

"You never can tell. These might be from our guys. In fact, unless this place is a famous parking spot, I'd say it's likely. Look, they drive up here after dark, say about nine-thirty. They have to wait an hour or so until all the cars leave and they sit around and drink and smoke. See all the butts?" She knelt and bagged a collection of these. "I figure three guys. One smoked Winstons, one smoked Camels, and one smoked those cheap, thin cigars. The amount of drinking's right for three guys, too. Now the cars are gone from your yard, so they're ready. Do they drive down? Where does this road go?"

"West of here it hooks into 130 west on the other side of Belo, or 11 north a little farther along. East of here was the way we just came, off 119 about a quarter mile from our drive."

"Wait a second—130? Does that go over some kind of bridge? A green bridge?"

"Yeah, it does. Over the Guyandotte. Why?"

"Because that's where Mose said he found the bloody boots. They stayed here, drove down to your place, did the murders, and what . . . ? Came back the same way, past here, and out to 130, across the bridge, where they tossed the shoes off the bridge, but not too carefully, because they landed on dry land instead of in the water."

"Yeah, that makes sense," Dan agreed, "because otherwise they would've had to go through the middle of town on 119 and someone might have seen them. There's not much traffic in McCullensburg after 1 A.M. But what does that do for us?"

Marlene was leaning against a pine and looking down the slope of the hill. A scrim of young pine and ash bordered the road, below which rolled a curiously even, glossy green carpet. "I don't know," she said. "Maybe it gives us their getaway route. On the other hand, they might not have bothered to move the car at all. They might've walked down this slope. It's not more than a couple of thousand yards and the slope isn't that steep. And that would've been better for them, assuming they knew about the driveway alarm and the lights."

"Maybe, but you can't walk that slope. It's a laurel hell."

"A what?"

"They don't have those in New York?" said Dan in mock surprise. "A laurel hell is an extremely dense growth of mountain laurel or some-times rhododendron, mixed with greenbrier and other creepers. Rabbits can go through it but nothing else. Sometimes they roll on for miles. This one is pretty small. I guess they could've gone around it, though, on the other side of that deadfall." He pointed to where a good-sized tulip tree had come down.

"Yeah, I guess," said Marlene, still looking downslope. "What's that?"

"What?" He came over to her and followed her pointing finger.

"That white stuff? Some trash. People fling stuff into laurel all the time. We call it West Virginia recycle. It makes a perfect dump."

Marlene went to her truck and came back with a pair of binoculars. She propped her shoulder against a tree and looked through them. "It's the heel of a sneaker. It's got what looks like a dark stain on the sole. I'm going to go get it."

"Marlene, it'll take you two hours to get down there and back. You got no idea what it's like in one of those."

"Nevertheless, I have a good feeling about this." She handed him the binoculars. "Stay up here and guide me." She started down the slope and before long discovered why they called it hell. The air was still, smelling of leaf mould, and breathtakingly hot. The laurel plants grew within inches of one another, so that each step was a contortion. Before she had gone five yards she was covered in sweat, wringing wet, stinging from dozens of scratches. Tiny flies rose from the damp earth and filled her nose and mouth and crawled into her eyes. The world contracted to the next stiff branch, the next tripping root. Several times she fell and had to stop to pick thorns out of her hands. Dimly she heard Dan's shouts, giving directions. She moved sluggishly in response. Her brain was frying. She could barely remember left from right. Time slowed and ground to a halt.

"There! You're right there!" came a shout. She stopped, wiped her eyes. Her palm, when she looked at it, showed a slurry of mud, sweat, and blood. She could barely recall what she was there for. Some punishment, perhaps. The brain wasn't working too well. The heat. What was he yelling about? There was nothing there, just green leaves and cruel branches inches from her face. She looked up. There was no sky, only more green, and something white, a flower or a fruit. She wiped her burning eyes again, blinked the sweat out of them. Not a fruit. The toe of a sneaker. She reached up and plucked it. A Nike, size eleven, well worn. On the sole, a curious design in red-black, almost calligraphic, that ran up onto the heel.

"Jesus Christ!" cried Dan as she staggered out of the laurel. He grabbed her before she fell.

"Bag it," she said, holding out the sneaker.

Back at the house, she didn't even bother removing her clothes, but stood shaking under the cold stream of the shower for ten minutes before she thought of undressing.

Forty-five minutes later she emerged in a robe, with a towel wrapped around her head, went straight to the refrigerator, got a beer, and moved to the porch, where Dan sat.

"Feeling better?"

"Much." She sat in a rocker, drank a long pull, sighed.

"You should have seen what you looked like when you came out of there. Red as a tomato and covered with dirt and blood. I thought you were going to collapse. People have, you know. Died in those things."

"I can believe it. How long was I in there?"

"A couple of hours. Campers look at a map and figure they can cut a couple of miles of trail by bushwhacking through the laurel. They don't usually try it more than once. How do you feel?"

"Like I've been whipped by chains. But we got our sneaker."

"Yeah, you did. I guess that's blood on it, huh?"

"I'd bet."

"What're we going to do with it?"

"I've been thinking about that. I think we should take it to Poole and get his advice."

"Poole? He's a drunk."

"Yes, when he's drunk. When he's not, he's a smart lawyer and he knows the situation here a lot better than I do."

Dressed in a crisp cotton shirtwaist and with the worst of the scratches covered up, she drove into town, which took longer than she expected because a moron in one of those pickups with huge tires dawdled in front of her and would not let her pass. Redneck fun. It took a while to track down Poole, but she eventually found him at the VFW hall. He was at a table in the back of the barroom, a high-ceilinged, dim, echoing place smelling of old beer. He was drinking bourbon with beer chasers. Being a private club, the VFW was allowed to supply him with his own bottle, whether or not he was actually a veteran of a foreign war. She sat at his table and plopped the sneaker in its plastic bag down on the table.

"I ordered the ham on rye," he said. "That's a sneaker."

She told him what she thought it was and where she had found it. "Ah, deeper and deeper, Ciampi. Why is it people never listen to good advice? What do you expect to gain from this?"

Good, she thought: he was at the expansive stage of his drunk. "The release of our client, for starters. The murderers came down from that ridge, broke in, killed the Heeneys, and walked back up to their car. One of them noticed he had blood on his shoes, so he chucked them into the laurel. I'll bet you a bottle of Jack Black that the blood on it matches up with one of the victims. That shit-cans the state's theory of the case."

"If Murdoch doesn't throw it out. He'll say you cooked it up. There's no custodial chain, and without one there's no probative value. If you give it to Swett, it'll just disappear."

"I wasn't thinking about Swett. What do you know about Hawes?"

"Hawes? He's new. Been in there six months. The old state's attorney was a guy named Hailey, an old drinking buddy of mine as a matter of fact. His evil ways caught up with him and he kicked off, and the governor put this kid in there. He's ambitious as Satan and he's smart enough to know he's never going to get anywhere by bucking the system."

"But is he bent? I should say, 'bent yet'?"

"I'm not sure anyone has bothered to bend him, but I'd say he's eminently bendable. The Majestic Coal Company hires a lot of lawyers, and they fund a lot of campaigns."

"Well, let's us go and find out," she said, rising and retrieving the shoe.

"Us? No, dear, this is your play. I don't want anything to do with it."

"I thought we were partners, Poole."

He threw a half shot of the bourbon down his throat and reached for the bottle. "No. You are an annoyance and I am the annoyee. That isn't partners." He carefully poured a shot. "Also, I am thinking of the original owner of that very large shoe. It looks to be a size eleven. Did you think that he might be a local resident? That he might harbor some animus against someone who was trying to pin a triple murder on him? That he might try to dissuade that person, or take some revenge? Revenge is big in Robbens County, Ciampi. It's what we have instead of youth soccer."

"Okay, suit yourself. But you better pray that Hawes isn't completely bent, because I'm going to tell him you gave me the Nike and that you know who owns it."

She had reached the door before she felt a hand on her arm. "You're not really . . . I mean, that was a bluff, right?"

"I rarely bluff, Poole." She turned to look him in the face. "You know, you're looking a little better than you did the last time I saw you. I think you're turning into a functional drunk."

"Thank you," he said as he followed her out. "I always wanted to be beaten to death while cold sober. You look like hell, by the way. What did you do to your face?"

"I scratched it in some bushes," said Marlene, her tone short. Marlene prided herself on not depending upon her looks to get things done (a false pride necessarily, the world being what it is), but did not appreciate having any shortcoming in that department pointed out. They walked the few streets to the courthouse in chilly silence.

The state's attorney had a suite of offices on the second floor of that building and a pretty red-haired secretary to put in it. Aside from that, there did not seem to be much going on in the office, which was, how-ever, nicely paneled and equipped with heavy, old-fashioned oak furni-ture. Poole greeted the secretary by name (Margie) and asked if Stan was free. He was not, he was in a meeting. Poole made to leave, but Marlene clutched his sleeve. "We'll wait," she said, and sat on a wooden bench under a glassed print of Washington crossing the Delaware. Poole sat grumpily beside her. She held the sneaker on her lap like a gift cake. The clock on the wall ticked, Margie typed slowly on her keyboard, Poole fell asleep, snoring gently. Marlene let the time flow past, pushed Poole away when his head slumped toward her shoulder, and tried not to imagine herself back in the choking laurels.

After forty minutes, the door to Hawes's office flung open and a large man in a blue suit strode out. He had a big jaw and a nose that looked as if it had been broken. His hands were big and red, as was his face. His hair was pale brown and freshly cut, as if he had just stepped from a barber's rather than a state's attorney's place of business. He was almost out the door when he caught sight of Marlene and Poole. He stopped short and smiled, showing big yellow horse teeth. There was definitely something horselike about him, Marlene decided, the kind of horse that kicked and bit. His voice was loud and confident: "Ernie Poole."

Poole snapped awake. He wiped his chin where he had dribbled on it and blinked at the big man.

"George," he said neutrally.

"How ya doing, Ernie? Catching up on your beauty sleep?"

"I have a hard life."

"Yeah, you want to take it easy, now. Don't strain yourself any."

Some more banter here, George's tone patronizing, hectoring, Poole's dry and his answers minimal. The interesting thing, Marlene thought, was that while George was talking to Poole, his eyes were fixed on her; pale, hard ones, like tin. She met his gaze without flinching.

"Nice seeing you, Ernie," George said, pointing a finger gun-fashion at Poole. "You take care now, hey? Stay healthy."

When he was gone, Marlene asked, "Who was that?"

"That was George Floyd, the business manager of the Mining Equipment Operators Union."

"Oh? I'm sorry you didn't introduce me."

"If you live your whole life without meeting George Floyd, you can consider yourself lucky."

"That bad, huh?"

"Bad? No, I'd say he was just an average degenerate sadist and crook. We have worse." He stood up as Margie told them they could go in now.

Hawes was behind his desk looking angry, although not necessarily at them.

"I have court in ten minutes. I hope this'll be quick," he said without offering his hand to them or a chair. Marlene sat down anyway, and Poole followed suit.

"Well, no small talk then," said Marlene. "We've discovered some new evidence in the Welch case and we'd like to share it with you."

"What kind of evidence?"

Marlene placed the sneaker on his desk and explained what she thought it was, how she had found it, and what it implied for the state's case against her client.

He gave it the briefest glance, waited until she had finished, and said, "What is this bullshit, Ernie?"

"Well, it's a shoe with blood on it, found near the scene of the crime. I'd say that wasn't bullshit. The blood can be tested. If it belongs to one of the victims, I'd say there goes your case."

"Oh, come on! A lawyer walks in here with a shoe that could've come from anywhere with blood on it that could've come from anywhere. That's not evidence. If she thought she found something, she should've gone to the police. As it is, there's no chain of custody. I'll oppose it and the judge'll back me up."

"That's not your role, Mr. Hawes," said Marlene.

He looked at her as if she had just popped out of the ether. "What?"

"That's not your role. Your role is not to disparage evidence but to establish the probative value of any evidence you come across, to make sure you bring the right people to justice. I bring you, as an officer of the court, a sealed bag, the seal signed by me and the son of the victim, in which bag is a shoe smeared with a substance that appears to be dried blood. We propose that it was disposed of by the real killers. Could I have concocted the evidence out of whole cloth? Yes, and opened myself to criminal penalties with a scam that any competent lab could detect. Would I do that? On a pro bono case? It's absurd on the face of it, and just as absurd is the idea that the victims' own son would conspire to allow the real killer to get off. Meanwhile, blood will tell, as the saying goes. They'll DNA it and age it and tell you that it flowed out of the body of one of the victims at about the time of the murders. They'll find carpet fibers that match the crime scene. They'll tell you it's genuine unfakable. It's particularly telling, since your own case rests entirely on finding blood on the shoes of a mental incompetent, which shoes are at least two sizes too small for him."

Hawes indicated the sneaker on his desk, using his chin. He seemed not to want to examine it. "That one'd fit him all right."

"Yes, but it changes your theory of the case a good deal, doesn't it? The murder then would involve at least two participants, one wearing a fairly expensive pair of Rocky-brand hunting boots, size nine and a half, and the other a fairly expensive pair of Nikes. It should be easy to check it. There can't be many pairs of such shoes sold in this county, and I think, in fact I'm sure, you'll find that my client never owned either type of shoe. He's more of a Goodwill dresser. The plain fact is you have the wrong man in custody. My assumption is you want the right man or men. I assume you don't want to railroad a poor dummy just to make a case and make nice with this courthouse and the people who run this county." She gave him a sympathetic smile. He did not return it, but did something more revealing. Good God, she thought, he's blushing. He's in the wrong business.

He cleared his throat. "I don't like the word *railroad*."

"Neither do I. But I want you to find who did the crime, and you *have* to know now that Moses Welch is not going to go down for it. Given this"—she picked up the bag with the Nike and let it thump down— "and given the general weakness of your case, no jury will convict, not with the defense we intend to mount. Correct me if I'm wrong, but you don't seem like the sort of man who wants to retire as state's attorney in Robbens County. Find the right bad guys and everyone will forget about this little excursion. But push this case to the bitter end and you'll end up looking very bad indeed. As in stinky bad. I'm on your side here, Mr. Hawes."

It took a while for him to respond, and as she studied his face, she thought that was a good sign. A lot of lip-biting and brow-knotting there, the signs of an intact moral center working hard.

At last he let out a long breath and began to talk technicalities and legal minutiae, which Marlene was happy to do for as long as he wanted. They left with a receipt for the evidence bag and an assurance that he would have it delivered to the state lab himself.

Outside the courthouse, Poole said, "Do you really think he's going to do what he said?"

"Yes, I do. I think he'll do the right thing. Don't you?"

Poole laughed and rolled his eyes. "Hell, no, I don't. I think he was on the phone to whoever owns him the minute we were out of there. That damn shoe is history."

"How cynical you are, Poole!" she exclaimed, laughing. "You should try to regain some faith. No, I think what we have here is a malleable kid up against his first real test of integrity, and I think he's going to pass it."

"And if not?"

"If not, I know approximately where the *other* sneaker is, and I will shout to the high heavens and hire a bunch of guys to find it while the TV cameras roll. Even Mr. Hawes knows that two sneakers make a pair. No, I think we turned a corner here. How would you like to come out to the Heeney place tonight? We'll have a cookout to celebrate."

Poole hesitated, looking away. "I don't know . . ."

"Oh, come on! It'll be fun. We'll get functionally drunk together."

He smiled. "Oh, in that case . . ."

They mounted the red Dodge, stopped off at the Pay 'n' Pack for supplies, and headed out of town on Route 119. After a few minutes,

Marlene said, "Say, Poole? Do you know anyone with an electric blue Ford 250 pickup on big wheels?"

"Where?" he said, startled, looking around.

"Right behind us. A couple of guys in the front. They've been driving around me all day. Who are they?"

"I have no idea. Say, you know, on second thought, I'm not feeling too good right now. My stomach. Could you just swing around and drop me at my house?"

"No. Who are they?"

"Cades. That's Earl Cade's pickup."

She checked her side mirror. The big truck was edging closer. Marlene tapped her brake and pulled to the right. The blue pickup came closer still. It towered over the Dodge, its heavy bumper and grille filling her entire rearview mirror. Her gaze flashed up the road, looking for a turnoff or a driveway, but there was nothing useful ahead, only a shallow roadside ditch and a line of phone poles. They had picked this place with care.

In the distance a tanker truck filled the oncoming lane. A grinding thump from the rear. The Dodge shook and swerved. She gripped the wheel, fighting for control. Another thump. Poole yelped and pressed his palms against the dash.

When she looked again, the blue truck was gone from the rearview, to appear immediately in the side mirror. Marlene looked out her window, but the giant tires raised the blue truck so high that she could not see anything but a sheer wall of shiny blue paint and chrome, which came ever closer. There was a crunch and tinkle as her side mirror tore away. Her right wheels were on shoulder gravel now, the pebbles machine-gunning against the underside of the Dodge. The oncoming tanker leaned on his horn. She heard the scream of air brakes.

We're going into the ditch, she thought. A phone pole ripped off the right-side mirror. She jammed on her brakes and jerked the wheel hard to the right. The Dodge fishtailed and plunged into the ditch, leaped into the air, crashed through a fence, and came to rest in a field, festooned with barbed wire.

The engine had stalled. There was no sound but its cooling tick, bird twitters, and heavy breathing. "Well, *that* was exciting," said Marlene at last.

"They tried to kill us," Poole gasped.

"Yes, but they didn't succeed. You should never *try* to kill anyone. You should either kill them or play nice." She opened the door.

"Where are you going?"

"Checking the dog and the truck," she called over her shoulder. The dog was fine, the truck less so, but drivable. She started it, shifted to four-wheel, and backed across the ditch and onto the edge of the road.

"They might try again," said Poole.

"I'm sure, which is why it's time to call for help."

9

"I WAS JUST TRYING TO GET YOU," SAID KARP. "YOUR CELL PHONE DOESN'T work?"

"This is West Virginia, the Mountain State," said his wife. "Here in Robbens County we have no TV except satellite and no cell phones."

"It sounds like my kind of place."

"No bagels, however, and I looked."

"They barely have bagels in New York anymore. How are you?"

"Not bad. The case is going well, but somebody just tried to kill me. That's why I called."

A silence. "How serious was it? You're not hurt?"

"Shaken up. They tried to run us into a phone pole on the road. I was with Poole, the local defense counsel."

"Maybe it's time to come home."

"Oh, it's just starting to be fun," she said lightly, knowing the tone would irritate him. It was a little game they played, had played for years. In philosophical moments she wondered why they didn't get beyond it, or if it was permanently fixed in the structure of their marriage, like a trilobite in chert. He said nothing, so she continued, "But why I called is, I was wondering if you got any information from Sterner. Whether the feds are going to move on the murder."

"They may, but the state is in it for sure. The governor would very much like to preempt federal involvement, in fact. They're appointing a special prosecutor with full powers, bringing in state cops. The governor's more or less decided to clean up Robbens County."

"That's a change. Any idea why?"

"It's time, I guess. The global village. People are starting to get more sensitive to killing and corruption, even in the backwaters. They want wild and wonderful West Virginia to be a little less wild and a little more wonderful."

"I'm impressed," she said. "Have they picked the guy yet? Or girl?"

"Not officially," replied Karp after the briefest pause. "The governor wants to examine the cut of his jib, but for all practical purposes, according to Saul, it's a done deal."

"Do you know who it's going to be?"

"Yes." Two beats. "Me."

"No, I mean really."

"Really," said Karp, aware of a rush of faintly sadistic pleasure. She was always pulling sneaky surprises on him, and this was a delicious turn-about. "I'm flying down to Charleston tomorrow. They're actually sending the state plane to pick me up at Teterboro."

An even longer silence. "Marlene?"

"I'm gaping. Wait a minute—you're leaving your job? What about the kids?"

"I'm not leaving my job. Jack was more than happy to lend me. The crocodile tears were falling so fast he had to wring out his tie. And Lucy can handle the twins until you get back there."

"Who says I'm going back?"

"Well, if I'm in charge of the prosecution, it's clearly impossible for you to be associated with the defense."

"Yeah, but the guy I'm defending isn't the guy. The case against him is a joke."

"If that's true, we'll obviously quash the indictment. And then you can go home."

"Home?" She said it like a foreigner trying an unfamiliar word.

"Yes, home. You know, among your pet children, your beloved dogs, the familiar felons. You can do the laundry, cook nutritious meals, and in the evenings embroider by the fire."

"You're loving this, aren't you?"

"Since you ask . . ."

"Rat! When is this all scheduled to happen?"

"Oh, you know, it's state bureaucracy, so figure weeks, not days. Will you promise not to get killed until I rescue you?"

"You know me, dear. It'll take more than a bunch of hillbillies to do me in. As a matter of fact, I might have this whole thing wrapped up by the time you get here."

Karp's tone changed. "No, be serious! There's no reason to poke into anything anymore until I get down there with the cavalry. Besides, you could screw up something." Oh, God, that was a mistake, thought Karp, the instant the words had passed his lips.

"Oh, well, I'll certainly *try* not to screw things up for you, dear. But I don't know, I'm such a total *klutz,* when it comes to legal procedure and all the other boy things. I swear, I don't know how you men keep all that stuff in your heads."

"I didn't mean it that way, Marlene, and you know it. You're just spoiling for a fight because you're miffed because you're going to have to give control of this thing over to me, which as you know has absolutely nothing to do with any assessment of your abilities. I'm sorry I said you might screw things up. I'm sure everything you've done down there has been in accord with the highest standards of legal procedure."

"Oh, I hate it when you try to wriggle out of it, when for once your true thoughts manage to slip out from under all the hypocrisy. Why don't you admit it? You really want a little wifey safe at home."

"Marlene, that is such *total* bullshit! I can't stand that whenever you're pissed at me, you trot out this absurd feminist cant. How long have we been married? In all that time, have I ever once—"

"Innumerable times. You really do want me to do embroidery."

"It would be a strange choice if I did," Karp snarled. "As far as I know, the only thing you've ever embroidered is the truth."

They went back and forth like this for a couple of more increasingly nasty rounds until Marlene hung up, leaving both parties feeling stupid, guilty, and irritable. Every long-married couple has a tape like this—some have whole racks of them—and they are wise who avoid pushing the Play button. Marlene knew she was a sneak who cut corners, when not actually committing crimes, but she wanted her husband to treat her like a model of legal prudence. Karp had spent nearly twenty years waiting for a call from some police agency telling him that his wife was either dead or under arrest for a violent felony. Most of the time he suppressed the anguish this caused him but occasionally it popped out, as now. The root of the pain was that each deeply loved the other, but wished the other different in this small way: why the divorce courts hum as they do.

"Bad news?" said Poole. He had heard the yelling from the porch. She glared at him and slammed a wedge of chopped chuck into a bowl hard enough to stun it.

"I see you've found the bourbon," she said, eyeing his highball.

"Yeah, I'm good at that. Trouble at home?"

"No. My husband has informed me that your governor is appointing a special prosecutor on the Heeney case and he's it."

A half smile appeared on Poole's face. "You're kidding, right?"

"No, I'm not."

"He's a prosecutor?"

"Yes. A big-time labor lawyer named Sterner arranged the whole thing."

Poole took a long swallow. "Well, I'll be damned! This'll be something to see. A hotshot New York prosecutor come to straighten out the hicks. He any good?"

"A lot of people think he's the best."

"I hope he's bulletproof, too."

"Don't be stupid, Poole. Nobody's going to do any more shooting. There's no way this arrangement you've got down here is going to stand up to serious public scrutiny. He'll find the idiots who did the crime, try them, convict them, and put them in jail for life. End of story."

"Maybe. But I'll tell you one thing, city girl. They brought the United States Army up here in '21. Fought them a little guerilla war up in the hollers, and it was a toss-up who won it. The folks up in Mingo and Logan laid down their arms when the troops showed up, but not here. Lot of people around here aren't too happy with the U.S. government."

"You mean like militias?"

"No, I mean families. They don't like people in fancy suits telling them what to do. They don't like the liquor laws, or the tax laws, or the drug laws. A lot of them got their own religion, too. They've been that way since 1790 or thereabouts. They'll take money from the coal company when it pleases them, and from the union, too, but mainly they do what they like. You'll see."

"Yes, we will," snapped Marlene. "Now, unless you want to help, scram out of here while I fix this goddamn cookout."

She fixed, Poole drank. It was not a fun affair. Marlene was grumpy, Poole drank and talked. Of the two sorts of drunk, he was the garrulous kind. Dan sulked. Emmett made sarcastic comments about Poole's stories. Emmett's girlfriend, Kathy, a small blond who might have been cloned from Rose Heeney, started using let's-split body language fairly early in the evening. Around nine, Emmett said they were going to go back to Kathy's to watch *Gladiator* on satellite, and they left.

"Young squirts don't know how to party," said Poole after they had gone, and launched into a rambling story about a memorable spree. He kept stopping and asking Marlene if she remembered old Joe Whitman and what he'd done with the cake some woman had made for some church supper, as if she were one of the old McCullensburg gang of his youth. She gave short answers, or none, but the odd thing was that she didn't think he was drinking that much, not enough for this kind of behavior. It was as if he was trying to live up to his reputation as a hopeless, drunken bore, while not really believing in it. He avoided her eye.

After several increasingly broader hints, Marlene decided to ignore him and tried not to think about what *she* was like when drunk, and whether she was even now on the first steps of the slope that led to this sort of display. She was clearing the picnic table using the kind of hyper-efficient and semiviolent motions women apply to household tasks when they are angry. Crash, clang. Dan hung around dutifully, trying to help, getting in the way. She was short with him, too, and finally he vanished into his room. She felt a pang of guilt and ruthlessly suppressed it. What was she feeling guilty about? She was doing them a favor! She had abandoned her family, and her business, and come here to this shitty little town, to get a half-wit out of trouble and hand the bad guys their lumps, only now it was her husband who was going to do that, so she was not only stupid but useless as well. Poole was still out in the yard talking away to the crescent moon. And nursemaiding a pathetic drunk, too, another thing she *really* enjoyed doing. She eyed the bottle of jug wine she had bought earlier, grabbed it, poured a juice glass full, stared at it, felt a tumult of revulsion in her gut, threw it splashing into the sink. No, coffee was the thing now, sober the both of them up and drag Poole back to his house; yes, cut off his booze and fill him with black coffee, a little sadism-stuffed virtue here, and why not? She loaded the coffeemaker, then the dishwasher, the latter with such enthusiasm that she smashed a large majolica serving dish.

Cursing, she swept up the pieces of bright pottery. You didn't get plates like this at the Bi-Lo in town, or at Wal-Mart, she could not help noticing. It was, or had been, a lovely moss green with flowers painted on it in shades of rust, tan, and yellow. Rose Heeney had selected it in some New York boutique, a bit of her native heath brought into exile. Marlene found herself sitting on a hard chair, crying bitterly into a dish-towel, and not just for Rose Heeney, either.

Then the dog growled. Marlene wiped her face and sprang to her feet, for it was that kind of growl.

Gog had been hanging around the kitchen, hoping she would allow him to preclean the dishes. Now he was standing stiffly, nosing the back door, the hair on his back bristling, making his bad-muffler noise. Marlene snapped the kitchen light off and looked through the back-door window. The floodlights illuminated a rough oval twenty yards out from the house; beyond that, the rural night hung like black drapes.

Marlene tapped on the door of Dan's bedroom and went in. He was lying on his bed with a set of headphones on, reading. He took the phones off and looked at her inquiringly.

"Turn off your light. Gog thinks we have company."

He sat up instantly and snapped off the lamp. "What should we do?"

"I need a big flashlight, if you have one, and your pistol."

He stalled for a moment, his eyes confused, but then leaped from the bed. A moment later she had Red Heeney's .38 Smith and a boxy camping flashlight in hand. She switched it on briefly to check the beam, then led him to the back door. They could hear Poole mumbling to no one by the picnic table.

"Stay by the light switch, watch me, and flick it off when I signal. I'll be outside in the shadow of the stairs."

"Shouldn't we call the police?"

"Yeah, that's a good idea," she said carelessly, "but watch my hand and stay by the switch." As he dialed the kitchen cordless, she went out-side with the dog and crouched on the storm door lying by the stairs. The dog was whining and panting eagerly.

A few minutes later, she saw two figures, one large, one smaller, pause on the edge of the lit area. They seemed to converse for a moment, and then they started toward the house, running in a ridiculous crouch, as if that would make them less visible against the floodlit lawn. The bigger one carried a shotgun. They were both wearing ball caps, but as they looked around, she could catch glimpses of their faces. The bigger one had a stupid, brutal look, like a child's sketch of the bogeyman: lantern jaw, shadowed with beard, a floppy mouth, a shapeless nose. The smaller was good-looking in a weedy country-boy way, the sort of look that had made the fortunes of Elvis and James Dean. Their eyes were hidden in the shadows cast by their cap bills.

When they had crossed half the yard, she raised her hand and brought it sharply down. The lights went off. "Get 'em, Gog!" she cried. The dog vanished into the blackness and she followed at a trot. She heard a cry and then a boom as the shotgun discharged. She stopped and turned the flashlight on.

Gog had the big man down, with his jaws clamped around the man's throat. James Dean was crouched, blinking, and waving a large silvery revolver around. Marlene put the beam on his face and said, "If you don't drop that pistol, son, I'm going to shoot you." She held her weapon in the light beam so he could see it. He hesitated. Marlene snapped an order to her dog. The man on the ground wailed and made interesting noises indicating a deficiency of breath. She said, "I could have the dog take his windpipe right out of his neck, and I will, if you don't drop the gun. Now drop it!"

After one longing glance over his shoulder, he did. She made him lie down and called the dog off the other man, who sat up rubbing his throat, which oozed blood. Marlene tossed the shotgun away as far as she could, picked up the dropped pistol, and called out, "Dan! Hit the lights!"

The lights came on and Dan walked over.

"You know these guys?"

"Yeah," Dan said. "That's Earl Cade and his brother Bo."

"Earl and Bo Cade, huh?" said Marlene. "So what were the Cade boys doing sneaking up on this house late at night, armed to the teeth? Hmm?"

"We warn't sneakin'," said Bo. "We was huntin'."

"Yeah," said Earl, "we was huntin', and you had no call to set that damn dog on us."

"What were you hunting for?" Marlene asked.

They looked at one another briefly. "Coon," said Bo.

"Yeah, that's right. Coon," said Earl.

"Gosh, I thought you needed dogs to hunt coon," she observed.

A look of confusion came over Earl's face, but Bo spoke up. "Shows you don't know much about huntin'."

"Well, maybe not," agreed Marlene. "We'll let the police sort it out. By the way, you guys murdered the Heeney family, didn't you? And you tried to run me off the road today."

She was watching Earl's face as she said this, looking straight at his eyes. These were very pale blue and practically vibrated with the effort to keep meeting her eyes, which she knew was a habit particularly stupid criminals adopted to fake sincerity.

"No, we didn't," he said.

"Mose Welch killed them folks," said Bo. She examined him, too. Same eyes, but a more skillful liar. Get them isolated from one another, and a halfway decent interrogator would have the whole story out of them in half an hour. She reached out her foot and tapped the sole of Bo's boot. There were old OD combat boots, cracked and stained. "They caught him wearing your new boots. It must've hurt to toss them away like that. You should've worn those old ones to the murder."

"I didn't kill nobody," he said. "And I ain't got any new boots to throw away."

A car sounded on gravel and red lights flashed against the foliage. Shortly there appeared a stout police officer in a tan uniform with a big American flag sewn to the left shoulder. He had a slack pie face and a boozer's lump of a nose, and his eyes looked squashed, as if he had just been awakened from a long sleep. The steel name tag on his breast identified him as Omar Petrie.

"What all's the problem here?" he asked, taking in the peculiar scene.

Dan said, "I made the call. We caught these guys sneaking up to the house with weapons."

Bo Cade said vehemently, "Damn it, Omar, we wasn't sneakin'. We was huntin' and she set that dog on us. It just about ripped Earl's throat right out."

At this, Earl started to get to his feet, the better to argue, but Gog barked at him and showed his impressive fangs.

"See! See!" Earl shouted, scooting away. "That's a bad dog, Omar. You ought to shoot him right now."

Marlene moved to put herself between the cop and the dog. "Officer, that is a highly trained guard dog and it's under my complete control." She lowered the timbre of her voice and ordered, "Gog! Off! Down! Stay!"

The dog seemed to forget about Earl Cade. He walked over to Marlene and dropped to his belly with an audible thump.

"See?" said Marlene. "He's perfectly safe."

"Who're you?" the cop demanded. He still had his hand on the butt of his pistol.

Marlene introduced herself. "I'm a guest here and doing some legal work for the Heeney family. The dog warned us and we saw these two sneaking up to the house. *Sneaking* is definitely the correct word. Three people were murdered in that house a little while ago and we thought we should take precautions. It could've been the murderers coming back."

Bo said, "Aw, shit, Omar, you know us! We ain't no murderers. Besides, they got the fella did it, that dumpy Mose Welch. We's just walking across the yard here and she attacked us. You ought to arrest *her*."

Marlene saw Petrie's eyes darting back and forth from the Cades to her. This is not going as it should, she thought.

The cop cleared his throat heavily and spat on the ground. "Well, what I see is one man chewed up by this dog and you got all the guns. Why don't you give them here for a start."

Marlene turned over the two pistols and Petrie stowed them in his capacious uniform pockets. Turning to the Cades, he said, "Boys, whyn't you all run along now. It's late."

Earl said, "What about my neck? That dog chewed the shit out of me. You just gonna let her get away with that?"

Petrie considered this. "You making a complaint here, Earl?"

"Damn right I am. And I'm gonna sue that bitch's ass for everything she got."

The cop nodded wisely. To Marlene he said, "I got to take your animal with me. Go put it on a chain."

"You are not taking that animal," said Marlene in an outraged tone. "That dog did nothing wrong. He knocked down and secured an armed trespasser as he's trained to do."

Petrie hitched up his gun belt and gave Marlene a cop stare. "You better do like I said, ma'am, or you're gonna be in trouble."

"I can't *believe* this!" cried Marlene. "You're arresting my dog for defending private property? Why don't you arrest me, too?"

"I will, if you don't get the dog into my car trunk right now."

"Oh, go fuck yourself!" she snarled, and turned to walk away.

Petrie reached out and grabbed her arm, hard, and jerked her back. This attracted the interest of the dog. Normally, he would not have broken stay for a major earthquake, but this was a special circumstance, the exception to the rule. He sprang up, barked, growled, and menaced. Petrie let go of Marlene, stumbled back a few steps, and unsnapped his holster strap. Marlene yelled, "Gog, hide!"

The dog whirled and ran. Petrie drew his pistol and took aim at the fleeing animal. Marlene flung herself on his gun arm. He grabbed her hair and yanked.

"Omar Petrie," boomed a big voice. "Let that woman go! She's not one of your roadhouse whores."

It was Poole, apparently cold sober and transformed. Petrie goggled and released Marlene's hair. She let go of his arm and stepped back. Poole walked up to the cop and laid an arm on his shoulder. "Omar, damnit, it's a good thing I was here. You almost made the mistake of your life."

"Where'n hell did you come from, Ernie?" asked the cop.

"I was in the kitchen pouring some coffee when this commotion started. I saw the whole thing through that window. These young Cades apparently got lost during one of their famous midnight expeditions. Ms. Ciampi here observed that old Earl was carrying a shotgun, and since she knew that two people in this very house had been killed with a shotgun, she was naturally on her guard. Now"—Poole lifted the flat of his hand to stall Petrie's objection—"as to the dog: Do you know what kind of dog that is? No, you don't. That is not just some yard mutt you can shoot because you're feeling a little cranky. That is a rare prize animal, Omar. That is a ten-*thousand*-dollar animal. Well, you shoot a ten-thousand-dollar animal that's just doing what it's told, apprehending prowlers on private property in the hours of the night, in the presence of a sworn officer of the court, which is me, Omar, then I think you're looking at a world of trouble. I'm talking lawsuits, here, big ones. The town ain't going to pay for no ten-thousand-dollar dog, and Sheriff Swett sure ain't, and who does that leave, hm? You want to set down and figure how long it's going to take to make that sum up, plus court costs and punitive damages, out of what you take off those girls down by Amos's out on Route 36? Why, some of those girls'll be grandmas before you paid it off."

Petrie was staring at him, as if at an apparition, Marlene noticed, and Dan and the two Cades were staring likewise. Poole clapped his hands briskly. "Well! Let's see now. This looks to me like a little misunderstanding. Miss Ciampi here's from away, so she might not comprehend our local mores and customs. No harm's done, except to Mr. Cade's neck, and a couple of Band-Aids'll put that right. A little disinfectant, too, if you got it. In fact, I believe, Omar, that the wisest thing you could do right now is to get back in your patrol car and drive away. Given the situation, I don't think Sheriff Swett would appreciate having legal attention being drawn to this *particular* house and family, if you catch my drift. What I mean is, this could be worse than what happened with Commissioner Jakes. Situation like this, the best thing to do is not to do anything." Turning to the Cades, he added, "Boys, why don't you just wander back where you come from. This business is all over."

At this Bo Cade immediately started off, but his brother rose and stood there like a dead tree. "What about my shotgun?"

Bo ran back and grabbed Earl's arm. "Goddamn it! There *wasn't* no shotgun, you idiot. Come along!"

But Earl jerked his arm away, roared out a curse, and flung a roundhouse blow at his brother's head, which was ducked. Bo kicked him in the shin. Earl shouted threats of murder and ran at him, Bo took off like a hare, and they both disappeared into the darkness, yelling curses at one another. Officer Petrie holstered his sidearm, adjusted his uniform, and gave everyone a look of malevolent stupidity. Without another word he strode off. They heard his engine start and then the rattle of gravel as he sped away.

Marlene said, "That was extremely impressive, Poole. Thank you. I guess there's still a little cherry vanilla left in the bottom of the carton."

"Thank *you*," said Poole. "I must be becoming a functional drunk. Or maybe it's that shotgun blasts at night tend to sober me up."

"But . . . they just walked away," Dan complained. "They snuck in here with guns and they just walked away."

"Yeah, well, I guess we could file a complaint for trespass," said Poole, "but you know Judge Murdoch would dismiss it in two shakes."

The phone rang in the house.

"Who's calling this late?" asked Dan.

"If you go answer it, you'll find out," said Marlene. Dan went into the house.

"We should pick up that shotgun," said Marlene. She used the flashlight to look in the tall grass at the edge of the yard and came back with the gun broken over one arm.

"A Remington twelve, fairly new. Do you think we're looking at the actual murder weapon?"

"Possibly," said Poole. "Although there are any number of murderous Cades and they all own shotguns. And every other kind of gun. I assume that pistol . . ."

"A .357 Ruger. Lizzie was killed with a .38 slug. I suppose it could've come from a .357. I take it that Officer Petrie will not put two and two together and submit the weapon for ballistic testing."

"You would assume correctly," said Poole. "In fact, I wouldn't be surprised if that gun found its way back to the owner before long." He looked away from her and up at the sky. "I can't stand these lights. It's like a prison yard. There's something shitty about having to put in security lights in a place like this. You can't see the stars."

"Are you a stargazer, Poole?"

"Yes. The sole advantage of getting drunk in rural surroundings is that you get to spend a lot of time lying on your back and watching the galaxies whirl around. You can tell yourself that you're small and meaningless and futile, which gives you an excuse for another snort. Not that you need an excuse."

Marlene went to the back door and snapped off the floods. Dan was on a stool with the phone clutched to his ear; she didn't disturb him but returned to the yard, where she found that Poole had settled himself in an aluminum lounge chair, staring at the heavens. The sky was still overcast, but the cloud cover was scudding, making holes for starshine.

Marlene whistled up her dog, who arrived bounding, to be hugged and made much of.

"You should give a nice lick to Mr. Poole, Gog," she cooed. "He saved your bacon, didn't he? Yes, he did! He said you were worth ten thousand dollars. And you are, and more. Go ahead, give him a big kiss."

The dog licked Marlene instead, kissing on demand not being part of his extensive repertoire, and settled heavily under the hammock where his mistress now reclined.

Poole said, "Speaking of which, I expect that this evening's events have pressed home to you exactly what we're up against here with respect to our so-called justice system."

"Old Omar is bent, you mean."

"No, it goes far beyond that. Bent is a useful descriptor only when you have the idea of the straight. But there is no such idea hereabouts. You need to think about a little banana republic set among these misty peaks, except instead of bananas it's coal, and instead of United Fruit, it's the Majestic Coal Company."

"I know that's what you think, but I still can't understand why the state would allow it. Or the feds. I mean, we had that kind of thing in the South, and it got cleaned up twenty years ago, and the same with the big-city machines and the Mob."

"Yes, but the critical thing there were complaints; people bitched about it, the press was involved. You know the old joke about the kid who didn't talk and his parents took him to all kinds of specialists, and no one could cure him, and one day, the kid is about ten and he pushes his plate away and says, 'I hate spinach.' And his parents get all excited. 'You can talk! You can talk! Why didn't you say anything until now?' and the kid goes, 'Everything was okay until the spinach.' It's like that. The level of expectation is so low, and the level of terror is so high, that there are no complaints. Until Red Heeney, and you saw what happened to him. The first plate of spinach, though. Now you arrive and dragoon me into it, and soon your hubby will come with the full power of the state. It'll be interesting. I may even stay sober occasionally to observe the high jinks."

"You have no great hopes, I take it."

"Oh, I think we'll get the boys who did it, the actual gunmen. As you saw tonight, we're not dealing with criminal masterminds. Probably half the people in the county know who pulled the triggers or know someone who knows. They'll toss them in the pokey, and the next squad of villains will appear ready for action. There's a never-ending supply, like cans in a soda machine. The Cades alone must have a dozen or so fellows like young Earl, shambling horrors with their eyes too close together who like to hurt people. The system, though, our way of life—changing that is another kettle of fish. It's like the transition from a society that's essentially barbaric, and based on fear and force, to a civil society based on laws and rights. It usually takes a century or so, and even then it's fragile, as the recent century has so hideously demonstrated."

"Well, I can appreciate that," said Marlene. "I'm a kind of feudal person myself. Odd for a lawyer, but there it is. *Dieu et mon droit,* et cetera, and Sicilian plots and revenges."

Poole turned his head to look at her. "Are you? And your husband, is he feudal, too?"

"No, he's extremely rabbinical when it comes to justice. Never ever personal, which is why he's so good at what he does. The methodical, perfectionist approach. I tend to drive him crazy."

"That sounds dull for you."

"Mm. But sometimes I crave dullness. It's like roughage in the diet, bran flakes, no fun but necessary for the organism. There's such a thing as excessively interesting."

"What would be interesting is if you rolled over here and gave me a big kiss," said Poole.

"Is that in the nature of a proposition, counselor?"

"It is. Or maybe more in the nature of tapping on the gauges to see if there's steam. I can't remember the last time I was (a) alone with a desirable woman on a soft summer's night, and (b) conscious. It gives me goose pimples."

"I'm sorry I can't help you there, Poole, although I confess to feeling flattered, slut that I am. And also let me say that while I have come real close in twenty-odd years of marriage, I have not yet slipped over the edge into infidelity."

"That's hard to believe. And you from the evil big city, too."

"It's hard for *me* to believe. And it looks like I will slide gracefully into the unattractive years with my honor intact. Maybe that's the upside of being a medieval-type person."

"Honor," Poole echoed, his voice sad and hollow. He lay back on the lounge and stared upward. "There's the Summer Triangle. Altair, Vega, and Deneb. Since you're not going to slake my lust, why don't you fix me a little drink."

"I think it's coffee time," said Marlene as she rolled out of the hammock. "By the way, who's Commissioner Jakes?"

"Duane P. Jakes. One of our fine county commissioners of a few years back. He had this thing about the space program. He thought it was making holes in the sky and changing the weather. Well, no harm in that. Duane was about average among our county fathers with respect to smarts, but the problem was he conceived the notion that the daily prop flight from Charleston to Knoxville was sent by NASA to spy on him. I mean, it stood to reason—the thing flew over his spread every day at about the same time, just when he was out feeding his hogs. So he started shooting at it with his rifle. The amazing thing is he actually hit it, so Omar and another deputy paid him a visit to get him to cut it out. Basically, it was a case of taking a rifle away from a loony old man, but Omar aggravated it into a real shoot-out. The deputy got shot, Duane got shot, and the town came in for the kind of publicity it would rather not have. I thought it wise to mention it in the present situation."

"It was, too." She leaned over and kissed him on the forehead before she left.

Dan was still on the phone when she walked in, and laughing. This was unusual enough to make her stop and stare. He saw this and brought himself under control.

"Here's your mom." He handed Marlene the phone. "It's Lucy." He vanished.

"I didn't know you were such a comedian," Marlene said.

"We were doing accents of weird people we know in Cambridge," said her daughter.

"For this you called in the middle of the night? Is anything wrong?"

"No, everything's dandy. We sold all the pups, and I got the Toyota running. Why I called is, I want to go on a road trip with the boys."

"To where?"

"Oh, I don't know, just around. I thought I'd take them on the car ferry to Bridgeport and see Tran and then maybe up to Boston, take them to the Children's Museum and Science Museum. I have a couple of things to do there anyway."

"How long would you be gone?"

"Oh, three, four days. They're antsy and it would do them good."

"And you love to drive."

"That, too. The car runs great. With the new tires it came in under a grand. I charged it to the farm."

"No problem. But, Lucy? When you get to driving, make sure your wheels don't turn southward. I don't want you and the boys down here. The situation is still too fluid. Did Dan tell you what went down just now?"

"Yeah. It sounds like something out of *Deliverance*. Do you think they'll try again?"

"Not in the same way. They're stupid, but not *that* stupid. You know your father is going to be playing Mighty Mouse in this cartoon?"

"Yeah, he told me. Are you going to come back when he gets there?"

"I don't know," said Marlene a little sharply. "It depends on the situation. Look, call me from Tran's or Boston or if you have any problems. Keep in touch. Meanwhile I have to go. I have to drive this guy back to his place."

"Okay, take care, Mom, and could you put Dan back on the phone?"

"Planning the wedding? I'd like to be involved."

"Mo-m."

"Okay, okay, here he is."

He had been hovering, and when Marlene handed him the cordless, he took it back to his bedroom. No, I will not hang around and listen in, she thought virtuously, and went off to pour the coffee.

"So," Dan said, "you checked in. Everything is approved?"

"Oh, yeah. I get a pretty loose rein. From her. My dad worries a lot more."

"Strange. It's funny. Mom always drummed it into us to let them know our plans, like if we weren't coming home for supper, or staying over. The other day, I drove out to Huntington to see a guy I went to school with and they asked me to stay for dinner and I said sure, let me call and tell them I won't be home. I had the phone in my hand, dialing."

Lucy had nothing to say to this that she thought would be tolerated by the other, so she stayed mum. He went on, "Could I ask you something dumb?"

"Sure. I'm an expert on dumb."

"Do you, um, believe in ghosts?"

"No."

"No? Why not? You believe in all that other supernatural cr—stuff."

"Because the spirits of the dead leave this world and other stuff happens to them. Also, it's insulting for you to imagine that, because I'm religious, I'm generally credulous or superstitious. It's like thinking that rocket scientists ought to believe in flying saucers."

"I didn't mean that," he said quickly, with genuine contrition. "Sorry, really I didn't mean . . . it's just . . . I mean weird stuff has been happening. Like calling home. I have this feeling that I'll call and Mom will pick up. It sends chills down my spine. But, okay, night before last, it's late, I'm reading in bed, totally absorbed, and all of a sudden I felt this *weird* feeling, like being light-headed, like when you stand up too fast? And I just knew that Lizzie was in the room with me. She used to like to be with me while I worked, or read. She had some games she liked to play on my machine. And I knew that if I had turned around, she'd be there in her quilted bathrobe, sitting in my chair. I mean the sweat was popping out on my face. And just then the hard drive kicked in, and my heart practically stopped, it was like she was there playing a game. I was just getting ready to turn and look when it went away. I mean the feeling. God, I can't believe I'm telling this to anyone! Did you ever, ah, have one like that?"

"Oh, sure, all the time. That's not ghosts, though. It's what we call the communion of saints. It's part of the Apostles' Creed as a matter of fact. I used to have long conversations with St. Teresa of Avila."

"You're kidding."

"Uh-uh, no lie. Starting from when I was about eight. For a while, I thought everyone could. I could see her and hear her and smell her, even."

"What did she smell like?"

"Onions. And roses."

"You spoke to her in English?"

"Of course not. In sixteenth-century Castilian Spanish, lisping all over the place."

"Oh, right, you can do that whole language bit. So, what are you telling me. Lizzie is some kind of saint?"

"Not at all. We just think that there remains a connection open between people who have died and people who're still alive, and there's an unseen world that can touch us and that's just as real as the one we can see. It's pretty complex and we're not encouraged to speculate about it in detail, or to try to penetrate the barrier. But it happens, there's contact."

"You don't think it's simpler to call that kind of stuff hallucinations?"

"Yes, if your purpose is to defend simplistic materialism. But that's a choice; it can't be proven scientifically one way or the other."

"But Occam's razor—"

"Yes, yes," she said impatiently, "Occam's razor, don't multiply entities beyond necessity, but that leaves open the question of what's necessary. William of Occam was a medieval churchman. He probably thought belief in the real presence was necessary, and certainly that God was. The bottom line here is that you've had an experience. You can call it an hallucination, which means that you consider that your brain is a machine with a screw loose, and that your sister is essentially erased from being, or you can believe that she still has her being in a state unimaginably different, but still real, and that your experience was also real, as real as the bed you're lying on."

"How do you know I'm lying on a bed?" he asked.

"Projection. I'm lying on a bed, so . . ."

"Gee, we're in bed together already, and we've barely met."

To his relief, after a brief pause, she laughed. "Yes, I'm such a slut, but I can't seem to help it. Men with their insatiable demands are ever at my heels."

He laughed, too, and after a moment said, "So, will I ever see you again?"

"In real life? Yeah, we both go to school in Boston. We could probably arrange it."

"I mean before that."

"I'm working on it," she said.

10

"MR. KARP? I'M WADE HENDRICKS," SAID THE MAN IN THE AIRPORT lounge. "From the governor's office?" Karp shook the proffered hand. "I'll be flying down to Charleston with you. We figured I could brief you on the way."

Hendricks was almost as tall as Karp, but rangier, and although he wore a blue suit, a certain stiffness about his bearing suggested to Karp that he had spent a lot of time in a uniform. Hovering behind him was another man who was actually in uniform, the green of the West Virginia State Police. "Trooper Blake will take your bag," said Hendricks, and Trooper Blake did. They all walked out of the gate onto the blazing tarmac and up a boarding ladder into a white twin-engined propeller aircraft. The plane held eight large, comfortable first-class-style seats, with the center four set opposite each other, so that the people sitting in them could converse face-to-face. Hendricks directed Karp to one of these and went forward through a curtain. Trooper Blake entered and sat in the rear. A uniformed woman came out from behind the curtain, closed the exit door, and popped behind the curtain again. The engines started with a cough and a whine. Hendricks reappeared, smiled at Karp, and buckled himself into the seat facing Karp. The plane taxied onto the runway.

"Is there a movie?" asked Karp.

"No, sorry," said Hendricks. "I got a copy of *Wonderful West Virginia Magazine* you could read, though."

"Maybe later. How long is the flight?"

"Well, it's four hundred and twenty-five miles as the crow flies, and that's usually about an hour and a half, but we've modified our flight plan to swing southwest, so you can see Robbens County from the air, low and slow."

"Will I be looking for murder clues?"

Hendricks looked startled for a moment and then registered that Karp had made a light remark. A slow grin spread across his face. "No, except maybe indirectly. The governor thought you might like to see what a strip mine looks like from the air, and also get an idea of the geography of the place. You being from away. You don't mind?"

"Oh, not at all. This is pretty exciting for me anyway. I don't get to fly much in private planes."

"No? Heck, most of the folks I see getting in the private jets and all look like lawyers."

"You might be right," Karp said. "I guess I'm not that kind of lawyer."

The engines roared, the plane sped down the runway and lifted into the air. Hendricks expounded on the virtues of the King Air 350, its comfort, its safety, its economy, its usefulness to the governor of a medium-sized state. Karp was not much interested in this palaver, but found the man worth study. Not the kind of face you saw much of in New York, but oddly familiar nonetheless. Karp recalled faces like that from the Saturday-matinee movies of his childhood—ten cartoons and two westerns—the faces on the people who hung around with Randolph Scott and Hoot Gibson, lean cowboys, the classic American stock, as alien as Martians to the little Italians and Jews yelling on the plush seats. He had the pale eyes, the small, straight nose, the lipless mouth, the strawlike hair. Karp saw him in a white hat. And a six-gun.

In fact, as he saw when Hendricks released his seat belt and stretched, there *was* a six-gun.

"You're a cop?" Karp asked, indicating the weapon.

Hendricks glanced down at his waist, as if he had forgotten it was there.

"Yeah, captain, state police. I should have said. Fact is, I'll be going down to Robbens with you."

"If I get the job."

"As far as I know, that's a formality, unless you call the governor a son of a bitch and piss on the carpets."

"I'll try to remember that. How did you get picked for this?"

"Just lucky, I guess," Hendricks said with a soft grin. "I was in charge of the security detail during the campaign, and we found we got along, and when he won it, well, he told me to stay on. Besides security, he's asked me to do a couple of chores for him the past year or so in the criminal justice line, and when this came up, he said I was it." Hendricks paused. "I'm from there originally. He thought it could help."

"You're from Robbens County?"

"Yes, sir. Coal-patch kid. When I was ten, my daddy sat me on his knee and made me swear on the Bible I'd never go down in the mines."

"And you kept your word."

"I did, too. When I was seventeen, I joined the Marine Corps. I did a hitch in the embassy guards and then my next hitch I got into the military police. Daddy was sick by then with the black lung, so I got out of the service and joined the staties, so's I could watch over him. After he passed, I stayed on. I liked the work, although, between you and me, I don't much care for the political end of it, which you have to if you're rising up. I'd rather just cop."

"A man after my own heart," said Karp. "But there's politics involved in this thing, isn't there? Or your governor wouldn't have reached out to a complete stranger."

Hendricks dropped his eyes, a shadow of unease crossing his face. "Well, I guess you'll have to discuss that with Governor Orne." With that, he reached under his seat and pulled out a fat, blue plastic portfolio with the state seal printed on it in gold. Handing it across to Karp, he said, "Here's all the information we have on the Heeney murder to date, plus we got some background material in there about Robbens you might be interested in. Why don't you read through it, and after you're done we'll talk." He stood up and dropped a large folding table down in front of Karp, then nodded and went to the rear of the plane, where he talked quietly to Trooper Blake while Karp examined the contents of the portfolio.

This comprised two three-inch loose-leaf binders, one containing all the documents relevant to the state's case against Moses Welch, and the other labeled "Robbens County: Historical Analysis and Situation Report." This latter had a governor's office seal on the cover, but no attribution or author. The Heeney case binder, neatly tabbed, began with a letter from the state's attorney, Hawes, to the attorney general, summarizing his case. Karp was particularly interested in the bloody sneaker, the finding of which he already knew about from Marlene. The lab had made a good DNA match on it and found that the stain on its sole was Rose Heeney's blood. Hawes had tried to put the best face on this discovery by postulating that the sneakers had actually been worn by the defendant while committing the crime. The boots must have been in the Heeneys' bedroom during the time of the murders, been splattered there, and stolen by the defendant. Karp snorted and paged through the data, trying to find any indication that Hawes had determined, whether through a search for receipts or checking records, whether anyone in the family had purchased such boots, or even some indication of what all the Heeneys' shoe sizes were. Nothing; nor had Hawes seemingly made any effort to determine the provenance of those boots, the only piece of evidence he had linking his suspect to the crime. Karp couldn't wait to meet Mr. Hawes.

After making some notes on the blank sheets thoughtfully provided at the back of the binder, he turned to the Robbens County report. He had expected the usual dry bureaucratic prose. Instead he found a fluidly written and absorbing history of what seemed to be a remarkable, if grim, piece of the nation. The county had been settled in the late eighteenth century, by Scotch-Irish farmers on the run from poverty or worse. They were feisty, independent, clannish people, the original pioneer stock that produced people like Daniel Boone and Andrew Jackson.

Those of them who might have been a little *too* feisty and clannish to invent great nations settled in the hills and hollows of the Appalachians and stuck. There they cut down the ancient forests of hickory, oak, and chestnut and built little farms and sawmills and fought the Cherokees and, on occasion, the agents of the United States, who tried to collect taxes on the corn liquor that was their principal source of income. The fields were small, rocky, and steep—not a prosperous sort of farmland, but at least they did not have to chop wood to keep warm. Great boulders of coal stood out from the hillsides, and many people started to mine it in a small way, for local use. In 1787, a vein of hematite was found near Ponowon in the western part of the county, and they started a furnace at Furnace Cove, nearby. They began making nails and ploughs, knives and fowling pieces. Around this nascent industry, small towns sprang up. Donald McCullen deeded land to the settlement that bore his name in 1793, and a few years afterward it became the county seat of Robbens County, that named for an otherwise forgotten legislator. For the next fifty years, the nation flowed around them westward, leaving the people to their strictly local concerns. Though poor, the people were nearly self-sufficient. Bartering was the rule in that economy. What little cash arrived in the place came from the stills. Corn liquor was the only product worth carrying over the rough trails that connected Robbens to the country of which it was nominally a part.

Among the people who arrived in the county during this period were Josiah Cade (b. 1810) and Ephraim Jonson (b. 1815). Cade settled on Burnt Peak, Jonson on Belo Knob to the east. Both married locally and raised families and attracted kin from other states and the old country. Cade had five sons and two daughters, and Jonson had four sons and one daughter. Somewhere around 1856, the two men fell into a dispute about a boundary between two adjoining fields. They went to law, and Jonson won his case. Cade was ordered to move his boundary markers. This he refused to do and ordered his sons Lemuel and Ransome to drive a herd of cattle to pasture on the disputed land. When this action was challenged by James and Peter Jonson, Ephraim's eldest sons, shooting broke out. In the affray, Peter Jonson was badly wounded, and Lem Cade was killed.

This was the origin of the Cade-Jonson feud, or war, as the report called it. In the next four years, two Cades and four Jonsons were shot from ambush. Barns were burned. Cattle were poisoned. Dogs were hung from trees. Shortly thereafter, actual war came to the region, when Virginia seceded from the Union and West Virginia seceded from its mother state. Although there were no formal contests of uniformed troops in Robbens during the Civil War, nearly the entire able-bodied male population of the town engaged in hostilities at some level. The report made it clear that the War Between the States was considered an excuse to escalate the War Between the Cades and the Jonsons. The surviving Jonson boys went to Harpers Ferry to enlist with the Union. Immediately thereafter, the surviving Cade boys trooped to Knoxville to sign up with the rebels. In the county, guerrilla warfare was continual for the duration of the conflict. Both sides easily obtained arms from the belligerents. By war's end only one son survived in each family—Moses Jonson and Ransome Cade.

Appomattox did not bring an end to the sniping and ambushes. Of the ten children, male and female, of Moses and Ransome, only two escaped murder long enough to survive into the twentieth century. Of the two, the report took particular notice of Ransome Cade (1864–1937), who brought a new level of ferocity and cunning to the feud. Devil Rance, as he was known, moved his clan away from its agricultural roots, replacing this as a source of income with a variety of criminal enterprises. He ran moonshine; he stole horses and rustled cattle; he could break a limb or a head for cash up front. He also ran a primitive protection racket among the local illicit distilleries. Most significantly, he consolidated the tribal property into a single hollow around Canker Run on Burnt Peak. This settlement was approachable only by a narrow, winding road and was surrounded on three sides by nearly impenetrable growth. From this fortress, Devil Rance fell like a robber baron upon his enemies and retreated with impunity. He held to the theory that the secession of West Virginia had been an illegal act, and that the state had no authority over him or his. Moreover, neither had the United States, since Virginia had seceded from the Union and the part of it that comprised West Virginia had never been legally reincorporated. It was not a theory that Karp would have liked arguing before a court, but Devil Rance was not all that interested in courts anyway. Courts had failed his tribe once; he was not inclined to give them another chance.

Into this parochial violence now barged the Gilded Age in the person of Thomas G. (Big Tom) Killebrew. Killebrew was a McCullensburg man whose family had been involved in small-scale coal mining for decades, all for the local market. But Killebrew was a traveling man and visionary. He had been to Knoxville on horseback and even to Pittsburgh. He had ridden on a railroad train and seen streets lit with gas. Quietly at first, and then brazenly, Killebrew began to buy up all the coal rights in Robbens County. Some people refused to sell, but Big Tom was not daunted. He soon concluded that the muscle that kept the moonshiners in line might be put to other uses. An agreement was reached with Devil Rance. Soon, after a brief terror, Killebrew had all the coal leases, save one. In gratitude, he gave his partner his very own coal patch, right up there near the Cade home place on Burnt Peak.

With the leases in hand, Big Tom ventured out to Pittsburgh again and talked with Mellons, and to New York to converse with Goulds. The result was the construction of the Huntington & Knoxville Railroad, which reached McCullensburg in the fall of 1889. Killebrew was, of course, a partner in the railroad, for the construction of which large numbers of Italian and Slovak immigrants were recruited. As soon as the railroad was finished, he began his mining operation, fittingly called the Majestic Coal Company.

Karp was distracted at the next chapter, an account of the worst labor violence in U.S. history, by a change in the motion of the plane. It was banking counterclockwise and seemed to be descending.

Hendricks was in the aisle, leaning over him. "How's that report?"

"It's fascinating. It reads like fiction. Is it on the level?"

"Like what?"

"Oh, here where it says fourteen revenue agents have gone missing in the county since 1900. Fourteen?"

"That's only the federals. We lost some state boys, too, over the years. They don't much like lawmen poking into them hollers up there. Plus, you got to consider that the county is stuck full of mines like a Swiss cheese, and you got boys up there with unlimited access to blasting compound. Stick a couple of bodies down a shaft and dump sixty tons of rock on top of 'em. What're you gonna do? Start digging with a pick and shovel? We know they run meth, they run pot, some corn liquor, too, but not as much as they used to. It's a bad situation. If you want to know the truth, the law wrote off Robbens County a while back."

"What changed your minds?"

"Oh, you know, new governor, new broom. You need to put your seat belt on now." Hendricks sat in the seat opposite and affixed his own. Karp looked out the window. They were flying at what he estimated to be fifteen hundred feet, over ground that resembled green corrugated cardboard.

"Are we landing?"

"No, but we'll be heading over Robbens any minute now. At this altitude we sometimes have to use evasive maneuvers."

"Evasive from what?"

"Ground fire," replied Hendricks blandly. "We have state markings. A lot of folks down there don't like official kinds of airplanes flying over them." He looked at Karp innocently. "Unless it makes you nervous. I could tell the pilot to get upstairs again."

"Not at all. I think everyone should be subjected to antiaircraft fire at least once."

Hendricks nodded, his face neutral. He pointed out the window. "Okay, you can see mining from here. We're still over Mingo. That's Mateawan down there. You heard of that, haven't you?"

"Yes. That's a coal mine?" It was a smudge of black and ocher the size of a town, intermittently veiled by greasy smoke, threaded by railways.

"Yeah, a Peabody operation, I think. In a bit, we should be coming up on . . . yeah, look there, see that big flat area?"

Karp did. It was a huge, perfectly flat oval, looking unlikely amid the rippled hills, as if God had dropped a soccer field for giants on top of the mountains.

"What is it?"

"It used to be a mountain called Thatcher. They chopped it flat and dumped the spoil in the hollers all around it, and smoothed it out and planted it with grass."

"They can do that?"

"Oh, that's a prize exhibit of reclamation. They fixed that one. Just wait, we're coming up on something real interesting."

Karp thought the interesting thing might be a controlled flight into terrain. A mountain was looming in front of them, whose top looked to be higher than the altitude of the plane. He stared at the approaching green wall; out of the corner of his eye he saw that Hendricks was watching him. A little mountain-state aviation initiation, then, he thought, and made himself yawn. When he could count individual trees on the mountainside and distinguish the very one upon which the King Air was about to impale itself, the aircraft twitched its wing up and zoomed through a break in the mountain wall. Karp thought he could see squirrels running for cover as the towering forest flew past.

"This is Conway Gap, and that's Majestic Number One," said Hendricks.

It looked like something had taken a huge bite out of the rear half of the mountain, leaving an orange and black earth pit that looked large enough to swallow New York City. Orange creeks ran off the sore and disappeared into the surrounding timberland.

"That's what they look like when you don't clean 'em up, and Majestic don't."

"Don't they have to?"

"Oh, it's the law all right, but try and make them. There's court cases been going on for ten years on this pit alone. See, what they do is dump the spoil from the hole down into the hollers. They bury everything, homes, farms, graveyards, whole little towns. Of course, the people've moved out before then. The mining ruins the water first, tears up the water tables and kills the creeks. And that's what you got left. You all have your coal, though. This here's downtown McCullensburg."

The plane dropped even lower and sped over a group of low buildings and a green square with a golden-domed courthouse in it.

"Not much to it at this speed," said Hendricks. "On the other hand, there ain't much to it on the ground neither." The plane circled the town twice, while the trooper pointed out the hills and highways, scars of coal patches, and the coffee stream of the Guyandotte River.

"We're passing over the murder house there."

Karp pressed his face against the glass and looked down with interest. A yard, a roof, a red truck in the driveway. Marlene's maybe. Then it was gone.

"One more beauty spot and then we'll put the pedal down and get us home," said Hendricks. The plane rose, rising with the curve of the mountain he had identified as Hampden. The top of the mountain was gone, leaving a great mustard-and-black scab upon which yellow trucks and bulldozers rolled. It looked like a sandbox occupied by a child unusually well supplied with Tonka toys. In the center was what appeared to be a white, rectangular, five-story office building.

"Majestic Number Two. There's the dragline," said Hendricks, answering Karp's unspoken question about what a five-story office building was doing in the middle of a mine. "They use a Bucyrus 2570, maybe the largest shovel in the world, although I hear they got one even bigger out in Wyoming."

"That thing *moves*?"

"Oh, yeah. It never stops, day and night. Every scoop is near four hundred tons. Those trucks down there? Cat 797s. Over six hundred tons fully loaded."

"I'm impressed," said Karp. "Every little boy's dream."

"Uh-huh. The reason I'm showing you this is to give you some idea. You want to bury a body around here, you don't have to go out at night with a spade and a lantern."

A few minutes later the plane heaved and rolled onto its side, climbing. Karp's belly lurched and he grabbed the seat arms.

"What was that?"

"Oh, Rudy probably saw a flash. He's real nervous when he flies over weed."

"Marijuana?"

"Yeah. It's getting as big as coal around here. We go down and chop it back some from time to time, but there're lots of hollers and not enough of us."

The plane climbed rapidly. Hendricks loosened his seat belt. He grinned. "Wild and wonderful. We'll be down in twenty, twenty-five minutes."

As they were. The trip to the capitol was swift, in a convoy of two state police vehicles. Karp and Hendricks rode in the back of one of them, with the captain pointing out the features of what looked to Karp like a nice little city on the banks of a not-too-clean river. The capitol itself was the usual massive gray-stone, gilded-domed structure. The governor was meeting them in his office there, instead of the one at the governor's mansion, in the interests of privacy, Hendricks explained.

"In case I piss on the rug."

"We're careful folks hereabouts."

"I might, though. I never met a governor before. The excitement . . ."

Hendricks laughed and opened a walnut-paneled door.

They were ushered in immediately. The office was modern and not impressively large, much like its occupant. Roy Orne was a small man with excellent barbering and a peppy manner. A young woman, trim in a fawn suit, her blond hair in a neat bun, was introduced as "my aide" Cheryl Oggert. Shakes all around, seats, offer of coffee, soft drinks, declined, the usual banter. Governor Orne asked how was the flight; Karp commented on the abundance of mountains. Laughs.

Time to turn serious: Orne asked if Karp had read the binders. What did he think?

"I think you got the wrong man. I think the people down there botched the investigation."

"Incompetence, do you think, or malevolence?" asked the governor.

"Hard to tell. Could be either. Based on the other binder, I would tend to bet on the latter. Otherwise it was a *really* dumb investigation. In any case their suspect is a joke."

"What does your wife think?"

Karp was taken aback. The governor had certainly done his homework. "Well, clearly, she believes her client is innocent," Karp said carefully. "As to malevolence, there seems to be plenty to spare. An attempt was made on her life the other day."

The governor looked grave, and a glance flicked between him and Hendricks. "Well. That's awful. Was she hurt?"

"No. Marlene is hard to hurt. Experts have tried. Of course, she'll be out of there once I get there, provided you want me. Speaking of which, why do you?"

"How's that?"

"Why do you want a prosecutor from out of state? It seems a bit extreme. I'm sure you've got plenty of fine lawyers in West Virginia."

"Well, yes, we do," said Orne. "But I'm kind of busy just now." The others chuckled, Karp allowed a smile. Orne continued, "Here's the thing, Mr. Karp. I've heard a lot about you from Saul. I don't think there's a prosecutor in the state that has your experience, hell, *half* your experience. State's attorney tends to be a young fellow's profession. We've got a man up in Wheeling's been there twelve years, and I doubt he sees three murder trials a year, and those're bar fights and domestics. We don't have any people skilled in unraveling a conspiracy."

"You think it's a conspiracy?"

"Well, let's see: a union reformer gets killed along with half his family in the most corrupt, antiunion county in the state. What're the chances it was a wandering drifter, like in that book, *In Cold Blood?* I'd say slim to none. Okay, that's one reason. Another is, if I assign a local, people are going to look at his political connections, either to me, or to my many fine enemies, or to Big Coal, or whatever. You on the other hand don't know one end of West Virginia from the other. That's an advantage. Also, Saul assures me that you don't play political games."

"Yes. People have said I have the political skills of a three-year-old."

The governor laughed. "That's good. We want the truth here, and let the bricks fly."

"Sounds good," said Karp. "Another reason might be that, if I crash and burn, I'm a stranger, and it doesn't cost you anything to dump me."

A tiny silence here. Then the governor chuckled. "Well, yeah, I guess that passed through my mind. And as long as we're being brutally frank, I'm also doing it to keep control of this mess, assuming that it might very well lead to some pretty powerful political factors in the state. I don't want the feds to have an excuse to come in here and piss all over another Democratic governor. This is a decent state, with solid liberal instincts, and it's tied to a nasty, regressive bunch of industries—coal, chemicals, power plants. It makes for a funny kind of politics, but just about everyone's now agreed that the old kind of Robbens County behavior just don't cut it anymore, and I mean to clean it up, and I need a pro to do it. Well, Mr. Karp, will you?"

"Sure," said Karp, surprising himself with the ease with which he committed himself. "Resources . . . ?"

"Whatever you need. If you want to hire people, there's money for that. Captain Hendricks will be part of your team, in charge of any detective and forensic work. You'll have priority at the state lab, of course, and a budget that should be adequate. Cheryl here will be your contact with my office and will go down there with you to handle the on-scene public relations. I assume you'll appreciate the help in that area."

"Saul must have ratted about my winning ways with the press."

"Well, no offense, but I think we're going to get a lot of publicity on this case, and I think the viewers would rather see her face on the screen than yours. When can you start?"

"How about the beginning of next week?"

"That's fine," said Orne. "Wade and Cheryl will form up an advance team and have everything ready for you when you get down there."

Orne rose, extended his hand. "Welcome aboard, Mr. Karp. We expect great things from you."

Karp looked into the governor's dark eyes; sincerity flooded from them, which made him feel good for a moment, until he reflected that Orne was a politician and that sincerity was easy to fake.

Lucy drove the refurbished Land Cruiser off the car ferry and onto the streets of Bridgeport, Connecticut, feeling quite uncharacteristically pleased with herself. She had fixed the car, obtained the plates, finished her various chores, whipped her brothers into finishing theirs, and escaped without either mechanical breakdown or dog-based emergency intervening. She had made one final executive-level decision just before leaving, and she was somewhat concerned that she had not called her mother to clear it, but Billy had agreed and she felt confident that she had done the right thing.

Zak the navigator, a street map unfolded across his lap, said, "Right in three blocks."

From the backseat came the tweedle of a Game Boy. Giancarlo was spread out with pillows like a pasha on a divan, his preferred mode of automobile travel. One of the nice things about traveling with the boys was that there was never any quarrel about who would get the shotgun seat. Giancarlo did not covet it, nor would Zak ride anywhere else.

The executive decision was about the dog Jeb. Jeb was a bonehead and varminty as all hell, which meant that he was suspicious of everything that moved, besides which, he was an escape artist of some talent. Billy had tried to break him of the habit of lunging at every stranger, with some success, but clearly Jeb would never make a personal guard dog good enough to sell as such under the Wingfield Farm label. The decision was to turn him into a yard dog. He would spend his professional career pacing behind a high fence hoping that some really stupid person would try to climb over it at night. Not a trivial decision either, because it meant that he would lose over half his value.

Lucy steered onto Route 25 and took it a few miles north to the Reservoir Road exit. A few more turns found them in a leafy neighborhood of middle-class homes set back from the street behind tree-shaded lawns. She spotted the right number and pulled into a long driveway.

"Don't get out," she said.

"Why not?" asked Zak, his hand on the door handle.

"It's good manners to wait," she said, a fib. In fact, she knew, weapons were probably pointing at them right now. She waited. Within three minutes, she heard a door open, steps on the brick walk; a handsome Vietnamese man of saturnine mien appeared at the driver's side window.

"Good morning, Freddy," she said in Vietnamese.

Freddy Phat smiled politely. He was always polite, but never friendly. Lucy imagined it was because he resented his employer's relationship with her as something that made that employer vulnerable. Which it did. "He's engaged, just now. Come into the house. Mrs. Diem will give you tea."

That person, gray-haired and severe, all in black, did so, at a wrought-iron table under an umbrella on the brick terrace behind the house. With the tea were croissants and sliced mangoes arranged in elegant spirals. The boys were not interested in the tea, but remained subdued under their sister's eye, and under the spell of the mysterious Tran, whom they had not seen since their infancy, but who was a legend in the family circle. They knew that he was a gangster, and since they had never met an actual gangster (aside from Mom), they were keen with anticipation. Giancarlo hoped to see a suitcase full of $100 bills. Zak wished to see a machine-gun in full blast. Both longed, without much realistic expectation, to watch a vehicle explode.

As if to pique them, a young Vietnamese man dressed entirely in black emerged onto the patio from the house, nodded to them, and walked past through the gate that led to the driveway. When he raised his arm to lift the latch, Zak said, "Wow, he's got an Uzi under his coat."

"Don't stare," said Lucy. "It could be a Skorpion. They use those more."

She watched the man depart. In her experience, Tran employed two sorts of people: either quiet, sad, hard men in their forties and fifties, veterans of the American war, old comrades and alumni of the regime's reeducation camps, like Tran himself; or people like the man in black, younger brothers and cousins of the former type, whose childhood the war had consumed, gangsters from the cradle.

"What should we do when he comes?" Giancarlo asked his sister in a subdued voice. "Do we have to bow or something?"

"A bow is always appropriate when meeting an Asian gentleman," said Lucy. "He doesn't speak much English. If you want to know something, ask me and I'll translate."

The boys had finished the last of the food and were, despite themselves, growing restless, when Tran stepped out on the terrace. He was wearing a white short-sleeved shirt and dark slacks, with woven leather sandals on his feet. Lucy immediately arose and embraced him, receiving the canonical three kisses on her cheeks.

"My dear, I am so happy to see you," he said, holding her at arm's length and studying her. "You have become a young woman overnight. As I have become an old man." This in French, in a peculiar colonial accent spiced with antique Parisian slang. He had been a student there and a Left Bank busboy, before he returned to the long war.

"You never age, Uncle," she replied, but she was surprised to observe many signs that he had. She had never thought much about it before, but she imagined that he must now be in his midsixties, or perhaps even older. Just slightly taller than she, he was still erect and sinewy, but his eyes had sunk deeper into their sockets and the skin was pulling away from the bones of his face. Their eyes met, and he smiled slightly, turning away. She felt a blush; he always knew what she was thinking.

The boys had risen. Tran said in slow English, "I hope you're not in danger, Lucy. You travel with such tough bodyguards."

She said, in the same language, "My brothers, Giancarlo and Zak. Boys, our uncle Tran."

At this Zak bobbed his head uncomfortably, but Giancarlo delivered a bow that would not have insulted the emperor of China. No one laughed. Tran nodded gravely and showed them around the garden, which was formal in the French manner: paths of white gravel between geometrically clipped hedges, neat flower beds, miniature fruit trees, and exotic tropical flowers in large wooden or ceramic pots. A small greenhouse held orchids, hibiscus, and cyclamen. A large fishpond, fed by a waterfall, contained huge carp, each of whom had a name. Tran showed them how to feed them by hand. Giancarlo found a paper bag and made an origami boat. Zak built a raft from twigs. They amused themselves and waited patiently for the gangster stuff to begin. Lucy and Tran sat on a stone bench in the russet shade of a Japanese maple.

"They seem to be fine boys. Exactly alike to look at, but very different as people."

"Yes. Totally different. It's a wonder to science."

"Remarkable! And you? Your studies progress well?"

"I'm not flunking out, another wonder. I spend most of my time on the languages and being a lab rat. Studying holds little interest, I'm afraid. It seems like a delay before I do what I'm meant to. The other students seem like children; that, or worried old people in young bodies. Of course, I don't expect to fit in anywhere."

"Oh, you poor child. Pardon me while I weep bitter tears."

"Well, it's true."

"Yes," he said after a pause, "but you should be used to your fate by now. Has anything vocational presented itself?"

"Rather an embarrassment of riches, Uncle. Offers from banks, from the UN. Also there are people who come to watch my demonstrations who are definitely not from the scientific community."

"Well, yes. You would be God's gift to any intelligence service. Are you interested in that sort of work?"

"Not at all, or rather not for a government. I might want to do something for the Church, though."

"You are still religious, I take it."

"Yes. Did you think it would fade?"

He looked at her consideringly. "Perhaps not. And what of love? Do you lie on riverbanks under blossoming trees with beautiful young men?"

"Oh, yes. I have a little machine, like in the butcher's. There are so many they have to take numbers."

"I am glad to hear of it. It should serve to distract you from an excess of piety."

"I am joking, Uncle, as you must know."

"Why must I? You seem fascinating to me, and delicious: slim, elegant, and graceful, when you are not distracted by self-consciousness. Very like our women, I think. Most Western women seem like cows to me. In fact, were we in a civilized land, like France or Vietnam, and were I only a little younger, I would certainly try to seduce you myself. I see I have succeeded in shocking you. This will only serve to confirm my reputation as an evil man."

Lucy was flustered, rather than shocked, since it had never occurred to her that *anyone* could find her delicious. Broaching the subject, however, brought thoughts of Dan Heeney to her mind, which had brought the color to her cheeks. Did Dan find her delicious? He had certainly not made a pass at her, although since no one had ever done so, perhaps she had missed it. It was just a phrase, after all. There may have been a whole series of obvious openings that had slipped by. The movies made it seem simple, but the movies also made shooting people seem simple, and from what she had observed of her mother's life, it was not at all thus. Maybe they lied about sex, too. She had an impulse to tell Tran all about Dan Heeney, but suppressed it. Why? She couldn't have said.

"Speaking of which," she said, to change the subject, "how is the gangster business?"

"Flourishing, although the Indians at Foxwood are cutting into the gambling somewhat. I have some more restaurants, and a restaurant supply business, and some other businesses. I have dispensed with the girls."

"Why?"

"It became annoying. One finds an unpleasant type of person in that business. I still extend protection to some ladies of a superior class, but no more happy-beer places. Then there are the loans, and protection for the Vietnamese community. If they did not pay me, they would have to pay someone else, who would undoubtedly be greedier than I am." He sighed. "I'll tell you what it is, my dear. I am used up and cranky *[grillé et grogné]*. I was not meant for this life, and the life I was meant for no longer exists. I don't even wear my own name anymore. I smoke more pipes than is good for me. My associates are perhaps getting nervous. From time to time, I must eliminate an overly ambitious young man, and what for? Even Freddy sometimes looks at me in a way he should not. I would despair to have to eliminate Freddy. Sometimes I think, 'Oh, Tran, drive to the airport, board a plane for Vietnam, and sit at a café in Saigon, smelling the air and drinking little cups of coffee until someone finds you and puts you out of your misery.'" A tiny pause. "Tell me, how is your mother?"

She was bored and irritated at the same time. She had not had a decent cup of coffee in ten days, since McCullensburg appeared to be in the vast Bad Coffee Zone of the United States, and she was drinking a little more wine than was good for her. Given the situation, she really had nothing to do. Her husband would soon come, and she suspected that one of his first acts would be to spring Mose Welch, which made her continued presence here otiose. And it was hot. And there were gnats.

Cursing without energy, she went into the house, took her second shower of the day, dressed carefully, and drove to town. Her only remaining useful activity was visiting her client once each day, to bring him a pint of chocolate ice cream and play a game of Chinese checkers with him. She had purchased the Chinese checkers herself in the Bi-Lo and taught him the game, and she did not let him win. Mose was getting better at it, though, either that, thought Marlene, or I am losing my marbles, so to speak. Or maybe playing Chinese checkers with a moron in a county jail is about my speed.

They had spectators, too. The cops came by to kibitz, and Sheriff Swett often found time in his busy schedule to stop by for a chat, as now.

"How're you doin', Mose?" called the sheriff heartily. "That pretty good ice cream?"

"It's pretty good ice cream, Sheriff," said Mose happily. "It's chocolate."

"Well, I can see that, Mose. You got it up to your eyes. I would say you look half like a nigger, but Ms. Ciampi here would report me for racial insensitivity."

"I would not, Sheriff," said Marlene. "I would give you a pass on that. I would report you for incompetence and corruption, maybe."

The sheriff laughed. "Well, then it's a good thing for me you'll be leaving soon."

"Yes, it is. Did you check out that pistol I took off Bo Cade?"

"Yes, I did. But I'm so incompetent, you probably don't even want to know what the state lab found out. I probably can't even read the report with my tiny little brain."

She moved a marble and gave him a considering look. "I take it back, then. You're not incompetent. You're competently corrupt. What did it say?"

"Wasn't the .38 that killed Lizzie Heeney, is what."

Marlene was somewhat let down by this news, but took care to disguise it. "Well, then, I'm sure you'll redouble your search for the actual murder weapon."

"Oh, hell, you know he could've pitched it anywhere in the county, down some mine probably. This is an easy part of the country to lose things in. Is that what you done, Mose? Pitched it down a mine?"

"Uh-huh," said Mose cheerfully, nodding his head and studying the board like Boris Spassky contemplating a tricky endgame.

"See?" said the sheriff.

"What can I say, Sheriff? It's just like *Perry Mason.* You've totally outsmarted my client." She moved another marble, hardly looking at the board. "Just between us, now, who do you think really killed the Heeneys? I kind of like Earl and Bo Cade for it, although it's hard to believe that they're organized enough to actually pull it off. There must have been someone else involved."

"I wouldn't know about that." Sheriff Swett grinned around his big teeth and rubbed his right eye with the heel of his hand. "And it ain't my job to speculate. I will tell you one thing, though."

"What's that?"

"I think your client just outsmarted you." He gestured to the board, where Mose was just placing a blue marble. He looked up, his mouth an O, and bounced on his bunk like a four-year-old. "I win! I win!" he crowed.

The sheriff and the cops and the other inmates roared. After a while, Marlene did, too.

"It must be something in your water," she said, and thought, grinning up at Swett, you just gave me an idea, Sheriff.

11

"WHY DON'T WE," MARLENE SAID, "FIND THAT GUN?"

"What gun is that?" asked Poole without much interest. They were dining at Rosie's in the courthouse square, McCullensburg. Rosie's served what Marlene always thought of as mom food, although Marlene's actual mom had not served the sort of food Rosie served, or rather Gus served, Gus being the current Rosie. Gus's meat loaf on Thursday was famous throughout the county, as was the fried chicken on Wednesday and the batter-dipped catfish on Friday. Sugar was the major condiment in Gus's cuisine, and grease the prevailing flavor. The food was, however, always served very hot, and in large quantities, which seemed to meet the needs of the locale, and Marlene's needs, too, as it was a welcome relief from the food *fascismo* prevalent at the time in lower-Manhattan upper-bourgeois circles. The place was friendly, the service was swift, the atmosphere was full of the good-natured joshing that passes for wit in the provinces, where everyone knows all the jokes and everyone else's foibles. Tonight, Marlene was going with the chicken-fried steak and mashed pot., w/peas; her partner had the open roast-beef sandwich, w/fries.

"The murder weapon," she said. "I think I know where it is."

A fork of Rosie's grayish roast beef was poised halfway to his mouth and stopped there when she said this. "Excuse me, but I thought we had agreed to leave all that to the pros from now on." He ate the morsel. He was eating better since Marlene had arrived. He wondered whether he would go back to being a nonfunctional drunk when she left.

"Yes," she said, "but this is practically a gimme."

"A gimme?"

"Yeah. It was the boots, and something Swett said this afternoon. He said the killers would've tossed the incriminating stuff down an old mine shaft, the gun, I mean. He suggested that Mose did just that. But they didn't, the actual killers didn't do that at all. They threw the bloody sneakers into the laurel and the bloody boots off the 130 bridge. Why? Because besides not being criminal geniuses in the first place, they were drunk. One of them tosses his sneakers in the laurel when he gets back to the car. The other one doesn't notice his boots are blood-covered until later, and he throws them off the bridge as they pass by, and at that point he remembers, oh, the gun, the pistol, they can trace that, so the pistol goes in there, too."

Poole looked at her narrowly, still chewing slowly. "If you're serious, I think our pollution is starting to affect your brain. That's not only a stupid idea, it's a McCullensburg-stupid idea."

"Oh? And why is it stupid?"

"It's pure speculation based on associating facts that have no logical association, like our fella who thought the weather had something to do with the moon shot. Shoes in the laurel, shoes in the river, hence gun in the river. Why not gun in the laurel? Or shoes in the river *but* gun down the mine. Or keep the gun. They don't like getting rid of weapons in Robbens County anyway. The people are poor, and they typically have so little to fear from the law. Plus, everyone in the county knows that Dummy Welch goes frogging under that bridge and sleeps there from time to time. Maybe the boots were a crude attempt to frame our client. Which worked, as it turned out."

"You never mentioned that before," said Marlene accusingly.

"The greatest legal mind in Robbens County is more functional than it was a short while ago."

"I think it's worth a look, anyway," said Marlene, deflated somewhat. "There's hardly any water in there this time of year, I'm told. Two, three feet at the most."

"And opaque. What were you planning to do, feel for the gun with your toes? And what if you find it? How is that going to help our client? You expect to find prints on it after weeks in the sort of corrosive water that flows through the lovely Guyandotte? You'd be lucky to find more than a rusted frame."

Marlene shrugged. "Maybe. It's always nice to have the murder weapon." She turned her attention to her steak, although her appetite had faded in the face of the resentment she now felt welling up in her. Now she was getting legal lectures from a man she was recently hosing down in a bathtub to get him sober enough to walk. It was unbearable, especially as the idea she had germinated was revealed as a stupid one, a typical bit of girl-detective nonsense. On the other hand, she had experienced odd ideas in the past that had paid off. She had figured out cases, including ones far more complex than this one, against far smarter criminals than these appeared to be. It was all very well for Poole to dismiss her smugly like that, like a man . . .

Marlene was by no means a doctrinaire feminist. She had never had many problems competing with men, and the one area where she admitted some inferiority was nicely evened up by a two-hundred-pound guard dog and, where necessary, a pistol. But just now, with Karp coming to take the whole thing away from her, and Poole acting as if he just had, some darker mud had been stirred up, thick and toxic like the sludge below the Guyandotte, and she started to obsess.

"Can I get you folks some dessert?" asked Mamie, the waitress. Unlike waitpersons in more civilized places, she did not describe what was on the menu, since nearly everything was displayed in cake stands on the lunch counter, and what Rosie's had on offer had not changed in twenty years.

Poole wanted blackberry pie. Marlene laid some money on the table and stood up. "I just remembered something I have to do," she said, and left.

She drove back to the Heeney place. "What do you think, huh?" she said to her companion. "Don't you ever have instincts where you know you're right? Of course you do. That's all you do have, is instincts. If you were half the dog you should be, you could dive into that river and come out with the goddamn gun between your teeth."

And more of the same. The dog let her rant and licked the fragrance of chicken-fried steak from her hand.

"Dan, have you got a magnet?" He was watching a Yankees-Orioles game on the TV, with a thick text on his lap and a beer at hand.

"What kind of magnet?"

"You know, a big, strong one, for dropping in water and pulling stuff out. Magnetic stuff."

"Yes, magnets don't work on nonmagnetic stuff. I speak as a professional physicist here. How about that one?" He gestured to the door to the dining room. At its foot was a black object the size and shape of a small brick, with an eyebolt growing from its center.

"The doorstop?"

"Yeah, we got it from mail order when we were kids. We used to use it to find stuff underwater."

"That's what I want it for. Can I borrow it, and some strong rope?"

"May I ask?"

"You may, but I'd be embarrassed to tell you. Did you ever get an idea that you knew was dumb, but you had to go ahead and try it or you couldn't get any peace?"

Dan felt himself blushing. His idea of that category was to get on a plane and drop in on Lucy Karp, unexpected and uninvited. "Yeah, most of my ideas are like that. You're looking for the gun, right?"

"You got it. Oh, also, do you have, like, waders?"

"Emmett had a pair. I think they're still in the cellar." Dan got out of the bed. "Come on, we'll fix you up."

An hour later, Marlene found herself on the muddy banks of the Guyandotte River, in the shadow of a green-painted steel-and-concrete bridge. The river here was not more than a hundred feet wide, at this season running sluggish and shallow between high, slaty banks. The water itself was red-ocher with an uninviting sheen on it like beetles' wings, and it smelled faintly like the cabinet under her mother's sink. Gog the dog was wisely not splashing about in it but patrolling the bank, investigating holes and sprinkling the shrubbery.

She knew that she now stood on the spot where Moses Welch had found the boots. Assuming they were flung at approximately the same time from a moving car . . . She swung the magnet around her head a couple of times and heaved it out into the river. Nothing. Then: a can; another can; nothing; a muffler; something too heavy to move; a piece of angle iron; a Delco alternator.

The light was starting to fade, as were Marlene's expectations that this project was anything but what it had initially seemed, a stupid waste of time. No, the murder weapon was not going to magically appear on your magnet, you silly girl.

The dog barked sharply, twice. Marlene looked around. A boy was standing ten yards away, at the head of the little trail that led down from the road. He was about twelve, Marlene estimated, thin, and weirdly pale, like a mushroom. He was dressed in worn bib overalls on top of bare skin, and his feet were in old sneakers with the toes ripped off. His hair was the color of dead grass, and like grass on a hummock it stuck up in all directions. The dog bounded up to him and gave him a sniff-over. He neither flinched nor tried to pet.

"Does he bite?" He had a thin, nasal voice.

"Yes, but only bad people."

"Does he mind?"

"Yes. Come here, Gog." The dog came down the trail and stood by Marlene. She flung the magnet into the water again, telling herself it would be the last one.

"What're y'doin'?" the boy asked after the magnet came back with a piece of auto chrome.

"Looking for something. Want to help?"

"It ain't there."

"What isn't there?"

"What all you're lookin' fer. It ain't there."

"How do you know what I'm looking for, and how do you know it isn't there?"

"He says," said the boy confidently. "*He* says, tell her she ain't gonna find nothing in that river. *He* says to take you up the holler and he'll tell you who killed them and how it was done."

Marlene felt the thrill sweat pop out on her forehead and her lip. "Who are you?"

"Darl."

"Darl? Okay, Darl, you got a last name?"

"I cain't say. You come on with me now. *He* said." Darl turned and walked up the bank. At the top he stopped and made a beckoning gesture. Marlene gathered up her magnet and line and tromped out of the waders. At the truck, she parked Gog in the back and let the boy into the passenger seat. When she was in herself, she asked, "Where to?"

"Just straight." He pointed. It was full dusk now; she turned on her lights.

They drove north on the highway, which flanked the river and the railroad tracks that stitched the valley. The boy said nothing and ignored Marlene's conversational gambits until: "Turn right here."

She turned onto a county road, whose number she didn't catch, and after a mile or so, the boy turned her right again onto dirt and gravel. It was now quite dark. Every so often, the boy would say "Right up ahead" or "Go left," and she would hump the truck, in four-wheel drive, up some primitive track. Branches whipped against the windshield. The truck rolled and heaved like a small craft in a seaway, its headlight beams sometimes pointing to the heavens.

"Are we almost there yet?" she asked finally.

"It ain't fur now."

She checked her watch. They had been driving for about ninety minutes, and she had no idea where she was, except that it was some-where on Belo Knob, the northern edge of it. After more driving, once along what seemed to be a rocky creekbed, the boy said, "Slow down here. Turn right."

She looked at him. His face seemed to glow in the dash lights, in a way that ordinary flesh should not. "Turn where? There's no road."

"There is. Just go through them bushes."

She hit the gas and wrestled the wheel around. Branches made shrieking sounds on the metal. It was a track at least, a steep tunnel through rank overgrowth. Then they were clear, and she felt on her cheek the changed air that meant open space. The high beams cast out across a small mowing, the grasses chest-high, and the edge of a struc-ture.

"That's it," said the boy. "You can shut your lights off now."

She did so, and the engine, too. The sound of crickets and the faint breeze in the grasses. A nightbird called. As her vision adjusted, she saw a dim light ahead, a window in a small building. She walked toward it, following the boy.

It was a farmhouse, long disused. Tall grass grew through the sun-bleached steps. There was no door. The boy made an odd gesture, like a headwaiter motioning toward a table. She entered and found that a sheet had been hung from a low ceiling, behind which there was a kerosene lantern, the only source of light. She could make out the sil-houette of a seated man.

"Sit down," said a low voice, an old man's voice, rough and rumbling.

A stool had been placed in the center of the floor. She sat.

"I got me a gun here, so don't go a-gettin' no ideas about coming round this cloth. You understand?"

"Yes. Who are you?"

"Never you mind that. I know what I'm talkin' about though, so listen good. I reckon you know that slow Welch boy didn't do those Heeneys."

"Of course he didn't."

"You'd like to know who did do it though."

"Yes, I would."

"It was Earl Cade, and Bo Cade, and Wayne Cade, and George Floyd. They done it on orders from Lester Weames, on account of that union business. Red Heeney was going to get an investigation of the union goin' and Lester couldn't stand that. So he had to go."

"How do you know this?"

"I know what happens on Belo Knob."

"Well, good for you, but so what? I don't know who you are, or where you got your information. Why should I believe you?"

"They was paid, warn't they? Cades'll kill for fun, but this wasn't no fun killin'. They was paid cash money, ten thousand dollars. Earl was boastin' on it. How'd he get that fancy truck of his? No Cade ever could keep a secret."

"But you're not a Cade." Marlene's thoughts went back to the barbecue supper with the Heeneys, back to things Rose had said, things Poole had let slip. The boy's not telling his surname. "You're a Jonson, aren't you? What's your name?"

He ignored this. "Listen. They cain't touch him, the law's no good around here. But you're from away. That's why I'm tellin' you. You check the money, Weames's money, you'll see."

"What about the pistol? The boy said you might know where the pistol is."

"Well, they didn't throw it down a mine. You look around them all, it'll turn up. Now, that's all I got to say."

The shadow moved, growing large, then shrinking as the man approached the lamp. Marlene heard a clink and a hiss of breath. The room went dark, leaving Marlene blinking at the ghostly afterimage of a white rectangle that shrank into nothing. She stood up, knocking over the stool, and fumbled in her pocket for her keys. She pressed the stud on the tiny key-chain light and the room glowed in its beam. No one was behind the sheet. A back door swung loose on a single hinge. She listened for footfalls or the sound of a car engine, but heard nothing more than the eternal crickets and the wind in the grass.

Through this grass she walked then, guided by her light. She found the truck, let the dog into the shotgun seat, slipped behind the wheel, and thought, idly rubbing the dog's ears to improve concentration. The hidden man had seemed to know what he was talking about. At the very least he had confirmed her suspicions. The question was going to be how to prove it in court. Not my department anymore; wait for Butch, and then what? Offer it up and depart? Probably. How did they know I'd be at that bridge? Somebody told them. Who knew? Poole and Dan. Couldn't be Dan, had to be Poole. Ask him, but not now. Now, should she continue her string of stupid moves and try to find her way off this mountain on steep, unmarked trails in the pitch dark, or should she just sit here with her dog and wait for morning light? She put the question to the dog and got the sensible answer she expected.

All of them were packed into the black Ford Explorer: Lucy, the twins, Tran, and two young Vietnamese men, part of a shifting crew that Lucy had started to call privately the Lost Boys. Freddy Phat drove. Where were they going? A surprise, said Tran. They drove briefly on the highway and then turned off into what looked like an extensive industrial district, a reminder of Bridgeport's glory days as the national machine shop and instrument maker. Most of the factories were vacant, their yards weed-grown, their windows staring, glassless. They stopped before a chained gate in a long chain-link fence around what seemed to be a large, derelict industrial property. One of the boys jumped out and unlocked the chain.

"What is this place, Uncle?" Lucy asked.

"It is a cement plant. I own it."

"I thought you were in the restaurant business."

"Yes, but one must *diversify.*" He used the English word. "Or so I have read. Besides, you know, I am a gangster, and all gangsters must have a cement plant."

"Are we going to observe you constructing a concrete canoe for a squealer?"

"Of course not. Such an event would not be suitable for your brothers. No, we are going to shoot."

The property was extensive. They passed a row of gray, peak-roofed buildings equipped with silos and smokestacks and came to a huge sandpit. A crude plywood table was at the lip of the pit and an old wooden swivel chair. Out in the pit against a mound of sand some twenty-five yards away stood a structure of two-by-fours like a giant easel. The Lost Boys got out of the SUV with a brown duffel bag and laid it clanking on the table. Then they went into the pit and stapled a number of silhouette targets to the two-by-four frame.

Freddy Phat lined up the weapons on the table, with stacks of clips and magazines, like cakes at a bake sale. There was an AK-47 assault rifle, a Skorpion submachine gun, a Beretta 9mm pistol, and a Colt .45 Gold Cup. Everyone put earplugs in. The two Lost Boys fired first, then Freddy Phat. Tran sat in the swivel chair and made comments in Vietnamese, mostly to do with not wasting ammunition, firing shorter bursts, keeping control. He did not seem all that concerned with the marksmanship of his staff. The twins and Lucy stood back and watched. The Lost Boys stopped firing and replaced all the shredded targets.

Then it was the twins' turn. Lucy watched Tran showing Zak how to fire the Beretta, placing his feet, arranging his hands on the weapon. Tran's horrible scarred hands against the smooth flesh of the boy's hand. She recalled Tran teaching her to shoot in the same way, when they were in the city. She was younger then than the boys were now, and mad for shooting.

Tran took Zak through all the weapons, crouching behind him supporting his arms when necessary. Zak's face was shining with joy. Then Giancarlo, just the pistol and the Skorpion, and then he said he had a headache and withdrew.

Tran turned to Lucy with an inquiring look. "No, thank you, Uncle, not today."

"You used to enjoy it so much."

"Yes. But now I don't think it's good for me to shoot, especially not at man targets. I can't not think about what the bullets are meant to do, to people's bodies. It makes me too sad."

He nodded and looked sad himself.

"But aren't you going to shoot?" she asked.

In answer he removed a small weapon from his jacket pocket.

"Oh, you still have the Stechkin," she said.

"Yes. You remember you were always plaguing me to let you fire it, and I would not. Would you like to now?"

"I don't think so," she answered, smiling. "I missed my chance, I think."

He turned toward the firing line, hefting the little weapon.

Zak asked, "What is that? Another pistol?"

"Yes, but a machine pistol. It's very rare. Most people can't shoot one very well."

"But he can."

"Yes," Lucy said. "Tran does most things very well."

Tran shot. In an instant the center of the target vanished into flapping rags.

After the shooting party, they all went to one of Tran's restaurants and in a private room had stuffed squid and garlic quails. Lucy was glad the boys had been trained from an early age to eat everything, and they did not disgrace her in the American fashion by demanding hamburger. After the meal they returned to Tran's house, where their host and his minions departed for their regular evening round of inspection, collection, and terrorization. Lucy took her brothers, who were hyped and restless, on a walk through the parklike neighborhood. They found a playground, a basketball court, and three kids of around fourteen playing horse in the fading light. Did they want to have a game, Lucy asked them, and after some nervous hesitation, they agreed. They had expected a walkover, a girl and two little kids, but the Karps had been playing b-ball together for a long time, and Lucy was as good a player as you were likely to find outside of a top-flight college team. Zak was an excellent shot and aggressive even against kids twice his weight, although he shot whenever he had the ball. Giancarlo was a born point guard and had inherited from his father an almost preternatural sense of what everyone on the court was likely to do next. They played until they couldn't see anymore, winning two, losing one.

Later, as Lucy tucked them into their sleeping bags in the guest room, Zak said, "This was the best day of my whole life."

"I'm glad you liked it," said his sister. "What about you, GC?"

Giancarlo and Lucy exchanged a look. "Oh, definitely the best day, superterrific," lied Giancarlo out of love for his brother. Only Lucy knew how much he disliked shooting.

She mooched around the house for a while after that, made herself some tea, smoked a cigarette in the garden. Then she went into the house and, like the good girl she was, called her mom.

But was not surprised, nor disappointed, when Dan Heeney answered the phone.

"Oh, I was thinking about you," she said.

"Really?" This was actually the first time that a girl had said that to him. "How come?"

"I was out with the boys and a bunch of gangsters shooting machine guns today and I thought, 'Oh, I'll probably talk to Dan when I call Mom tonight and he'll ask me what I was doing and I'll say that, and he'll say, "No, really." ' "

"You're making this up." He laughed.

"Yeah, or, 'You're making this up.' No, *really*. My strange life. What's hopping in McCullensburg?"

"Oh, well, I don't know where to start. There's so much to do. We caught B.B. King's concert at Amos's roadhouse and brothel. Pavarotti's at the VFW hall. Most nights I just drop in at Rosie's to check out the wits and glitterati who assemble there nightly—Woody, Jay, Leo. It's like *People* magazine."

She laughed. "I mean *really*."

"Oh, *really?* I'm studying matrix algebra and astrophysics. Working on my world-famous pyramid of Iron City beer cans. Waiting for this damn thing to resolve."

"My dad'll fix it."

"Yeah, that's what *my* dad thought," Dan snapped bitterly, "and look what it got him."

Lucy thought that between the two dads, hers struck her as the more competent fixer. She let the thought pass, but the mere mention of the case strummed the ever-tuned strings of responsibility in her, and she said, "Well, it'll work out somehow. Is my mom there?"

"No, as a matter of fact, she's out."

"Out? Where is she? It's pretty late."

"Oh, you know—McCullensburg, the city that never sleeps. I don't know where she is exactly. She had some whacked-out idea about using a big magnet to troll the river for the murder weapon. She thought she'd figured out exactly where it is. I thought it was kind of dumb, myself."

"It probably was. She can go off on an idea sometimes. That's how she lost her eye, you know."

"I didn't. What happened?"

"This was before they got married. She started obsessing about my dad's ex. She thought they were getting back together. Then she found an envelope addressed to him, from the city where the ex was living, and she opened it to see whether anything was really going on, and it was a letter bomb, meant for my dad, from this maniac. The funny thing was, she was the DA's expert on letter bombs at the time."

"Weird. She's sort of a strange woman, if you don't mind me saying so."

"Not at all. Which makes it odd that she has such perfectly normal children. Look, I'd like to chat more, but I hear my host is arriving. Would you do me a favor? Have her call me when she gets in—it doesn't matter how late it is. Okay?" She gave him the house number.

"Sure. Fine. By the way, you said you'd work on us getting together this summer. Any progress?"

"I promised my dad I would stay away until they catch the bad guys. Because of the twins."

"Uh-huh. Well, I guess it's going to have to be back at school."

"Oh, I don't know," said Lucy, "two Karps on the case, those guys're doomed."

Midnight. Lucy sat cross-legged on a cushion in the plain finished basement of Tran's house, using *yenhok* needles to prepare a pill of black Chinese opium for her host, who was reclining on a couch. She manipulated the tarry mass over the blue flame from a brass alcohol lamp, shaping and heating it all the way through, as he had taught her. It was curiously relaxing work. The lamp provided the room's only light.

She placed the pill in a long, carved pipe, brass-bound bone with an amber mouthpiece, and handed it to him. He took two long sucks from it and fell back against a cushion.

"You are good at this," he said after a while. "An opium chef as we call it. Do you feel corrupted?"

"Not at all. It seems a very innocent pleasure. And I like to see you relaxed."

"You're a good girl."

Another long pause. "And I am a very bad man. But when I take *nha phien* with you, I seem to float into another world, as if I am living a story different from the actual story of my life. As in the *Tale of Kieu*, the story of Kieu and the bandit chieftain. Do you remember that?"

"Yes. The bandit chieftain was really a decent man, forced by necessity into a cruel life. I always thought of you when I read it."

"Our sorrowful national epic. We Vietnamese are connoisseurs of sorrow, you know. We make the Russians look like the French. Or the happy Americans, the fortunate people. My hope is that the boys I bring over will in time learn something about this."

"Who are they?"

"Sons of my old comrades. Southerners, of the NLF. I find as many of them as I can, and whoever remains of the people I served with, and their families. We were all disgraced after the war. Insufficiently grateful to our northern comrades, too many bourgeois tendencies, our grandfathers could read, perhaps. We had imagined we were fighting for a better life, so we all had to be reeducated. It turned out that what we were fighting for was to give absolute power to a bunch of fat bastards who sat out the war in Hanoi bunkers. Imagine our surprise!"

"How can you get them out?"

"Oh, in Vietnam now anything can be arranged with money. The country is one great bazaar. The granddaughters of the Vietcong are selling themselves to fat Germans in Saigon hotels. Nothing changed. All the wars, twenty years of them, so that the pimps can be Vietnamese instead of French. Or Americans. You should have dropped dollars from your bombers instead of bombs; it would have been cheaper." He took another long drag and closed his eyes.

"You don't have to continue in this life," she said. "You could go anywhere. Start over."

"I do start over, my dear. Every night when I smoke my pipe I have a beautiful and quite different life."

"And then you kill more people."

"In fact, the last time I killed anyone it was rescuing you, do you recall? From those Chinese in that shop by the beach."

She felt a flush of shame. "I'm sorry, Uncle. I was being a prig. Who am I to judge you?"

He said nothing for several minutes. "No, I am far from offended. I believe that had I not met you and your mother, I would not have been a real person anymore. As it is, my goal is to keep violence"—he drifted for a moment—"to a minimum. If I died before I had to kill another person, I would be happy."

At this he fell silent. She stayed with him, drifting off herself into a semisleep, touched a little by the drug fumes, a state that provided just a taste of the famous silky dreams.

From which she was startled by a ringing phone. She climbed the stairs to the kitchen and picked up the receiver.

"*Hai ba ba, nam sau bon bay.*"

"Lucy?"

"Yeah. Dan?"

"Uh-huh. What was that?"

"The number in Vietnamese. Is my mom okay?"

"Yeah, well, that's why I'm calling. It's two-thirty and she's not back. I called Poole's and she's not there either. I checked the cops and the hospital, too. I'm a little worried and you said to call . . ."

"Yes. Thank you. Do you know where she went?"

"She said something about the bridge on Route 130, north of town."

"Okay, good, I'll take it from here. You should get some sleep."

"You'll *take* it . . . ?" he exclaimed, disturbed by the coldness in her tone. "What're you going to do?"

"Call my dad, for starters. Don't worry about it."

"Aren't *you* worried?"

He heard a long sigh over the wires. "Of course I'm worried. But I'm used to this. In my family we don't get all upset when someone goes missing. My dad calls it Karp Disaster Mode. I have to go now."

Karp had the answering machine on, so Lucy had to call six times before the accumulated disturbance penetrated her father's sleep.

"What happened?" No preambles at 3 A.M. He could feel his heart thump.

"I don't know. I'm at Tran's with the boys. Dan just called. Mom went out looking for a piece of evidence and hasn't come back."

"Oh, crap!" Karp knuckled his face, took a couple of deep breaths. "Okay, I'll get something organized. You have your cell phone?"

"Yeah. We were planning to go to Boston tomorrow. Should we come back home?"

"No, there's no reason for that yet. I hope. Just keep the phone up. You okay?"

"Fine. You'll call me as soon as you know something?"

"Right. Take care."

He punched off and found the number Hendricks had given him. A machine answered. Karp spoke to it, trying to control the urgency in his tone, so that he did not sound like a hysterical husband. He took a shower, then dressed and called airlines. He found a Continental flight to Cleveland out of La Guardia at six-thirty with a connection to Charleston that would have him there at ten thirty-eight. Only first class was open. He took the seat, one way. It cost about the same as a round-trip to Buenos Aires, coach.

The phone rang as he was putting on his jacket. He told Hendricks what had happened, and his travel plans.

"Okay, I'll have you met at the airport," said Hendricks, "and I'll get a team down there. You say she was headed for the bridge over the Guyandotte?"

"Is that on 130?"

"Yeah. We call it the green bridge."

A pause. "What do you think? Should I worry? I mean, it's only one night . . ."

"No, you did good calling me. It pays to be worried if the Cades start messing with you."

The plane was delayed, as planes always are at La Guardia. Fortunately the turboprop was delayed at Cleveland, too, so that Karp, at the end of a desperate sprint to the gate, was allowed to stumble sweating out onto the tarmac and climb into the little plane.

They were waiting for him at Yeager Airport in Charleston, three Broncos with state markings and their engines running, and a dark sedan with Hendricks, in full uniform and dark Ray•Bans, leaning against the fender.

They shook hands. Karp tossed his bag in the trunk and jumped in the back with Hendricks.

"Any news?"

"I got the barracks at Logan working on it. She was there. Someone saw a red truck go by yesterday evening, headed north on 130. We've got troopers looking, but no luck so far."

The motorcade took off with sirens and lights. Forty-five minutes later they were at the state police barracks in Logan, just over the border from Robbens. There Karp observed that two of the Broncos were full of men in black jumpsuits and baseball hats.

"You expecting a war?" Karp asked.

"Something like that," said Hendricks. He left Karp in an office while he ordered his troops, Karp feeling useless and starting to feel stupid as well. From a distance he heard the thump of a helicopter, which added to the impression of a major, semimilitary operation.

Cheryl Oggert came in, looking crisp as a saltine in a tan shirtwaist dress. She had a paper bag in hand, containing coffee and sweet rolls.

"I wouldn't impose state police coffee on you," she said. "How're you doing?"

"I'm fine. What're you doing here?"

"Public relations."

"And spying for the governor."

"That, too. Are you worried?"

"Hendricks thinks I should be. On the other hand, Marlene is pretty resourceful."

"I hope she is. Are you going out with the search?"

"I'd like to. I haven't wanted to be a pain in the ass, though. Hendricks seems like he's fairly busy."

"You should go. I'll take care of it, if you want." She smiled and patted his hand.

Marlene had forgotten about the mosquitoes. She had no repellent, and even though she rolled all the windows up, they got in, attacking in squadrons. Sleep came in unsatisfying dribbles. She awoke stiff and itching to thin, silvery light coming through windows made opaque by condensation. Cursing, she staggered out of the truck into a heavy morning fog that had swallowed the farmhouse she had been in the previous night. Gog circled around her, sniffing. She found a clean rag in the truck and wiped the windows, using the soaked fabric also for a face wash. Inside, she cranked up the engine and wiped the rearview mirror, during which exercise she caught sight of her face and yelped in dismay. It was like a contour map drawn in scarlet, welts upon welts.

After driving slowly around the little clearing for some time, she found what she thought was the track up which they had come in the night. It was more like a tunnel than a road, but the sight of broken branches and deep tire tracks convinced her that she was going the right way. She had, of course, completely forgotten the directions of Darl, but this did not seem to be an insurmountable problem.

"It stands to reason," she explained to the dog, "if I pick the road that tends downward every time we meet another trail, then eventually we'll hit the river valley and the main roads, or if not, we'll still get off the mountain and reach the land of baths, whiskey, and Lanacane. And dog food. See, that's the advantage of partnering with a species that has higher mental functions. You could never have figured that out on your own, could you?"

After an hour or so of driving, during which the fog burned off considerably, she found herself on a steep, rocky road, little more than two ruts, with rank growth and even small trees growing up between them.

"This is what they call a divided highway in West Virginia," she said. "The ruts are divided by lovely ornamental sumacs. But lucky us, it's dropping real steep and I have a good feeling that just around this curve we will be able to see . . ."

She hit the brakes a little too late, just after she had become aware that the road had disappeared. What lay ahead was a great tangle of sunken, disturbed earth and fallen trees, as if a giant had pressed his foot down hard upon the earth. The truck tilted; Marlene screamed; the dog whined. Metal screeched upon rock, a heavy branch smashed against the windshield, as the truck skidded at a terrifying angle, down, off the road and into the churned-up area.

And stopped with a bone-jarring thump, nosed into the upended root ball of a toppled hickory. After she had stopped shaking, she got out to inspect the damage. The rear differential housing was wedged upon a boulder, leaving the rear wheels clear of the ground. The front wheels were buried to their upper rims in mud.

"Well, this truck needs a nice rest. It's not going anywhere without a wrecker. What we need, Gog, is a colorful Neapolitan dogcart, to which I would hitch you, and you would pull me in a leisurely fashion back to civilization. But you forgot your colorful Neapolitan dogcart, didn't you? You *always* forget your goddamn dogcart. What kind of best friend are you? A piss poor one. This is absolutely the last time I am taking you on a fun trip like this."

And so on as she labored up the slope. At the top she continued downward on what had been the shoulder of the putative road. Gradually, however, the ruts became fainter, the growth between them became more mature, until she found herself facing a twenty-foot-high mountain ash growing between the vague traces of wheel marks.

"Excuse me," she said to the tree, "could you tell me where I could catch the downtown D train?" Turning to the dog, she said, "This is entirely your fault. I will never listen to your stupid ideas again!"

Hendricks came into the office. "I'm going to go talk to someone who might know something about this. You want to come along?"

Karp did. They got in a Bronco with three of the black-clad officers. Hendricks drove.

"Where are we going?" asked Karp.

"See a fella I know." That was all Karp got during the forty-minute drive. They passed the green bridge and then headed west up increasingly primitive roads. Karp tried to recall his airborne geography lesson.

"We're on Burnt Peak, yes?"

Hendricks looked at him. "You got it." He turned into an overgrown driveway.

In a clearing stood a double-wide mobile home, painted pale green. A mud-covered white Mazda pickup sat in the yard, beside a scatter of toys, an inflatable pool, some bikes, a yellow mutt dog, and a towheaded boy of about seven, wearing swim shorts.

The dog barked. Hendricks got out of the Bronco and allowed the dog to sniff at him. To the boy he said, "Your papaw in there?"

A nod.

"Well, whyn't you go on in there and tell him Wade Hendricks wants to talk to him."

The boy ran into the trailer. A few minutes later a large-gutted man in an undershirt and stained green workpants stepped barefoot out onto the mobile home's concrete apron.

Hendricks advanced and shook the man's hand. "Russell. How you keepin'?"

"Pretty fair," said the man, not smiling. His chin indicated the Bronco. "I guess you ain't visiting."

"No, I'm not. This's police business. We're looking for a woman gone missing. Her name's Marlene Ciampi. She was Mose Welch's lawyer. The one from away."

"I heard about her. She's gone missing, you say?"

"Went out last night to the green bridge and didn't come back."

"Uh-huh. Well, how about that. She's got that Dodge four-by, ain't she? Red?"

"That's right. You seen it?"

"No, I ain't. I worked the late at Majestic last night. I'm just now getting up. You're here because of her runnin' the Cade boys off."

"That's right. You heard anything about maybe they was plannin' some get-even?"

"Tell you the truth, them boys is always running their mouths. I don't pay them much mind. They was red up, though. Earl, mostly. That lady needs to watch her step, I guess. But I didn't hear of no actual what you might call a plan."

Some polite talk about people Karp didn't know followed this exchange, and then Hendricks returned to the car and they rode off.

"What was that all about?"

"Oh, Russell is a good fella to talk to if the Cades have got up to any mischief."

"He's a Cade?"

"Related to them. It's good news, though. We're probably not dealing with foul play. On the other hand, if she decided to go cruising around these hills at night . . . well."

"An accident?"

"Maybe. More like she got stuck. Some of those roads peter out to nothing, or they're busted up by landslides or fall-ins."

"Fall-ins?"

"Yes, sir. All these hills are riddled with mine shafts. The pit props rot out and the shafts collapse and the land kind of sags. And there are fires. We got underground fires burning for years up here. They hollow out a whole rise and then the land just collapses like a rotten pumpkin. Then you got your sloughs. A slide blocks a creek and the water pools up and makes a little swamp. You go into one of those, and you might have a worry getting out. And there's rock slides—"

A squawk from the radio interrupted this dire catalog. Hendricks picked up the mouthpiece and talked and listened to what to Karp was incomprehensible garble.

Hendricks hung up the instrument. "They spotted the truck. It was stuck in a fall-in, but there was no sign of her. Up on Belo, the north side."

Three hours later, Karp, now in sodden shirtsleeves, tieless, his city shoes covered with mud, was leaning against the side of a Bronco, drinking from a plastic water bottle, when he saw his wife, or what seemed like his wife, striding down the dirt road, trailed by her dog and a couple of uncomfortable-looking troopers. Her face was mottled red and she was covered in stinking black mud from shoe (she had but one) to crown.

She spotted him. "One laugh and you're dead," she snapped, "and you probably forgot to bring bagels."

12

"THEN I TRIPPED ON SOMETHING," MARLENE SAID, AND TOOK ANOTHER sip of gin and tonic, "a root, or a goddamn alligator, and went headfirst into the swamp. When I got out of it, I leaned against a tree and screamed for, I don't know, three hours? Then the dog barked and I heard your guys thrashing around in the bushes. They must have heard me." Another pull on her drink. "At which point I was discovered by this major countywide search you organized, adding the last possible increment of embarrassment."

"People get lost up here all the time, Mrs. Karp," said Hendricks.

"Marlene, please. And you're Wade, right?"

"Right. Couple of times a year we got to go up some mountain and find a hunter. Sometimes it's people who lived here all their lives. They fall in holes, they get tangled in some laurel and get exhausted, heatstroke, hypothermia, depending on the season, or they get wrecked like you did. It's no big thing, really."

They were in the living room of the Heeney house, Marlene, Karp, and Hendricks. Marlene was freshly bathed, with her hair in a towel and wearing a black T-shirt with a calligraphic design on it and her only pair of clean shorts. She wanted a nap, and more than that, she wanted the previous twenty-four hours not to have happened.

Hendricks looked at his notepad and thumbed back through some pages.

"You said the boy said his name was Darryl?"

"Sounded like Darl. You think there's any chance of finding him?"

"Maybe. Lots of Darryls in these parts. This man behind the sheet—how come you asked if he was a Jonson?"

"Just a guess. The Jonsons are feuding with the Cades, right? If someone wanted to rat out the Cades for the murders, I figured it might be the other clan. Also . . . the way the boy talked, calling the man *he* in a funny way, like he was a leader or something, more than just an older relative."

Hendricks tightened his chin, causing his upper lip to protrude, and knotted his brow. Another of his portfolio of Gary Cooper grimaces, Karp thought. "Well. It might could be. It could be you talked with old Amos Jonson. That would be something."

"Why?" Karp asked. "Who is he?"

"No one's seen him for a while. He's the only survivor of the Jonsons of his generation. I guess he must be in his late sixties if it's him. He had four brothers and a sister, all dead." Hendricks looked directly at Marlene. "Killed."

"By the Cades?"

"That's what people say. Two of them were passed off as mining accidents. No one was prosecuted. The last brother, name of Jonathan, was shot by Ben Cade, right on his own front porch. His sister, Dora, said she saw the whole thing. Well, they had to bring old Ben in on that. A couple of days before the trial, someone tossed a couple of sticks of dynamite through her bedroom window. Killed her and a couple of her kids, as I recall. So they had to let him go. That was when Amos sort of disappeared. Of course, there are still lots of Jonsons around, even if they keep sort of a low profile. He could've been staying with his kin all this time."

"Can we find him?" Karp asked. "According to Marlene, he's got lots of answers. Would he testify, do you think?"

"I would doubt it," said Hendricks after a silence.

"Right," said Karp. "And I expect that this guy Floyd and the three Cades would have alibis provided by all the merry Cades and various henchmen and would not be forthcoming out of, say, remorse."

Karp received the expected laconic agreement and clapped his hands briskly. "Well! Assuming that Marlene's guy is not just some kind of grudge horseshit, we now know who done it. Not a small thing, but on the other hand, we have *bubkes* on anyone from a purely legal standpoint."

"Pardon, *bup* what?" said Hendricks.

"*Bubkes,*" said Karp, "a term widely used in the New York bar to signify an insufficiency of probative material. The point is, an anonymous message from a probable clan enemy is almost worse than nothing at all. That leaves the possibility of forensic evidence linking one or more of these guys to the crime. We have prints at the scene. I assume these scumbags have prints on file?"

Hendricks made an assenting noise. "The Cades do. I don't know about Floyd."

"We'll find out and see if there're any matches. Next, we have the famous sneaker. We'll check that for biological traces of the last wearer and do a DNA workup. Also, we have the famous boots, expensive and new. We'll check around town and see who bought a pair like that recently. The murder gun, if it's still available, would be nice. Juries always like to see a murder weapon. Wade, I'd like your guys to go over all the evidence collected the first go-around. My assumption is they didn't bust their humps over it when Mose Welch stepped into the frame."

"As we speak," said Hendricks, "they're reviewing the material at the Charleston lab, and I got people going over the grounds outside right now."

Marlene added, "I've got beer cans and bottles from that overlook, too. It'd be interesting, at least, if any prints on them matched the prints found in the house."

"Good idea," said Karp. "What I'd like to do now is . . ."

A young man came into the room. He was wearing plain clothes and rubber gloves, which identified him as one of the crime-scene people in Hendricks's outfit. He stopped short and looked at Hendricks inquiringly.

"What's up, Frank?" asked Hendricks.

"We found something, Captain. I thought you'd want to take a look."

They all followed Frank out through the kitchen to the back stairs. Marlene saw that the storm door that had lain by the side of the stairs since the murders had been moved aside, and that in the damp, grassless earth near the stairs were two near-perfect impressions of boot soles. Marlene recognized the wavy tread pattern as being from the size-nine-and-a-half Rocky-brand boots found with Heeney blood all over them, and said so.

Hendricks looked down at the impressions. "Damn it all, Frank, how in the *hell* did this get missed the first time?"

"No excuse, sir. Just pure sloppy work. Nobody thought to move the storm door to see what was underneath it."

Hendricks looked to have a few other things to say to old Frank. Marlene could see muscles working in his jaw, and a dark flush was spreading up from the jawline. She said, "Say, Frank, could you generate a body weight from that print? By how deep the boot sank into the soil?"

The technician looked up at her with relief, and perhaps gratitude on his face. "Yes, ma'am, we could. A range, anyway. Within five or so pounds."

"Well, if it's all right with Captain Hendricks, if you could do that test right away and it turns out that the fellow who made them was much less than two hundred pounds, I can probably get my man out of jail."

The technician looked at Hendricks, who nodded abruptly. "Go do it," he ordered.

To the Karps, he said, "I got to run into town now and see how they're doing on our temporary headquarters."

"We have headquarters?" asked Karp.

"Yeah, in the old Burroughs Building. An insurance company used to have it. They went bust and the state grabbed it up for the taxes. They still got all their furniture and equipment in there and the building's still in good shape. I got people cleaning it out now, putting phones in and all. I assumed that was okay. It's right near the courthouse. Trooper Blake's got an unmarked standing by and he'll drive you anywhere you need to go."

Karp found himself nodding in agreement, keeping the surprise off his face and suppressing any expression of what he knew to be petty annoyance.

"Good. That's real good, Wade."

"Also, we've arranged quarters for you. I was thinking it wouldn't look that good for you all to both be staying here, I mean it being the murder scene. There's a kind of lodge west of town, Four Oaks. They rent it out for groups, industry and church groups having retreats, what passes for the tourist industry here. I arranged a cabin. I'll be staying there, and some of my guys and Cheryl, too. If that's all right?"

"I'm overwhelmed. Thanks," said Karp. Hendricks took his leave, and Karp and Marlene went back into the house, where Marlene refreshed her drink.

"Well," she said. "No flies on Captain Hendricks."

"No. I feel like a nature film where the queen ant is being shoved into position by the worker ants, my swollen abdomen being wiggled into position so I can lay the eggs. I guess I'm staying."

"You hadn't planned to?"

"I haven't planned anything since Lucy called. I've been responding to the crisis, which turned out to be a noncrisis."

"And you feel dumb because I'm just raddled with bug bites instead of smashed to pieces or kidnapped by desperadoes."

In answer he sat next to her on the couch, threw an arm around her shoulder, kissed her cheek.

"Ugh, how can you stand it? I look like an illustration from a medical textbook. I should have one of those black rectangles across my eyes."

"My bug-bitten beauty," Karp said tenderly. "I've missed you. Call me old-fashioned, but I used to like coming home to the happy family every night."

"Or the unhappy family, on occasion, if you recall."

"Even that. Anyway, it seems that since I'm here now instead of next week, I might as well put my game face on and play. Have you thought about what you'll do?"

"Well, I'll see my client out of jail and the charges dismissed, which should be a matter of days. Beyond that, I don't know. Leap on my horse and vanish with a hearty 'Hi-yo, Silver.'"

"Why not stay?"

"And do what?"

"Nothing. It's summer. Take a break. You went from busting your hump as a corporate mogul to busting your hump as a struggling dog farmer. Why not kick back?"

He cupped his hand to his ear. "Listen . . ."

"What? I don't hear anything."

"My point. No howling animals. No gormless employees requiring direction. No darling children yammering for attention. We haven't been alone together since Christ was a corporal."

"Yes, and if I stay, *I'll* be alone together, and you'll be consumed with your case."

"Oh, consumed, conshmumed! Look, darling: it's *one* case—count it, one—instead of the fifty I usually have to follow. Two, the people who did it are morons operating under the assumption of impunity. They've made a million mistakes, and they'll make more. Their hillbilly asses are mine. Three, as you just saw, I apparently have the entire Wehrmacht at my disposal. Four, no political horseshit to cope with. Compared to what I usually do, this is flower arrangement."

"Wait until you're here awhile," she said sourly. "Things won't seem so simple. This is a truly weird place."

"Why, because they talk funny and there're no Chinese restaurants?"

"No, really, Butch! There's a strange feel to it. Everyone's polite and helpful, at least when they're not trying to kill you, but you get the feeling that everyone knows a secret that they'll never tell. And there are little looks you catch, like in a family when someone mentions insanity, and everyone but the guest knows about Auntie Rose up in the attic. It's funny, but I've been trying and trying to think of where I had that feeling before and I can't quite recall it. But stick around and you'll see."

"Yeah, we'll see," said Karp dismissively. "Meanwhile, you'll let me know."

"You'll be the first. Where are you going now?"

Karp was up and moving toward the door. "I think I'll have Trooper Blake drive me to our new home, where I will take a shower and change my shirt, and then I'm going to show the flag to the state's attorney."

"Use short sentences," said Marlene, "and talk slow."

State's Attorney Hawes did not salute the flag when Karp carried it into his office late that afternoon. He looked as if he wanted to burn and trample it, the way Iranians so often do to Old Glory. He sat behind his desk with his jaw (and, Karp assumed, his ass as well) as tight as could be and gave curt answers to Karp's polite questions about the triple murder.

Karp remembered about talking slow. He let a little silence descend, after which he said, "Mr. Hawes . . . Stan, if I can call you that?"

Hesitation, a short nod and a grunt.

"Good. I'm Butch. We seem to have got off on the wrong foot, so let's roll the tape back and start again. If I were you, I'd be pissed, too.

You picked up the biggest murder case in the last decade, and all of a sudden I show up, a big-time out-of-town prosecutor, and it looks like the big boys in Charleston think you can't handle your job. And on top of that, it's becoming more and more likely that you indicted the wrong guy."

"I can convict him."

"Well, you might be able to and you might not. That's not the point. I'm just now starting a complete review of the forensic evidence, and I would bet your next two paychecks that we come up with enough material to absolutely exonerate Moses Welch and shine a pretty bright spotlight on a couple, three other people."

"Who?"

"Earl, Bo, and Wayne Cade, plus George Floyd. Since Floyd works for Lester Weames, I'd assume he gave the order."

"Where'd you hear that?"

"It's around. Amos Jonson says that's how it went down."

"Hah! Jonson would say the Cades killed JFK."

"I agree. But the fact remains that Bo and Earl tried to kill my wife the other day and came around the Heeney place with weapons, in the hours of darkness. That's suggestive to me that Jonson or whoever was not just whistling 'Dixie.' Now here's a prediction. We will find their fingerprints at the crime scene, and on cans and bottles found at a lookout place above the crime scene, and we will find that the blood-covered boots that are virtually your whole case against Moses Welch were purchased by a member of the Cade family, and if we're a little lucky, we might get DNA evidence off the two pieces of footwear we have that were soaked in the victims' blood, evidence connected to the bunch that we like for it. That would constitute a pretty good case, wouldn't it?"

"A lot of ifs." Sulkily.

"Uh-huh. Look, Stan, I know you wish I would just dry up and blow away, but I'm not going to. So there's two things you need to know about me. One is, I've tried and won over a hundred homicide cases, some of them against the best defense lawyers in New York. I am extremely good at this, not because I'm a genius or a better lawyer than you are, but just because of that experience. Two is, I have absolutely no political or ego-building agenda here. As far as I'm concerned, this was your case and it's still your case, and I will direct the PR lady that the governor sent down to present it that way to the press. I am perfectly content to lurk in the background while you win it." Karp's face broke into a grin. "You're looking at me like I'm trying to sell you a condo in Florida."

Hawes's face relaxed a trifle. "It *is* a little rich. Why the hell did you come down here, then?"

"The truth? I got some political problems with my job in New York that I'm not ready to deal with yet, and this was an opportunity to carve out some space. The main reason, though, is Saul Sterner. You know who he is?"

Hawes shrugged. "The union lawyer?"

"That's the one. He's an old friend. I studied under him in law school. He asked me to do it, and it's kind of hard to keep from doing stuff Saul asks you to do." Karp paused and was relieved to see that Hawes was working this over in his mind, that he was entertaining the idea that this was maybe not going to be a complete disaster. A rather too transparent face for a lawyer, Karp thought, but in the circumstances an advantage.

"So do we have a basis here?" Karp asked. "For now, you're willing to accept that I'm not bullshitting you?"

"Do I have a choice?"

"There's always a choice. In your case the choice is cooperating with me and learning something about your profession and ending up a hero, or being a hard-ass and nursing a wounded ego and ending up looking like a jerk. But I don't think you're a jerk, and more important, I think you're basically honest. My wife, who you've met, has the best scumbag detector in North America, and she says she's getting a low reading in your case. However, to be frank, I think you're a good bit brighter than she thinks you are. I mean, Moses Welch? For that kind of crime?"

Hawes flushed a little and dropped his eyes, but said nothing.

Karp went on, "And as long as we're being frank, I have to say this, too: nearly everybody who starts out in this business makes the mistake you made. The cops bring in a guy and they say, 'He's the one,' and you look at the guy and the evidence and who's on D and you make an assessment: Can I win? The answer looks like yes and so you go forward, because it's a hot case, and you need a win. And when new evidence

starts to show up, like it did here, that your guy is wrong, you start to figure out ways to get around or to discount that evidence, so as to keep
your case in the win column. It's done every day. It's lazy and it's rotten,
and it's the reason why the prisons in this country are filled with innocent
mental retards who were defended by drunks or incompetents and prosecuted by people who wanted a win more than they wanted to honor
their oath of office."

"Thank you for the lecture."

Karp ignored the sarcasm. "You're welcome. I expect it'll be the first
of many. The fact of the matter is, you swung at a sucker pitch and
fucked up, and what you do when you fuck up in this business, if you're
a mensch, is you admit it and bust your hump finding the right scumbag
the next time. As it is, you're getting off easy. You should try fucking up
big-time in New York City, when you got four major networks and the
New York Times putting you in the crosshairs. What kind of ball did you
play?"

Hawes goggled at this change of pace. "Who says I played ball?"

"Every prosecutor I ever met played a competitive team sport."

After a long beat, Hawes said, "Baseball. High school and college."

"Varsity?"

"Yeah. Third base. I had a tryout with Charleston. The Alley Cats,
Class A with Toronto."

"How'd you do?"

"Good field, no hit. I went to law school instead. Let me take a wild
guess: you played basketball."

"You got it. High school all-American and two years at Cal before I
screwed up my knee. You're a local boy, I take it."

"Born and raised. My dad managed the Exxon out on Lincoln at
130."

"So you know the situation: the unions, the miners, all the corruption horseshit."

Hawes nodded.

"And you wanted to be state's attorney so you could clean up the
evildoers and bring civility and justice to benighted Robbens County. Is
that a bitter laugh, Stan?"

"My main goal was to last long enough to get a decent job a long way
away from Robbens County. And it ain't horseshit, neither. These guys

don't fuck around. And I got a wife and two kids." Hawes's eyes passed briefly over a framed picture on his desk.

"You were actually threatened?"

"I was talked to in a friendly fashion."

"By who—Weames?"

"No, Weames don't do the talking. Floyd."

"My wife's met him. I hear he's a sweetheart."

"Mm. If I ordered a carload of sons of bitches and they just sent him, I'd sign the invoice."

"You think he's the type who'd pull a trigger?"

"I don't know about trigger, but George likes to hurt folks."

"How about the sheriff? I assume he's up to his ears in it."

"Oh, yeah, but Swett's in a different class. Swett's a good-natured slob, good-natured for a Cade, I mean. His mom's Ben Cade's cousin, which would make him a second cousin of your alleged perps."

"Ben Cade being the Cade patriarch."

"You got it. Then we have Judge Murdoch. He's a Hergewiller."

"Not a Cade."

"No, the Hergewillers are a lot more high-tone than the Cades. Rudy Hergewiller was the sheriff here during the first Robbens County war. His people've been on the more legal end of union busting around here ever since. Your boy Poole is a Hergewiller on his mother's side."

"He's not my boy," said Karp automatically, but filed the fact away. "I assume the judge's on the graft like the sheriff."

"Yeah, but it's not even graft the way you're thinking. The company takes care of the sheriff and Murdoch like they've taken care of everyone with any power in the county since Big Tom Killebrew bought the place. It ranges from cases of whiskey at Christmas to bags of cash. It's accepted, like, I don't know, the hot dogs at a company picnic."

"And what does the company buy for this money?"

"It gets to do what it wants. It keeps it being 1910 inside the county. That was a good year for them and they don't see any reason for changing just because the rest of the world has moved on a little. Mainly it's controlling the union, the workers, that and the environmental stuff, although there they have to deal with Charleston and Washington a lot more."

"And how about you? Do you have any bags of cash?"

"I have an envelope of cash. I'm not important enough for a bag."
Hawes reached into a bottom drawer of his desk and came out with the
classic fat manila envelope.

"I found this in my desk drawer two days after we arrested Mose. No
note, nobody saw who left it there. It's two grand in hundreds."

"That's pretty cheap to buy a state's attorney on a triple murder. Did
you get bought?"

"I don't know. I guess I was waiting for one of the usual suspects to
show up—somebody saw them do it, or some piece of evidence no one
could ignore. When Welch waltzed into town in those boots . . ." He
shook his head, as if to clear it of fog. "I can't rightly recall what I
thought. Relief. Okay, it wasn't one of *their* killings, it was just some
damn imbecile, a misfortune. I wasn't going to get any calls in the middle of the night—'You know what we want you to do, Stan.' Then I got
that envelope."

"I notice you didn't spend it."

"No. And we could use the money." He picked it up and let it drop,
sighing. "I guess I could have it cast in a block of Lucite, with a label, like
a desk ornament."

"Before that, I'd recommend handing it over to the staties as evidence. Speaking as your legal adviser, now."

"I guess," said Hawes, putting the envelope back in the drawer. "So
what do we do now?"

"Wait on the forensics. Speaking of which, the state guys came up
with a couple of footprints off that boot of yours at the murder scene."

"Don't tell me. It was worn by a man half the size of Mose Welch."

"We don't know for sure, but that's the way I'd bet," said Karp. "But
you knew that."

"Well, what do you want me to do, apologize?"

"Yes. To Welch and his family, and in public. You're bad, you take the
shit."

Hawes looked off to the side until most of the red flush had departed
from his cheek. He gave a curt nod.

"Good," said Karp. "So, if the crime lab stuff shows what we think it
will, that'll be enough for a warrant on the Cade boys and maybe Floyd.
Then we'll see if Floyd will rat out Lester Weames."

"That'll be something to see, Willie Murdoch issuing a warrant to arrest the Cades and Floyd. Maybe if they signed their names in blood on the bathroom mirror."

"Well, we'll just have to see," said Karp, and then, with a meaningful look: "I always like to give everyone a chance to do the right thing."

"Hi. It's me."

"Well, it's about time," said Marlene. "Where are you?"

"Back at the farm."

"You were supposed to keep in touch. We haven't spoken since my miraculous escape from the killer mosquitoes. What is it, a whole week?"

"Six days. Sorry. We've been running around a lot, and by the time I thought about it, it was too late. I actually did call a couple of times, but you weren't in."

"I'm not in now. We've moved, or *I've* moved. The state stashed us in a corporate lodge. It's pretty nice if you're really into intense boredom. On the upside, my client is sprung."

"That's great! They found the real bad guys?" Lucy's excitement as she said this was rather greater than what could be explained by an abstract passion for justice.

"Well, we have a good idea of who they are, but there seem to be difficulties with the judge. How was your trip? The boys behaved?"

They were angels, it seemed. Lucy spun out the story of her trip, studded with amusing anecdotes. The boys had risen to the occasion of contact with their sister's peers, older but not really grown-ups, with surprising charm. They had done Boston with a minimum of whining. GC liked the Fine Arts; Zak had loved Bunker Hill. Both had loved the Museum of Science and the Aquarium. It was just the kind of conversation with her daughter that Marlene liked, a cheery tale of normal children behaving normally to the world's eye. Marlene did not much care what the world thought of her, but she wished very much to be reassured that she had not screwed up her kids too badly. Lucy had learned to provide such assurances whenever they were remotely possible, as now. It *had* been a nice trip.

"So I guess you'll be coming home soon," said Lucy.

"I don't know. Plans are a little vague just now. Your father seems to regard this as an opportunity for a second honeymoon."

"That's nice."

"Yes, but when the phrase *second honeymoon* has entered my mind, which I confess it has from time to time, I usually envisioned the Côte d'Azur or Tuscany, not McCullensburg, West Vee Ay. Also, strangely enough, he seems to want me involved in the case. We had a little council of war the other day to review the forensic results, and Stan Hawes, the state's attorney here, objected strenuously to my presence. I'm not one of his favorite people. Your father took him aside and said that we needed all the brain power we could get on this and that I was the second-smartest person he knew, and now that the Welch kid is history, I was clear to stay."

"That must have made you feel good."

"I guess. Second-smartest isn't bad."

"Who's the first?" asked Lucy.

"That's what Hawes said, and Butch said, 'We'll get *him,* too.' He was talking about V.T."

One St. Andrew's Plaza is where the U.S. attorney for the Southern District of New York is quartered, just a block or so south on Centre Street from the building where Karp had spent most of his working life. It was still steaming in the City when Karp entered the cool of the lobby. He had thought it was hot in West Virginia, but a few weeks in the mountains had sufficed to make the nearly solid air of the City's streets a shock to his system. The gold lettering on the door said Criminal Division, Asset Forfeiture and Money Laundering Section, New York Branch. Karp went in and told the secretary that he had an appointment with her branch chief, Mr. Newbury.

"Nice office, V.T.," said Karp as he shook hands. It was not a particularly nice office, for a federal bureaucrat of some standing, but small and overfull of GI furniture, and with one narrow window. There was, however, a set of original Daumier prints on the wall, and a large framed poster showing the final scene in *Little Caesar,* Edward G. Robinson dying in the gutter, with the caption being the film's famous last words, "Is this the end of Rico?"

"My palatial office, as my staff calls it," said the other, waving Karp to a seat. "The problem is I am housed in the U.S. Attorney's Office but not of it, therefore of low pecking order when it comes to goodies. I report directly to the criminal division in D.C."

"And you're here because of . . . ?"

"It's where they keep all the money," said Newbury in a confidential voice. He was a small, elegant man, handsome in a peculiar old-fashioned, old-money way, like a model in a 1920s cigarette ad. He was from a famous New York family of hoary antecedence, with its wealth so extensive and encrusted with verdigris that it was simply no longer a consideration. He had started in the DA's office at about the same time as Karp, an unlikely enough event for one of that pedigree, and with even greater unlikelihood he had become Butch Karp's best friend. Karp had not seen him for some time, but it was not entirely friendship that had brought him here. V.T. Newbury was one of the nation's premier experts on dirty money.

After some chatter about personal things, Karp brought up his current occupation, laying out the case itself and the peculiar sociopolitical matrix in which it was embedded.

"So we have enough to arrest and probably convict at least three of the perps, Earl and Wayne Cade, they're cousins, and Bo Cade, Earl's brother. Floyd was more careful, but I don't think it'll be much trouble getting the Cade boys to roll on him. The problem is the judge, a guy named Murdoch. Completely in the tank to the people who apparently own the town and who, indirectly or not, set up the hit on the victims. The state cop I'm working with, Wade Hendricks, thinks that as soon as we ask for a warrant and show our cards, this turd is going to warn them off and make a lot of trouble with the warrants, and in general screw up any chance that we'll be able to get these guys. So, why I thought of you is, I need another judge."

Newbury mimed looking in drawers and under the drift of papers on his desk. "Gosh, we had a bunch of judges stashed here the other day, but they must all be out at the fumigator's."

"What I mean is, the guy takes home eighty-two five per year. He paid cash for a sixty-grand car, and since he got into robes, he's bought hundreds of acres of property plus a twenty-room house. How are they getting him the money?"

Newbury wore an incredulous look. "You want me to initiate a prosecution against a county judge for taking bribes?"

"No, of course not. I just want the goods on him. I want enough documentation to knock him out of the box. Look, these guys are crude. They've been screwing this county so long that they've almost forgotten it's illegal. It won't be multiple anonymous transactions via Nauru and Liechtenstein. It might even be actual big cash deposits, naked. All I need are bank records, or sources of funds if they used noncash transfers."

"Why not go to the state on this?"

"Too long to get them moving, too political. I don't know who we can trust. The governor agrees."

Newbury nodded. "I see. And our legal basis would be . . . ?"

"Our long friendship. Come on, V.T., think up a plausible entry. You're a fed, aren't you?"

"Well, yes, your federal government, where the Fourth Amendment is just a slogan. Still . . ." Newbury looked off to the side, seemingly studying the poster of the dying Hollywood gangster. Karp waited confidently as his friend's remarkable brain ticked away.

"Robbens County," Newbury said after a minute of this. "Where have I heard that name recently?"

"The murders maybe? There was some coverage . . ."

"No, murder is of little interest to us here in the white-collar world. Whacking is so blue-collar. Of course, now that the Russians and the Viets are getting involved, this may change, but . . . no, I'm positive it was more recently, the other day, I think. Some report . . ."

He flicked through a set of vertical files and pulled out a slim sheaf of papers, scanned them briefly. "Yeah, here it is. This is about the methamphetamine production and distribution system in the Northeast, and it looks like your Robbens County produces a good deal of crank. Do you think that might be the source of some of Judge Murdoch's extra disposable income? Say yes."

"Yes," said Karp.

"Well, then on the basis of a knowledgeable and anonymous informant, I feel justified in adding Judge Murdoch as a subject of the investigation we're currently running on meth-gang money laundering."

"And about time, too. How long before you know something?"

"If they're as dumb as you say? A day or two."

"That fast?"

V.T. gestured to the *Little Caesar* poster. "It's part of the wonder of RICO. The Racketeer Influenced and Corrupt Organization Act is the neatest thing to come along since they closed down the Star Chamber. We practically have general warrants to fish and fish around anyone named until we find something. Your judge is a gimme if he ever used the banking system. We could make toast out of Learned Hand."

Karp walked north through Foley Square, keeping as much as possible in the shade of the tall buildings. He passed 100 Centre Street, easily resisting the impulse to drop in and see what was going on. He passed the Tombs and spared a thought for what it must be like to be imprisoned without air-conditioning, without even a fan, in this oppressive heat. Sympathy, but even more bafflement. Despite all the years he had spent in criminal justice, Karp had never developed a workable psychology of crime. Okay, you had your lunatics, but most of these slobs were rational actors. They thought risking *that* horror was actually worth some marginal gain, so they broke into buildings, stole cars, passed bad checks, stuck guns in ribs. Many of his colleagues, Karp knew, thought that the criminals didn't mind jail and prison, that it was a rite of passage for lower-class youth of a certain stripe: no big, as they said. Karp didn't believe that. He believed that criminals were able to suppress in their minds the inevitability of punishment, as we all suppress the *other* inevitability, quite successfully, for most of our lives. For jail *was* inevitable. Virtually no one did just one crime. Crime *inevitably* became habitual, and sooner or later Leviathan would notice and chomp! Into the stinking, sweating cages. Helped along by cops and such as Karp.

He crossed through Chinatown. Everyone, it seemed, was out on the street, except those in the sweatshops, literally sweating today no doubt, just like the jailbirds, although these had committed no crime except being born poor in Asia. He passed vent fans that blew out air only a little hotter than that filling the narrow streets. Did South Asians suffer as much from the heat or was that racism? He passed little groups of men in T-shirts or wife-beater undershirts, with rags knotted around their heads, all smoking. The breath from the doorways was scented with boiling rice, anise, venerable greases. Crosby Street was less crowded. Here it was almost entirely industrial, except for his building, which had been converted to residential lofts. There was also one sad Chinese brothel and gambling den, his neighbor.

The loft was breathless as a tomb, oven warm. Quickly he gathered clothing, filled two large suitcases, called a cab. He stripped, took a brief shower, dressed again in fresh clothes. He had the cab take him to Penn Station, where he caught the Metroliner to D.C. He fell asleep somewhere in New Jersey and slept until Baltimore. From Union Station, he cabbed out to National Airport, to the general aviation terminal. The West Virginia King Air waited on the apron. Inside was Governor Orne and a party of state bureaucrats and legislators. Karp took a seat in the rear of the plane, attracting some inquiring looks but no conversation.

Shortly after takeoff, the governor came aft and sat down next to him.

"How'd it go with your pal?"

"Fine," Karp said. "The fix is in. Have you got a replacement in mind? I mean, assuming Murdoch agrees to go quietly."

"Oh, he'll go. He may whine a little, but he'll resign. Bill Murdoch doesn't want to go anywhere near prison, and he knows I'll stick him in Mt. Olive, and not in any of the country clubs we got now. Cheryl tells me you got suspects."

"We do." Karp laid out briefly who they were and the case against them.

"Good. I want Floyd, though, and I want Weames. I don't want to leave this with a bunch of pathetic hillbillies taking the fall."

"We're in agreement then."

"I thought we would be. As far as a replacement, I have a man I think will do fine. He's retired from the state supreme court, name of Bledsoe."

"Retired?"

"Well, he's old but he can run me into the ground. The thing about him is he don't scare. Speaking of which, I hear you might run into some trouble actually arresting these fellas."

"Wade's been making noises like that. He seems to want to avoid a Waco situation."

"So do I. I don't have the manpower or the budget for a siege. If it comes to that, we'll have to bring the feds in, and avoiding that was the whole point of this exercise. I realize Hendricks is in charge of the police work, but I'm looking for you to provide the subtle angles. Wade sometimes lacks subtlety, and he's got no sense of resources. He's a get-the-job-done kind of fella. Hell, that's one of the reasons I came to Washington this trip. I think our LEAA grant's going to be cut, and God knows where I'll find the money to keep your operation going. So speed . . . you know? If you can manage it, I sure would appreciate getting this behind us as soon as possible."

"We could just grab them and hang them."

The governor looked startled, then laughed. "Bite your tongue, son. We don't have a death penalty in this state. We can't afford one, tell the truth. I'm counting on you for—what did we used to call it?—all deliberate speed."

The FedEx package from V.T. took a week to arrive, during which time Karp had essentially nothing to do: deliberate speed indeed. Marlene went to New York for a meeting of her foundation board and returned to find Karp in a lounger by the pool at the lodge, picking through papers.

"Is that it?"

"Yeah, Judge Murdoch's ticket to retirement. How was your trip?"

"Sure are a lot of people in New York, and those tall buildings. When are you going to use that?"

"Now."

"Will you change out of your bathing suit?"

"Yes, this is a pinstripe occasion. I've always wanted to fire a judge."

13

THE PRESS LOVED IT. WEST VIRGINIA DOES NOT ORDINARILY GENERATE A lot of news aside from car wrecks, so that the local TV stations and newspapers seized upon the doings in naughty Robbens County like the castaway upon his coconut. The results of this interest shone from the screen in the living room of the Karps' cabin at Four Oaks, the evening after Judge William Murdoch announced his retirement for reasons of health. The team—Hendricks, Hawes, Cheryl Oggert—had gathered to watch with Karp and Marlene.

"Oh, we have a logo!" Oggert exclaimed. "The great PR nightmare. I never had a logo before."

"Mazel tov!" said Karp, and smiled at her. The logo, floating above the sculpted hair of the anchorpersons at WOWK (Huntington-Charleston), consisted of three red skulls and crossbones, superimposed over a stylized dragline, under the caption (with the sort of gore-dripping letters associated with B horror movies) "Blood on the Coal." The coverage started with a look at a crime-scene photo, the blood-stained bed in the Heeneys' bedroom, ten seconds of the funeral, with inset photographs of the three victims, a shot of Moses Welch being arrested, then one of him being released. A shot of Hawes eating crow and announcing the expectation of new arrests, some excited blather from the anchor, then stock footage of Murdoch as a state senator, with a coda showing him with wife and kids, giving ten seconds of resignation speech. He had health problems and wanted to spend more time with his family. Knowing comments from the anchors, suggesting otherwise.

After that, a round of applause in the room, as their own Cheryl faced the press on-screen, announcing the appointment of Justice Honus Ray Bledsoe, late of the state supreme court, to fill Judge Murdoch's shoes until a new election could be arranged. A still photo of that jurist appeared over the anchor's right shoulder.

"What a face!" crowed Marlene. "He looks like an engraving on a Confederate twenty."

There was indeed something stern and nineteenth century about the man, the bristling eyebrows, the grim, lipless slash of the mouth, the odd peaks that decorated the spare, bony face. Then the image was gone, replaced by an inserted talking head, a political reporter standing in front of the state capitol. What does Charleston make of this, Barbara? Barbara allowed as how Charleston was all agog. Murdoch was not just a county judge, it seemed; he'd served three terms in the senate and had plenty of powerful allies. He was known as a good friend of big coal. Rumors of corruption? No plans for any prosecution? Not now, according to sources. Connection with the triple murder and the union troubles in Robbens? Too early to say, Jim. Jim gave us all a sincere smile, and the scene dissolved to a car crash involving a truck and a family car and the miraculous escape of a baby thrown from the latter. But first this.

Karp muted the set as the commercial came on. He looked at Hawes. "You know this Bledsoe guy, Stan?"

"Only by rep. Vinegary but fair is what I hear. He's from around here originally."

"Everyone's from around here originally," said Karp. "I'm surprised it doesn't have the population of Brooklyn. Meanwhile, I think you all did real good, defined as keeping my name out of the news."

"Don't think they didn't ask," said Oggert. "The print guys, especially. The story is you're a technical consultant to Stan here. The *Charleston Gazette* is doing a feature on the crime-fighting Karps. I told them no interviews."

"You told them right," said Karp. "Wade, can we pick up these guys anytime we want?"

Hendricks waited his usual couple of beats before answering, his face knotting around the mouth, pursing, unpursing, lower-lip chewing, a half frown, cheeks sucking in, then releasing. "Well, I have some fellas generally keeping an eye out for them, but I don't have the resources for a twenty-four-seven tail on all four of the suspects. Floyd is no problem. He's in the union offices every day and he lives right outside of town. The Cade boys are another story. First of all, they can't hardly be followed up onto that mountain. Burnt Peak I mean. Once they're up there, there's a million ways they can get off it, and there's no traffic and no concealment for a following car. Unless you want them to know?"

Hendricks saw Karp make a negative gesture and went on, "If we can pick them up in town, that'd be good. If we have to go up the mountain . . ." He made a shaking gesture with his hand, stuck out his lip consideringly, shrugged.

"You think they'd resist?"

"They might. Ben Cade swore the last time that he wouldn't let the law touch him or his again. He don't believe in the state of West Virginia much."

Hawes said, "I'm a little tired of hearing that. What's wrong with going up and getting them? You've got enough cops."

Karp thought, wrong move, Stan, but said nothing.

Hendricks gave Hawes a considering look, not hostile, but not interested, either. He did the business with his face again; those muscles seemed to be linked to his thought centers. "Have you ever been up there on Burnt Peak where those Cades live?"

Hawes indicated he had not.

"Burnt Peak," said Hendricks reflectively. "I been there. You come up off the county road onto a dirt switchback that climbs up the face of the mountain through big outcrops of greasy shale. That whole mountain is pretty well coaled out. What they live in is the remains of the old coal patch, plus they got some newer double-wide trailers. They had to take 'em apart to get them up there. Any one of them switchbacks, three men with automatic rifles and dynamite could hold up an army. Well, maybe not a real army, but let's say the whole of the West Virginia State Police. I guess there's eighty or so living up there, a little more'n half of them men, all Cades. Got a nice spring and a big diesel generator. They never took the public power when it came in 'round the Depression. Old Devil Rance said he wouldn't have it, and he didn't need it, 'cause he had all the old plant from the Canker Run coal mine.

No phones either. Anyway, the compound, or village I guess you could call it, is built on a big shelf that trails off into a bunch of hollers all full of laurel. They got some fields they cleared, but nothing much, mostly vegetables and some cows and hogs. Ben likes to have animals around, is what I hear. It makes it more Old Testament for him, flocks and herds. It would take a month to climb up through those hollers, if no one was shooting at you, that is, which I guess they would be, if they didn't want you up there. Which generally they don't. I won't even mention the dogs, big packs of vicious dogs they keep, let 'em run wild in the woods. Over on the back, that's the northwest side of the mountain, you got the leavings of the first strip mine in the county. That whole section is chewed away. It looks like a stairway, with each step maybe four hundred feet high, and a lake at the bottom. You could get up there if you were mountaineers."

"I thought you were all Mountaineers," said Marlene.

Hendricks did a grin 'n' head bob to acknowledge the joke. "No, I mean those technical rock climbers. Rangers."

"You're trying to tell us it'd be rough, I mean, dragging them out," said Karp.

"Rough, yeah, for a full-scale military operation prepared to take major casualties. Which we're not prepared to do right now, even if we had the resources. Speaking of military, the Cades ain't poor. They had that coal, and they had their rackets, moonshining and now marijuana and meth labs . . ."

"How do they get the product out? Car?"

"Well, no, they know better than to try that, because we'd stop them just on general principles. What they do, we think, is pack it out to a county road feeding into Highway 712 around Ponowon and their contacts pick it up there. There's a grocery store outside Ponowon where they get messages and use the phone. The drug boys got a tap on it, but the Cades are pretty careful about what they say. There's trails down that mountain, but they're all trip-wired and booby-trapped. People around here tell their kids to stay off Burnt Peak, and they do. Occasionally someone goes up there and don't come back." Hendricks looked at Marlene. "Marlene here'll tell you that ain't hard in these parts, even if no one means you any harm. Anyway, about their money. Ben Cade is sort of a famous miser. He's supposed to have a lot of gold, so he'll be sitting pretty when the country falls apart, which he expects it to. But a lot of the time they trade their dope for weapons. They're well armed, maybe they even have heavy machine guns and rocket launchers." Hendricks looked at Hawes again. "So that's the answer to your question. I heard that the ATF was planning a raid up there a while back, but after Waco they kind of lost interest. Women and kids and heavy weapons? No one wants to go there again."

"But they come off the mountain, don't they?" Marlene asked. "The guys we're interested in don't seem to have any problem showing themselves."

"Uh-huh, that's so," said Hendricks, "but since you all let Mose Welch loose, they haven't stirred from home. And if you swear out warrants against the three Cade boys, I can guarantee you they will disappear permanently, or at least until this show goes home and things get back to normal. For them, I mean."

"It would be good," said Karp reflectively, "if we could lure them out. And grab them up in town or on the road."

"Lure them?" Marlene asked. "I could do my Streisand medley from the bandstand in the courthouse square. Do you think they'd be attracted by sophisticated song stylings?"

"I think we need to hold that in reserve, dear," said Karp, "if all else fails." He got up and paced. Everyone watched him do it. "Let's see," he mused, "we know these people aren't rocket scientists, so how hard could it be to *schmeikel* them?"

"Pardon?" said Hendricks.

"Oh, *schmeikel?* An old Norman French legal concept meaning to cozen, deceive, gull, shaft, bamboozle, generally in financial matters but by extension in any negotiation. And now that I think of it, you said something interesting there a while ago, Wade. You said the Cade boys holed up after we let Welch go. Because they're afraid we'll go after them next, since they really did it. Also, let's assume they have a leak or leaks letting them know all about the evidence we have pointing their way."

"Leaks? What leaks?" said Hawes.

"Hey, in a small place where everyone is related to everyone else, most of what we're doing will become general knowledge before long.

Believe me, it happens in New York and Washington, too. But this, what we're planning now, absolutely can't get out. It can't go beyond the five people in this room plus one."

"Two can keep a secret if one is dead," observed Marlene darkly.

"Yes, thank you," said Karp, "good advice from the Sicilian delegation."

"Who's the plus one?" asked Cheryl Oggert.

"The new judge. He'll have to be in on it. I'm hoping that with enough hoopla and verisimilitude we can roll them, even if they hear rumors to the contrary. You're going to have to be the key man in the deception, Stan."

"Deception? I don't follow," said Hawes, scowling. "What are you talking about?"

"Oh, sorry. I thought it was obvious. The *schmeikel*. You have to go into the tank, and let them know that you're going in. You have to find another Mose Welch, but a more plausible one, a more shocking one, and Cheryl here has to grind out publicity on it and all of us have to have our pictures taken, grinning like idiots. Once we've seemed to settle on the new suspects, and once Stan has told Floyd that he's aboard, our real scumbags ought to come down from their impregnable mountain stronghold to join in the fun, just like they did when we had Welch."

Everyone was silent for a moment, digesting this. Then Hendricks asked, "Is that legal? Arresting someone like that just to get someone to come out of hiding?"

Karp forbore to roll his eyes. "No, Wade, we're not *really* arresting anyone. The persons involved will of course be volunteers. Legally, the whole thing will be a nullity. It's analogous to those scam contests the cops in New York and the feds use to pull in fugitives. The cops send an official-looking letter to the fugitive's last known address—congratulations, you've won the lottery, come to such and such an address and pick up your check. Or it's season tickets to the Yankees. The mopes show up and get nabbed."

"They actually fall for this?" asked Oggert incredulously.

"Every time. And these are streetwise hoods we're talking here, not . . ." Karp searched for a nice way to put it.

"Dumb hillbillies?" suggested Oggert.

"Thank you," said Karp with a grin, and to the group: "Well, what do you think?"

"It might could work," said Hendricks. "Who were you thinking of? I mean for the phony killers."

"Ideally, like I said, it should be someone both plausible and scandalous, so that the fake carries some weight. We want big publicity on this, and we want the Cades to really believe that they dodged the bullet again, that Stan here is bought and wired. I also want them to think it's amusing. I want them to *want* to come to town and sit around in bars and chat about ain't it awful how—"

Marlene interrupted, "I know who you're thinking of and I think it's disgusting. How *could* you?"

"It's right, Marlene. You know it's the only way to go."

"It still stinks on ice."

As the three others observed this exchange, confusion grew on their faces. Hawes said, "Would you mind telling us what you're going on about?"

"Sorry," said Karp. "My wife is objecting to my plan, which she figured out because she knows my devious ways, as I know hers."

Marlene said, "He wants to use the boys. The Heeney boys."

Karp saw the ripple of revulsion replace the confused looks. He ignored it. "If they'll agree," he said. "And if the judge will go for it."

Judge Honus Ray Bledsoe had not enjoyed retirement much, although he had a generous pension, a comfortable house with a garden in which he grew roses. The roses won prizes; they dared not do otherwise. He read widely; he gave an occasional interview; he recommended bright local kids to law schools; and he was bored. He had left the high court bench at age seventy-eight as he had promised himself he would. By no means a fearful man, he admitted to himself that he feared the loss of mental powers he had seen among many of his older colleagues. Appointed judges may in most places serve for life, and it is a sad peculiarity of their status that usually no one in their milieu is comfortable with telling them they have become senile, while many may benefit from manipulating them in their infirmity. The problem, Bledsoe thought, was that the victim of advanced age was the last person to know he was losing his sharps, and in his case no one was around anymore he could trust to tell him. His wife would have told him, but she was dead. His kids all lived away, and besides, they thought he was immortal, which he knew he was not, but was eighty-three all the same. So when Orne had called him about cleaning up Robbens, he had agreed to do a job he had thought about on and off for four decades, provisional to an interview, during which they had discussed points of law (Orne had been his clerk) and the events of the day. At the end Bledsoe had asked Orne in his characteristically blunt manner whether the governor thought he still had all his marbles, and Orne had said that in his opinion the judge had more marbles than anyone else in the state of West Virginia.

Armed with this opinion, he had driven himself, in his 1985 Cadillac Seville, from his place in White Sulphur Springs to Windy Grove in Robbens County, where he shacked up (as he said) with Marva, his baby sister, who was living in the ancestral home. After a day of rest to recover himself (on Marva's insistence, actually, since he felt fine), he had reported to the Robbens County Courthouse, where he terrified the staff, who had become used to Bill Murdoch's slack ways. Judge Bledsoe disliked slackness, nor was he overly fond of fancy lawyers, especially fancy lawyers from New York, especially very large fancy lawyers from New York. Judge Bledsoe was, on the outside at least, a rather small man.

Karp thought he looked, close up, like a rooster. The TV photo had been taken some years ago, it seemed. He had a cowlick, for one thing, which stuck up like a silvery crest, and wattles that got red when he was annoyed, which Karp thought might be most of the time. Maybe it had been a mistake to let Hawes do most of the talking. They were in Bledsoe's chambers. Bledsoe had recorded his dissatisfaction with the conduct of the investigation so far (although Karp thought that was really none of his business) and with the arrest and detention of Moses Welch. His wattles had reddened at the mention of bribes, and reddened more when Karp had explained (in approximate terms) just how Murdoch had been dispatched. When they told him about the plan to apprehend the Cades, the red moved up his jaw and blossomed on his cheekbones. Karp imagined that if it reached his crown, it would detonate, like a thermometer in a cartoon.

"You want this court to participate in a public fraud?" Bledsoe asked, his voice quiet but deadly.

Hawes hemmed; Karp interjected, "Your involvement will be minimal, Judge. You have no reason to speak to the media and can refuse to comment if asked. Obviously, you're one of the few people who need to be apprised of the plan. Also you'd be issuing the warrant. We'd want to have Sheriff Swett do the arrest."

"Why?"

"Because Swett will leak it to the Cades as genuine."

"If Swett is corrupt as you claim, then get rid of him."

"Good idea, but after the Cades are in custody."

"So your plan is to fight corruption by chicanery."

Karp took a deep breath and kept his face neutral. "Yes. Because given the time frame the governor has set, there are only two other alternatives. One is to let them get away with it. The other is to go up onto Burnt Peak and drag them out of there. I assume being a local man you know what that would be like."

"I'm not afraid of Ben Cade."

"I'm glad of that, sir. I am. I have it on expert advice that doing the dragging would cause the biggest bloodbath since the Robbens County War, even assuming we could get official permission for an assault. I'm as big a fan of legal niceties as you are, Judge, but I wouldn't want that blood on my hands, if there was any alternative. And I think we have one here."

Karp and Bledsoe played the staring game for a while, the judge's mouth line bending down into a hair-thin parabola.

"This how they do things in New York, Mr. Karp?"

"When necessary, sir."

"All right. I want all this documented and signed by you two and anyone else with cognizance of it. Who does what when and where and to whom. That includes the putative suspects. I assume they're on board?"

"More or less."

"What does that mean?"

"We're working on the details."

The judge grunted. "Well, make sure they know exactly what they're getting into."

"Yes, Judge," said Karp. "And, Judge? That would be a document you'd want to take some care of."

Bledsoe shot him a fierce look, then tapped his breast pocket, slowly, thrice. "It'll sit right here, Mr. Karp. I think that'll be all for now."

Bledsoe turned pointedly to some papers on his desk. Karp got up immediately and left, and after a moment's hesitation, so did Hawes.

Out in the hallway, Karp said, "What's the matter, Stan? You look like you've never been contemptuously kicked out of a judge's chambers before."

"Never like that. I don't think he likes you much."

"No, he made that very clear. Which is just another reason for me to take a low profile and you to take a high one. On the other hand, I have the impression that Judge Bledsoe is the kind of judge who, if he doesn't like a lawyer, makes an extra effort to be scrupulously fair, as opposed to the kind who in similar circumstances will try to fuck you up. Let's get out of here. I want to talk in the open air."

They found a bench in the courthouse square, in the shade of a huge oak. Karp said, "I meant it about you being the center of this thing. You have to convince Floyd that you're going to do everything you can to pin this on anybody but the people who did it. Besides that, you're going to have to play a corrupt bastard in front of a TV audience, the town, all your friends, and your family. And you can't tell anyone about it until we have those people in custody. You understand that? Not your wife, not your parents."

"And you're wondering if I can do it."

"Yeah, a little. I'm a control freak and I'm giving up control. It makes me jumpy. I guess I want to make sure you understand how miserable you're going to be. And also this: undercover work, which is what this is, is the worst work in the world. I've seen it a million times in the cops. A decent guy pretends to be a scumbag all day, pretty soon he finds it hard to go back to being a nonscumbag. Every undercover detective I know has been divorced at least once." Karp allowed a moment to let this sink in. "But if we're lucky, it won't last long."

"I can do this," said Hawes. "I'm not worried about that. I'm not worried about a failure. What I'm worried about is, even if this works, and we get them, and we can convict them, and Floyd, and the rest, and you're back in New York City, I'll still be here. I'll still be here with my family. And the Cades will still be up on that mountain, mad as hell, and looking for someone to hurt."

Karp nodded. He didn't have a good answer to that.

✻   ✻   ✻

This conversation stuck irritatingly in Karp's mind and nagged at him during the even more unpleasant interview he and Marlene had that evening with Emmett and Dan Heeney, in the living room of their home.

"You must be out of your mind if you think we're going to do that," declared Emmett at the conclusion of Karp's pitch for the idea. "Get arrested for killing our family?"

"It's not a real arrest," said Karp patiently. "It's a scam. I explained that the Cades are holed up—"

"I heard you. That's not our business. Hell, maybe now *is* the time to blast those Cades out of there. Let 'em drop napalm on 'em, I don't give a rat's."

"Well, but that's not going to happen, Emmett. The only way, the only practical and realistic way to bring those men to where we can get at them is to show them that they have nothing to fear, that the law has made a big mistake again."

"Okay, but why us?" said Emmett sulkily.

"It's the most convincing scenario. It'll get the kind of publicity they won't be able to ignore. And, frankly, it's so outrageous that they won't believe it's a scam. Also, you have an interest in it. I'd have thought you'd be glad to do it."

"Well, you thought wrong." Emmett crossed his arms.

Marlene said, "Emmett, I know it's an awful thing to ask you to do, and I was truly disgusted when Butch brought it up. But he's right when you consider the alternatives. What you need to do is think about what your dad would've wanted you to do. What would Red Heeney have done?"

Emmett made no response to this. A silence ensued. Then Dan said, "He's worried about Kathy."

"I am not!" snapped Emmett.

"Yeah, you are. You're thinking of what she'll be thinking while everyone else thinks you killed our family. And you're thinking about what her parents will say, what the town will say."

"Oh, that's such horseshit! You always think you know what I'm thinking."

"I do. And what am I thinking, huh?"

Emmett looked startled. "Well, too bad, you can't, you weren't even here when it happened."

"No, but I could've hired it done," said Dan. He said to Karp, "That's a plausible scenario, isn't it? Everyone knew my dad and I didn't get along. So we say I hired a drifter to do it. I didn't want him to kill my mom and Lizzie, but he did, and then I confessed just now out of remorse. You're still looking for the drifter. Would that work?"

Karp's glance flicked briefly between the two brothers. "Yeah, that would work fine, if that's how you want to do it. We could put out fictitious wanted posters of the make-believe drifter."

"Ah, that's so dumb," said Emmett. "How in hell would someone like him find a damn contract killer? Not one person in this whole town would believe it. The Cades would laugh themselves sick."

Dan said, "Well, you don't know dick about it, do you? Butch is the expert. He thinks it'll work."

"You ain't doing it," said Emmett with finality. "If anybody does it, it'll be me."

"What do you think," asked Karp somewhat later as a trooper in an unmarked police car drove them home, "was that a little brotherly manipulation we saw there?"

"Who, Dan? I don't think so. He really would've done it because he's genuinely noble. He's Rose Heeney's kid down to the bone. Plus, he doesn't give a shit what anyone in this town thinks about him. Emmett does. He'll do it, mainly to stop Dan from doing it. But ten to one, he'll tell his girl."

"No bet," said Karp, and then dejectedly, "This is not going to work, is it?"

"It might," Marlene said, but without enthusiasm. "But I never want to hear another lecture from you on the ends not justifying the means. Meanwhile, it'll depend on how fast the McCullensburg grapevine is against how stupid the Cades are. You have a shot. Even if it does work, however, you're not going to love it, are you?"

"No. The idea that once we have probable cause for an arrest, we can't in fact arrest an individual without the potential for a huge disaster . . . it makes me break out in hives. I hate it. And I hate what it makes us do. Like this crap with the Heeneys."

She saw how upset he was, and instinctively she leaned closer to him, ran her arm through his, clutched his hand. "Yes, you're a law-and-order fellow, with law first."

"What's wrong with that?"

"Nothing. But the concept clearly hasn't penetrated to every corner of the world, including here. We can but hope things improve. You know, you're going to laugh, but ever since I got here, I've been having a sort of déjà vu, a sense that I've been in this kind of place before. You recall I mentioned that earlier? And I just tonight figured out where it was. It was something you said when we were planning this. The mountains, the lawlessness, the families, the vendettas . . ."

"Where was it?"

"Sicily. No wonder I felt right at home."

"Sicily, huh? Gosh, Marlene, you really know how to cheer somebody up."

"Thank you. It just occurred to me also that the miners are not going to take the arrest of Emmett very well. For the dissident faction, he's sort of the crown prince, the son of the martyr."

"What are they going to do about it?"

"No, you're still thinking New York. There, when people protest, it's a bunch of liberals with placards. In extreme cases, a riot, stores get trashed, and everyone goes 'Oy vay!' Here they use dynamite and everyone's armed to the teeth. But I have an idea."

He waited. "Are you going to tell me what it is?"

"No. You'll know if it works, though. I don't want to jeopardize my reputation for perfection."

Giancarlo Karp awoke before dawn to find his sister in the bedroom he shared with his brother. She was stuffing clothes into a couple of duffels.

"What are you doing?" he asked.

"Packing some stuff for you guys. We're going on another road trip."

"Where to?"

"West Virginia. Listen, as long as you're up, get some clothes on and go down to the kitchen and make a bunch of sandwiches. I want to leave right away and not stop. And fill the red cooler with ice."

Zak sat up in bed. "We're going away again?"

"Yeah," said Giancarlo. "We're going to West Virginia to see Mom and Dad."

"Among others," said Lucy.

The murder of the Heeneys had attracted some modest national attention, but the news that the family had been killed by one of the two sons set off a media tornado. On a slow summer newsday it had led at six on all three major networks, and the *Times* ran it front page above the fold, column left. Lucy had seen it the previous evening on the eleven-o'clock and had immediately called Dan Heeney fifteen times over three hours, receiving a busy signal each time. Only then had she thought to call her parents. After some arguing with the night manager, she had been put through and engaged her sleepy father in an unsatisfactory conversation, consisting largely of (from him) the unhelpful statement that he couldn't talk about it. She had then slept badly for a few hours and awakened with the resolve to drive immediately to McCullensburg.

She went out to the barn, fed and watered the dogs out of guilt, and let Magog out of her pen. Billy Ireland was in bed when she barged into his room and then barged out again when she saw Marjorie Rolfe was in it, too.

"Sorry," Lucy said. "Look, I have to leave. I'm taking the boys to see my folks. Will you be okay?"

"Well, yeah, for a while," Ireland said. "Are the bills paid?"

"Yes. Also, I want to take Magog. The pups don't need her anymore and I think she'd appreciate the break."

"Hell, she's your dog," said Ireland, "I just work here. Have a nice trip."

They passed Alex Russell as they headed out the drive. "See ya later, agitator!" Giancarlo yelled as they sped by.

The old-style Toyota Land Cruiser was not built for speed, but she kept it at a steady seventy-five from Jersey west through Pennsylvania and down into Charleston, stopping only once for gas, and twice, fuming, in rest stops, so that the boys could empty their absurdly small bladders.

"Why are you angry?" Giancarlo asked her after the second of these.

"I'm not angry."

"Well, you're driving like a maniac, you don't talk, and you're bossing us around like we did something wrong. That's what Mom does when she's angry."

"I'm sorry, guys. I'm upset, not angry at you."

"What about?"

"You remember Emmett Heeney from the beach? Lizzie's brother?"

"Is he the one you like?" asked Zak.

"No. That's Dan," she said automatically. "No, that's not . . . what I mean is, the cops down there are saying that Emmett was the one who killed the Heeneys and Lizzie. It was on the news, and I can't reach Dan for some reason, and Dad won't tell me what's going on. That's why we're going down there."

"How could he murder his parents?" Giancarlo asked. "Was he crazy?"

"I don't think he murdered them at all," said Lucy firmly. "I think it's a horrible mistake."

"Is Dad going to find the real ones?" asked Zak.

"I hope so."

From the backseat, Giancarlo said, "He will. Don't worry, everything will be fine."

An hour later they were descending the steep grade on Route 130 south that the map said led into McCullensburg when they saw red lights flashing ahead and traffic stalled. They stopped behind a tractor-trailer and waited. After ten minutes, Lucy got out and walked along the shoulder. The trucker was standing on his front bumper, looking down the line of vehicles.

"What's the problem?" Lucy asked. "An accident?"

"Nah, some trouble down in the town. I was just talking with some drivers on the CB. The damn coal miners are having some kind of damn riot in town. They drove some coal haulers into the junction of 130 and 119 and parked them there and they blocked the railroad, too. Traffic's backed up for miles in all four directions."

"What are they rioting about?"

"Oh, the cops arrested some union fella for killing his folks, and his buddies think it's a frame-up. What it is, is a damn pain in the butt. I should've been in Williamson half an hour ago."

"Is there any way to get to 119 east of town without going through the junction?"

"Well, yeah, if you want to go over the top of the mountain. You hang a U-ey right here and drive on back till you get just outside of Logan, hang a right, and follow the signs to Gilbert Corner. Shoot on through there and in four, five miles you hit the highway. I'd do it myself but the bridges won't hold my weight."

She did as the trucker suggested. Twenty minutes later she was in first gear, four-wheel drive, climbing a dirt road. Zak had a road map spread out on his lap, complaining that the road they seemed to be on did not exist and that they were lost. Giancarlo was spinning a tale about them getting permanently lost, wandering through the desolate mountains until they ran out of gas and then having to eat human flesh. Lucy paid attention to neither of her brothers. The news about the riot was good; it meant that substantial numbers of people thought the charges absurd.

"There's the highway, smarty-pants," she said as their wheels rolled onto the blacktop. "Intuitive driving once again triumphs over map-bound patriarchical worrywarts."

"Dumb luck," said Zak. "And I have to pee again."

Several cars, a police cruiser, and a couple of news vans were parked at the turnoff to the Heeney house.

"Sorry, miss," said the trooper. "You can't go through there."

"Why not?"

"Family's having some trouble. We've been asked to protect their privacy. There's a wide place just ahead where you can turn around."

"I know about the trouble. We came all the way from New York."

"And you are . . . ?"

"Lucy Karp. I'm Dan Heeney's, um, fiancée."

The trooper looked the car over, saw the boys, the dog slavering in the window. He said, "Why don't you follow me in."

He got in the cruiser and turned down the drive, Lucy following. She watched him knock on the front door, saw Dan come out and talk to the trooper, saw the smile break out on his face, his vigorous nod. Lucy got out of the Toyota. Dan came running down the steps, threw his arms around her, and planted a kiss on her mouth.

"Darling," he sighed. "I've longed for this moment."

The trooper was observing them from his cruiser. Satisfied, he drove off.

"He's gone," she said. "You can let go of me now."

"What if I don't want to?"

"Oh, stop it! I had to say that or he wouldn't let me in. The road is full of reporters. Will you just tell me *what* is going on?"

The boys and the dog jumped out. Dan, releasing Lucy, made much of them and Magog, after which he said, "We better go in unless you want to be on TV. I think they've got a crew up on the mountain there."

Dan played host, to Lucy's great impatience. He poured drinks, showed them the house, settled the boys in front of his computer with Quake II. When he and Lucy were alone on the living room sofa, he said, "Relax, it's a scam."

"What do you mean, a scam?"

He explained. She listened, her face still, not interrupting. When he had finished, she asked, "This was whose idea? My mother's?"

"I don't know. Your dad was pitching it pretty hard. Why?"

"I don't know. It just sounds like something she would think up. So I seem to be the prize schmuck of the Western Hemisphere. Why didn't he just *tell* me on the phone?"

"I think because they're keeping it really close. The desk clerk at Four Oaks likes to listen in, it's well-known. In fact, your dad made a big point about not discussing the deal on the phone at all." He met her eyes. "You're sorry you came, right?"

"Of course I am!" she cried, and then seeing his face, she said, "No, of course, I didn't mean that. Oh, I don't know. When I heard the news, all I could think about was how awful it must be for both of you, and I dumped what little logical process I have and just tossed the twins into the car and drove. My mother will go crazy. She's the only one allowed spontaneous excesses in the family."

"It was a nice kiss, though," he said. "You have to admit that. Maybe not worth an eight-hundred-and-sixty-mile drive, but . . ."

"Oh, stop it!" Then a grin broke out on her face. "Yes, it was. My feet sweated."

"That's supposed to be an infallible sign." He moved closer on the sofa and dropped an arm around her. "We could try it again. Then it would only be a four-hundred-and-thirty-mile kiss."

She found herself on her feet. "Maybe later. I have to get in touch with my folks before they find out from someone else and go nuts." This was not the real reason, though.

"What's the situation now?" asked Karp. "Is it as bad as it looks on the TV?"

They were in the Karps' cabin at Four Oaks: Karp, Marlene, Hendricks, and Oggert, all of them looking grim and flicking eyes toward the live coverage on the room's television.

"Well, it's a mess," said Hendricks. "The local troop is trying to straighten out the traffic tangle, rerouting and all, but what I'm worried about is the mob down at the courthouse. That's Willie Pogue up on a D8 in front of the courthouse demanding they release Emmett right now or he's going to take the jailhouse down and pull him out."

"Who's Willie Pogue?" Karp looked at the screen. A fiftyish man with a mane of white hair and a florid face was haranguing the crowd through a bullhorn from the nose of an immense yellow earthmover.

"One of Red Heeney's pals. I guess he's the head of the dissident faction now. There's about eight hundred miners out, with wives and kids. Some of them're armed. The sheriff's in full combat mode, and there's a bunch of security guys from the company standing around, also armed. Deputizing mine security is kind of a tradition in Robbens County. That happens, all bets are off."

"Can't you do anything?" asked Marlene.

Hendricks shook his head. "I don't believe I have a horse in this race unless the governor tells me different. The local troopers are pretty much tied up, and I don't have enough men to get between that mob and a bunch of scared cops."

"And we have no idea where the Cades are right now?" asked Karp.

"No. I pulled my cars back so it'd look like we weren't interested in them anymore." He stared briefly at the TV. "We didn't count on this."

"No," said Oggert. "And if this keeps up, someone's going to get hurt, and if that happens, we will get absolutely no support from the governor. He'll repudiate the bunch of us. Maybe it's time to pull the plug."

"Pull the plug?" said Karp.

"Yeah. Release the kid, say we have new evidence that exonerates him. Take a breather and then play it straight against the Cades."

"That gets us back to the siege business, Cheryl. I thought we all agreed that was the worst case."

"Yeah, but that was before this happened. Even if it comes to a siege, at least we'll be the good guys. I'll tell you right now, no one is going to take responsibility for cops or miners killed pursuant to a fraudulent arrest. The lead will be 'Cops Too Chicken to Go after Cades, Four Dead in Phony Arrest Riot.' Uh-uh."

"No. We're hanging tough," said Karp. "And you can tell the governor I said so."

Oggert glared at him and seemed about to say something when Hendricks cleared his throat. "Uh, also, Butch? You ought to know this, too. We had a call from Murchison, the trooper who's watching the Heeney place? Do you know a Lucy Karp?"

Karp felt a hammer descend on his diaphragm. "Yes, she's my daughter. What about her?"

"Well, she showed up at the Heeney place a little while ago, in a car with two little kids and a big dog. She said she was Dan's fiancée, so Murchison let them through. He said they looked like they knew each other pretty good."

"The mom is always the last to know," said Marlene. "Oh, *shit!* That stupid girl!"

"Calm down, Marlene," said Karp. "She was worried, she came, we'll deal with it. Why don't you call the Heeney place and talk to her?"

"Oh, I'll *talk* to her all right," said Marlene, and departed for the suite's bedroom, slamming the door behind her.

"Look, something's happening!" said Oggert.

The others turned their attention to the television. Karp cranked up the volume.

Marlene came out of the bedroom. "I can't get through on the phone. What's going on?"

The screen showed Pogue in the cab of the D8. A plume of black smoke shot from its stack as he revved the engine. The voice of the TV reporter was strained and barely intelligible over the roaring of the giant earthmover. Pogue was heading toward the line of helmeted, flak-jacketed deputies standing behind sawhorses placed around the jail entranceway. The scene rolled and jumped as the cameraman ran along-side the great treads.

"That's a hell of a machine," said Karp.

"Yes, sir, it is," said Hendricks. "It weighs forty tons. It'd go through that jailhouse like a knife through pie." The ten-foot-high blade of the Cat edged ever closer to the sawhorses, moving slowly but inexorably. The deputies had gas masks on now. Their shotguns now pointed at the Cat and the crowd around it. Karp could make Swett out, unmasked, talking into a radio. A sawhorse crashed over. The deputies sighted their weapons. Swett was handed a bullhorn by a deputy and started to talk into it, but the soundman from the TV station was not in position to pick up what he said. Karp and the others could imagine it though. Pogue had his bullhorn, too, and said something back about release Emmett Heeney and we'll talk.

Then the door to the jail opened, and a gray-haired man in a dark suit walked out, carrying a briefcase. He shouldered through the line of deputies, stepped over the toppled sawhorse, and climbed up onto the yellow snout of the D8. The soundman was already poking his furry sausage out on its pole, so they were able to hear: ". . . it, Willie, turn this damn thing off and give me that bullhorn. They *are* letting him go. Now give me that damn thing before someone gets hurt." The engine sound cut off.

"Who the hell's that?" asked Hendricks.

"It's Poole!" cried Marlene.

The camera got its range and zoomed in a little. It was indeed Ernie Poole, who now raised the bullhorn to his mouth and gave a speech. He said who he was, and that he was representing Emmett Heeney. He said that the cops had tried to frame Mose Welch and he had got Mose Welch off free, and now they were trying to frame Emmett, and he would get Emmett off, too. There was no evidence worth looking at against him. He said that he guaranteed that the charges against Emmett would be dropped, unless they wanted to kill him, too, in which case you were at liberty to push the courthouse over. Laughter. But you had to go home now and move this equipment away, too, because what they want is a riot with gunfire, so that they can claim that a stray shot killed Emmett Heeney. Are you going to let them do that? *Noooo!* the crowd moaned. Poole said he'd applied for bail, and that

Judge Bledsoe was inclined to grant it, but he'd said that no one would be released until order was restored, because old Judge Bledsoe did not want anyone to think he was acting out of fear of a mob. Poole said that the judge was an honest man, not like some of the judges we've had around here, and that he would see justice done, and now he was going to go back into the jail and sit with Emmett until they were both released. Vast cheering from the crowd, and in the room grins and applause.

Poole got down from the Cat, and the producer shifted to the on-scene guy, who started to tell everyone what they had just seen. Karp muted the sound. He looked at Marlene. "Way to go," he said softly, so that no one else heard.

14

LUCY DROVE THE LAND CRUISER DOWN THE HEENEYS' LONG DRIVE, smiled and waved at the state trooper, rolled slowly through the gauntlet of newsies, who pointed cameras and microphones at her and yelled questions. Does he think his brother did it? How does he feel? That's what they always asked. How do you *feel* now that your kid's been eaten by the bear, your mother hacked to pieces by a maniac? She thought it was because everyone felt dead inside and thought they could jump-start their own withered hearts by some transfusion of pain from the victims of a catastrophe. Surely *they* felt something. It was a kind of vampirism; maybe that's why tales and movies about vampires were so popular just now.

Past the media encampment she gave it the gas, and once the vans and cars had vanished in the rearview, she called, "You can come out now." The boys were clapping and giggling as Dan climbed out from the rear compartment, where he had been concealed by a beach blanket and Magog the dog. He sat in the rear, next to Giancarlo.

"How far to the border?" Dan asked.

Lucy met his eyes in her mirror. "Not far but the Nazis are everywhere."

Giancarlo said, "You have dog slime in your hair."

Dan touched his head, examined his wet finger, and touched it to the boy's nose, provoking a giggling battle.

Lucy said, "If you two can't behave back there, there's going to be no ice cream."

"He started," whined Dan.

"Are we there yet?" whined Giancarlo.

"Where *are* we going anyway," Zak asked.

"To see Mom and Dad," said Lucy, to a chorus of boos.

"We want to go to Six Flags," said Dan.

"She never takes us anywhere fun," said Giancarlo. "She's terrifically mean, too. She scratches us with her nails."

"Do you *like* her?" asked Zak.

"Yeah," said his brother, "you kissed her on the mouth."

"I did," said Dan, "but it was yucky. I'm never going to do *that* again."

"If you get married, you *have* to," Giancarlo said knowledgeably. "Girls love it."

"Well, if that's so, I'm never getting married," said Dan.

This nonsense continued during the entire drive to Four Oaks, which lay west of McCullensburg. The traffic leading into town was still heavy, although it seemed to be flowing smoothly again. News vans were still in evidence around the courthouse.

Outside of town, the countryside was rolling hills, and more of what Lucy thought of as country. They passed fields with black-and-white cows in them, cud-chewing and stupid in the shade of big trees, and once a roan horse running across a green meadow.

"Pretty area," Lucy remarked. "I didn't expect this."

"South county," Dan said. "The seam gets thin here and it's still mostly agricultural. It's where the richer folks live."

He leaned forward and placed a hand on her shoulder, near her neck. "You're looking for a big sign on the right."

This was nice, she thought, a tiny sliver of normality: driving along a country road, a man with a warm hand on your shoulder, a couple of kids, going to visit Mom and Dad in the country. An exotic treat, like smoking opium would be to regular people. She wished he would keep his hand there, she wished she had the nerve to raise her own hand and cover his.

Which then removed itself and pointed. "There it is."

A certain chaos then ensued: greetings, fond looks, stern looks, arrangements made for sleeping quarters for the new arrivals. Gog came bounding out to sniff Lucy and the boys, and especially Magog, who curled her lip at him. He was twice her size, but the strange politics of dogland made her dominant, except when in heat. Lucy found that Four Oaks had more or less been taken over by the murder investigation, and it was agreed that Dan should stay there until things settled down, and Emmett, too, after he was released on bail. Marlene was cool to Lucy, while doting on the boys, which Lucy did not much mind. She saw the eye play that transpired when Marlene saw Dan and her together, and Lucy could see the wheels spin. Her mother did not like plots, except when she was in charge of them. Beneath the surface jollity the atmosphere was tense at the lodge because, Lucy suspected, of the difficulty of guarding the secret that now lay at the heart of the investigation. Her father greeted her distractedly and soon went off to confer with the cop, Hendricks.

There was a pool with a slide and a couple of diving boards there, and they all went swimming. Lucy discovered the delights of horsing around in the water with a young man, with its many opportunities for little touches on naked or nearly naked skin. Marlene was stretched on a lounger, supposedly reading, with her sunglasses on. Lucy could not therefore tell where her mother's eyes were and so felt them upon her constantly.

"Let's go somewhere else," she said into Dan's ear as they drifted together.

Hendricks came into the room with an expression on his face that Karp assumed was what passed for excited, which meant that Hendricks had for the moment stopped looking like Lincoln contemplating the slavery question.

"They been spotted," he declared.

"Where?"

"Someone called it in from a gas station on 712. That's north of Burnt Peak."

"All three of them?"

"They didn't say. But they were driving that monster truck Earl Cade's got, and there was someone sitting in the bed of it. So figure one in the shotgun and the driver. That's three, and it's likely it's them."

"What're we doing?"

"I've got cars moving to plug the main roads back up there and a couple cruising on 130 north of town. That's the best I can do. I'll move the car I've got at the Heeney place now that the boys're going to stay here, but we're still short. I'd hate to ask a single trooper to take on all three of them. Anyway, it looks like your plan worked all right." A twist of the mouth that might have been a smile appeared on the captain's face.

"Where are we going?" Lucy asked. They had slipped away in the Land Cruiser, Lucy with a pair of shorts over her Speedo suit, Dan in a T-shirt and his cutoffs. Dan was driving north out of town. He drove the clumsy vehicle accurately and at speed, without a belt. No one in this part of the state wore seat belts, and the highway code apparently demanded that the dotted centerline on the blacktop be aligned with the hood ornament, especially on hills. She admired this sort of driving, as she admired the golden curls flapping around his face. The mastiff was curled up asleep in the back.

"First Forge," he said. "It's a kind of park near Ponowon. There's a carousel and rides, and a lake, and a reproduction of a colonial iron-works. I thought you were the kind of girl who would enjoy seeing a guy in a wig bending red-hot bars."

"It's something I've always dreamed of. What I really hope, though, is that they'll have a dim room full of glass cases and wall boards with yellowing labels, and a lot of old, dusty machinery."

"Well, you're gonna get your wish, little lady. I don't think there's a better collection of hand-cut screws and carriage bolts anywhere in West Virginia."

"Be still my heart!"

"Yeah, but really it's nice, in a tacky way. Sincere. Dad used to take us there all the time, and that's where they always held the Labor Day picnic, the great event of Dad's . . . um . . . calendar . . . no, what's that church word?"

"Liturgical year."

"Right, that. My mom would always roll her eyes at me when he wasn't looking. Anytime she could, she'd grab us up and zoom into D.C. for a day of tromping through art museums, and we'd go to a concert in that room at the National Gallery with the fountain, and zoom home again to cook supper."

"Did you like it?"

"We liked the Natural History and the Air and Space all right, not the art so much. Lizzie liked the art." He was silent for a long interval. She watched his face. He is transparent as the air, she thought. You can see what his heart is feeling. Without thinking she moved closer to him and put her hand around his neck. He jumped and shuddered.

"Wow. Shit, I was about to bust out crying there for a minute. What a drag."

"It's not a drag," she said. "It's grief. You're supposed to feel that way."

"You're not going to tell me they're all having fun in heaven and I shouldn't worry?"

"Of course not! 'Blessed are they who mourn, for they shall be comforted.' Even Jesus wept."

That was interesting, she thought, he can pull down a screen over his face, but it takes an effort. He doesn't want to hear any of that stuff. She regretted her outburst.

More silence and then he switched the radio on, found a country station. "You don't mind? It's the onlyiest kand of music we get here in bee-ootiful southwestern West Virginia."

She smiled and shook her head. They drove, they listened. Dolly sang about the coat of many colors my mother made for me. He took her hand. This is not happening, she thought. I am not out on a date with a gorgeous boy who likes me. She rolled the words *date* and *boy* around in her mind like a baby playing with something shiny and new. To test whether it was really happening, she reviewed the modal suffixes of Korean in her head. I want to go: *ka-go shipsumnida;* I must go: *kaya huminida;* I ought to go: *kaya haeya hadda* . . .

"What are you thinking?"

She started and turned toward him. He was smiling. "You were someplace else. What were you thinking?"

She felt herself blushing. "I was reviewing the modal verb modifiers of Korean."

"Really. Are you having a test in Korean tomorrow?"

"No, it's a habit, like picking cuticles."

"Uh-huh. You realize you are an extremely peculiar person. I kind of resent that."

"You do?"

"Yes. I used to be the most peculiar person in Robbens County, and now you butt in. I'll have to think of something really weird."

And more of this kind of silly, delightful talk, until they pulled into the parking lot at First Forge. It was full of families and smelled of fried things and burnt sugars and the stink of burning coal from the actual forge. They watched a fat, red-faced man in a wig make a shovel blade. They walked giggling through the dim room and got glared at by the guardian. They ate fried chicken. Then they took a ride on the Tunnel of Love.

"Gosh, this is a first for me," said Lucy as their little craft, pink and spattered with hearts and crudely figured cupids, was yanked through the heart-shaped entryway.

"Oh, you're just saying that to make me feel good."

"No, really. I didn't think they had them anymore. I figured the sexual revolution had put them all out of business."

"They had a sexual revolution? No one told me."

"I bet you've been on Tunnels of Love with lots of girls."

"Oh, yeah, hundreds. Miles and miles in the dark with 'Moon River' playing on cracked speakers. There's no detail of tunnel of loving I haven't plumbed . . ."

After saying this, he kissed her neck, her ear, drawing her to him, mouth on her mouth. His hand slipped around her shoulder, wiggled under her arm, fingers slid under the stretchy fabric of her suit and settled on her nipple. Time became stretchy, too, as the love pod moved for hours up a minor tributary of the Orinoco.

Suddenly she pulled away. "Whoa! My gosh!"

"What?"

"Whew! Nothing, I was being overcome by lust."

"What's wrong with that?"

"I just didn't expect it, is all. My experience in these things is fairly limited. Approaching zero, as a matter of fact."

"Now must be the time, then."

"No, I don't think so. If we keep this up, I'll want to drag you into the bushes for purposes of fornication."

"That sounds like a good plan," he breathed into her ear. The hand snaked again.

"No, it's not," she whispered against his cheek. What an absolutely remarkable smell he had.

"And why?"

In a whisper, too: "Because it's a *sin.*"

"You're joking."

"I am not."

He pulled an arm's distance away from her and looked at her. His eyes had adjusted to the dimness and he could make out her face, its expression woeful, vulnerable, mouth slightly open, the thin lips fatter than they had been with all the kissing, her eyes almost reflectant, like an animal's.

"I don't understand."

"You'll laugh if I tell you."

"I won't, honest."

"It's connected. My gift. I mean the languages. I have to abjure sex until I'm married, I mean if I ever get married. Otherwise, it'll be taken away from me."

"You mean . . . like that thing with the girl and the unicorn?"

"Yes, pretty nearly."

"Lucy, that's insane. You have a . . . a rare genetic variation, that's all. Like people who can extract ten-digit primes in their heads or tell you the day of any date, or become chess grand masters. You can't lose it because you think you're violating some medieval rule."

"Yes, that's what Morrie Shadkin says."

"Does he want to get you into bed, too?"

"No, although he does want to marry me. I pointed out to him that he's already married and has two kids. He says, 'Lucy, that's *such* a technicality!' He hates to let me out of his sight. He'd go nuts if he knew I was in dangerous, uncivilized West VA."

"She drags me into the Tunnel of Love to boast about her other boyfriends."

"Oh, Morrie's not a boyfriend. He's the neuroscientist who's trying to figure out how my brain works. Anyway, about your rare genetic variation—the experts of the whole world have looked into my head, CAT scans, fMRI, PET scans, and, yeah, there are small variations, but not explanatory variations. Physically, I'm the same as anyone else, but I can do stuff that no one else can do, except another freak, a fifteen-year-old boy in Russia. So forgive me if I regard it as a gift of the Holy Spirit. Look, what if you knew that if you did something, it would mean that after you couldn't tell a quark from a lipton?"

"Lepton."

"Lepton. How would you feel?"

"I'm prepared to risk that."

"Well, I'm not. And besides, it's wrong. Do you love me?"

"Love you? Christ, I just met you."

"Yes, but you're willing to use me to slake your lust. So say I want to slake my lust, too, and so we slake them, and slake them, and then we get bored with it after a while, or find someone who's more attractive or more interesting, and the whole thing starts over again with someone else."

"All right, fine!" he snapped.

After some silence, she said, "You're pouting now."

He was inclined to pout. He was horny as the devil and he was attracted to her without really understanding why. He had never been attracted to such a girl before this, and it irked him a little. He was a modern kid and had enjoyed plenty of sex from an early age. While it was true that he tended to go for girls who wanted a different sort of boy, he had never had much trouble scoring. His high school had, of course, been full of girls who were born-again and self-consciously Christian, and he had mocked them along with the rest of the bright crowd he had hung out with. This one, however, was not like any of them. He found now, somewhat to his surprise, that he did not want to pout, did not want to push her away, wanted . . . something, he didn't quite know what. Without thinking about it, he flung his arm around her again and gave her a squeeze. "Oh, well, so we'll be pure. I can't believe this. This is like 1903."

She relaxed against him. "Or 1403. Look, we're emerging." There was brightness ahead around a curve, and then a heart-shaped slice of the real world, glowing and making them squint their eyes.

"Where's Lucy?" asked Karp.

Marlene blinked awake and looked around. "Isn't she in the pool?" She sat up and saw that Lucy was not. The twins were there, playing with a ball and a net set up at the side of the pool. "I must have dozed off. The sun got to me." She sat up, rubbed her face, looked around. "Mm, I don't know. She was with the Heeney boy. They're probably off in the bushes somewhere, playing doctor."

"Yeah, psychiatrist, maybe. I just wanted to tell you I'm going out with Hendricks."

"Anything going on?"

"We had another sighting. They bought a case of beer at a grocery in Selden. That's north of here at the junction of 712 and 11. They look like they're getting ready to liquor up and come to town. Wade is gathering the forces. Also, Hawes called. Bledsoe sprung Emmett on a hundred grand bail. He's coming here, but it looks like it might be over by the end of the day, if Wade does his job."

"You want to be in on the kill, do you?"

"Yeah, I do. I deserve it." He sat on the edge of the lounger. "Speaking of which, are you going to tell me how you psyched Ernie Poole up from *Death of a Salesman* to Clarence Darrow?"

"Oh, that. You know, womanly wiles, tee-hee."

"Really."

"I went to his office, where he was trying to climb into a bottle, but had only got a leg in so far, and I told him I knew he had got Amos Jonson to drag me into that shack with his story, and then I expatiated on how you were going to cream Emmett Heeney in court. And he cursed out Hawes for a corrupt fuck, and you and me for fools. He was pretty eloquent, and I said Hawes wouldn't be a factor, you'd be running the case, and you were ten times the lawyer he was, even when he was cold sober, and I walked out."

"That was it?"

"Yes. It came down to a penis-measuring contest between you and him, as I find most litigation does in the end. He's nuts about me, the poor sap, and I manipulated him shamelessly. It's going to break his heart not to be able to beat you up in court."

"He couldn't beat me up in court on his best day and my worst," said Karp, winking John Waynesque.

"Right. I rest my case."

"Now that we've done the cultural riches of the greater McCullensburg area," Dan said, "how about looking into the lowlife?"

They were walking with their arms around one another by the side of a little lake, on a kind of sandy promenade. There was a bathing beach full of shouting children, and the smell of barbecue fires, broiling meat, and charcoal starter fluid. Lucy had never done this with a boy before, but thought she could get to like it. Small town, girl and boy, summer, a lakeside carnival, the hallucination of innocence. She understood that it was hallucinatory, America having given up innocence along with unleaded gas, but she was enjoying it nonetheless. And the badinage.

"There's lowlife in McCullensburg?" she said, miming wonderment. "I'm shocked! *Shocked!*"

"Yep. There's a roadhouse on Route 11 just outside of Selden. They got a pool table and a jukebox with all country favorites. A couple of pinball machines, too."

"You can see my eyes are sparkling, I guess. Did you also hope to get me drunk, so as to make me more pliable?"

"Be honest? Yeah, it had crossed my mind. There's a motel right behind the roadhouse." He hugged her more closely. "Come on. We're young. It's summer. Look at these people." She looked. They seemed to fall into two general classes: parental couples jiggling with fat, mostly lard-pale except for the blue-collar sunburns on the men—face, neck, and lower arms—and rail-thin teens in gaggles and couples, poking and pawing one another. He meant the adults.

"Soon we'll be fat and ugly, too, with mortgages and bratty kids. You want to look back and think you never once did anything just because you had the urge? Seize the day, Lucy!"

To his surprise, she giggled. "Seize the *day?* My God, you're such a pagan! You should be wearing a helmet with horns on it and a greasy beard. Look, let me explain something. If you believe that you're basically an animal, and you're only going to live a certain little bit of time, and for most of it you're going to be in decline, then 'seize the day' is the right take on life. On the other hand, if you believe that your real destiny is entirely outside of time, and that you were made to be with God forever, then the right take is 'sufficient unto the day is the evil thereof.' In other words, forget the crap from the past and what you're plotting for the future, such as, in your case, getting into my pants. Live for eternity, which means, among other things, behaving in a certain way."

"What I can't believe is we're having this conversation. You are honestly, really, not going to have *any* sex at all until you're married?"

"Uh-huh." She gave him another of those light-filled grins. In the bright sun her tan eyes seemed disks of flashing gold. "At which point, I expect to be completely insatiable. They'll have to pry me off it with a sharp tool. And who can tell, you may be the lucky man."

At these words he felt a thrill go through him, lust mixed with terror. She added, "But meanwhile I would love a beer in your low dive."

"You would?"

"Uh-huh. I trust you, and also I have a big, ferocious dog with me. And I can outrun you."

With that, she spun around and took off, racing along the edge of the lake, with the black dog at her heels. Dan stood there for a moment, slightly stunned, watching her run, those long legs graceful as birds' wings. She was like something out of a fairy tale, the kind of girl who might, in some shady wood, turn into a deer or summon a unicorn to her lap. Heart thumping, he began to run after her.

The roadhouse was a low, windowless, concrete structure, painted tan, plopped like a discarded brick on a gravel lot. Lucy put Magog under the Land Cruiser with a pan of water and a handful of dog biscuits and followed Dan through the olde-saloon-style swinging doors. Inside it was surprisingly cool, smelling dankly of old beer, the air stirred by ceiling fans, the light dim and colored by several beer signs over the bar and a large TV with the volume off showing a stock-car race. Pinball noises and the click of pool balls came from an adjoining room. In the saloon proper half a dozen country boys and a fat woman in a halter top were engaged in serious drinking. They looked up briefly when Dan and Lucy entered and then went back to their drinks. Dan sat Lucy at one of the eight tables and brought a pair of Coors longnecks from the tired-looking blond woman at the bar.

"So," he said after a long swallow, "do you feel your virtue giving way yet?"

"It's pretty depraved. We don't have anything this bad in New York."

"Just wait. You might get to hear some uncouth language in a while. Someone might even hurl a sexual innuendo."

"Well, let's hope it doesn't happen. I don't want to have to change my underpants *again.*"

"Yes, and you're always making that kind of dirty remark. I mean, if you're going to be a prude, you ought to act like one. How come you're not grim-faced and shockable like the born-againers at McCullensburg High?"

"I'm sorry if I inflame your lusts even more than they are by my preternatural physical beauty . . ."

"And you keep knocking the way you—"

He stopped abruptly. Something had gone wrong with his face, the expression frozen, the color draining from it so that his lips looked almost blue. He was sitting facing the door. She had her back to it, and he was staring past her shoulder. She turned to look and saw three men walking in, just past the swinging doors.

"Oh, shit!" said Dan under his breath.

The three men went to the bar and loudly demanded beer. They were obviously already drunk: two big ones—one rawboned with an ugly weasel-sneering face, the other huge, neckless, gut hanging over the broad belt of his jeans—and one smaller with a pretty-boy face bleared by drink, with sleepy, sly eyes. Some altercation at the bar. The woman didn't want to serve them. The pretty boy vaulted the bar and extracted a double handful of beers from the cooler. They leaned against the bar and drank, glowering at the occupants. The other drinkers had fallen silent.

The no-neck said, "Hey, Bo. Go put some music on. This place is fuckin' dead."

Bo went to the jukebox. It started to play Merle Haggard's "Okie from Muskogee."

Lucy knew who the men were without being told. She had more acquaintance with killers than most girls her age, and she understood what she was looking at. Next to her, Dan sat frozen, staring at them.

They must have felt the stare, or else their eyes had now adjusted to the gloom of the barroom, for the ugly one said, "Hey, Wayne, ain't that Dan Heeney sittin' there?"

The big one stared and showed brownish teeth, a gap-toothed grin. "Yeah, Earl, I believe it is. How're you doin', Heeney? I hear your brother's in trouble. Hey, boys, let's go cheer old Dan up."

They clumped over to the table and hovered. Wayne said, "Now, Heeney, I want to know why Emmett'd do a mean thing like that? I mean, killin' his folks and his pore little sister. You all must've had a piss poor upbringin', what d'you think, boys?"

Earl said, "Yeah, and his brother's sittin' in the jail, and he's out drinkin' with some damn ugly girl. Heeney, you must be getting some kinda fierce pussy, to go out with a girl that plain."

Wayne said, "Yeah, now that you mention it, Earl, I don't believe I ever have seen a girl that flat-chested. You need to put them things back in the oven for a while, honey, get a little more rise outen 'em."

Then, to everyone's surprise, Lucy said, in a loud, clear voice, audible throughout the bar, over the music. "Yes, I used to worry about it myself. 'Oh, why don't I grow breasts?' I cried about it for years. Now I've come to accept it as my fate. And isn't that the real secret of happiness? To love your fate? *Amor fati,* as we say in Latin. How much happier you would be, for example," she added, looking directly at Earl, "if you truly accepted your ugliness and lack of intelligence. You would not feel impelled to take out your rage by doing sadistic and cruel acts."

Someone sniggered at one of the back tables. Lucy now looked carefully at Bo Cade. There was something off about him that she found interesting, something that distinguished him from the other two. He had composed his face into a contemptuous sneer, but it had no depth. "It's true," she said in the same tone, "what you feel is real. You're not like them. It's hard to go against your own blood, but sometimes you have to. Drinking doesn't help, really."

Bo opened his mouth in shock and then shut it with a snap. The others seemed not to have heard any of what she said, although Earl was conscious of having been insulted, and his slow brain was contemplating revenge. Wayne understood only that this little bitch who should have been quaking in terror was not, and it made him cranky. He was a good deal quicker than his cousin Earl, however, quick enough to see something pass between Bo and her, although not to understand it.

"Hey, little Bo, she likes you," Wayne said. "Why'nt you ask her to dance? I bet she's a real good dancer. Lady, you touch that fuckin' phone and I'll rip it off the wall and shove it up your sloppy old cunt." This last shouted to the bartender, who had been edging toward the pay phone on the far wall.

Wayne resumed, "Yeah, I want to see some dancing. Bo, go play that song again, and we'll see if Miss Smart here'll dance for us. Go do like I said, Bo."

Bo hesitated and then went and put another quarter in the slot.

When the music started again, Wayne said to Lucy, "Now, get up and dance!"

"I don't care to, thanks," said Lucy.

"Well, I don't give a shit what you care to, honey. Just for being pert, you can dance nekkid. We'll see if you got no hair on your pussy like you got no titties."

When Lucy didn't move, Wayne grabbed her left arm and jerked her to her feet. Dan came out of his chair with a bottle in his hand, but Earl was ready for him and landed a solid punch on the side of Dan's head that knocked him sprawling. He got to his knees, and Earl kicked him in the ribs.

"Don't you ever watch movies?" Lucy asked. They all stared at her. "Every single movie you ever saw, a bunch of thugs goes into a place and abuses respectable people, and every time, something terrible happens to them. You're those guys now, and something terrible will happen to you if you don't stop this right now."

Again, they seemed not to hear what she said. Wayne said, "You better shuck out've them clothes, honey. Or do you want old Bo to take 'em off for you?" Wayne gave her arm a shake to make his point.

Lucy sighed, raised her fingers to her mouth, and produced a piercing, three-toned whistle.

Magog entered the barroom at a dead run, at which point Lucy shouted a command in a language only she and the dog understood. She also pulled against Wayne's grip, at which the man instinctively jerked back. This improved Magog's target picture. Without breaking stride, the dog hit Wayne Cade in the groin with a mouthful of teeth. Wayne went over backward, his mouth open wide enough to swallow a grapefruit. The dog gave a sharp jerk of her massive head, like the jerk a terrier makes to kill a rat, producing the sound of tearing cloth and a high-pitched scream.

Magog then backed off a few steps and dropped on the floor a sodden mass of denim, Jockey-short stuff, blood, and tissue. Wayne writhed with his hands against his crotch, making the sort of sounds he had not made since he was weaned.

Earl reached under his shirt, brought out a revolver, and took careful aim at Magog. Lucy shouted something. Magog started to move and Earl fired. Dan Heeney rose slowly to his feet.

It is extremely hard even when cold sober to hit a black dog moving toward you at speed in a dim room, and Earl's bullet did not connect. His second shot also went wide, into the ceiling in fact, because Dan hit him over the head with a chair, and Magog launched her 110 pounds through the air and landed mouth-first on his forearm. Earl screamed and dropped the gun.

"Magog, off!" cried Lucy. "Heel! Dan, come on!"

After a second's hesitation, because he really wanted to hit Earl again with the chair, he ran after her, shaking his head to clear it.

Outside, they both stopped short, blinking. Four state police cars were lined up head to tail, forming a barricade across the parking lot. Helmeted troopers crouched behind them, pistols and shotguns at the ready. One of the troopers was making frantic "come here" motions. Looking wildly around her, Lucy saw that a team of police in helmets and flak jackets, carrying short-version M16s, were flattened against the walls of the bar on either side of the door.

Lucy and Dan did what the trooper wanted them to do and went behind the line of cars. At that moment, Earl Cade came running out, clutching his revolver in his left hand, his right hanging loose and bloody. Twenty voices started yelling at him to drop it, to get down, get down! Slowly, it seemed, it dawned on Earl that they were addressing him and not someone else with a gun in his hand, and also that enough firepower was pointing at him to stop a battalion. He let the gun fall and lay down on the gravel. Some troopers rushed forward and grabbed him.

"What'd I do? I ain't done nothin'," wailed Earl.

The assault team rushed into the saloon and soon emerged with Bo Cade, in handcuffs. Shortly thereafter, a paramedic van pulled into the lot; two paramedics pulled a gurney out of it and went in.

"Hi, Dad," said Lucy.

"Are you all right?" Karp asked. She saw how pale his face was and ran to embrace him.

"I'm fine. How did you know I was in there?"

"We didn't, until I saw your truck in the parking lot. I almost had a heart attack."

"You were following the Cades?"

"A trooper saw their truck and called it in. What were you doing in that place? I thought you were at Four Oaks."

"Dan took me. He's been showing me the McCullensburg sights."

Karp turned on Dan a paint-scorching look. "You think that was smart, zooming around the county with a bunch of killers on the loose?"

Before Dan could answer, the paramedics emerged from the building with Wayne Cade on their gurney. They stopped to talk to a tall trooper with gold glinting on his shoulders, then packed the man away in their van, with a trooper for company.

Hendricks walked over to the Karps and asked, "What happened in there?"

Lucy answered, "That big one, Wayne I think his name is, tried to sexually assault me, and Magog bit him." A child of two lawyers, she was ever alert for torts.

"Bit him, eh? I'll say!"

"Is he badly hurt?" asked Lucy with real concern. "I called her off right away."

"Oh, he'll live. But I guess it'll be a while before Wayne's interested in that sort of thing." To Karp, Hendricks said, "You'll want to see them right away."

"Yeah. You know the drill. Keep them separate, and the Miranda stuff. Let's have that gun tested. Make sure they're comfortable and take care of their medical needs. We'll talk to Wayne later in the hospital."

"I guess my wife won't be leaving me now," said Stan Hawes to Karp as soon as Karp walked into his office. "And I can take my kid to Little League again."

"Was it that bad?"

"Pretty near. Anyhow, it worked. I guess we need to talk to those boys."

"Whenever you want." Karp hesitated, then said carefully, "You know, I've done this a lot. Maybe I should take the lead interviewing the first one."

"I got no problem with that. On the other hand, I think I got more experience with boys like the Cades than you do. I guess you don't have many like them in New York City."

"Good point.We'll feel our way. You want to go downstairs now?"

"You know, as a matter of fact, I'd like to get something to eat first." Hawes stood up and slipped on his suit jacket. "I haven't been eating all that well since I became a corrupt son of a bitch. Christine's been flinging a frozen dinner at my head and calling it supper. Let's go down to Rosie's. The Cades'll keep for a while."

The restaurant was crowded, much to Karp's surprise. There was no velvet rope, but they had to hang around in the entryway for a table to be cleared.

"It's Friday," Hawes explained as they took their seats, "catfish on the menu. Gus's catfish is famous. He's got a tank in the back he keeps them in. He brings them up from a farm in North Carolina."

"Well, I do love a mess o'catfish."

"I bet you do, country boy like yourself."

"What's with all the old guys?" asked Karp, surveying the room.

"Pension day today. They're all old miners. Basis of the economy, besides coal itself. Another one of our local traditions. There's your Lester Weames fan club. The union's been screwing them for generations and they love it, because he hands them a cheap pension every month. Plus occasional odd jobs. A great and generous man, Lester. Another reason I brought you here. Look over there, those fellas at that big round table in the corner."

Karp looked. He did not recognize any of the eight men at the table, but he thought instantly of Marlene and her flash of déjà vu. He had seen tables like that in Italian restaurants in his neighborhood at home. The men were dressed a little better, and a little more formally than the other diners, and they had a sleek, confident look as they dug into the greasy fried fish and downed bottles of beer. Three of them were larger men than average, with hard, stupid faces. The table was making a good deal of happy, aggressive noise.

"Man in the yellow golf shirt with the little round glasses, that's Lester himself. Over one to his right is George Floyd. The others are his buddies in the union management, and his goons. I guess you can tell which ones are the goons."

Karp inspected them for a moment. "They seem to be having a good time. I guess us arresting the Cade boys isn't affecting their appetites. I assume they know?"

"Oh, yeah. Swett must've been on the horn to them five minutes after we brought them in."

George Floyd said something and everyone laughed heartily. Karp imagined that this was not an infrequent occurrence when Floyd made a joke. Weames seemed quieter, almost studious; perhaps it was the glasses. He looked like the sort of nondescript accountant who turns out to have forty-three dismembered women in his basement. Weames glanced up from his fish. His glasses glinted. He said something to Floyd, who raised his head and stared over at Karp. Their eyes met. Floyd said something to Weames and laughed, and then their whole table laughed and turned to look at Karp and Hawes.

The waitress cut off their view. Hawes said, "Don't need no menus, Maggie. We'll have the catfish specials. That all right with you, Butch?"

"Sure, why not." Karp smiled at the waitress.

The fish was extremely tasty, he had to agree. He could not help noticing that, as the various tables of pensioners finished their meals, they would go up to Weames's table for a word or two. Paying homage. George Floyd stood, pulled a fat roll of currency out of his pocket, and peeled off a half dozen bills, licking his thumb and snapping it down to pull each one off. Karp had seen the gesture a hundred times on Mulberry Street in Little Italy.

"In the event that Lester ever becomes a defendant here," Karp observed, "it's not going to be easy assembling a jury, is it?"

Hawes grinned at him, a satisfied grin. "Ah, finally, the penny drops."

15

THERE WERE NO FORMAL INTERVIEW ROOMS AT THE ROBBENS COUNTY jail, so they had Bo Cade brought to the deputies' lunchroom, a fluorescent-lit, windowless nine-by-twelve with a Formica table and several mismatched straight chairs. Its air was warm, stagnant, reeking of burnt coffee and microwaved pizza.

"Do you like catfish, Mr. Cade?" was Karp's first question.

Bo looked confused, then nodded warily. A trick question, his face declared. He still smelled strongly of beer, but no longer felt drunk. Being arrested for murder often has a literally sobering effect.

"Good," said Karp. "I brought you some catfish from Rosie's." He handed over a paper sack. "We can talk while you have your supper. I think the sheriff can spare a soda, too."

Karp and Hawes watched Bo eat catfish and drink RC. "Pretty good, isn't it?" said Karp. "I never had catfish before today, but I'm a fan now. I don't think it's usually on the menu in the prison system—correct me if I'm wrong, Stan."

"No, I wouldn't think so," said Hawes, "not at Mt. Olive. Or not fresh like Rosie's anyway. Maybe you'd get some soggy frozen fish fingers, though."

Cade stopped chewing. "I got nothin' to say to you. I didn't do nothin' and I don't know nothin'. I don't even know why I'm here."

"Uh-huh," said Karp, "I hear what you're saying. Well, let me do something then. I'm going to read to you off this sheet of paper, and then I'm going to ask you to sign it if you understand what's on it." Karp read off the Miranda rights and asked, "Do you want to see a lawyer now, or would you like to talk with us some more?"

"Hell, I told you I don't know nothin'. Why'd I need a lawyer then?"

"Good, then sign the form." Bo signed. Karp said, "Okay, Mr. Cade, let's talk about your situation. On May twenty-eighth of this year, you went into the Bi-Lo in town and purchased a pair of Rocky-brand hunting boots, size nine and a half. We have a copy of the receipt and the clerk remembers you. You wore those boots the night you killed Mr. and Mrs. Heeney and Elizabeth Heeney."

"I didn't kill—"

"Right, you didn't do nothing. But just hold that for a second. Subsequent to the murders, upon finding the boots were spattered with blood, you threw them off the green bridge on Route 130, where they were found and worn by Mose Welch. You also left several good sets of fingerprints at the Heeney home. Now, we have done a detailed analysis of the interior of the boots—"

"Hey, now, wait a minute! I thought you got that Emmett Heeney for all that anyway."

"No, actually, that was a ruse."

"A what?"

"A trick. A swindle. We pretended to arrest Emmett Heeney so that you boys would come down from Burnt Peak and we could arrest you without having to go up there and drag you out, with the chance that someone might get hurt."

Bo Cade gaped.

"Yes, I thought it was pretty smart, and it worked," said Karp. "As I was saying, we took apart one of your boots. Do you know what DNA is, Mr. Cade?"

"Yeah, the forest rangers."

"No, that's DNR," said Hawes. "The Department of Natural Resources. DNA is a chemical found in your body. It's different for different people. If we got some DNA from a crime scene, we can compare it to the DNA in your body and tell if you were there."

"Thank you, Stan," said Karp. "Well, Mr. Cade, it turns out that when you wear boots, little flecks of skin get shed through your socks and stick to the leather. We've extracted some of those little flecks from your boots. Now, naturally, some of them belong to Mose Welch, because he wore those boots, but others of them we've found belong to someone else. I would bet a lot of money that when we compare that DNA to a sample from your body, it'll match right up. Also, we've got good footprints of where you stood on the night of the murder right outside the Heeneys' back door. Our lab people can tell the weight of whoever made those footprints with your boots, and I would also bet a lot of money that they're going to come up with exactly your weight. So we have what we call a good circumstantial case. That means we can put you in your fancy boots at the Heeney home the night of the murder, where you got them splattered with Mrs. Heeney's blood right after you killed her."

"I told you I didn't kill no one."

"Yes, you did. But the problem here is you're the one we have. You're the only one with bloody boots."

"Oh, hell, Earl had blood all over his shoes, too. He throwed them away into the laurel."

A considerable silence followed this remark. Karp let it hang, then said, "Uh-huh. He killed the Heeneys with his shotgun, didn't he?"

Bo hesitated, looking sullen. Karp waited, his expression neutral. Bo said, "I ain't got nothin' more to say to you."

Karp said, "I see. So that means *you* were the one that shot Lizzie Heeney in the head? That's funny, because I didn't figure you for someone low enough to shoot a ten-year-old girl while she was sleeping in her own bed."

"I did not! I didn't do no killin' at all," Bo shouted. In a smaller voice, he added, "It was Wayne did the little girl. I didn't think they was gonna kill all of them."

"Uh-huh. And where was George Floyd while all this was going on?"

"How'd you know about him?"

"Mr. Cade, I know *everything*," said Karp, smiling gently. "I'm only asking you these questions because you're a kid in trouble and I'm trying to catch you a break. I know you didn't kill anyone. But you're going to go away for murder unless I hear it from your own lips that you weren't pulling any triggers that night and you sign a paper that says so. Then I can go to the judge and get you off. But you have to tell me the whole truth about what happened so that I can tell him that *your* part of the story is true, okay?" Karp passed a pad of yellow paper and a ballpoint across the table. Bo Cade looked at it, glowered briefly at Karp, then took up the pen. *I dindt kil no one,* he wrote, the pen clutched vertically in the crotch of his thumb. *It was Gorge Floyd got my broter and my cousin Wayen and me to do it.*

Two hours later, Karp and Hawes were in the latter's office waiting for Bo Cade's handwritten confession to be typed.

Hawes still seemed a little stunned. "Boy, I thought they'd be tougher nuts to crack. You were pretty smooth."

"Oh, right," said Karp, eyes to the ceiling, "the battle of the Titans. I was rolling dumb kids twice as bright as Bo Cade before he was born. No, the real sweat on this case is going to be getting Floyd, and then getting him to rat out Mr. Weames. In fact, as soon as that confession's done, I've got to get a hold of Judge Bledsoe, have him issue a warrant for Floyd, and a warrant to search his personal effects and any bank accounts to which he has access. You can take a statement from Earl. I don't think he'll give you any trouble. I presume Wayne is still having his testicles reattached?"

"That's what I hear. He won't be ready for questioning until tomorrow late at the earliest."

"Yes, I should be sadder about his misfortune, but somehow . . . anyway, then I will whistle up Captain Hendricks and go bring in Mr. Floyd. But no catfish dinner for Mr. Floyd. He's already had his catfish."

George Floyd did not dwell in a mobile home like so many of the people who employed him, but in a large, distinctly stationary two-story brick home on nicely kept grounds in the southeastern, more genteel regions of the county. It was hard to find a place in Robbens County unscarred by coal, but a good number of people had persevered, it seemed, and the community of Peale was the result. Peale was ten miles south of McCullensburg on Route 11. Here were located the substantial estates of the coal barons, the Killebrews and the Hergewillers, as well as the (somewhat) less imposing homes of the union grandees.

Armed with warrants for arrest and search, Karp arrived at Floyd's house in the evening, accompanied by Captain Hendricks, two Blazer-loads of green-clad troopers, and a crime-scene van from the state lab at Charleston. The frightened housekeeper tried to keep them out, but was bullied out of the way with threats and waved papers. Some forty minutes later, Floyd himself pulled up in his Chrysler. Karp watched Hendricks arrest him in his own living room, while troopers dismantled his home. It was a good arrest, the rights read out properly, no violence, or rather, no obvious violence. Karp had, of course, heard the expression *if looks could kill,* but had not often seen a demo so vivid as the one he got from George Floyd, who kept looking at him as Hendricks snapped the handcuffs on. Floyd's face had turned an interesting shade of lavender, tending to scarlet along the cheekbones. His pale eyes bulged and his lips were drawn back over his big yellow teeth, as if preparing to rend living flesh. He didn't say anything dramatic, as they do in the movies, neither protesting his innocence nor promising dire consequences.

After Floyd was driven off, Karp hung around to watch the search. Troopers carried out boxes of papers and one locked four-drawer filing cabinet.

"Find any guns?" he asked a technician.

"Yes, sir. Rifles, shotguns, a couple of semiautomatics."

"Not a .38?"

"Not yet. We're still looking, though."

Karp nodded and the man went out of the house. After a moment Karp followed him. Puffy clouds had appeared, bringing a gentle mountain breeze. It had turned cooler, too, nice weather for strolling around the grounds. The sun was behind the mountains, but the day still hung on in the long twilight of high summer, still plenty light enough to find things. Karp strolled, observing men probing flower beds, going over the lawn with metal detectors. The man he had spoken to and another man were in the center of the backyard, inspecting a birdbath made from some black, glossy stone. Karp wandered over and inspected it, too.

"That's a birdbath," said Karp.

Karp's pal smiled. "Yes, sir. It's a birdbath someone moved not too long ago. Lookee here." He knelt and indicated a tiny width of naked earth forming a crescent around the base.

The man addressed his colleague. "Bob, let's get the digital over here."

"Wise move," said Karp. "There might be something under it. Unless an extremely large robin used it."

"I'd almost rather believe that than that the man buried a murder weapon in his own backyard."

"Oh, about now I'd believe nearly anything," said Karp.

The other man came back with a fancy Sony digital camera and began to click it. Karp helped the technician lift the bath proper off its pedestal. When the base column was rolled away, they saw a round patch of naked earth. The technician probed it with a trowel.

"Was that a clink?" said Karp.

The photographer snapped away as the trowel uncovered a revolver wrapped in a Bi-Lo clear plastic bag.

"You think that's it?" asked the technician.

"Would you bet against it?"

The man laughed. "Not me."

"Me neither," said Karp. "How long will it take you to generate prints of these pictures?"

"Couple of minutes. We got a laptop and an ink-jet in the van."

"Everything's up-to-date in West Virginia," said Karp. "I'm impressed."

The man gave him a grin and went off. The other technician lifted the weapon. "Looks like a Smith .38, three-inch barrel."

"Any chance of prints?" Karp asked.

"Well, sir, we'll check, but I kind of doubt it. This puppy's been in the water. It's got rust on it, look here. Probably down in the mud, too. You can see it stuck to the cylinder."

Karp could. It was greenish and it stank of chemistry.

Karp drove back to town with Hendricks, followed by their motorcade. Karp was silent, so silent that Captain Hendricks broke a life-long habit and opened a conversation.

"Something wrong? I thought it went pretty good."

"Oh, no, it went great. I'm thinking about that pistol."

"It's on its way to Charleston with results asap."

"Right. I'm assuming that we'll find it's the gun that killed Lizzie. If it is . . . it doesn't make any sense. According to Bo Cade, his cousin Wayne used it on Lizzie. According to your technician, someone tossed it into the water. If both of those things are true, how in hell did it migrate to George Floyd's birdbath?"

"Floyd took it from Wayne on the night of the murder?"

"Unlikely in the first place, but suppose he did. Then he throws it into some lake and then thinks, hey, the bottom of a river isn't that good of a hiding place, I think I'll . . . *duh!* . . . dredge it up and bury it on my property, and I'll stick a birdbath on it, because the cops never think to look under birdbaths."

"Criminals do stupid things," said Hendricks.

"Yeah, they do. And to tell you the truth, the first thing I thought when we found it was something like that. This whole murder has been amateur hour anyway, and I thought, it's the impunity. They never thought there'd be a serious investigation, so they were sloppy. George probably had it in his bedside drawer, and then when we picked up the Cade boys, he said uh-oh and shoved it under the birdbath. I'd still believe that, if it wasn't for the mud. That gun was at the bottom for a while, in slimy, polluted mud. What I'd guess is that the boys threw it into a local body of water sometime after the murder, and someone saw them do it and picked it up and sometime later buried it where we found it. Someone was trying to implicate Floyd."

"But . . . Floyd *is* implicated," Hendricks protested. "By Cade. So . . ."

"Yeah, so why go through the trouble of framing a guilty man?"

"Unless Floyd did it himself, to mess up any case against him."

"Yeah, that crossed my mind, too, but if you don't mind me saying so, that's a little too deep of a game for Robbens County. In any case, it tends to cloud the value of our presumed murder weapon. It's a complexity, and I like it simple. According to Bo Cade, Floyd never had the pistol anyway. The whole thing ranks way up there among stories I would prefer not to tell a jury."

Upon arrival in town, Karp went immediately to see Stan Hawes. "How'd you do?" Hawes asked.

"Found the murder weapon. It was under a birdbath."

"A black birdbath? Shiny?" Karp nodded; Hawes snorted. "That's kind of ironic."

"Why? This is a famous birdbath?"

"Oh, they had a testimonial for George a couple of years ago, fifteen years of distinguished service to the union. It's carved out of slate from Majestic Number One."

"That's interesting." Karp told him about the mud and the rust. "It adds to the theory that some third party was trying to make a point. How'd you make out with Earl?"

"Oh, Earl rolled right over when I confronted him with Bo's statement. He got all red up about it. According to him, it was Bo that shotgunned the Heeneys. He was just along for the ride. Confirms that Wayne did the little girl, though, and that Floyd was there. Also confirms the payoff, twenty-five hundred cash to each. He spent his fixing up that truck. Back to the gun: This is not good for the good guys, is it?"

"No, not necessarily. Let's wait for what the lab has to say before we start worrying too much, though. Have you been in to see Floyd?"

A hesitation here, a hint of embarrassment. "No, I was . . . I mean I thought we could go in and see him together."

"Sure, let's talk for a minute about how we're going to play him. I think double-teaming is the way to go with George. And let me order some muscle from Wade. I don't much trust the jailhouse guys."

Floyd had taken off his jacket and tie and rolled up the sleeves of his white-on-white shirt. His forearms were massive and flecked with brownish hair. He rested them on the coffee-room table, their muscles flexing as he clenched his fists. Behind him, flexing even more massive forearms, stood Curtis Vogelsang, the largest state trooper in southwestern West Virginia. A much smaller jailhouse deputy, Peagram by name, sat on a chair in a corner.

"Here's what we got, George," said Karp breezily as he sat down. "We have two confessions to the murders of the Heeney family, from Earl and Bo Cade. They say you organized the whole thing. They say you were there in the house supervising the proceedings."

"I was at a meeting. Twenty guys will vouch for me."

"All on your payroll, I have no doubt. We'll see how much they vouch when we explain the perjury statutes to them. Also we have this." Karp passed across a sheaf of ink-jet printouts—the photographic record of the finding of the .38 under the birdbath. "That's a .38 there, George. If it proves to be the murder weapon, you're in big trouble."

To Karp's dismay, Floyd barely glanced at the photographs. He grinned and said, "That's horseshit. Someone planted it. Maybe you, or your little dickhead friend there."

"No, you know it wasn't anything like that," said Karp dismissively. He stared for almost a minute at Floyd silently, as if examining a specimen. He had found it a useful technique before this. Then he said, "It *is* interesting though. Although we know you're an asshole, I can't quite believe you're *that* big an asshole, because I couldn't help noticing that you walked in here with your shoes on the right feet, and also neatly tied with bows. We know you're an asshole because only an asshole would have planned a murder with a bunch of half-wit hillbillies for triggermen. And of course they screwed it up, and of course we grabbed them, and of course they ratted you out instantly. But you were smart, in just the way that assholes think they're smart. You told them to throw away the gun because you saw on the TV somewhere that we could match bullets to guns. You didn't take the gun and throw it away yourself. You're not capable of that much intelligence, you pathetic sap! No, you *told* your witless accomplice to throw it away. But this moron actually had more sense than you. This moron planted the gun on you, so that if anyone ever asked any questions, they could say, 'Oh, George did it. George shot a sleeping little girl.' And you're going to go away for it, for the rest of your miserable life. You know, George, they don't like child killers in prisons. You'll be at the bottom of the pecking order in the joint, instead of at the top like you are here. When you go up, you better bring a large jar of Vaseline and a frilly negligee—"

George Floyd actually shouted *arrgh* like they do in comic books and came out of his chair at Karp, knocking the table aside. They grappled. His clawing hands came within millimeters of Karp's throat before Trooper Vogelsang whipped a mighty arm around Floyd's neck and strangled him back into his chair. Karp cocked a fist and went for Floyd, but Hawes got in his way and pushed him back. "What are you, crazy?" Hawes shouted. "Don't ever talk to a prisoner that way in my courthouse again! Who the hell do you think you are?"

"I'm in charge of this investigation," said Karp in as authoritative a tone as he could manage.

"The hell you are! This is my courthouse, goddamnit, and right now you're not welcome in it. Get out!"

Karp did a glare and then spun on his heel and walked out, slamming the door behind him. Outside in the narrow corridor he straightened his clothes and took a drink from the water fountain. The guard on duty looked at him curiously as he signed out of the jail.

"Having some trouble?" the deputy asked.

Karp replied, "Just torturing the prisoners, Deputy Wyatt," and walked up the stairs.

He thought it had gone fairly well. Because he had a genuine sympathy for evildoers—he could not have stayed married to his wife had he not—Karp was extremely, famously effective as the good cop and hardly ever got the chance to be the bad one, as he had just now. He did not think he would ever get to like it, although he knew some perfectly decent people who doted on the role.

It was dark when he left the courthouse and walked the few streets to the Burroughs Building. As he had expected, the lights were burning still. Hendricks and his team had taken over the largest room in the place. At desks and at makeshift trestle tables, several detectives were methodically ploughing through George Floyd's papers.

"Did you find the diary, yet?" Karp asked Hendricks.

"What diary is that?"

"The one with the entry 'June 26, pick up frozen yogurt, kill Heeney family.'"

"Oh, *that* diary. No, not just yet. Floyd seems to be a cagey fellow. Most of what we looked at so far is copies of routine union business and personal stuff. How did you make out with the man?"

"I did my crude New York monster impression. Stan is soothing him as we speak. Somehow, I doubt we'll get much. We don't *have* much except the confessions."

"And the pistol."

"Could've been planted. *Was* planted, more likely, and, boy, would I have loved to have found it all oiled and fingerprinted under his Simmons. But anyway, whether or not Floyd was at the scene, he's definitely the guy who set the whole thing up. He *paid* for the whole thing. You serve that subpoena for the bank stuff yet?"

"Right after we got it, Floyd's personal account. Mel Harkness is going over them now. It might take a while."

"As long as it takes. We're looking for seventy-five hundred dollars, if the Cade boys aren't just blowing smoke. Seven point five K cash."

"Follow the money?"

"That's what they say. The weak point of every criminal enterprise. It'll probably be in the union accounts, though. We need those, too."

Karp went to the room he was using as an office and called Marlene at Four Oaks. Not in. He sat back in his chair, a cheap old-fashioned job, not nearly as comfortable as the big judge's swivel he used in New York. He swiveled. It squeaked. He tried to make it play a tune while he tapped out "The Yellow Rose of Texas" on his teeth with a pencil. The phone rang.

"Butch? Stan."

"A full confession. Remorse. Tears. You stroked his head and said, 'There, there.' "

Hawes laughed. "Not quite. I had to take some abuse, but I calmed him down. He thinks I'm still one of the boys."

"Yeah, that's why you were the good guy. What's his story?"

"Outraged citizen. He allows as how it might have been suggested around the Cades that Heeney was trouble and that no one would cry their eyes out if he got hit by a truck. But planning his murder? Heaven forbid! It was like that old movie with what's his name, Richard Burton?"

"*Becket*," said Karp. " 'Who will rid me of this troublous priest?' He mentioned that?"

"No, I was thinking of it while he was lying. His story is the Cade boys got the idea that Floyd and the union bosses wanted Heeney dead and they thought they were doing a favor. He wasn't there, didn't know nothing about it until it happened. A pretty good defense, I thought. At trial, it'd come down to the gun and the testimony of a couple of con-victed felons, or three. And they tried to implicate him because they knew he had the county wrapped up and they wanted to get off."

"Uh-huh. Unfortunately, that's not the way it works. Their play was to hold out for a deal before they ratted out George. But you're right, our case versus. Floyd could be a lot better. Did Weames come up at all?"

"I broached the subject. Funny expression on his face, like wheels were spinning. But what he said was Weames didn't have anything more to do with it than he did."

"Truer words were never spoken," said Karp. "How about that two grand in the brown envelope?"

"Never mentioned. But he contrasted me as quote 'one of us' with you, 'the Jew bastard.' I blamed you for everything."

"Right move. Okay, we've gone about as far with him as we can right now. Let's wait for the physical evidence to firm up and we'll see where we go from there. But my sense is that this is going to be settled when we find the payoff. That's the key."

After he got off the phone, Karp called the inn again and again found no answer. He walked out of the Burroughs Building and looked down the street. McCullensburg shut down early. The courthouse was dark, as were the Market Street businesses. Traffic was light. It had been a while since the catfish supper and he was hungry. In the middle distance golden arches gleamed. He walked a couple of blocks and went in. There he found three-quarters of his missing family.

He slid into the booth and snatched up the plastic movie-marketing toy in front of Giancarlo. "My monster!" he said, clutching it dramatically to his breast.

"*Garçon!*" Marlene called. "*Encore de Happy Meal!* They were whining for Micky D and they wore me down. I called you but you weren't in the office."

"I was fighting crime. And all of a sudden I realized that what I really wanted was not justice but a cheap plastic Disney figurine and a thin, tasteless burger."

"Dad, I have news for you," said Giancarlo. "You're a grown-up."

"No toy?"

"No. As a matter of fact, I think I'm outgrowing Happy Meals myself," said Giancarlo. "You can give it to Zak. He'll be ordering Happy Meals when he's forty-two."

The response to this from Zak was a quick knuckle to the ribs. Giancarlo flinched and yelped. "Dad! Zak punched me!"

"Yes," said Karp. "You abuse him verbally and he responds physically. A few minutes pass. Then you abuse him verbally and he responds physically. A few minutes pass. You abuse him verbally and he responds physically. Do you see a pattern here?"

"He's not supposed to hit me."

"No, and you're not supposed to insult him either." Karp handed back the toy. To his wife he said, "Have they been like this for long?"

"Only all day. I tried to drown them but they were too slippery. I heard about your big-boy day from Emmett. He came by after they sprung him. How's Lucy?"

"She seemed perfectly cool. Apparently the dog intervened before anything really nasty went down."

"Yes, that's what they're for," said Marlene. "In any case, dingdong the witch is dead. The bad guys are in custody. My work here is done."

"Planning on leaving?"

"I guess. It's not really fair to stick Billy with the whole burden."

"Oh, hell, Marlene, take a break! Have him hire some more people. You've got the money and the whole thing's just a tax dodge anyway."

"We can't leave now, Mom," Zak interjected. "Emmett promised to take me hunting. We're going to go hunting at night, Dad, with real shotguns and dogs."

"When I'm dead, you can go hunting at night, darling," said Marlene sweetly. "It's not just a tax dodge. It's a tax dodge I have a substantial emotional investment in. It's my profession. I'm good at it and I like it."

Karp sighed and slid out of the booth. "Whatever. Do what you like, you always do. I'm going to get a couple of Big Macs."

He *had* been hungry, he decided, after the first Mac had vanished, and it had made him unnecessarily cross. The boys had left for the McPlayground just outside. Giancarlo had done a drawing on the back of the place mat, made with the crayons supplied by the franchise. It was a typical Giancarlo product, monsters in extraterrestrial landscapes. Karp was no connoisseur, nor could he draw a straight line himself, but even to his eye his son's artwork was more sophisticated than he imagined was typical of ten-year-old boys. The crayoning was layered, smudged, and mixed to yield colors not in the Crayola box, and the line was vigorous and confident. Where did it come from? he wondered. Another disturbing miracle, like the languages. Zak seemed to be the one normal kid, if saying four words a day and wanting to shoot everything moving was normal. Karp felt Marlene's eyes. Around a wad of the second burger he said, "Sorry for snapping. Besides the brats, how was your day?"

"I worked on my tan. I hated three teenagers who showed up at the pool for their sleek limbs. I swore I would never wear a bikini again. I flirted with Trooper Blake and reneged on my swear about the bikinis on his unspoken advice. I arranged for the truck to be deposited at Buddy's

Body and spent a good deal of time waiting for Buddy to get to where he could look at the damage and let me know how long it would take him to fix it. Buddy is a deliberate fellow, which I guess comes naturally when you weigh three-fifty. Have you noticed how many remarkably fat people there are in this town?"

Karp looked around the restaurant to confirm this. "Yes. Are you afraid it's catching?"

"Frankly? I am; it may be something in the air. Buddy was telling me about Alma Knox, whose Chevy he had right there in the shop. Alma got into a little fender bender out on Route 11 that squished the latch on the driver's-side door. Well, Alma could not actually slide across to the passenger door to exit the vehicle. They had to call fire and rescue to cut her out with the Jaws of Life. In any event, I got to sit in the shade of Buddy's Body for a good long time, drinking diet RC and occasionally easing my bladder, while the rich life of McCullensburg flowed around me. Buddy's junkyard is one of the places to see and be seen, it turns out. A parade of codgers, mainly guys with few teeth and tobacco stains on their stubble. Very polite gents, all retired miners looking for junk parts to keep their 1978 Pontiacs humming. Apparently they occasionally get a little bonus of some kind from the union pension fund, and they all just got one and were blowing it on Delco alternators. They weren't fat, though. Would you still love me if I weighed three hundred pounds?"

"Of course, dear."

"How incredibly sincerely you lie. You must be a lawyer. On the strength of that guarantee, however, I will risk another french fry." She chomped. "In any case, Buddy says it will take the better part of a week to fix the truck, and there's no point in leaving before then."

"Good. When you're tired of McCullensburg, you're tired of life. I assume that our daughter has not reappeared?"

"Oh, her! Speaking of my work being done, that's the one good thing about this whole adventure. I don't have to resign myself to having raised a sociosexual failure. I *will* have grandchildren before I get Alzheimer's. I will!"

"She's still with that Heeney kid, huh?" Karp grumbled. "What, you think that's serious?"

"I saw a couple of looks pass that would've melted plastic."

"From him you mean?"

"Mutual. They were sliding their limbs over one another in the pool like spawning grunion."

"And you approve of this?"

"Darling, he goes to MIT, plus I'm almost a hundred percent certain he's not a junkie and not HIV-positive. He doesn't belong to a cult, he doesn't pick his nose, he doesn't weigh three-fifty, and he has excellent table manners. What more could a mom ask?"

Karp had stopped listening at *HIV-positive*. Mental pictures he did not wish to entertain entered his mind. "Wait a minute, you think they're . . ."

"Fucking their brains out? I deeply and profoundly hope so. And about time, too."

Lucy and Dan had made their police statements, and Dan had been examined by paramedics, after which Lucy had volunteered to drive Dan back to his house. Lucy drove south on 130, Dan slumped in his seat, not speaking.

"What's wrong? Are you in pain?"

"No, I'm fine."

"I hate it when people say 'I'm fine' when they don't mean it, especially to people who are supposed to mean something to them. If you have cancer and the mailman asks how're you doing, then 'fine' is an appropriate answer, if false. But I really want to know."

"Well, what do you expect, cheerful? Happy? I just got the shit kicked out of me by a bunch of guys who probably killed my family. And they probably were going to do something really bad to you, and I didn't do shit."

"Yes, you did. You hit an armed man with a chair and while you were hurt, too. He might have shot Magog if you hadn't done it. I thought it was incredibly heroic."

Here he gave her a quick look to see if she was serious. He determined that she was, which was fine; but still the association of his sense of what he knew himself to be and the concept of heroism had a profoundly jarring effect on him, as if he had just been informed that he was adopted. He was not a hero; he was a shy bookworm; his father and brother were the heroes.

"The dog was the hero," he mumbled.

"Of course," said Lucy matter-of-factly. "That's what she's trained and bred to be. She'd give her life for me without a thought, assuming she thinks at all. There are people like that, too, I guess, people who just, like, jump into danger without thinking. Like a dog. You can call that heroic, and people do, but that's not really all that impressive, when you think about it. It's like being strong because you happen to be six-seven with a big frame. Well, *yeah*? It's really much more impressive when someone who's careful and thoughtful and imaginative does something courageous, because you know it was moral strength that got them over all their fears. Like my mother—she does brave things all the time, but you know it's really all in the nerves. She just acts without thinking. My dad's brave, too, but he suffers, before and after: 'What should I do, did I do the right thing?'"

"And which one are you like?"

"Both, I guess. I act without thinking a lot, but I still suffer." She laughed. "The worst of both worlds."

"You're just trying to make me feel better."

"True. Am I succeeding?"

"Mm. Try harder." This time they both laughed.

"But really," she said, "I meant it. If you hadn't behaved well, I would have told you that, too."

"Yeah, all the time I was thinking, take the girl, do whatever you want, just don't hit me again."

"No, you weren't."

"No, I wasn't thinking at all, except getting hold of a gun or weapon and killing all three of them."

"Yes, and if you'd done that, we wouldn't be sitting here."

"Oh, you don't approve of revenge?"

"It's not me that's in charge of approving or disapproving," said Lucy. "I'm obliged to love my enemies, being a Christian; you're not. But it would've changed you. You don't think it would've, and the movies and everything tell you it doesn't. The good guy kills the villain and hugs the girl, music up and fade to black. But that's not the way it is in real life, and believe me, I know. When you strike your enemy with a sword, the blade goes through your own body first. St. Augustine." She slowed the truck. "Is this the turnoff?"

"Yeah, but don't turn. Keep going on 130. I want to show you some-thing."

"Ooh, yet another wonder of Robbens County! I have goose bumps already."

"Yet another," he agreed, and sat back in his seat. Somehow, the darkness that had lately borne him down was gone. He placed his left hand on her thigh below the hem of her shorts and felt a tide of glad-ness when she removed a hand from the wheel and placed it on top of his.

"Dan handwich," she said, "on thigh."

Dan had heard the phrase *she made him happy* many times, but until just then he had thought it to be a mere figure of speech or hyper-bole. Before he could think about it or reduce it to the level of strategy, his usual way with girls, he heard his voice saying it: "You make me happy." And blushed.

She nodded. "Uh-huh. I know. You make me happy, too. You won't believe this, but I was actually thinking just that, and how funny that phrase is. I was also thinking, I don't know where we're going, but I hope it's hours and hours."

It was only twenty minutes, though, before he directed her to a left turnoff. The asphalt lasted only a hundred yards or so, as usual, and then they were on oiled dirt and gravel, *rat-a-tat-tat,* steeply back and forth up the mountainside. Then off that road up a rutted track to a clearing dotted with little twisted pines and gray boulders on a field of whisper-ing, pink-tinged ocher grasses.

"This's Mount Knox, the highest point in the county," he said. "You can see almost the whole thing from here." Hand in hand they picked their way among the boulders, the dog casting before them, nose asniff.

He helped her clamber up a whaleback boulder resting against a much higher mass of naked rock. "You're looking north. You can make out the town there."

"Yes, the storied towers of McCullensburg, and their promises of romance and adventure. What's that smear?" She pointed to where a dirty tent of yellow-brown haze hung under the dome of the sky.

"That's the pit. Majestic Number Two, Hampden Mountain. That mountain used to be nearly as high as this one until they cut the top off it. What do you think?"

She looked at the splotched landscape, scarred by coal working and obscured by colored smokes. "*Terribilità.*"

"Come again?"

"It's what they said in the Italian Renaissance for the mighty works of men. Iron furnaces and foundries. Horrible, but also terrific, what puny man has accomplished and so on."

"Yeah, I've felt that. I didn't know there was a word for it, though."

"Oh, there's a word for everything, just about, in some language."

"And you know them all, huh?"

"Yes. Or will." She bent down, scooped up a stone, and flung it into the void.

They tossed stones for a while. Then he said, "Come on, I want to show you something else. This is the real reason I brought you up here. Hold on to my hand, it's tricky."

He led her down a narrow path around the base of the cap rock. The tops of forty-foot pines waved like meadow grasses far below. The path curved south, then climbed upward over a set of natural stairs. She saw that the southern rock face of the peak had fallen away, leaving a high, rectangular niche, open at the top and flanked by a pair of horizontal ledges.

"It's like a huge chair!" she exclaimed.

"Uh-huh, it's called Aaron's Throne. This last part is a little rough. Watch where I put my feet. And don't look down."

He clambered up the vertical base of the throne, and after a moment she followed him. It was not as hard as it looked. Dan helped her onto the seat of the throne, an area three yards square, covered (to her great surprise) by short, soft grass. Below, Magog complained about not being able to follow.

"This is incredible," she cried. "It's like fairyland."

"Yeah, now turn around."

She did and gasped. Green and purple-blue, the corrugated mountains stretched in waves to the limits of vision, their hollows boiling with white mist. In the middle distance a large bird cruised some invisible torrent of air. There was no sign of man's mighty works at all.

He came up behind her and clasped his hands around her waist. "This is what this country looked like before people got here. The Throne is set so you look over the south end of the county and into Virginia. That's Jefferson National Forest to your left. Pretty, huh?"

"It's gorgeous. Is that an eagle?"

"Turkey vulture. But we do have eagles and hawks. We can sit down and lean against the back wall. It's just the right time of day for the light show."

They sat. They watched. The beams from behind them lit up the hills in odd colors, converting the view into something like a Maxfield Parrish landscape. They lay down on the grass. They chewed on each other's faces, wound tongue around tongue. His arm was up to its elbow in her baggy shorts, his hand exploring the country he had glimpsed for a second on the train, before everything . . .

"Whoops," she said, and rolled away, spinning on her long axis several times. She stopped a yard or so from him, looking up at the sky, catching her breath.

"What's wrong?"

"Nothing's wrong. I'm about to sink into uncontrollable carnality, and as I think I mentioned on the love boat, I can't do that." Silence. She turned her head. "Oh, now you *are* pouting."

"Well, it's not fair to me. I mean it's not natural."

"You could procure a trollop," she offered. "To afford you carnal release."

"I don't want a trollop. I want you. Besides, wouldn't you care if I did? Procured one."

"It would pain me, but I'd try to live with it. I would offer it up, as we say. And I *am* yours, except in that way. As you very well know." She reversed her rotation and ended propped upon an elbow, looking down into his face. "Look, I have a feeling this is big-time, and I don't want to mess it up, and I don't want it to be some boring fifties-type thing, us grabbing at each other and me pulling back and you getting all cranky."

"We could do other stuff."

"Oh, right, blow jobs, the prep school solution. You're missing the point. The point is not to release it, because I know and you know that, once we start, we'll be on each other like minks and that'll be that. The thing is to raise the energy from here . . ."

And to his amazement she bestowed a gentle squeeze upon the bulging crotch of his jeans.

". . . to here." She placed her hand under his shirt, on his beating heart. "Do the same to me."

"Under your . . . ?"

"Of course." He did so. She was extremely warm to the touch. The beat was firm and rapid.

"Now look into my eyes. Let the energy flow up from your sex organs to your heart."

"How come you talk like a book? How come you know this stuff?"

"Do I talk like a book? Maybe. It could be the languages, a taste for precision. I like words. I can't bear the inarticulate yawp that passes for conversation. Complaint. Boasting. Sarcasm. Tag lines from sitcoms. How about those Sox? But language is sacred. It has glory, even in ordinary speech. The way most people use it, it's like a winged horse pulling a junk wagon. As for this"—she pressed on his chest—"this is how I whiled away the long, lonely years waiting for you. My mystical readings. It's working, isn't it?"

"Yeah. It's weird. Did you ever do this before?"

"Of course not. This is my maiden flight. Don't talk now. In a little while time will stop. Don't be frightened."

16

"WHAT DID THE JUDGE SAY?" ASKED KARP.

"Judge is not inclined to issue our warrant," said Hawes. "Judge says we haven't demonstrated the involvement of the union to the degree necessary to open the union books and the personal accounts of all the union's officers to the extent we asked for."

"Christ! Why in hell does he think the Heeneys were killed? We have Floyd involved. What else does he want?"

"Something besides the Cades," said Hawes, and added gloomily, "You have to admit he's got a point."

They were walking down a pale green corridor smelling of disinfectant that could have been any hospital in the world, but was in fact the Robbens County Medical Center. They were going to visit Wayne Cade.

"I don't admit any such thing," said Karp. "I should have been there. I assume the Sewer was present?"

"Yeah, he was in good form, too," said Hawes, letting pass the small dig. He had grown a thicker skin in the weeks of working with Karp. "Very eloquent about the importance of the Fourth Amendment to our vital freedoms."

"And Bledsoe bought it."

"Well, yeah. He made the point, which was hard to argue with, that he'd been on the state court of appeals and the state supreme court for twenty years, and if an appeal had come up based on the exclusion of evidence produced by the present subpoena, he'd have been inclined to reverse. Seward pointed out that the only connection we have with the union is through Floyd, and the only inculpation of Floyd is the testimony of a pair of half-wit felons. Hell, they could've said the mayor was there, too."

"He probably was, in this town," said Karp darkly. "Well, fuck it anyway, we knew it was a stretch. We'll just have to find the money some other way."

They had arrived at a door guarded by a Robbens County deputy. Officer Petrie looked up from his ragged *Guns & Ammo,* glared briefly, and with a motion of his head informed them that the occupant was available for interview.

They found Wayne Cade propped up in his hospital bed watching a NASCAR race on a television hung from the ceiling. He was still huge, but not as ruddy as he had been. Tubes entered his mound of bedclothes at several points.

"You want to shut that thing off, Wayne?" said Hawes. "We need to talk to you."

"I got nothin' to say," said Cade, nor did he still the roar of the track.

Karp reached high and flipped the power switch off. He said, "Your cousins say you shot Lizzie Heeney in the head while she was sleeping. You want to comment on that?"

"Yeah. My comment is fuck them, and fuck you, too." Cade stared at Karp. His eyes, like those of all the Cades, were small, close-set, tin-colored. "That's your girl, ain't it? The one with that dog tore me up?"

Karp said nothing.

"Yeah, you're that one. You're that Jew lawyer from New York. Okay, here's a comment, lawyer man. When I get out of here, I'm gonna find that dog and gut-shoot it, and throw it on a slow fire, and skin it while it's still wigglin'. And then I'm gonna do the same thing to her, after every man I can drag in has fucked her up the corn hole."

"Not a helpful attitude, Mr. Cade," said Karp. "It speaks to a lack of remorse. When had you planned on accomplishing these deeds? You know you're going to spend the rest of your life in prison, don't you?"

"That's what *you* think, shitheel."

"Well, Mr. Cade, given your current legal position, ordinarily I'd have to say you have a lot of balls, but in your case . . . exactly how many do you have now?"

Cade roared, clenched his fists, made a move to leave the bed, grimaced in pain, and fell back on his pillows, yelling, "Petrie! Goddamnit, Omar, get these goddamn people out of my face!"

"We'll try him first," said Karp after they left the room. "A conviction will give us a nice base for going after George Floyd and Lester."

"You're pretty confident," said Hawes.

"Yeah, aren't you? We have good forensics, prints at the scene, his prints on the cans and bottles along with those of the other two we know for sure were at the murders. We even have an I.W.Harper pint with all three of their prints on it, overlapping. Also, since all the DNA stuff from the shoes came back positive, there's a lock on Bo and Earl, and the bottle prints mean Wayne was at the party. We have the two cousin confessions. He killed the child with a gun. We have the gun, too."

"But no prints on it, and no knowledge of how it came to be buried at Floyd's. We do know it was in the Guyandotte. They compared the mud on the gun and got a match."

"Yeah, my darling wife was right on the money there, if a little late. And for sure I'd dearly love to have whoever saw them toss the piece and fished it out. And planted it on George. But you can't have everything."

"I don't like it, though. It's just the kind of thing that screws up a case."

Karp waved a dismissive hand. "But we don't need that for Wayne. We got Wayne without his gun."

Emmett Heeney was driving the old red Farmall tractor, with Zak on his lap, steering and crowing with joy. The tractor towed a little stake-bed trailer on which bounced Emmett's brother, his brother's girlfriend, her dog, and her other brother. Also in the trailer were tools of various kinds, fishing equipment, weapons, and a large picnic hamper. The Heeneys had acquired nearly forty acres along with their farmhouse; today Emmett and Dan were providing a tour of the land.

It had not been a farm for a long time. As Dan explained, Red had not been interested in land and had been a little wary of accepting the title of landlord—so bourgeois! Rose had raised a garden, but the rest of the land had been allowed to follow the natural succession and had grown up in thickets of dogwood, white oak, bay laurel, above which young yellow pine were beginning to tower. There was still a good-sized apple orchard, which they now passed, descending a little hill toward a shallow stream that ran through a sparse, pale forest of beech and willow. Emmett stopped the tractor. They all unloaded and walked along a narrow trail through the trees and over an earth berm. There was a little pond there, made by damming the stream, with lilies in the water and a tiny beach.

They ate barbecued-chicken sandwiches and potato salad and drank beer and lemonade. After lunch, Emmett took Zak to the pond's edge and taught him the first lessons in fly casting, and to call dragonflies snake doctors. Then Emmett went with tools to repair the dam and clear culverts. Giancarlo sat on a rock with his pad and markers and drew the pond and the surrounding woods, adding to it many creatures not normally denizens of West Virginia. Dan and Lucy put in an hour's work helping Emmett. Afterward, they sat against a log cooling off, talking or not as the mood struck them. They were for whole minutes at a time extremely silly, which delighted both of them, since neither had logged much time in that country. Lucy had almost forgotten the extreme unlikelihood of her situation, and that the delight was likely to stop before too long. Dan, for his part, was still wondering why the colors were so extraordinarily bright, why time had become variable in its pace, why he was never bored anymore, why music seemed more lovely and compelling than it once had. In common with many alienated bright kids, he had taken LSD a time or two. This was like that, but not like as well—the intensity and peace without the speediness or paranoia. Somewhere in the lower reaches of his overintellectualized mind, the L-word began its slow rise to the surface.

Zak caught a bass, which was admired, as was Giancarlo's drawing. Later that afternoon, Lucy went a distance away from the campsite to pee, and after emerging from the bushes, she heard Zak's voice coming from above.

"You can't find me."

She looked. "I can't. Where are you? In the tree?"

"In the deer blind. Emmett showed me." There was a rustling forty feet above, and the boy's delighted face showed in the leaves of a tulip poplar. "Come on up. It's great!"

Lucy found climbing rungs on the tree's other side and climbed up.

"Wow, you're pretty invisible. What're you going to shoot?" The rat rifle was couched in his arm.

"Squirrels. They're considered varmints. You could eat them, you know. Emmett's going to show me how to make squirrel stew. I almost got a crow, too. Emmett's going to let me nail it to his barn if I do. And he's got a hunting bow, too, he showed me. This is what they use this blind for, bow hunting. It doesn't have a season. The deer come down to the stream there, through the laurel. They have paths."

She riffled his hair. "You're having a great time, aren't you?"

"Yeah, I never want to leave."

"Oh, yes, I know just what you mean."

When Karp returned to the Burroughs Building, he was not amazed to find his wife there, in the room with the state detectives, kibitzing and making herself useful, which was useful indeed. Karp did not believe there were three people in the country he would rather have involved in a criminal investigation than his own dear one, as long as she stayed continually under adult supervision. For the past several days Marlene had realized that she was not, in fact, made to lie around pools. Working on her tan was not enough work, it appeared. So she had started to show up and was accepted immediately by the staties as a colleague. Word had spread about her speckled background.

Virtually all the person-power Karp had at his call had been directed at a single goal: tracing the $7,500 blood money to a source of funds controlled by George Floyd, Lester Weames, or both. He found her working on just this with Mel Harkness.

"Any luck?" Karp asked, kissing the top of her head.

"Zilch. I am prepared to state that at no time in the past six months did either of the two scumbags in question withdraw that sum in cash from either private or union bank accounts. Those that we know of, anyway."

"Mel?"

"I don't get my head kissed?"

"Maybe later. Is she right as usual?"

"She's right," said Harkness, a rotund, balding, bespectacled state police detective who looked like an accountant and was an accountant.

"We got pretty excited there for a bit. We found a ten-grand check to cash written out, but then there was a ten-grand cash deposit a day later."

"Why would they do that?"

"Can't say. But if there's no net withdrawal, we can't attribute it to any illegal payoff. Of course, there's a million ways they could have done it that we can't trace. They could have used a kickback from a purveyor. They could have private accounts. The company could have slipped them the cash. They could have cashed in their piggie pennies . . ."

"Unlikely," said Marlene. "I would be inclined to doubt that either of them spent their own money on this. Weames has a rep for cheapness. Neither of them spend their own money for anything, as far as I can tell. Car, travel, meals—it's all out of the union account. And perfectly legal, too. It has to be union cash, and since your judge won't let us look at the union books . . ."

"He's not my judge," said Karp. "But let's think about this. They didn't expect an investigation by us, but they had to know that the feds would be interested in the union, since Red had said he was going to bring them in. The feds would want to look at the union finances, therefore they have to be a little careful. So no big cash withdrawals. What do they spend their money on, anyway, the union?"

"Mainly pensions and health," said Harkness. "Salaries. Mortgage on the hall. Bonuses. Research. Very straightforward as far as the bank is concerned. It could be cooked as hell, but we can't tell from this."

"Well, we'll just have to follow up every check they cut and make sure it's legit."

"Better call in the marines, then," said Harkness.

"He doesn't have marines," said Marlene, "just us." To Karp she said, "I bet you wish you were back chasing Beemer and the congressman now."

"What congressman was that?" Harkness asked.

Neither Karp answered. They were staring into each other's eyes, combining brainpower in a way that they hadn't in a while.

"Smurfs," said Karp. "Why didn't we think of that?"

"The old guys' spending money," said Marlene. "The bonuses." He grabbed her, they kissed.

Harkness stared first at one, then at the other, a confused look on his face. "What're you two talking about?"

"We just figured out how they did it," said Karp, moving, looking for a phone to call Wade Hendricks.

Royal Eberly lived in the coal company house he had been born in, a four-room wooden affair with a sagging porch. It was painted baby blue with white trim. Red geraniums bloomed in number-ten cans on the windowsills and in the center of a white-painted truck tire in the tiny front yard. A faded American flag flapped gently above the heads of Karp and Hendricks and Eberly, the latter rocking in a straw-back rocker, the others in straight chairs. Mr. Eberly was sixty-nine; Karp thought he looked eighty: hollow-chested, sunken-eyed, hands so knot-ted with arthritis that he needed both of them to hold the jelly glass of iced tea. They were all drinking very sweet iced tea as Mr. Eberly talked about the old days in the deep mines. He had worked with Hendricks's daddy right here in this coal patch, Racke Creek, forty-eight years, man and boy.

Mr. Eberly was a loyal union man. He thought the world of Lester. Lester had come up to the holler himself when Mrs. Eberly passed a few years back. Last time the whole family was together. A shame. His daughters had moved away, something he had not expected. People used to stay with their kin. Mr. Eberly blamed it on the television. He didn't have a dish himself. Radio was good enough, music all the way from Nashville. He used to play a fiddle himself away back in them days, but now the arthritis had stopped that pretty good. He didn't have that old-timer's disease though, thank Jesus, he could recollect good as he ever done.

Hendricks said, "Now, Royal, I hear you all got a bonus to your pen-sion a couple of months back. Do you recollect that?"

"Sure I do, and it come in right handy. New tires on the truck. New muffler, too. I still got some left. It warn't no bonus though. It was research."

"Research?"

"Yessir. What they said. How we'ns was all getting along and such. Give us a paper, you had to make little crosses in the boxes, with a pen-cil, if'n you had a 'frigerator and a TV. How you spent your time, an' all. I didn't mind on account it was the union askin'."

"And they paid you for this?"

"Yessir. A thousand dollars." He shook his head. "Lord Jesus, that's how much I made my first two months in the mines. Age of sixteen and one week old. Course, they wanted half of it back. One of the union boys, Jordy Whelan, drove me into the bank and I cashed it."

"Did they say why you had to give half of it back?"

"Oh, some gummint foolery he said. I didn't really follow it, tell the truth." A worried look appeared on the worn face. "There ain't nothing wrong, is there? I mean, I won't have to give none of it back, will I?"

"No, you won't," said Hendricks. "That enough for you, Butch?"

"Yes." Karp spoke a few formal words into the tape recorder and switched it off.

They interviewed six other pensioners that afternoon, all with the same story. The bank records showed that fifteen checks for $1,000 each had been cut and issued. Each recipient had given half his check back in cash to Jordy Whelan. The Cades said $7,500 had been paid out for the murders. The math was simple.

They drove by the union hall the next morning, with a Bronco-load of staties for backup. These were not necessary, as Jordy Whelan came along with no difficulty. Karp recognized him as one of the bruisers present at the catfish dinner at Rosie's, sitting with Floyd and Weames.

"This ain't about not showin' up for my speed ticket, is it?" Whelan asked from the back of the unmarked.

"No, it's not," said Karp. "It's about some union stuff. Have you worked for the union long, Mr. Whelan?"

Whelan placed a forefinger the size of a spark-plug socket on his upper lip and thought. "Six years, about that. What kind of union business?"

"We'll talk about it later," said Karp.

They took him to the back of the Burroughs Building and into a dis-used office full of furniture from a bankrupt firm. They all sat on swivel chairs around a dusty fake-wood conference table.

Jordy looked like an offensive tackle, an appearance supported by his having retained his high-school-team crew cut, a hairdo that left the sides of his head nearly bald. He looked to have added twenty pounds or so since the glory days, mainly beer-gut.

"What exactly is it you do for the union, Mr. Whelan?" Karp asked when they were settled, provided with coffee or RC, and the tape machine was running.

"Administrative assistant, Local Four. That's the Majestic Two mine."

"And your duties?"

"Oh, you know, keep everything runnin' smooth. Sometimes I drive Mr. Weames places, and interviewin'. Sometimes."

"Interviewing?"

"Yeah, you know, talk to the members, see if everything's okay. Check on the pensioners. How come you're asking this?"

Karp in reply read off a list of fifteen names from a typed list. "Are these names familiar to you?"

"Sure. They're pensioners. Alwin, Murphy, Eberly, all those guys. What about them?"

"They say that over a period of five days sometime in June of this year, you drove them to several banks in this county to cash checks the union had given them, and that you then took half of the proceeds of these checks, in cash."

"Uh-huh. What about it?"

"You've done this before?"

"Sure. It's the givebacks. Some of the old guys don't have cars, so I drive them."

"Givebacks?"

"Uh-huh. See, it's like when you go to the grocery store. The food, say, comes to twenty-four dollars and you give the girl a check for fifty, and she gives you it in cash, so you have, you know, for gas and cigarettes."

"Right. And who told you to collect the givebacks?"

"Oh, that was Mr. Floyd. He's the business manager."

"And you handed the money to him? It came to what?"

"Seventy-five hundred, all told. Uh-huh, and I gave it to him it must've been a Friday, because the checks always go out on Friday and I recall it took a whole week to collect from all those old boys."

"Did he say what he wanted it for?"

"Uh-huh. The basement in the union hall needed sealing and the guy was going to give us a break on the job for cash. Oh, and the rats, too."

"Rats."

"Uh-huh. Rats in the basement. He said it was for an exterminator."

"Thank you, Mr. Whelan," said Karp.

Whistles, cheers, hoots of laughter, filled the Burroughs Building when Karp played the tape for the assembled team.

"No further questions, Your Honor," said Marlene.

"Yes," said Karp, "I have had many golden moments in court, but this is going to have a special place in the scrapbook."

"I want to be a fly on the wall," said Stan Hawes, "when Seward gets this stuff. He'll want to deal."

"Oh, he may *want* to," said Karp obliquely. Hawes met his eye, then looked away. They had an unvoiced understanding. Hawes would do most of the trial work and get the credit and front to the press, but Karp would decide the major strategic moves. Karp could see that Hawes still bore a trace of resentment about this, but Karp was careful not to rub his face in it, and Hawes had enough sense not to bring the subtle hierarchy into the public gaze. There was a little eye action with Cheryl Oggert, too, Karp noted. Maybe Stan manipulating around the edges? Who knew? thought Karp; who cared?

"Well, it looks like the police part of the operation's just about over," said Hendricks. "I guess the governor's going to be happy about that."

"Yes, he will," Oggert agreed. "I get a call from his budget people every other day. It's like we're going to have to close the schools if Robbens County keeps draining resources. I told them you'd be able to release everyone back to normal duty as of the end of this week."

"This is wise?" asked Karp. "We don't want to depend on the sheriff too much."

"We won't," said Hendricks. "We'll keep the detectives, and we'll still keep priority at the lab. But we don't need thirty-six troopers anymore. What I mean is, we already arrested all the bad guys."

"Your show, Wade," said Karp. "I just work here."

Three days later, after the defense had perused the Whelan testimony, and after some remarkable findings had come in from the state laboratory, and after Wayne Cade had been transferred to the jail, still refusing to talk to anyone, including his state-appointed lawyer, a call came in from

Floyd's attorney, Milton Seward, asking Hawes for a meeting. Karp insisted it be held in the makeshift conference room in the Burroughs Building, rather than in Hawes's office in the courthouse. When the state's attorney expressed annoyance at this, Karp explained, "I'm the bad guy, Stan. Let me *be* the bad guy, with the meet in the bad guy's castle. They still think you're a patsy. I don't want them to discover you're not until George is sitting at his trial. It'll be a Clark Kent moment for you."

"This is how they do things in New York?" said Hawes grumpily.

"Yeah, it is, and, you know, people around here ask me that a lot, I notice. It seems to be polite code for 'Is that some kind of Jew trick?' Answer: yes, it is. So, when we go in on this, I'm going to ask you not to contribute anything. I want you just to sit there and look uncomfortable."

"Well, hell, *that* won't be hard," said Hawes sourly.

Milton Seward was known as the Sewer among the members of the West Virginia bar, both because of his frequent use of salty language and because one of his first major cases had been the successful defense of a group of speculating contractors and councilmen accused of rigging bids for the construction of the Wheeling waste-water treatment system. He was arguably the state's premier defense lawyer at the time, a status to which he frequently adverted.

When he arrived, with his client in tow, Karp again noted that of the two canonical premier defense-lawyer personae—(1) slick, pinstriped $2,500 suits, French cuffs, handmade shoes, $200 haircuts; (2) custom-made, monogrammed cowboy boots, cattleman suits, funny Stetsons, sideburns, lots of heavy jewelry—the Sewer had chosen the latter. Waal, Ah'm jest a shit-kickin' good ole country boy who made good: that was the message. Karp thought that the people who chose (2) did so because they were generally short little fucks and the cowboy boots gave them as much as three inches.

"What the hell you tryin' to pull with this goddamn horseshit, Karp?" was the Sewer's opening gambit.

"What goddamn horseshit would you be referring to, Mr. Seward?" Karp inquired.

The Sewer flung a sheaf of bound paper on the table. "This. This Whelan so-called testimony. You can't use this."

"And why not?"

"Because the whole fucking thing is a tissue of lies coerced under pressure, plus declarant is a mental incompetent. Jordan Whelan has an eighty-six IQ."

"Making him smart enough to be a bagman for your client, but not so smart that he'd ask a lot of questions. His testimony, which was in no way coerced, a fact we can demonstrate without a peradventure of a doubt, is amply confirmed by the testimony of a number, fifteen to be precise, of union pensioners, each of whom received a thousand-dollar fee for so-called research, half of which fee was given back to Mr. Whelan, who then gave it to your client, who gave it to the three Cade boys, for which remuneration they murdered the Heeney family."

Seward chuckled, as if Karp had told an amusing joke. George tried to paste a smile on his face, but it came out like the grimace of a man who had just bitten down on a bad oyster. "Well, Lord fuck a duck, you New York boys sure can come up with the stories. You know as well as I do that there is no way on God's earth you can connect that union money with whatever money, if any, got passed to the alleged murderers. It's all fuckin' smoke, Karp."

"Not quite smoke, Mr. Seward. I wouldn't call DNA evidence smoke."

"What the *fuck* are you talking about, DNA?"

"Gosh, Stan, didn't we turn that over yet? Well, it just came in from Charleston last night." Karp handed a thin manila envelope across the desk. Seward made no move to pick it up.

"It turns out that little Bo Cade had five twenties left from that payoff when he was arrested. Did you know that your client has a habit of licking his thumb when he peels money off a roll? Well, he does. I observed him doing it myself. And when we took a close look at those twenties, we found some saliva traces on the bills. And there was enough cellular material in the saliva traces to give us DNA lines. It's amazing what they can do with tiny little bits of organic material today. I guess your client, being an honest fellow, hasn't kept up with the very latest in criminalistics. Now, we haven't matched that DNA with anyone yet, but since you look like a betting man, Mr. Seward, with that fancy outfit, I'd like to bet you, say, a thousand dollars that we get a match off your client there. What do you say?"

"Ah, that don't mean shit," Seward exclaimed. "Fifty different people could've touched one of those bills."

"All the bills," said Karp. "Same traces on all five bills." There was a brief, delicious silence.

Then Floyd leaned over and whispered something in his lawyer's ear. The lawyer whispered something back. Karp loved to see whispered consultations like this. It was so hard for even experienced rogues to get their lies straight on short notice.

"Not admitting anything at all at this time," said Seward, "but my client directs me to discuss the possibility that other individuals were involved in plotting these murders."

"For example?"

"Other individuals, *an* individual associated with the union. At the highest level. Suppose we were to say that this individual was the prime originator of the murder plot, who made the money available, who directed the murders, who used my client's good offices as an unwitting intermediary."

"You're talking about a plea in exchange for testimony, are you?"

"Well, what the fuck do you think I'm talking about? I'd like to know what your position would be on that?"

"My position on that would be that if your client pleads guilty to the top count of the indictment, murder in the first degree, and if he testi-fies to the material involvement of Lester Weames, we will place that fact into the cognizance of the sentencing judge."

"You're fucking joking." Seward had a face made up of semispheri-cal units, not unlike that of W. C. Fields—little round nose, little round chin, full cheeks—and now all these turned rosy.

"I am deadly serious."

Seward looked at Hawes. "Stan, what the fuck . . . are you gonna sit there and let him get away with this? I mean, are you the goddamn state's attorney here, or what?"

Hawes said nothing. Seward turned on Karp again. "Okay, then lis-ten to me, Mr. New York! You got a lot of horseshit, is what you got. I don't give a fuck what kind of DNA trickology, what kind of lying testi-mony from a bunch of no-account hillbillies, you bring into court, I will personally guarantee you that no Robbens County jury is gonna convict George C. Floyd for these murders." He stood up. "Let's go, George. We're done here."

✧   ✧   ✧

"He might have a point," said Hawes. "Those citizens who don't think George Floyd is man of the year are scared silly of him."

"You're thinking change of venue?"

"It's worth a look."

"No, it's not. The whole point of this exercise is to bring justice to *this* county. Justice has to be done in this place, and seen to be done. If we have to run somewhere else, it's not the win we need."

"We could lose."

"Bite your tongue, and cheer the fuck up, Hawes. We are going to pull George C. Floyd's shorts down in open court and whip his heinie for him."

They walked out into the main suite. Harkness seemed to be the only one at a desk. The chair Marlene usually occupied was empty.

"Where's Marlene?" Karp asked.

"Oh, she's gone. She got a phone call and just dropped everything and ran off like her hair was on fire. She said to tell you she was going to the city, but she didn't say which one."

Karp knew which one. He learned the rest of the story early that afternoon, when Lucy showed up at the office.

"Mom called me," said Lucy. "Billy called her here and said that Jeb had got off the property and bit Mrs. Winchell next door. She got the truck out of the shop, drove herself to Charleston, and got a plane back to the City through Pittsburgh."

"Oh, Christ! There goes the college fund. Was the old lady badly hurt?"

"Oh, no. She wasn't like *attacked*. According to Billy, Jeb just likes to roam, and he roamed into Mrs. Winchell's backyard, and her Scottie dog went for him, which of course Jeb ignored, and then Mrs. Winchell came out and tried to shoo him off with her cane, and I guess that constituted assault with a weapon in his dog mind, and he gave her a nip on the hand. Really it wasn't his fault."

"Uh-huh, and I bet your mom will be making just that argument in front of a judge and a contingency-fee lawyer who's already picking out the color of the Rolls. Why did she call you and not me?"

"Sheer mortification, since you were always going on about something like this happening and ruining us. Also, she wanted me to collect Gog. I'll be watching both of them at Dan's place with the boys. The boys are in paradise. We're going huntin' 'n' fishin' this afternoon. I figured you didn't need to worry about them while you're involved here."

Karp raised an eyebrow. "You're, um, planning on staying there, huh? Setting up light housekeeping?"

"Yes, and what you mean by that is, are you sleeping with him? What do you think?"

He studied the ceiling tiles. "Your mom thinks it's unbridled teen lust out there."

"Yes, I know. It's sort of gross when your *mom* leers at you, nudge-nudge, wink-wink, and I wish she'd cut it out. The problem is she's been preparing practically her whole life to be the understanding and helpful mom of a gorgeous lust bucket like she was when she was my age, and what she gets is virginal me, floating slightly above the ground. It must be quite vexing." Lucy paused and gave him one of her deep looks. "You really don't want the details of my—ha ha!—sex life, do you?"

"No. As long as you're okay."

"I'm okay." She smiled. He recalled that she was smiling a lot more nowadays, not the dry and sardonic smile she had formerly affected, but a real grin, from which light flared. "I'm actually real good."

Karp watched her walk out. Floating, yes. She had a bounce in her step that he had not noticed before. He hoped it was love, although personally he thought that Dan Heeney was not fit to tie the laces of her shoe. After he thought this, he had the good sense to laugh at himself.

He stuffed a number of documents and scrawled-upon legal pads into a cardboard folder and walked over to the courthouse. There for the next several hours he consulted with Stan Hawes about their strategy for the Wayne Cade trial, which amounted to teaching the younger man how to prevail in a high-profile homicide prosecution without seeming to teach him anything. It was subtle and tiring work. Hawes was bright enough to understand he needed help, but he was also a competitive and politically ambitious young lawyer, and his mind was at least partially on the greasy pole rather than totally devoted to the case at hand. Karp had observed this in such lawyers before this. It pissed him off, and he could not afford to be pissed off just then.

At three, they both went down to the courtroom to answer motions before Judge Bledsoe. Wayne Cade had a public defender, a man named Rob Sawyer. Sawyer had a new blue suit, a law degree nearly as old, and a light trace of acne on his cheeks. The motions were the usual pro formas: exclusion of evidence, deficiencies in the warrant, quash the indictment. Hawes answered them well enough, and Karp thought that Bledsoe would have no problem in deciding all of them in the state's favor. While Hawes was up arguing, Karp noted that young Sawyer was having difficulty attracting his client's attention. His client was more interested, seemingly, in Karp. Karp met his stare, which was predictably malevolent. Then Cade made a choking gesture and bared his teeth in a nasty grin. This was actually quite unusual. Karp had tried people who could eat Wayne Cade for lunch, and typically the really hard boys had no personal animus at all against the people whose job it was to put them in jail. Things were apparently different among the Cades. Karp rolled his eyes and looked somewhere else. He felt embarrassed for young Sawyer.

After court, Hawes and Karp went back to Hawes's office. Bledsoe had promised to rule the next day and had announced that, without objection, he wanted jury selection to begin the day after. He expected a speedy trial, with no obstructionism.

At 5:32, they were just about to knock off and go get a bite to eat when they heard a series of popping noises coming from below.

"Someone's got firecrackers left over from the Fourth," Hawes observed, and was startled when Karp leaped up and ran headlong from the room.

Dan Heeney had Emmylou Harris playing out of his computer speakers, "Sweet Dreams" the song. He was lying on his bed watching Lucy Karp lip-synch the song and play air-guitar accompaniment. That Lucy liked Emmylou Harris seemed to him the final benediction on the relationship. For her part, Lucy was not conscious of ever having heard Ms. Harris before arriving in West Virginia, being in the main a world-music sort of girl. She had decided, however, that country was actually world music from the United States. And she actually spent a good deal of time gyrating and lip-synching, in a dozen tongues, in the privacy of her room. That she was now doing it in front of a boy was to her mind a greater intimacy, almost, than getting naked.

The song ended; he applauded; she took a modest bow.

"Can you actually play anything?"

"No, not a thing. My mom tried to teach me guitar—she's good at it—but I could barely get through the first two bars of 'Go Tell Aunt Rhody.' I have perfect pitch, of course, but I could never figure out how to read music. A tragedy, huh?"

"I can play the banjo."

"You can? Oh, play something!"

"I might later, if you're good. You know, you look a little like Emmylou Harris used to."

She sputtered out a startled laugh. "Oh, yeah, I get that all the time. People stop me in the street. Except for . . ." She grabbed up the CD and consulted the face thereon. "She has shining, perfectly straight raven locks and I have curly brown fuzz not unlike pubic hair. She has razor-sharp cheekbones; mine are barely visible. She has a cute little absolutely straight nose; I have a hideous contorted bassoon; she has lush red lips; I have thin pale objects that resemble stretched rubber bands reaching nearly to my ears. She has a broad, noble brow; mine slopes backward like that of early man. She has huge, lustrous dark eyes; mine are tiny and resemble dog poo in color. Aside from that, we could be twin sisters." She grinned at him, put a hand on her hip, cocked it, and said, "You must be in love, me bucko."

He slid away from that one, saying, "I hate it when you dis yourself like that. You have unbelievably beautiful eyes."

She nodded and batted the mentioned units ostentatiously. "Yes, I do. It's my pathetic one good feature, and I'm proud as Lucifer of them, God forgive me." She flopped next to him on the bed.

"Do you always tell the truth like that?" he asked.

"Uh-huh. I never lie, but the truth is not for everyone. My mom says that a lot, when lying. But I think I'm beginning to see what she means."

"I like your mouth, too."

"Unfashionably slitlike though it is?"

He was demonstrating how much he liked it when a sound came from just outside the door, from where the two mastiffs had been lying, facing away from each other like a pair of bookends. It came from both dogs, a kind of growling whine. Lucy jumped up, cold sweat breaking out on her face. Another sound now, tires on gravel, the roar of an engine.

"Get the boys, Dan!"

He got off the bed. "Why, what's wrong?"

She ran out of the room, out the front door, confirming what she had feared.

She ran back to Dan's doorway. "Get the boys! Go, now! Get them and hide in the woods!"

"What are you talking about?"

"It's the Cades, a bunch of them. Go out the back!"

"But what about—"

"I have the dogs. Oh, please, just don't stand there, for the love of Christ, *go!*"

He found himself running out the back. Lucy said something to Magog, who dashed out after him. Lucy and Gog went out onto the porch. She sat in the rocker and placed the dog next to her, talking to him gently. He was whining continuously and his back hairs bristled.

There were three of them in a dirty green Ford pickup truck. Someone she didn't recognize was driving it. The two passengers were Wayne and Earl Cade.

They parked at the foot of the driveway, where it joined the access road. It was twenty yards away, but the wind was right and she could hear what they were saying.

The driver said, "Goddamnit, Wayne, we ain't got time for this."

"Henry, you listen here. I'm gonna shoot that dog there, grab up the girl, and blow up that house. It won't take but a minute. Just set here and I'll be right back."

Wayne walked toward the house. He was walking slowly and carefully, she observed, with a somewhat bowlegged gait. He had a large revolver in his hand.

He stopped in front of the porch steps. "Well, honey, here's what's gonna happen now. I'm gonna gut-shoot that dog of yourn, then I'm gonna take you and your dog back to my home place, and I'm gonna cook it on a slow fire and skin it while it's still alive. Then I'm gonna—"

"It's not my dog," she said.

"What?"

"No, this is my mother's dog. *That's* my dog." She pointed.

Wayne heard the sound of running claws behind him and a shout from Earl. He whipped the upper part of his body around to his right, his gun hand extended.

Magog was already airborne, but easily made a slight midcourse correction. She knew Wayne from before, knew he was a bad actor who would not, for some reason, learn his lesson, and so when she clamped her jaws down on his forearm just behind the wrist, she gave him the full twenty-six hundred foot-pounds. The pistol went flying; so did Wayne. As the other two Cade boys scrabbled in the cab of the truck to grab their weapons, Lucy called the dogs to her and disappeared into the house.

Giancarlo had just caught a largemouth bass that must have weighed a pound and a half. He detached it from the hook and ran to call his brother, who he knew was sitting in the deer blind waiting for a target for the rat rifle. He approached the tulip tree where the blind was and was all set to shout when he heard heavy, running footsteps and the voices of men in loud conversation. He stopped and remained still, the fish held in his hand.

Two men came around the curve of the trail. One held a shotgun, the other a pistol. Giancarlo heard Dan Heeney call his name from the direction of the pond. The men heard it, too. They looked up and saw Giancarlo. The man with the shotgun raised it and pointed it at him. Still clutching his fish, Giancarlo dived into the laurel. Earl fired both barrels.

Up in the blind, Zak had seen this happen, and without thinking he laid the crosshairs of his scope on Earl Cade's head and pulled the trigger.

"Oww! Goddamnit! Oww!"

"What in hell is wrong with you?" Henry Cade cried. His cousin Earl had dropped his shotgun and was doubled over holding his hand to the left side of his head.

"Something bit me or stuck me. Goddamnit, that hurts!"

"Lemme see it," said Henry, and pushed Earl's hand away. A small, round wound an inch above his left ear was bleeding slightly. Henry laughed. "Looks like a pellet hit from your own gun. Must've ricocheted off've somethin' and hit you in the head."

"Ah, shit, Henry, that never happened to me before. How in hell could a thing like that happen?"

"Well, you prob'ly never shot no little boy before neither," said

Henry sagely. "C'mon, let's get ol' Wayne put together and get shut of this place. I swear, between the two of you . . ."

"We all're still gonna blow up that house," said Earl, kneeling down carefully to retrieve his shotgun.

"Yeah, and you better be quick about it, 'cause I think I hear sirens."

Magog sniffed him out in the laurel hell. When Lucy went in, following the dog, she found him lying on his back with his eyes closed. For a glad instant she thought that he was kidding, pretending to be asleep, but he did not stir at her voice or touch, and when she shrieked and clutched him to her, she found that he was all soaked with blood from the crown of his head to the backs of his knees.

17

HAVING BEEN MARRIED TO MARLENE CIAMPI FOR A LONG TIME, KARP had been exposed to more small-arms fire than the average attorney. Thus he had known instantly that it was the popping not of fireworks coming from the direction of the jail but of automatic weapons; hence the sound of a jailbreak. Halfway down the stairway, this impression was confirmed by an explosion that shook the courthouse and brought a blizzard of plaster dust upon him as he raced along. When he arrived at the door that led from the courthouse to the jail proper, he paused. No shots. A sound of flowing water. Shouts. A thin cry for help. He went through, down the flight of stairs, and into the dark and smoky wreckage of what had once been the jail's front desk and reception area. A figure approached through the gloom. Karp saw that it was a man wearing a blackened and torn county deputy's uniform, one of the jail guards. Peagram?

"Peagram! What happened?"

The man stared at him uncomprehendingly. "Sheriff's dead. They shot him dead."

The man swayed. Karp grabbed him before he fell and helped him sit against the wall.

"Who shot him?"

"They had machine guns. Sheriff come out with his pistol, told 'em to get outa his jail, and they just blew him away." The man put his face in his hands and started to sob.

Crashing noises. Through the murk poked a shotgun, followed by the comforting form of Trooper Blake, accompanied by a pair of McCullensburg volunteer firemen in yellow reefer coats. They moved around, looking for survivors, making a lot of noise.

"What the hell happened?" Karp asked the trooper.

"We don't exactly know, sir. Some folks out there said it was the Cades. Three truckloads of them. I guess the prisoners are gone."

"That would be my bet. Where's Captain Hendricks?"

"Chasing a couple of their trucks, I think. I was in my cruiser when I heard the shots and the explosion, so I just took a look and headed for the smoke. One of the deputies told me that Captain grabbed up all the men he could find, troopers and detectives and all, and went off after two of the trucks. They were headed north out of town on 130, probably making for Burnt Peak."

Karp felt his gut wrench. "The other truck went east on 119, didn't it?"

"Yessir, but I don't think anyone went after them. Almost all of our people are back on regular duty. We put it out on the radio—"

"They're after my daughter. Come on!"

Karp ran out of the jail, sidestepping and stumbling over wreckage, passing a stream of firemen and paramedics coming in. When he reached the street entry, he was happy to find Blake right behind him, shotgun at high port. They pushed through the growing crowd to Blake's cruiser and got in. Blake hit the lights and siren. In two minutes they were at the junction of 130 and 119, and Blake was screeching into a tight left turn, accelerating to ninety on the two-lane blacktop. Karp looked at his hands. They were filthy with plaster and soot. Blood, too, from Peagram's uniform. They were shaking. From somewhere ahead came the boom of an explosion.

They could see the column of dust and smoke through the trees as they sped up the access road in a shower of gravel. Karp leaped from the car while it was still rolling and ran toward the house. Half of it was gone, a tumble of smoking wreckage. The kitchen range sat scorched in a flower bed. The front door was lying flat on the porch. A piece of paper fluttered from a splinter of the shattered doorframe. Karp snatched it up and read: "Dad: We're going to the hospital. All safe except GC, badly shot. Earl, Wayne, another Cade, first two wounded. L."

He read it twice more, but it kept saying the same thing.

✿   ✿   ✿

Two pictures on the wall of the waiting room, one a print of a kitten hanging by its claws ("Hang in There, Baby!") and the other the familiar Rockwell of a boy getting a needle in the butt. Cheery, but Karp was not cheered. The room was small, carpeted in blood-colored industrial, and furnished with plastic chairs, orange and white, a white couch in tatty vinyl, and a white Formica table, with two ragged *People* and a week-old local paper strewn on it. It was lit by three long fluorescents, one dim, one flickering. Karp was not a great believer in hell, but thought that, if it existed, hell might be like this.

Zak was asleep in his arms, a fitful sleep from which he awoke often with a cry and looked wildly about. Then Karp tried to comfort him, unsuccessfully he knew, because the only real comfort would be to tell him that it had been a bad dream, that his brother was not being oper-ated upon by unknown doctors in this mingy little hospital. Karp shifted his burden and looked at his watch. Eight thirty-five. The last time he'd looked, about an hour ago, it had been 8:28.

He had made the call earlier. After he had passed the doleful news, blurted it out, there had been no curse, no cry of alarm, from his wife, just a silence so long that he thought that the line had gone dead. I'll be there as soon as I can, she had said, and then the line really had gone dead. He wondered vaguely how long that would be, even if she left the Island immediately. The surgeon's name was Small. Karp knew nothing about him; for example, that Small had lost his license for drunken slic-ing in another state. There wasn't any time to find out. No one had come to talk to him or tell him what was going on. Not a Jewish doctor, either. Bigotry, he knew, but there it was. Lucy was gone, he did not know where; she had run out of the place after they had watched the draped, still, intubated figure of Giancarlo being wheeled out of the ER toward the elevator. But he could guess.

Every time the brushed-steel doors of the elevator across the hall slid open, he looked up. Those doors had swallowed his son and they were taking their time about giving him back, or producing some mes-senger from the medical gods in whose hands he lay; that would be good, too.

He checked again. Eight thirty-seven.

✿   ✿   ✿

Lucy was running along the street, Third Street, wiping the tears away every few strides. It was twelve blocks, she had been told, from the medical center to Holy Family. She didn't trust herself to drive. Also her Toyota was smeared with blood, as she was herself; it was all over her hands and arms, and on her shirt and shorts. She'd never worn shorts into church before, a mark of respect, although she knew people came to church in anything nowadays. What does God care what you're wearing? But they'd howl if the priest wore a skirt.

Here was the church, a squat, sooty-brick building in an eclectic style, a little Gothic, a little Romanesque, a little Baroque, ill-assorted and ugly as nearly all Catholic parish churches in America were. It always made her a little sad that the organization that had sponsored the greatest architecture in Europe had given up on beauty in that department. The great front doors were for show, but a side entrance was open. She crossed herself with the water from the font and went inside.

Dark and empty, lit by small sconces on the walls and by evening light coming through stained-glass windows, crudely done in sentimental nineteenth-century style. The Good Shepherd. The eponymous Family. A crucifixion, Christ taking a little nap in a somewhat uncomfortable position. It had been Vatican Two'd, however: the altar, a carved wooden table that looked as if it had been made for a coal baron's dining room, was squarely in the center, with dark wooden chairs arranged around it on four sides. A Mary chapel; a St. Joseph chapel; a glass case with a dusty doll in it—the Infant of Prague. The sanctuary was where the old altar had been, in a deep niche in the east wall. She went there, bowing to the altar as she crossed the aisle.

Prie-dieux in four rows faced a cylindrical brass tabernacle, highly polished, with late-Victorian embellishments of angels. She knelt, pulled a jet rosary from her bag, and cranked it up. Praying at God, this was called, letting the familiar automatic words send you into a kind of trance, pushing out the distractions of the selfish self, opening the heart. You were supposed to contemplate the words as well, envision the various mysteries, although Lucy did not do that now. She wanted only to clear the page so that she could inscribe on a virgin surface a message, or receive one.

The outgoing message was simple. Whatever you want, take it all; stupid to say that really, it's all from you anyway, but take it back. The languages, poetry, music, sex, not that I've ever had any really, but take that too. Dan and any other Dans lurking in the future, happiness . . . wrap it up and ship it out, make me mute, stupid, paralyzed, I'm already ugly, take it, but just, and I know you don't like bargaining, we're supposed to love whatever you do to us because you're good, that's the whole point, isn't it? But this is too much, even you'll agree, this good and sweet little kid, have mercy, have mercy.

Talking *to* God, this is called. Lucy had been doing it for as long as she could remember, and for as long as she could remember, God had talked back. There had been actual visions, voices, to the extent that her priest, a sensible and pragmatic fellow, had become a little concerned, for the Church has never been entirely comfortable with that sort of thing. But he had thought it would fade with age, and it had. Two years and more had now passed without Lucy's receiving what is technically known as a consolation. Now, instead, she was receiving a desolation. To those serious about religion, these are even more to be prized than the gaudier epiphanies, and Lucy knew this very well, but her present pain had pushed this knowledge from her mind. She wanted comfort; she had always *had* comfort; she was getting none now, and she was beginning to grow cross. She was quite terribly spoiled, in fact, and when one is spoiled by Omnipotence, one is spoiled indeed.

She threw claims into the scales: her time on her knees, her many good works, her self-denial, her faith . . . Nothing. She felt nothing, except the muscle stiffness and a stuffiness in her head. She was talking to someone who wasn't there; from this commonplace it was only a short jump to thinking: talking to someone who doesn't exist. She felt a chill. An explanation presented itself: she was crazy, just like Mom, a fanatic, always had been. There *was* no one there. Maybe there had been once—who knew?—but it was gone. Giancarlo would die or not, according to chance and the skill of his doctors. That tabernacle was remarkably ugly. I've lost my faith, she said to herself, amazed. It was just here in my purse and now it's gone. Her chest felt tight. She had to . . . what? Hide? From God? But there wasn't any.

She stood up, feeling light-headed. Dan Heeney was standing outside the sanctuary.

"I thought you'd be here. Are you okay?"

"Yeah, fine. Just, you know, praying." For the very first time she felt embarrassment at saying this.

"Uh-huh. I stopped by the hospital. He's still in the OR." She looked different, he thought, diminished in some way. He attributed it to the catastrophe. She was not looking at him. "What's that thing?" he asked, pointing to the tabernacle. "It looks like an espresso machine."

"It *is* an espresso machine," said Lucy, sliding toward hysteria. "It's the very espresso machine that Saint Paul got a double tall latte out of just before he hit the road to Damascus. You're very fortunate to have it here in McCullensburg." She had to get out of the church or she was going to do something awful. She walked rapidly out, not pausing at the altar as she always did. In the small lobby she stopped with the feeling that she had forgotten something. Wallet, bag, sunglasses, keys, all there, what was it?

"You okay, Lucy?"

"Yeah, just a little . . ."

"You have dirt and blood on your face."

"Do I?" She checked her image in the glass of the church notice board. Then she pulled out a bandanna, dipped it in the font, and wiped the stains from her face.

"Can you do that? I thought that was holy."

"It doesn't matter." She walked out of the church.

He had a motorcycle, a canary-colored Suzuki dirt bike. "Get on. I'll take you back to the hospital."

"I didn't know you had a bike."

"I don't. It's Emmett's. After you left, he picked me up at the hospital and drove me back to the house. We took some of the good stuff out of the ruins. The garage fell on my mom's car. I guess it's my car now. Or was. This was out behind the garage. Not a scratch on it." He threw a leg over the machine and started it, the sound startling on the quiet street. Crows flew from the neighboring trees, complaining.

Suddenly she felt deep shame. "You've lost everything. Oh, Danny, I'm so sorry."

"Yeah, well, what can you do? Cry? I didn't lose my computer, though. And I still have the family pictures. They threw the dynamite into the kitchen, and the appliances and the sink took a lot of the blast. Get on now and hold tight."

She did and did, pressing the side of her face flat against his back. She thought she could hear his heart beat over the roar of the engine. He was real at least. No, don't stop at the hospital, just drive, just drive, we'll give up everything for love, have a life together, we'll worship each other, like pagans, like Americans . . . no, she thought, I'm not good enough for him.

As they rode up the drive to the hospital parking lot, they heard a roaring that nearly drowned out the sound of the motorcycle. A small helicopter was coming in for a landing atop the six-story building's roof. Dan switched off his engine and they watched it land.

"That'll be Mom," said Lucy, and felt a peculiar and perverse pride. I'm like her, now. Took a while. Will she be *pleased?* Lucy found she didn't much care.

"Should I come in?" Dan asked.

"No, I don't think . . ." She saw his face fall. "No, I need to . . ." She had lost the ability to talk to him. She wanted him to go away now. He saw this. He shrugged, nodded, turned away.

Zak was now stretched full-length on a vinyl-covered couch with his face on Karp's jacket. A number of people had come by to see Karp. The lawyer Poole, to express his condolences. Cheryl Oggert, to express the governor's. Besides that, Oggert wanted Karp to talk about the legal situation regarding Floyd and Weames, angling to see if something could be pulled out of this disaster. Karp was polite, monosyllabic; she soon left.

Hendricks came by later with a number of other state troopers. He had not, as it turned out, come just to offer comfort, but when he spotted Karp, he walked over, shook his hand, and did so. Karp thought Hendricks looked uncharacteristically rumpled, bleary. His eyes were red-rimmed. He sat down heavily in a chair next to Karp.

"You get them?" Karp asked, more out of sympathy than because he still cared.

"No. I'm sorry to say we didn't. We only got one roadblock out ahead of them and they blew right through that. They had a five-ton truck they stole from a coal company lot. Then we followed them up Burnt Peak, on that road, and they dropped the side of the hill there with dynamite right in front of my lead car. Road's full of big rocks. So that was that.

Two of my boys're dead and two are here. Pruitt and Vogelsang are the ones didn't make it. I got to go call their families, I guess. Never happened before, never had to make that kind of call."

Hendricks seemed dazed. Karp, however, although normally a sympathetic sort, was not inclined to be so just then.

"Meanwhile, could you tell me how the *fuck* this was allowed to happen? A jailbreak in broad daylight?"

"What can I say? They kept it real close. Normally, you get a sense of what them boys are gonna do, and I got informants in the family. You recall I took you to see one of them."

"Russell."

"Him. But there wasn't a peep about this. They blindsided us, that's for damn sure."

"So what happens now?"

"Well, there's no way in hell the governor's gonna keep the feds out of it now. We don't have the resources to put a siege on a whole mountain. I'm not sure anybody does, if you want the truth. I mean Waco, that was a bunch of houses on the flat, in the desert. Ruby Ridge, that's the other big case, you had terrain, but there was only two men with guns, three if you count the kid they shot. Now put them two together. You got a, hell, figure a whole platoon up there, forty men, with all the dynamite they want and heavy automatic weapons. Plus you got the mine shafts. That hill's riddled with 'em, so it's perfect defensive territory. They know the shafts and the good guys don't. If this was a military operation, say in the Pacific or Vietnam, you'd chase them off the surface with artillery and air strikes, and then you'd go in with infantry, at least two hundred men, I'd reckon. If you got any serious resistance, you'd take major casualties: twenty, thirty dead and more wounded. Then you'd just blow the tunnels, seal 'em up inside. But we sure as hell ain't gonna do nothing like that. We ain't gonna take those kind of casualties, not with cops. And we ain't gonna use artillery, not with women and kids involved. You know, when you think on it a little, the gun nuts are right. You get you enough crazies and enough automatic weapons, and if you're in some rough country and you got enough food and water, well, then you got yourself your own country if you want it."

"That's what the Cades have now, their own country?"

"Pretty near. We'll block off the roads, of course, but there's no way on God's green earth we can stop up every rabbit trail off of that mountain. It'd take the whole West VA state police. So they'll keep being able to sell their dope and bring in reinforcements and food. Hell, it ain't much different from the way they live now. They could hold out for years up there if they want to. And I think Ben Cade wants to. He's been easing up to this kind of thing for years. We hear stories, you know. Girls, runaways, picked up and took away up there. For his wives." Here he paused and stared at his dusty shoes.

"So, the truth is, this is our problem, here. We let it grow like a boil for years and now it's time to pop it, come what may. I wanted to say, though, and all the boys think the same, and all the people I been talking to in town, we're all real, real sorry your boy got hurt. It wasn't none of your fight, and you came in and helped us out, and this happened. I guess after what happened to Lizzie Heeney I should've known the Cades were mean enough to gun down a little boy, but I reckon it's still a shock. I had half a dozen men come up to me and say, Captain, if'n you need another gun, just ask. And those that pray are praying for him. I know it don't mean much, but I wanted to say it. I'm sorry." Hendricks's steely blues locked on Karp's eyes. They looked teary. Karp did not think he could hold it together if Gary Cooper went all blubbery on him. He firmed his jaw and said, "Thank you." They shook hands. The captain left.

Karp's daughter and his wife arrived almost simultaneously, Marlene stepping out of the steel doors, Lucy coming down the corridor.

Karp gaped at his wife. "How did you get here so fast?"

"I leased a helicopter." Embraces, brief ones.

"How is he?"

"Still up in surgery the last I heard. They said they would contact us."

She checked her watch. "It's been five hours." She gave him a quick, appraising look. Everyone had a weakness, she knew, even hypercompetent people like her husband, and this happened to be all matters medical as they related to his family. His normally mighty powers of assertion seemed to flee when the kids were sick and the white coats were pontificating. That was why she had moved mountains and spent money like water to speed her way back here.

Marlene now took over. She made a scene, several in fact. People started moving a good deal faster than they were wont to at the Robbens County Medical Center. In short order the commotion arrived at the doctors' lounge, where Edward Small, MD, was taking a brief nap after operating on the kid. He had actually done a good deal of gunshot work in his time, although he usually left the cranial stuff alone. Stick a drain in there and either the patient would live or would die. Of course, it mattered which one—they were not heartless—but either way there would not be consequences for the docs. Robbens County Medical Center was essentially a medicaid/medicare mill, with a sideline servicing the stingy union health plan and telling injured miners they were fit to go back to work and not to bother suing the company. Anyone who could afford to pay got treated in a real hospital in Charleston or D.C.

Small had heard the helicopter land, but assumed it was something to do with the police who were hurt. It never occurred to him that one of his patients would have a relative rich enough to arrive in a private helicopter. Informed that this was the case by a frantic nurse, he hurried downstairs.

Small was a pink-faced, heavy, balding man of around sixty. Marlene sized him in a trice as a genial loafer, competent at routine, but not one to take pains, and definitely not good enough for her boy. Small told them how the surgery had gone. He had removed double-aught pellets from Giancarlo's legs and back. The good news was that no vital organs had been struck. The bad news was that he had a pellet lodged in his brain.

"When will you remove it?"

"Well, we don't think that's advisable now," said Small, addressing his answer to Karp. "With these cerebral wounds, we think it's advisable to wait and let nature take her course." A little chuckle here. "You know, despite all our advances, and at my age I've seen an awful lot of them, Mother Nature's still the best healer."

"What tripe," said Marlene. "I want him moved out of here. I intend to fly him to New York."

"He can't be moved," said Small with some satisfaction. "You can't move someone out of ICU. He wouldn't make it to Charleston, much less New York."

They went back and forth about this for a round or two until Karp put his vote down for not moving, after which she demanded to see the

CAT scans of her son's brain and looked at them, as did Lucy, who had a lot of experience looking at CAT scans. She pulled her daughter aside.

"What do you think?"

"I don't know, Mom. I'm not a doc, but it looks awful. It's in his occipital lobe and it's all swollen."

"I don't mean the pictures. I just wanted to know he'd at least taken them. I don't buy this crap about not going in and fixing it. I want a second opinion. You know brain surgeons, don't you?"

"I know people who do. I'll call Morrie."

She did. Morrie Shadkin, called at his home, was horrified to hear what had happened and yet more horrified (though he did not mention this) to learn that the precious brain of Lucy Karp was wandering around in range of people shooting bullets.

"Lenny Polanski," he said. "He's the best brain-trauma surgeon in the world, if you believe him. I got him through physio our second year at P and S, absent which he would not be a surgeon at all, but humping refrigerators in his old man's warehouse. He owes me big-time. You say the kid can't be moved?"

"No. We'll fly your guy and his team down here. We have a helicopter."

Shadkin said he would get back to her, and after fervent urgings that she watch out for herself, he hung up.

Then they all trooped into the ICU to look at Giancarlo. At the sight of her son lying still and dead-white in the mesh of tubes and blinking machinery, Marlene lost it, giving way to operatic grief, and frightening the personnel. After this, Karp was back in charge. He made the necessary arrangements with the hospital (Small had heard of Polanski and was awed), getting the helicopter to a parking place, and its pilot housed in a motel, and transporting his family back to Four Oaks. Marlene and the two children, who seemed to have regressed nearly to infancy, were put to bed, the former with half a bottle of Scotch and pills, the latter with meaningless, calming words.

Karp himself did not sleep for a long time. His mind, like a small animal expelled from its accustomed burrow by a flood, sought familiar shelter and found it in legal strategy. Assume the Cade boys were lost indefinitely. Could he still construct a case against Floyd? If yes, could he then involve Weames, if Floyd kept mum? But would Floyd keep mum if such a case could be constructed? As he pondered, bits of data floated into his mind. A chance remark by Harkness, some incidents from the recent past. Toward dawn, as he slipped into exhausted sleep, something like a plan had formed in his mind.

In the morning he awakened from a dream in which the events of the past two days had been a dream. The return to the horror of the reality hit him with the force of a shot to the gut, bringing nausea. Marlene was already gone. He ate a glum breakfast with Lucy and Zak and took them to the hospital, where the staff reported that the boy was stable but comatose. Marlene, to his surprise, was not there. He sat for a while watching his two sons. Zak was staring at his brother with an intensity that Karp found difficult to watch. Something was wrong with Lucy, too, a dullness of spirit that was quite unlike her. To be expected? He didn't know. Of all the people in the family, he had expected his daughter to be the most capable of dealing with tragedy. Wrong again, it seemed.

He freely admitted to himself that he could not. Shameful, but undeniable: he could deal with life or death, but not this shadowland.

"I'm going out for a while," he said to them. "I'll check in."

"Sure, Dad. We'll see you later. Have you heard from Mom at all?"

"No, and that's one thing I want to check on."

Outside, breathing full breaths again, he couldn't help noticing that Marlene's helicopter was gone from its place in the parking lot.

Marlene stood on the lip of an enormous grassy tableland that had once been the south peak of Hogue Mountain, watching her helicopter drop in for a landing. It was a Gazelle SA 341J, an ex–British navy aircraft from the seventies, and still the fastest helicopter in the world. Two and a half hours more or less from Bridgeport to this shithole. Billionaires would have to find another unit to get them to the Hamptons.

It landed and Tran Do Vinh got out, crouching as everyone always did under the spinning rotors. He greeted her with the traditional cheek kisses and expressed again, as he had on the phone earlier that day, his profound regrets about what had befallen her son. He spoke to her in French. "You know, I have never before been in a helicopter, though I have seen many and shot down a good few. That hill on which your adversaries are emplaced seems a formidable position. The pilot flew quite low and we received fire, though fortunately took no hits. How can I assist you?"

He was thoughtful when she told him what she wanted done. "Marie-Hélène, I personally am at your complete disposal," he said, "but an operation of the type you describe, an almost, one might say, military operation, will require many men, expensive weapons, logistical supplies . . ."

"I'll advance whatever you need."

"Yes, of course, but the men . . . these are no longer soldiers fighting for a cause. And the young ones I am afraid are mere gangsters. They will not wish to endure casualties without some tangible—"

"There is gold," she said. "A good deal of it, I'm informed. Ben Cade has been a criminal for decades, as was his father before him. They put their profits into gold because they believe that soon all paper money will become worthless."

"Oh, gold!" He laughed. "Oh, well, that's a different story entirely. With gold all things are possible. We Asians love gold. We also fear the ephemeral nature of paper, with rather more reason than M. Cade, I think. Given gold, I should have little trouble organizing the necessary people and equipment. What I do not have and need are maps, detailed maps, including maps of all local mining operations, at least one to ten thousand in scale."

"I can get you those. Are you familiar with computers?"

"Alas, not I myself, but I have people. They operate a pornography site, 'Asian Teens XXX.' You will send the maps to me in this way?"

She nodded.

"And I assume this operation will require a certain settlement with these fearsome Cades, besides relieving them of their gold. Escorting them to the authorities, perhaps?"

"No. I want them killed."

He was not quite sure he had heard her, for a strong breeze was whipping the grasses.

"Pardon?"

"Kill them," she said more clearly. "Kill them all."

Lenny Polanski arrived on Marlene's helicopter the following day with two others, an oriental man and a striking blond woman, all three wearing Hawaiian shirts and sunglasses. The great surgeon seemed like a cross between a retired middleweight prizefighter and a stand-up comedian. He was blocky, tanned, foulmouthed, crop-haired, and athletic in stride and gesture. Karp loathed him on sight. In the dingy waiting room (Dr. Small having hovered and having been curtly dismissed), Polanski introduced to the Karp family Dr. Chao, who will be passing gas at this party, and Ms. Vava Voom, the world's hottest scrub nurse, who will be cooling my brow, so to speak.

Polanski focused on Lucy. "You're that kid, Morrie's superstar with the languages. Say something in Lithuanian."

"Do you speak Lithuanian?" asked Lucy.

"I don't know, I never tried, ha, ha, ha!"

"If you don't make my brother better, you ape," said Lucy, smiling, "I will have you killed in a particularly unpleasant fashion," in Lithuanian.

Ms. Voom held out her hand to Marlene, who shook it. "I'm Anne Rasmussen. He's a horse's ass, but he really is the best brain surgeon in the country. We can't take him anywhere." Lenny cracked up at this.

Karp was not amused. "You know, maybe this isn't a good idea. I mean, this is a child's life we're talking about and I don't appreciate it being treated as a joke."

"Hey, listen, dad," said the doctor, "do I come into your courtroom or whatever and tell you how to act? Ever since I saw M*A*S*H, I wanted to be the pros from Dover—you know that scene? Where the two docs barge in wearing Hawaiian shirts, cure the congressman's kid, and leave? No? Hey, check it out, a great scene! So the first thing you folks have got to do is lighten up. I know you're worried. I'd be, too, if I was in the shit-bag hospital. But I took a look at the kid's snaps—"

"Giancarlo," said Marlene.

"Right, Giancarlo, his snaps, and it's a no-brainer, so to speak, ha ha. I mean, first of all it's a pellet, obviously at longish range, not the usual shot to the head from a pistol at point-blank, so there's less damage generally. We have minimal penetration, not much bleeding, there's no major circulatory damage—"

"Why is he still in a coma, then?" asked Marlene.

"Brain swelling. What do you want? He got shot in the head, okay? A couple of days being knocked out is absolutely normal here. Okay, we go in, we take out the pellet, we repair the good stuff, we snip the bad stuff, we sew him up. These guys here could have done it if they weren't such patzers. Kid's going to be fine, you'll see." Polanski beamed, and it was hard for the Karps not to share his bravado.

"What about impairment?" Karp asked.

Polanski made an elaborate shrug. "That I can't tell you. I've seen people lose a chunk of brain the size of a Big Mac and live a perfectly normal life, and other people just get a tap on the skull and they never move again." He pointed upward. "That's not my department. Your kid's going to get the best surgical care available, but what happens after that, with the brain . . . if you believe in God, he's in charge of that part, not me."

At that, Lucy burst into tears and fled the room.

"Hey, what'd I say?" asked Dr. Polanski in dismay.

Everyone was being extremely nice to Karp. He had not had so many strangers so solicitous toward him since his senior year in high school, when the basketball coaches had come around. He went back to the Burroughs Building two days after the New York team had operated and departed. Giancarlo was as well as could be expected. He looked like he was sleeping peacefully. His color was good, his breathing regular. But he would not awake.

The Burroughs Building had been transformed in Karp's absence, for Captain Hendricks and Cheryl Oggert had lent most of it to the FBI, who had over a hundred agents on the scene now, under the command of a bullnecked person named Ron Morrisey. Morrisey treated Karp like an invalid, or someone with a contagious disease, leprosy, for example. He was not invited to the big-time strategy meetings Morrisey held with the state boys.

Still, Karp tried to show at the office in between bouts of watching at Giancarlo's bedside. Once there, he mostly sat at his desk with his feet up and tapped on his teeth with a pencil. Sometimes he tapped on the desk with two pencils. The plan he had come up with, he now saw, was absurd. It was based on George Floyd having a credible fear that he was going to be convicted of murder, and Karp had to admit that inculcating such a fear would require not just a paper confession, but the prospect of an actual live Cade sitting on the witness stand, pointing a skinny white finger at the defendant. Which Cade he did not have. Which Cade was sitting up on Burnt Peak, thumbing its nose, or noses, at the legions of troopers and agents below. Karp had tried to find out whether Morrisey was planning an assault, and if so, whether he had some way of extracting Karp's two confessors, but Karp did not, it seemed, have a need to know these plans. Cheryl Oggert was not helpful, either. The governor would not apply pressure here; the governor was starting to distance himself from the whole mess.

On Thursday (and it was hard to believe that only three days had passed since the raid), Karp and Marlene and the town's notables attended the funeral of Sheriff J. J. Swett. A surprising number of non-notable townspeople also showed for the event. Several people, including Lester Weames and the mayor, stood up and lied about Swett's character and achievement. Karp noted substantial negative murmurings among the crowd during Weames's presentation, which made him feel a little better. Ernie Poole, who was there and drunk, seemed to sum up the general feeling when he said in a loud enough voice, "He was a corrupt old bastard, but he did the right thing in the end, God rest his soul."

After the funeral, the Karps went back to the hospital. Marlene took over the watch from Lucy. Zak, who had hardly eaten a bite in three days, refused to leave his brother's bedside. Karp obtained a chocolate milk shake and threatened to send the boy to a distant state if he did not consume it.

After an almost silent meal with Lucy (What's wrong? Nothing.), Karp went back to his office in the Burroughs Building. Needing to pretend to himself that he was doing something productive, he called Raymond Guma in New York.

"You're still alive?"

"Yeah, barely," said Guma. "I'm smoking dope now."

"How is it?"

"Eh. I don't get what the kids see in it, to tell you the truth. It helps me eat, though. I get it off this Jamaican from that place on Third. Jerked Chicken, we deliver. What's happening in Podunk?"

Karp told him. Guma said, "Jesus, Butch, that's awful. Terrible! Poor little kid! The bastards escaped, huh?"

"For now. Look, Goom, failing something better, I got a little idea you might be able to help me with."

"Anything."

After Karp had finished the exposition, Guma said, "Well, this end maybe I could help with. It could work. We'd have to get the locals involved, probably not a problem, you being you and me being me."

"What about Eddie Bent?"

"Eh, maybe a little sticky there, but Eddie owes me some big ones over the years. Your big problem is gonna be convincing Lester that what's-his-face is going to roll on him, which is going to be hard to do at this point. Absent the hillbillies."

"I know. I'm working on that. But could you set things up in the City, just in case?"

"Will do, buddy," said Guma, "unless I die first. Or unless I come down off this high and decide it's horseshit. I'll let you know."

That night Karp awakened at three-forty. He looked at the little vial on Marlene's bedstand and contemplated, for the first time in his life, taking a downer. He rejected the idea. He got out of bed, slipped the lodge's terry-cloth robe on, and began to pace the room.

Click.

He stopped, startled. Something had struck the sliding glass doors. *Clack.*

Someone throwing pebbles against the glass. He slipped behind the curtains and looked out. Beyond the little concrete apron and its plastic chairs a sloping lawn dropped to a line of bushes. In front of the bushes stood a slim figure, glowing like marble in the light of a gibbous moon. Karp slid the door aside and stepped out on the apron. The figure made a beckoning motion, silently. Karp felt a chill; it was like something out of a fairy tale. A scatter of rubber zori lay at his feet, his family's, one large, two medium, two small. An extra pair of zori? Image of giving away little clothes. No, don't think about that now. He slipped into the largest ones and headed toward the figure.

As he came closer, he saw it was a boy, an incredibly pale, wheat-haired boy, dressed in bib overalls and a white T-shirt.

"You're Darryl," Karp said. "You talked to my wife one time."

"Uhn-huh. You foller me, now. He wants to say sompin' to you."

Karp followed the boy down a dark pebbled path through the bushes, to a picnic area: a lawn, some tables and grills, a duck pond. Seated at one of the tables was an old man.

Karp sat down. The boy stood behind the old man.

"I'm Amos Jonson," said the man.

"I guessed you were. You spoke to my wife."

"Yessir, that was me. I wanted to talk to you. Startin' off, I want to say I'm sorry for your trouble. I hope your son's all right. I lost two of mine, so I know what that's like."

"We have hopes for a recovery, but he's not out of the woods yet."

The man nodded. "Since I heard, I been considerin' what to do, and I come up with this. I been hiding for a long time, with Darryl here. In an old shaller mine on Belo. Afeared every minute the Cades were gonna send someone to get me, or Darryl. And I got to thinkin', here's this feller comes from away, to help get those Cades, all legal, like nobody ever tried to do before, not since eighteen and fity-six anyways. And then they shoot down his little boy. I considered and I contem-plated and I said to myself, 'Amos Jonson, are you still a man, or are you a slug worm crawlin' in the dark?' It got so I couldn't hardly stand myself. So I come here tonight."

"What have you got to tell me, Mr. Jonson?" said Karp out of a cracker-dry throat.

"I seen it all. Me and Darryl here. We was frog-jiggin' under the green bridge. Two cars come over the bridge and stop on the crown of it. We hid oursels. I seen it was George Floyd's big Chrysler car and a Ford pickup. George gets out of the car and goes over to the pickup. He has words with a man in the pickup. The man gets out. I see it's Wayne Cade. They have more words, cussin' and arguin'. Finally, I seen Wade give George a pistol. Then George goes over to the winder of the pickup and talks some to whoever's in there. I couldn't see that feller at all. But the feller passes out a pair of yeller boots. George throws the boots and the pistol into the river. The pistol goes in the water, but the boots land on a little spit that's there when it's low water. Well, sir, then they go off. Me and Darryl look at the boots, but we don't touch 'em, 'cause we can see they're covered in blood. Then Darryl goes in and feels around with his bar feet and fishes out the pistol. We seen where it fell by the splash. Then I thought, well, George dropped his gun in the river, we ought to do him the favor of giving it back to him."

"So you hid it under the birdbath."

"Darryl done it," said the man. "Tell him, Darryl."

Darryl bobbed his head. "Uhn-huh. Next night I went down to his house. I got me a Bi-Lo bag from the trash and put the gun in it, and then I calculated, where should I lay it? I saw that old birdbath he got there, and I said, that's the place, 'cause I'd alus know where it was, do you see? And then I stopped and said, I should ought to have a memorial in it."

"A memorial?"

"Yessir. So no man could say, no, that ain't the gun he throwed in the river, it was some other gun look jest the same. So, I took my clasp knife and screwed the handle plate off'n it, and I took this small piece of paper that was in the bag, like the Bi-Lo gives out when you trade?"

"A receipt."

"Uhn-huh. Well, sir, I wrote it with a pencil on that little small piece of paper: 'This gun throwed in the river at the green bridge by George Floyd and I pulled it out,' and under I put my name, Darryl Mark Jonson, and what the date was, which I got from a newspaper that was in the trash, too, and then I screed it up small as small and put it in the handle and screwed the plate back on. And then I buried it under the birdbath."

Karp said, "Darryl, would you like me to give you a great big kiss?"

"Nosir," said Darryl coolly, "but thank you kindly anyhow."

18

"TELL ME AGAIN WHY THIS ISN'T AN ENTRAPMENT," SAID STAN HAWES.

"Because we're not entrapping him into the commission of a crime," said Karp. "We have no legal interest in any crimes he may be contemplating or conspiring to commit. We're only using the contemplated crime as a predicate to get him to admit to our agent the details of a crime that he actually did arrange, to wit, the murders of the Heeney family."

"I don't know. It sounds kind of complicated. I especially don't like using my office to engage in a . . . I guess it's a fraud, isn't it?"

"It's no different from what we did to bring the Cades into town."

"Yes," snapped Hawes, "and look at how great that turned out!"

Then Hawes recalled what had happened to Karp's son and his face colored. "I'm sorry. I didn't mean . . . okay, let's start over here. You say we have a much better case against Floyd now, with the gun and the Jonson testimony, and I agree. Seward and Floyd will want to deal, but you don't want me to make a formal offer."

"No, no deal with Floyd. I want him to take the full hit. We won't need his testimony against Weames if this works. That's the whole *point,* Stan. But Lester has to believe that a deal is imminent, which is why you have to leak it to him and spread it widely around the courthouse."

"And then Lester calls George, and George says, 'What deal? Ain't no deal, Lester.'"

"And will Lester believe him? Why should he? Do you really think that there's so much love and loyalty between these two crook bastards that Lester Weames will credit that Floyd would be willing to spend his whole life in prison to keep his dear friend Lester safe from harm?"

"Okay, okay, let's say you're right. Lester now believes he's going to get the shaft from his good buddy. Why should he go to New York City and hire a killer, like you say? Why should he go and try to hire *your* killer?"

"He's not *my* killer, Stan," said Karp, trying for patience. "But I have it on reliable information that there are very few people at the top of this profession. A number of these people based in New York have been questioned by people you don't want to know who they are: Did a guy answering Lester's description come by last June, July, and ask about doing a hit and backed out when he heard the price?"

"Why would a professional hit man give out that kind of information?"

"He might if the people who asked him were good and regular customers." Karp's statement hung in the air for several long seconds.

"Oh," said Hawes, his face wrinkling with distaste. "And you think that explains why Lester went to New York then and pulled ten grand out of the union account and put it back in again?"

"It's the only explanation that makes sense. He went to hire a pro. It was too expensive, so he figured he'd save some dough and get it done locally. So he brings George into it. George, get someone to whack Heeney. George says, okay, boss, but we got to be careful with the payoff. We'll use the giveback money. Lester didn't think of that himself when he pulled out the ten grand. George is the moneyman, after all. Now Lester needs to get rid of George."

"And you assume he's going to go back to the same guy?"

"Yeah. It's not like there're four columns of these guys in the yellow pages. Besides, I plan on having him sent a flyer in the mail."

"A flyer?"

"Yeah," said Karp. "A bunch of clips about the Heeney murders and the arrests with a friendly note: 'Hey, next time, hire the best, regards, Mr. Ballantine.'"

"This is the hit man?"

"More like a hit-man broker, according to my sources," said Karp. "There'll be a number for Lester to call."

❀ ❀ ❀

Karp went from Hawes's office to the hospital. They had moved Giancarlo to a sunny room on the second floor. As Karp passed the nurse's desk, he saw that the piles of toys and cards and flowers had grown. The townspeople had adopted the boy as a symbol of their current travail and, perhaps, their guilt. People had tied yellow ribbons around their trees. Deputies were wearing little yellow ribbons on their badges. Marlene wouldn't let any of the material into the child's room.

She was there, sitting side by side on straight chairs with Zak. She rose when she saw Karp enter.

"Are you going to stay? I have to go out." She had a frantic look on her face. Zak didn't stir; Karp saw that his lips were moving.

She moved past him into the hall. He turned and followed her, putting his arm across her shoulders. It was like grabbing a phone pole.

"Marlene, what's wrong?"

"What's wrong? What's *wrong?* Excuse me . . . ?"

"I mean what's going on? We haven't talked in days, it seems like."

"Okay, let's talk. Nice weather but we could sure use some more rain. How about those Mets!"

"Marlene, don't be like this." She had her hands clutched together. He felt her trembling.

"No, I'm sorry. I don't know how I should be. I keep replaying it in my mind. If only I . . . if only you . . . if only Lucy. I started this. I am the *cause* of this."

"That's stupid, Marlene."

"Right, stupid Marlene." She looked into his eyes. Her realie was teary and red-rimmed, but the other seemed full of pain, too, a familiar hallucination.

"I stare at him all these hours," she said, "and I think what if this goes on for ten, twenty years? It happens. I can't deal with it, Butch. And he talks, Zak, he talks to Giancarlo, and it's like he's listening, too. He's going crazy like his mother. Lucy walks around like a zombie. . . . I don't know. Do you remember, whenever we'd have a fight, you and me or me and Lucy, Gianni would make us stop, he'd jolly us out of it, or throw a phony tantrum? How he always wanted us to be 'regular'? We're flying apart." Her voice choked. "I need some air."

She broke away and ran down the hall. Karp went in and sat down next to his son.

"How're you doing, kid?"

"Okay. He's still here, Dad." Zak's face was pinched and his tan had gone yellow, like old newspapers. "He's still here. He wants to come back but there are these nets, like in fishing. I'm helping him."

The fear sweat popped out on Karp's face. He patted the boy's shoulder. "I'm sure you are."

Lucy drove. She drove most hours that she wasn't sleeping or at the hospital, with Magog beside her in the shotgun seat, the dog's head lolling out the window, tongue flapping in the breeze. Driving passed the unbearable hours, presenting a pathetic illusion of freedom. Once she took the road up to Aaron's Throne, but shied at climbing to the vista itself. She thought she might throw herself off, and was afraid. Mostly she frequented the bleaker parts of Robbens County, parts with which it was unusually well supplied: yards full of rusting machinery, deserted coal patches, dreary villages of fallen-down miners' shacks, the great pit of Majestic Number Two itself. She would stroll along the lip of the workings, dodging from time to time immense coal trucks roaring by that showered her with grit. She watched the dragline scoop away the mountain, and the monstrous D11 Cats shove the spoil over the lip into the defenseless hollows, obliterating streams and deserted settlements, sterilizing the country under a pall of rubble. During these hours she thought often of a famous *New Yorker* cartoon, the one showing a featureless waste studded with trash and old tires, under the caption "Life without Mozart." She had a copy pinned to a corkboard in her room in the City. It did not seem as amusing as it once had.

Gradually over a week or so, the first sharp pangs of utter despair scabbed over. She began to consider how she would spend her life, deprived as it now was of something greater than Mozart. She had no experience of living without God. The question of what else to worship arose, for she understood that everyone worshiped something, the usual gods in her society being power, money, sex, fame, and the sacred Me. She had good models: her father worshiped the law and the family; her mother the same, plus justice, minus the law. They seemed to have done all right in life. Not for her, though. The usual secular gods had little appeal, except sex, and she cringed with shame at the memory of how she had tormented that poor boy. She certainly did not believe in justice. Or mercy. A line from Weil flickered through her mind, the one about there being four proofs of the mercy of God here below: the consolations of the saints; the radiance of these and their compassion; the beauty of the world; and the complete absence of mercy.

How to live, then, on the endless, trashy plain. Usefulness still appealed to her. She could use her gifts. Be a humble lab rat for a while, she owed Shadkin that much. After that, what? Some distant place helping the hopelessly miserable, a Graham Greene sort of burnt-out life. Thinking of what was owed, she found her wheels turning back toward the town, and once there, toward a house she knew on Walnut Street, where Emmett Heeney lived with his girlfriend, and recently, with his brother, Dan.

The house was small, wooden, red-painted, shaded by maples. Dan had been put up in a room above the garage. She climbed the creaky outside stairway and knocked.

"I'm surprised to see you." Dan was wearing a grubby T-shirt and cutoff jeans. He hadn't shaved in a while, and his face was wary.

"Can I come in?"

"Sure." He stepped aside. "I wasn't expecting company."

Obviously. The room was littered with take-out cartons, cups, and wrappers and smelled of unwashed clothes, man, and fast-food greases. She sat down in a rocking chair, on matted clothing. It was the same rocker that had stood on the Heeney porch.

Besides the rocker, the room contained an iron bed, unmade, with flowered sheets bunched in the center, a straight chair, an overflowing trash basket, and a deal table on which stood Dan's computer. The computer had a paused game showing on its screen—a gunsight pointed down a dark corridor.

"I called you at the lodge a bunch of times," he said. "Then I gave up."

"What've you been doing?"

"Oh, having a ball. Reading astro for next year. Playing Doom. Hanging around on the Net. You know, the usual nerd stuff. How's your brother?"

"The same. It's driving all of us crazy. I'm sorry. I mean about not calling. That was mean."

He shrugged. "Hey, no biggie. It's not like we were engaged or anything." She was silent. He examined her more closely.

"What's wrong? You're not sick, are you?"

"No, I'm not sick." Her voice was dull. Why had she come here? To share the torment? Why don't I just fuck him and get it over with? At least I would be doing someone some good. As soon as this thought appeared, she felt something shrivel in her and thought of her mother.

"Your mother was by a day or so ago," Dan said conversationally, as if reading her mind.

Her head snapped up, as if she had been stung. "My mother? What did she want?"

"Just some maps. When she first got here, I showed her some hi-res topo and side-scan sonar maps of the county. Mine shafts, coal seams, and all that. She wanted me to cut her a CD of a couple of sections— Burnt Peak, surface and sub. She paid me, too." He paused and looked closely at Lucy again. She had stiffened, was chewing nervously at her lip.

"Did she say what they were for?"

"Yeah, she said the cops needed them for their operation against the Cades. It's proprietary stuff from the company. The cops won't have anything that good. That's what she told me anyway. What's wrong now?"

Lucy had jumped up, leaving the rocker swaying. "Quick, where's the nearest phone?"

"In the house. Who do you want to . . . ?"

But she was gone, running down the outside stairway. He followed. She ran through the back door. She was on the phone when he came in, twiddling a credit card in her hand, tapping her foot, mumbling impatiently.

"*Chao ong, Ba Diem?*" said Lucy, and then began speaking rapidly in a twittering, tuneful language.

When she hung up, her face was tight-jawed and grim. "They're all gone. And she doesn't expect them back. Oh, Christ, that stupid woman!"

"What? Who's all gone? Who were you talking to?"

"I called Bridgeport. Tran's house."

"That Vietnam guy?"

"Yes. He's gone and his whole army's with him. I talked to his house-keeper. She said Tran told her I might call. He said to tell me not to worry and he'd be in contact later."

"I don't get it. What army?"

She took a deep breath. "The maps. I think my mom has arranged for Tran to attack the Cades on Burnt Peak. God, how come I didn't see it! All that sneaking away, the helicopter jumping up and down . . ."

"You think he's really going to do it?"

"Yeah, I do. Look, Dan, can you print out those maps you gave my mother?"

"Sure, but why—"

"Please, just do it! There might still be time to stop them."

Dan pushed some buttons. A DeskJet hummed and clicked into action and sheets of brightly colored paper slid out onto a tray.

"Show me how to read them."

They spread them on the bed, and he pointed out what the false colors meant and how the subterranean views related to the standard topographic ones, and the various structures, old mine workings, and the place where the Cades had their stronghold.

"What are you going to do," he asked as she pored over the maps, "tell the cops?"

"Why would I want to do that?" She put her finger on a sheet. "What does it mean when a red line is broken like that?"

"A cave-in, usually. The red lines are voids, shafts or adits, the ones that go transversely. Here, see, where the red line intersects with green, it means the shaft hits the surface. Where it intersects with brown or black or gray, it means the shaft hits rock or coal."

She kept studying the maps, flipping from one sheet to another. Fifteen minutes passed this way, with only an occasional question.

"Lucy, if you're not going to call the cops, what're you planning on doing?"

"I'm going to go up there. Here! Look at this!"

Her finger traced a red line. "There's an opening on the west side of the mountain. And it goes through to a shaft that opens right in the middle of these structures. Is that right?"

"Yeah, that'd be the old Canker Run mine. What do you mean you're going to go up there?"

"This has to be it. It's the only place where a road comes close to an abandoned mine tunnel, and they'd want that. They'll be hauling heavy stuff. It's a way to penetrate the perimeter the cops must have around the mountain. You say people around here don't know about all these shafts and things?"

"Oh, they know about them, but not how they interconnect. Most of these tunnels were dug by wildcat miners, back before Majestic consolidated the county. This here's the first and only—"

"Right, and so no one will be watching this hole. When they come out, they'd be west and above where the Cades are, good observation and a strong position in case of counterattack. They could assault through this dead ground to the south or down this creekbed from the northwest." She sprang to her feet and gathered up the map sheets, folding them neatly and sticking them in the back pocket of her shorts.

"I have to go," she said.

Lester Weames dialed the number he had been given, the one from that package. He rubbed his chest. He'd had heartburn on and off ever since the thing had arrived and he'd realized that Mr. Ballantine knew who he was and what he had done. Somehow this was even more disturbing than George Floyd's defection. George he could deal with, but Ballantine was a complete monkey wrench, a shocking surprise.

The phone rang twice. A gravelly voice said, "Weames."

"How . . . how did you know . . . ?"

"It was you? Weames, you're dealing with a professional organization here. Naturally, we have a phone line for each client. It's not like we do a volume business. When the job is done, we cancel the line. Speaking of jobs, how did you like the low bidder you used?"

"Okay, I was wrong. I made a mistake. I need to clean some things up. Your message . . ."

"Yeah, we can help there. Listen, so you don't feel bad, it's not that unusual. A lot of our business is cleaning up after do-it-yourselfers. You remember the bar where you made the appointment the first time?"

"Yeah, it was—"

"No names on the phone. You be there tomorrow, the bartender will give you an envelope so you'll know where to meet my associate. You will be carrying fifty large, in hundreds."

"Fifty? But . . . ?"

"Price has gone up, Weames. Inflation. Or do I hang up now?"

"No, don't! Okay, fifty. And I'll be dealing with just you, right?"

"No. But Mr. Schaeffer has my full confidence. And Weames? This is it. We don't give you no third strike. Fifty large or don't show."

Ray Guma broke the connection, then called a number on his other telephone.

When it was answered, he said, "Bingo."

"He bought it?" asked Karp.

"Seems like it. I got Vinnie Cicciola from the Five going to do the interview. He looks more like a goddamn ginzo mobster than the ginzo mobsters."

"You did good, Goom."

"Hey, it keeps me interested. The docs say that's a good thing. How's the boy?"

"No change."

"Are you nuts? You can't go up there by yourself," cried Dan Heeney. "And that's all she wrote. You need to go to the cops with that stuff."

She seemed about to object, and for a moment he saw a flash of the former Lucy, but then she shrugged, her shoulders slumped, and she said, "Yeah, I guess. I'll go do that. My dad'll know what to do. Thanks for the help. I'll see you."

"Yeah, see you round," said Dan to her back as she walked out.

Lucy drove the Toyota west on 119, but instead of going right on 130 toward the center of town, she continued past the junction with its little forest of signs and arrows. She drove west, past the hamlet of Till, past Mt. Bethel, almost to the Kentucky line, before she turned north at Marblevale. She was now several miles to the west of Burnt Peak, outside the zone of police activity, which centered on Route 712, the road that ran along the mountain's western edge.

She stopped often to check her bearings against the map and against the big floating compass on the dash. Southwest of Ponowon she left the blacktop and took the dirt roads that wound through the hollers, climbing through a landform called Jubal Ridge, a lower corrugation running parallel to Burnt Peak and five miles to its west. It was surprisingly easy to find, for the little road bore the marks of heavier traffic than it was used to. Some vehicle, a large truck or trucks, had snapped off overhanging branches, scarred the bark of roadside trees, and marked the way with deep, fat ruts in the softer places. These signs led her to a hole in the side of the hill. Brambles and some small bushes that had grown up before it had been hacked down and cleared away. She took a six-cell flashlight from under the seat, and a plastic bottle of water from the side pocket of the door. She filled a large tin basin with water and ripped the top off a ten-pound bag of Purina chow.

"You have to stay here," she told the dog. "We don't want you to get shot. I'll be back soon. Stay, Magog!" The animal whined in protest, but Lucy calmed her with hands and voice. Then she switched on the flashlight and descended into the pit.

It was a crude shaft, most likely dug nearly a century ago by a little group of men with picks and shovels, earning a little extra money to supplement their incomes from the land. The floor sloped slightly downward; the ceiling dripped in places and was supported by props made of chestnut logs. She followed it until it was intersected by another adit, at a slightly lower level, this one much larger and clearly made by more modern machinery, an accidental intersection with a newer and hungrier mine, sucking at the same rich seam. She did not need to consult the map. On the soft dust and mud of the floor were the marks of many feet, and also of narrow wheels. They were using bicycles, which made sense. No one on earth had been more successful hauling heavy military supplies by bicycle than the Vietcong.

She followed this trail for many hours, climbing up or down where tunnels intersected, pausing occasionally to rest and drink from the bottle. Now she noticed other signs, too, cigarette butts and crumpled food wrappers. Not very military after all; she recalled that Tran always shredded his butts.

She became aware of a strong chemical smell and of noises ahead. She began to sing, in Vietnamese, a song from the war that Tran had taught her:

When he was a child, his father died
His mother left him all alone,

Yet he grew well, like a healthy plant,
In wartime now he lives for himself
The boy makes himself into a man, by himself
Never mourning the orphan he is.

A flashlight beam shot out of the blackness ahead, blinding her. She stood still, turned off her own light, and held her hands high. She heard footsteps approach. Squinting around the glare, she made out the face of Phuong, one of the Lost Boys. He was staring at her in amazement. Held tightly under his flashlight was a submachine gun pointing at her.

"Hello, Phuong," she said cheerily. "I've come to visit Uncle Tran. Would you kindly take me to him?"

"Anything new?" asked Marlene when she came in to relieve Karp at the hospital.

"No, he's always the same. Zak says he's dreaming. How're you holding up?"

"Marvelous. The press is out in force. There's no news from the siege, so they've discovered Giancarlo. I had twenty cameras shoved in my face coming in here. How do you feel?"

"I'll get some more security."

"Oh, the security's fine. Deputy Petrie is in charge. He likes pushing people. He's got a yellow ribbon tied to his badge. We're a national spectacle."

"Marlene, cripes! I feel like I've a lance piercing through my chest. I can give a shit about a so-called spectacle."

Momentary stone silence filled the room. Then Karp said matter-of-factly: "I have to go back to the City tomorrow."

"What is this now, Saturday? I've lost track of the days."

"Yes, Saturday. Mac and cheese at Rosie's, that's how I can tell."

"This is for the scam on Weames."

"Right. Guma came through."

"Good old Goom. Well, I wish you luck. If it works, can you get a conviction?"

"Oh, yeah. I got both of them if it works, without any deals. They'll both go for the max."

"What is that? Being eaten alive by army ants?"

"No, just life."

"Fuck life." She looked at the still boy on the bed.

Phuong led Lucy through the mine tunnel, which became gradually lighter, until they came to a section illuminated by large fluorescent fixtures and stinking of phenol and acid. Here there were fifty-five-gallon drums of chemicals, and rows of plastic garbage cans rigged with hoses and duct tape. Racks of steel shelves held cartons and brown bottles and laboratory glassware. Lucy had never been in an illegal meth lab before, but Billy Ireland had described them to her, and she figured she was in one now. A former meth lab. A good deal of destruction was apparent, bullet holes, smashed and punctured equipment, the marks of fire, dark stains on the duckboards they walked on, spatters of red-black. She could reconstruct the events these suggested. The Cades, or their employees, had been peacefully making poison when Tran and his people had burst in among them.

They arrived at an elevator cage. Phuong used a phone attached to the wall, and immediately Lucy heard the sound of a large motor. The boy motioned her into the cage. It was large enough for twenty men and moved fast enough to blur the black walls outside.

Tran was waiting for her at the head of the shaft along with Freddy Phat and several other Vietnamese. They were wearing black cotton pajamas and military web gear. Tran had his Stechkin in its big wooden holster on his hip; his face was wooden, too, and unsmiling. In French he said, "You know, this is the first time that I have not been happy to see you. I am quite displeased. Why have you come?"

"To try and stop you. I'm sorry you're angry."

Tran took her arm. "Come with me."

He led her past the staring, glowering men, through a door to a large room, wooden, painted flaking green and gray. Tangles of rusting pipes and smashed enamelware lay in heaps—some kind of bathhouse for the miners. Out into the air again, across gritty, black soil, to another building, also wooden, unpainted gray, with most of the windows smashed out. A loud noise of flies. Lucy saw that the flayed and gutted carcasses of a dozen large dogs hung from the eaves of an adjoining building. He took her to a room, formerly an office. On the wall, the same map Lucy had carried, with a plastic sheet over it, marked with grease pencil, and a calendar showing a train and the month of October 1977. There was a bench, a table, some chairs. They sat.

Tran said, "You see we are quite comfortable here. It was lucky for us that the Cades maintained the lift for their drug laboratory. I had visions of having to climb up five hundred meters in the dark, with all our equipment. They maintained as well the water and the electrical generator. And the dogs were a benefit, as well. We brought very little food, you see."

A volley of shot sounded from a distance, answered by several short bursts of automatic fire.

"Yes, the war has already started. They know we're here, of course. They're rather dismayed, I think. They thought their rear was secured by the strip mine. I think they had no idea that the network of tunnels debouched ultimately in an area outside their control. Your mother was clever to discover it. As were you, to be sure."

"Is that why you're doing this? For her?"

"To an extent. My own reasons are, as usual, complex, but my people are doing it for the gold. And now the drugs as well."

"I don't understand. You said you were sick of killing."

"Well, yes, but you understand, much of that sentimentality was the drug talking. In the light of day, I am just another bloodthirsty bandit chief. It is not a constitutional regime, I am afraid. The old guard is loyal to me, naturally, my old comrades, but the young guard . . . I am afraid Freddy has them in his grip. He is more stylish and modern than I am. This brings us to the problem of you."

"What do you mean?"

"We will go into action soon, perhaps tonight. From this action, either Freddy or I will not return. If it is Freddy, he will certainly kill you, or worse. But I can't let you go either."

"You can't?"

"No, because you will inform either the Cades or the police of our plans, which I dare say you know as well as I do." He paused and gave her an amused inspection. "Don't you?"

"The dead ground to the south, the creekbed to the north. A diversion at one or the other, and strike at their flank."

"Excellent. What a *coup de l'oeil* you have, my dear! It's a pity you are not coming with us."

"You're *enjoying* this?"

"To an extent. It makes a change from breaking the arms of defaulting gamblers. Besides, my old comrades always enjoy killing Americans."

"There are women and kids down there," said Lucy. "Families. It's a village, not a camp."

"Oh, well, we could not possibly attack a village with women and children in it. That would be wrong. Tut tut tut." For a moment he showed her his shark look, his dead-souled eyes.

"This . . . this can't be about the war."

"Everything is about the war." Then Tran grinned. "Let me show you my treasures." He led her to another room, where equipment was standing in neat piles.

"We have a mortar, one of yours in fact. And fifty rounds. Here you will recognize the M60 machine gun. We have three. These are RPG-7 rocket launchers—"

"Stop it!" she cried. "I'm not interested. I think it's all hideous. You're planning on murdering maybe eighty, a hundred people, and you're treating it like some kind of jolly game? And you're not like that. You're not like Freddy Phat. You're kind, and you love poetry . . ." She started to cry and bit her lip and turned away so that she would stop and not shame herself.

"Yes, well, Mao liked poetry, too. It's quite irrelevant. Seeing the good in everyone is a virtue, to be sure, but it may be misleading. I am horrid, *au fond,* as you must know, and your country helped make me so. It thus has a certain pleasing symmetry, this thing."

A dull boom echoed among the hills. Another. A sustained burst of machine-gun fire.

"They are attacking again, I suppose. I must go. While I decide what is to be done, I must secure you. You can keep our prisoner company."

"What prisoner?"

"Some young fool who tried to penetrate our lines last night with some dynamite bombs. You might ask him where the gold is kept. Otherwise he will tell us later under circumstances far less pleasant."

"You intend to torture him."

"Indeed."

"That's contemptible."

"Yes. But necessary just now. And I am good at it. Freddy is not so good at it because he likes it. That is the unfortunate choice. Come along."

He led her down a corridor to a rusty steel-bound door. "They must have kept their payroll here. It makes a fairly good dungeon. Go through. I will see that you are fed later."

He closed the door behind her, and she heard it lock. Shafts of dusty sunlight came through glassless, barred windows. In the center of the room was a man hanging from his bound wrists tied behind his back, his toes just touching the floor. He was naked except for a pair of camouflage-patterned briefs. She approached him, her Swiss army knife already pulled from her pocket. She sliced through the supporting rope. He collapsed at her feet, groaning. She cut the cords that bound his wrists. She looked around the room. On a long table was a length of thick, rubberized electrical cable, below the table a plastic bucket full of water. She carried the bucket over to the man, knelt, dipped her bandanna in it, and washed his bruised and swollen face.

He opened his eyes. Recognition dawned and he shied. "You!"

"Yes. Lucy Karp. You're Bo Cade."

"Jesus H. Christ! Every damn time I get my ass handed to me, you're somewheres around. Why in hell is that, huh?"

"Because you hang around in bad company probably. You remember I tried to warn you. How are you feeling?"

"Like I been kicked by a horse. Are you in with them all? Those chinks?"

"They're not chinks. They're Viet Kieu."

"What?"

"Vietnamese living here."

"What the hell do they want with us?"

"Your gold, for one thing. Another thing is that one of you shot my little brother. There's a revenge angle. My mother is Sicilian."

"What does *that* mean?"

"The Mafia is Sicilian."

"Your ma's in the Mafia?"

"No, but she has a sort of private mafia, and these are them. Look, we probably don't have much time. I need you to tell me where the gold is."

"Hell, no, I won't!"

"Yes, you have to, because here are your choices. You can tell me, and then I'll help you escape. Or you can refuse to tell me, and in a little while they'll come back and torture the truth out of you and then they'll kill you."

"They ain't gonna make me tell, I don't care what they do."

She sighed. "Oh, for Christ's sake! They'll break you in twenty minutes, you poor sap. You think your cousin Wayne is mean? Wayne is a church lady compared to these people."

"Oh, yeah? Well, let me tell you something, girlie. When my kin get finished with them, they're gonna be sorry they ever messed with the Cades."

"There won't *be* any Cades after tonight. Oh, God give me strength! You've heard of the war in Vietnam?"

"Yeah, my uncle Ralph got kilt there. What about it?"

"Those men out there, they're Commie Vietcong sappers, you dolt! They will go through the Cades like a blowtorch through a newspaper."

He was staring at her, his mouth slightly open. "I could get out anyway. You couldn't stop me. I could take them bars off with that fancy knife you got."

"Yes, you could. But I'd yell and they'd come in here and stop you."

"I could fix it so you didn't do no yellin'."

"Could you? Well, go ahead, then." She lay the open blade down on the floor. "See what happens."

Warily, he reached for the knife. She said, "Let me give you a hint. The man who's running this operation is a good friend of mine. If you manage to hurt me, he will stop everything he's doing and track you down. Then you'll die in the kind of pain you can't even imagine. Plus, you'll tell them everything they want to know in the first five minutes."

He stared at her, looking for fear or some trick in her eyes. But he didn't find anything like that. He grappled with that knowledge. Everyone was afraid; specifically, everyone was afraid of the Cades, and within the Cades there was a defined hierarchy of fear, with Ben Cade at the top. He himself was fairly low down in the order, liable to be beaten on by his brothers and his uncles. In turn he got to beat on his smaller cousins and any women, although he found he didn't like doing it all that much. In his mind there grew the desire to know the secret she had.

"You want to know why I'm not frightened, don't you?"

He felt a chill run through his body. He replaced the knife. She said, "It's a long story, but you'll never get to learn it if you're tortured to death or get killed along with the rest of your kin. Your old life is finished, but you could have a different life."

"Yeah, in jail."

"Yes, you'll have to go to prison, maybe for years. But you're young. You'll get out of prison. The world is a lot larger than Robbens County."

He felt a long sigh escape from his throat. "It's in the big house. In his bedroom. There's a trapdoor in the floor that leads to a shaft. . . ." It was complex, involving a descent into the underlying mines, turns and backtracks, and a number of booby traps that had to be disarmed. He told her all this in a low, dead voice. When he was through, and she had asked a few clarifying questions, she rose, checked out the barred windows, and chose one where rank growth pressed against the building. She thought of what Tran had said: "a fairly good dungeon." But a strong room was meant to keep people out, not in. The bars were screwed in on the inside, of course, and she used the screwdriver on her knife to remove them.

"Get into some thick laurel and stay there," she said. "I think it'll all be over by tonight, or tomorrow at the latest. Good luck." Without a word, he boosted himself over the sill and was gone in a rustle of weeds.

Lester Weames got into La Guardia at around two on Sunday, rented a Taurus, and drove into Manhattan. He drove through the City slowly and carefully, to a bar on Greenwich Street. He told the bartender he was looking for a Mr. Schaeffer. Last time he had been looking for a Mr. Ballantine. The bartender gave him a plain envelope and turned away. Weames noticed that the man did not look him in the eye, just like last time. In the envelope were driving directions to Rector and West Streets, near the Battery Parking Garage. He drove there and parked. An August Sunday afternoon in the financial district; you could fire a machine gun down the street and not hit anyone. The only other car on the street was a white Cadillac Seville. He picked up his briefcase, walked over, slid into the backseat of the Cadillac. As before, Frank was singing low on the stereo and the AC was maxed out. Weames felt the sweat prickle as it dried on his face.

The man in the front seat checked Weames in his rearview. As before, he didn't turn around.

"First things first. You got the fifty large?"

"Yes. Right here." Weames opened his briefcase and lifted up a fat manila envelope. The man in front raised a restraining hand. "Not so fast. We haven't decided to take your business."

"What the hell! What're you talking about?"

"Because the problem's not so simple anymore. You screwed up so bad that half the FBI's down there. If we're going to take the extra risk, we need to know what happened, the planning, who did what, and what went wrong. Otherwise, no deal."

"Hell, it's no big story. I told George Floyd to get rid of him, Heeney, and George hired a gang of goddamn slows to do it, and they left evidence all over the place, and the cops caught 'em. That's it."

"You told Floyd to do it. You told him to get rid of Heeney and his family, or just him?"

"I told him to get everyone in the house."

"Why?"

"Because it makes more of an effect. Man might take a risk himself, but not if he knows his family's going to get dead, too. It's better for business."

"And this Floyd supplied the money."

"Yeah, from the union. Untraceable, except the damn fool goes and licks it all before he gave it out. Now he's going state's evidence on me."

"Which is why you want to take him out. He's not in jail?"

"No, out on bail. He's living in his house. Got a couple of union security people with him, but they ain't much. You can take them out, too." Weames hesitated. "Or would that be extra?"

"No, that's covered. Bodyguards are always covered in the sticker price. Okay, Mr. Weames, I think we can do business. You're going to hand me fifty thousand dollars now, in exchange for which you want me to arrange the murder of George Floyd. Have I got that right?"

"Yeah, as soon as you can."

The man held his hand up.

Weames placed the envelope in it. "When do you think you can get it done?"

Mr. Schaeffer did not answer, but took the bills out of the envelope, riffled them, rolled down his window, and waved the wad out at the empty offices, as if trying to attract a wandering stockbroker.

"What're you doing?"

"It's an old Italian custom. It takes the curse off blood money."

"I asked you when you're gonna do it. I'm thinking I need to fix me up with an alibi for the time."

Squeal of tires. A car pulled up alongside on the left, the right-hand door flew open, a big dark man in a suit slid into the seat beside Weames. He felt queasy fear. A face appeared in the window next to him. Mr. Schaeffer swiveled around in his seat and pressed the button that rolled down the rear window.

Karp said, "Hello, Lester. How about moving over and letting me sit down?"

The big dark man put an arm around Weames's shoulders and jerked him across the seat. Karp got in. Mr. Schaeffer was grinning and showing a gold NYPD detective's badge.

Karp said, "Lester, this is Detective Cicciola of the New York police. He's going to arrest you for conspiracy to commit murder, which is a major league felony in the state of New York."

"This is entrapment."

"Oh my, Lester, you've been watchin' too many crummy TV crime shows. When a scumbag like you is 'ready,' 'poised,' 'wanting,' and 'predisposed' to engage in the criminal activity, entrapment goes out the window. Lester, we got you on tape. You're goin' down as big time as it gets for the Heeney slaughter and the Floyd attempt. While you're in custody, I wouldn't be surprised if the state of West Virginia attempted to extradite you for ordering the murder of the Heeney family. What I can assure you of is that the New York district attorney's office will make no objection to that extradition."

"I want a lawyer."

"And you shall have one, my murderous little hick," said Karp, "but it will not do you much good."

19

TRAN ENTERED THE STRONG ROOM. HE WAS CARRYING A STEEL BOWL with a cover and a pair of chopsticks on it and a steel mess-kit mug from which steam rose. The aroma from the bowl reached Lucy. She felt liquid rush into her mouth and her belly quivered. Tran placed the things on the floor, then removed the cover from the bowl.

"*Pho*. And tea."

"Thank you." She picked up a sliver of meat with the chopsticks. "Not dog, I hope."

"No, it's dried beef. I recalled that you did not care for dog."

Lucy was already slurping away at the *pho*. Between bites she asked, "How is your war going?"

"Well. There are about twenty-five of them on a little knob in front of their settlement. A stupid position and easily outflanked. When night falls, we will have them." A pause. "I assume you have the information we require. I could not help noticing that our prisoner is gone."

"Yes. You planned that, didn't you?"

"I thought it was a reasonable assumption that you would act as you did. You are a clever child. I hope I didn't terrify you too much."

"You did. You still terrify me. And you really would have tortured it out of him?"

"Of course, or Freddy would have. But having been tortured, I find I have lost my taste for it. In others, you know, the same experience heightens the taste. I am glad not to have to do it."

"What will happen now?" she asked in a tone that suggested she didn't much care.

"Tonight we will do our operation, return here, and go through the tunnels with our prizes. A truck will be waiting. You should not be here when we return."

"Because you might be killed."

"Yes. Freddy will certainly kill you if you remain. He will almost certainly try to kill me, and therefore I must arrange that this doesn't happen."

"You'll kill him."

"Not I. Someone else. Someone he believes has been suborned, but has not. It is quite complex and boring. We Vietnamese! In any case, you will not observe the last charge of the 614th Battalion of the National Liberation Front's popular forces. We were five hundred and fifty in 1965. Ten survived the war's end, of whom four are here with me today." He stood up. "I will look in on you before we depart. There is a guard at the door. No one will disturb you for the next few hours."

He waited for a moment, as if expecting some comment. She was, however, silent, and he left.

She drank the tea. It grew dark outside, and darker still inside. She loved him and he was a devil. What did that make her? She rocked back and forth with the pain of it. Her brother was probably dead by now, or a vegetable. There was no help in this world or out of it. She fell to the floor, arms outstretched, face against the dusty, splintered planks. Priests lie this way when they are ordained, but she was not thinking of that. Her head hurt, a nauseous pounding behind her eyes. She pressed her forehead against the floorboards, as if she could press clear through the wood, down to the earth, down to its hot bowels and be lost. There was no time, no light, the universe was nothing, deep stupidity, suffering, meaningless death, forever.

"Help me," a small voice said to nothing. Lucy was surprised to find that it was her own voice. "Help me," she said again. After that, silence, the blood in her ears, pain.

An odor touched her nostrils, cutting through the dry-wood and dust smell of the boards. Roses, heavy and sweet, and something sharper. Roses and onions.

Lucy lifted her head, groaning. She saw a woman dressed in dark robes, with a white wool coif around her face, sitting on a chair. She was cutting pieces from an onion with a small knife and eating them. The woman looked uncannily like her mother—dark, large, luminous eyes, thick brows, a straight, perfect nose, the mouth full and sensuous. The skin of her face was smooth and fine like her mother's; unlike hers, it was adorned with three small moles.

"You're a hallucination. Go away." Lucy said this in Spanish.

"If I am, then you are mad," said the woman in the same language, with a thick Castilian lisp. "Do you feel mad otherwise?"

"I don't know. I don't know anything anymore."

"So you claim. In the meantime, you are performing works of mercy at the risk of your own life. That is the behavior of a good Christian, not a maniac."

"Why are you eating an onion? I didn't know they ate onions in heaven."

"There is much about heaven of which you are unaware, child. Although you are as full of pride as Lucifer, at least you haven't claimed that."

"I'm not proud. I'm miserable."

"That is one of the worst forms of pride. I know it very well."

"Permit me to doubt that," said Lucy. "You're a saint. God spoke to you every day."

"He speaks to everyone every day, but only those who listen hear. Now you will listen to me, you silly girl, since you still seem to require these hallucinations as you call them. Our Lord has allowed you, of his grace, to suffer some tiny part of what He suffered, as much as a single tear is to the whole ocean. And what do you do? You cry, you pout, you complain, you have the affrontery to throw back in his face the gifts He has deigned to bestow on you. And why? Your brother is hurt? He will live or die according to His will, blessed be His name. Are you the keeper of heaven, to bar the way when He calls a soul to Him? Ten thousand times you have prayed, 'Thy will be done.' Was that a lie? Did you mean, Thy will be done as long as it is pleasant for me? Don't you know you must give thanks for your afflictions as well as for your graces? *More* thanks, to tell the truth. If he lives, rejoice. If he dies, mourn. Such is the life of us below. You speak of saints; what can you possibly comprehend of how the saints suffer? You know, at one time I was in danger of being called before the Inquisition, and I found this amusing, because nothing they could have done to me with their racks and red-hot pincers could equal what our Lord laid upon this poor body, out of His mercy. Many times I twitched like a crushed worm on the floor of my cell, my head bursting, my entrails all afire, praying myself hoarse for an end to the agony, and there was nothing, nothing answered. You know what I mean now, don't you?"

"Yes."

"I was in such a state, lying in a pool of my own tears and filth, when His Majesty came to me for the first time. So what is the lesson? He waits for us in the darkness; there we seek Him. The light, if it comes, is a pure gift, and we cannot summon it, however we may try. Kings are not summoned, my girl, although you imagined in your infernal pride that it was so. Now you have learned something, and you feel like you have been flayed. It won't be the last time, I can assure you."

The woman leaned forward in her chair, leaned and came much closer to Lucy than the geometries of ordinary space and matter would normally allow. She dropped her onion in Lucy's hand.

"Consider the onion, my dear. Its many layers. And when the layers have all been peeled away, what?"

The woman was gone. The onion sat in Lucy's hand, cool, weighty, pungent.

She heard the door swing violently open; Tran burst into the room, pointing his Skorpion.

"I heard voices," he said, peering into the dark corners. "Two voices. Who were you talking to?"

"Teresa de Alhuma."

"Who?"

"Teresa of Jesus, of Avila, saint, Doctor of the Church. Don't worry, she died in 1582."

"Hm. I should have known, this being you. My little sister used to talk to our grandmother's ghost and swore to me that she talked back. I never heard it myself, but my sister was otherwise never known to lie. Hien was her name."

"Your sister's?"

"Both of them were called Hien."

"What happened to her? Your sister."

"She became a Buddhist nun. She immolated herself in front of the American embassy in Saigon, in 1966. We are going out now. Wait until we are gone and then leave the way you came. I will arrange for the power to be left on. The elevator is easy to operate. Your flashlight is outside this door." He dropped down on his haunches next to her, squatting in the easy Asian way. He was dressed in black cotton, with a floppy black hat, bandoliers of magazines across his chest, and a pair of big Zeiss night glasses around his neck. It was what he must have looked like during the war, she thought.

He said, "If it should happen that I perish, I would like you to do me one last service. It is ridiculous, I know, but I find that it still gives me comfort. I would like you to collect my bones and deposit them at Tan My. It is our ancestral village, just a little south of Saigon, near the river. Mrs. Diem has the details and will contact you at need, if you are willing, that is."

"Of course." They both stood. He kissed her on both cheeks; she hugged him, smelling her childhood in his scent, her own wolf.

"What power you have, my dear," he said, "to make me feel even for a few moments like a human being again. It is almost better than opium. I am truly grateful. Good-bye."

"God bless you, Uncle," she called after him. She sat on the chair, her mind quite blank. But the crushing despair was gone, too. The world was flowing again with all its horror and beauty. She sniffed at her fingers. Onions.

"How's your siege coming along?" Karp asked.

"Hell, it ain't my siege, it's the damn FBI's siege now," said Hendricks. "I'm lucky they give me the time of day."

"But you don't expect it to be over anytime soon?"

"I would doubt that, unless they come up with a new plan."

The two men were in the back of a state police vehicle, returning from the Charleston airport. Night was closing in; the driver had switched on his lights. They had seen Weames booked and jailed in Manhattan, and Karp had made the calls that would grease the extradition process. If Weames had a good delaying lawyer, and he would, the process might take weeks. Karp didn't care, as long as the mutt stayed behind bars. Maybe the word would get around Rikers that he'd had a little girl killed. That would be of more than sociological interest to Lester.

"One thing that they can't figure out is the Chinamen," Hendricks was saying.

"Come again?"

"The Chinamen, or some kind of oriental fellas. Morissey's been sending a chopper over the mountain pretty regular to take film, and he's got a couple of guys in black clothes, orientals, running for cover. He said it looked like something out of an old Vietnam news show. He asked me if there was any Asian gang activity in the area, and I told him that besides the Chinese restaurants in Charleston, I didn't think we *had* any Asians in this part of the world."

"Oh, fuck!" said Karp. "That *stupid* woman!"

"How's that?"

"Wade, we need to go to the FBI command post," said Karp. "Right now."

"The command post? You mind telling me why?"

"They're not Chinese. I think they're Viets, and I think my wife arranged for them to be there. Could you tell him to step on it, please?"

They made good time until they hit the access road up the mountain, after which it was a slow crawl through herds of media. Huge vans sat in cornfields and on the shoulder, beaming nothing much to an anxious world. Searchlights probed the passing police car. Karp was recognized, of course, and the car was pursued by newsies holding cameras, mikes, tape recorders. How's Giancarlo? they screamed. Is he dead, is he talking, *how do you feel?*

The FBI command post was in a forty-foot-long mobile home, squashing a lot of young corn, surrounded by generator trucks, pole lights, and enough antennae and electronics to launch the space shuttle. Ahead, on the road proper, an army-green armored bulldozer was making slow progress clearing boulders off the road.

Morissey was not pleased to see them, and less so when he heard Karp's theory.

"That's crazy," he said authoritatively. "Your *wife* sent in a team of Vietnamese gangsters for revenge against the Cades? How the hell did they get in there? On little fairy wings? That whole mountain is sealed up tight as a bank vault."

"My wife is very resourceful," said Karp.

"You're suggesting that she's conspiring to commit murders?"

"I have no knowledge of any murders. Nor do you. I'm reporting my suspicions to you as officer in charge of this operation, which is my duty as a citizen and an officer of the court. The main thing I want to avoid is any more people getting hurt."

"That's very good of you, Karp. Your federal government appreciates it. What you really have up there, in my opinion, is an Asian drug gang transporting dope. Or trying to. They got stuck up there when we locked the mountain down. Now, if you'll excuse me . . ."

Outside the command post, Hendricks said, "Nice fella. What do you think?"

"Of his theory? I liked the one about fairy wings better. Look, I'm going to hang around here for a while. If you've got stuff to do . . ."

"I got some sandwiches and Cokes in a cooler. Why don't we sit on that rock over there and have us a picnic. Maybe we can learn something watching how the big boys do it."

They sat and ate as men in FBI jackets and SWAT attire and combat-dressed National Guardsmen strode or rode by. Pole lights were emplaced in the woods and along the road, giving the scene an air of carnival. They watched the bulldozer for a while, then went back to the car. Karp dozed. He awakened to gunfire.

"Sounds like something's going on," said Hendricks. "Sounds like a firefight. Those just now were machine guns, I think. Damn! That's artillery. Mortar fire."

"Yes, all your drug gangs have mortars nowadays. Let's go see what the FBI has to say about all this."

When they found Morissey, he seemed a good deal less confident than he had been, and nearly glad to see Karp's face again.

"I may owe you an apology," he said into his shoulder. "One of our people picked up a kid wandering along Highway 712 in his Skivvies. We just got finished interrogating him. He says he's Bo Cade. He says your daughter's up there in some old mine buildings along with the whole Vietcong. According to him, she's best buddies with the chief Commie in charge. You know anything about this?"

"Not a thing," said Karp with his stomach up around his throat. "They never tell me anything. Did he say whether she was okay?"

"She was alive and well when she helped him escape. We'll need to talk about this at some length, but not now. First light I intend to send a couple of teams up through those woods. Then we'll find out what the holy hell is going on here."

When she heard the firing and explosions die down, Lucy let herself out of the strong room and moved among the buildings. The moon was nearly full and she hardly needed the flashlight. She found a place near the wreck of the coal tipple where she could climb onto the roof of a machine shed and lie down on her belly. Some hours passed. She dozed and was brought to full attention by the sound of men moving through brush. There was a line of them, not as many as there had been, some of them carrying stretchers, some in groups of four struggling with heavy chests. So they had the gold. She strained her eyes to see whether Tran was among them, but the distance was too far to make out anything but silhouettes. She heard the sound of the lift motor and the squeal of its gearing.

She slipped off the roof and went north, using the flashlight now, until she came to a nearly dry creekbed and began walking along it. After ten minutes, she found her first corpse, one of the Lost Boys. She didn't know his name. A little farther there was an older Vietnamese, Vo, who had kept the house in Bridgeport, and who had survived fifteen years of the French War and then the American War, only to die in his enemy's country. She said a prayer for the repose of his soul. Farther on, at just the place she would have chosen, her flashlight picked up a thick carpet of brass. This was where they had placed one of the flanking machine guns. Beyond that, she found the Cades, in small groups or individually, looking like dreamers in the moonlight, or smashed beyond humanity, like props from a horror movie. She passed a place where the ground was torn and bushes were uprooted, and where she had to walk carefully to keep from stepping on viscera and chunks of former people. This was the kill sack. The Cades had been pushed from both flanks back to what looked like a good defensive position, and then the mortar bombs had started to fall on them. Some, she found, had run and been cut down by automatic fire, probably from a squad that had infiltrated to their rear. There was another black-clad corpse, but his head had been so smashed she could not tell who it was. She rolled it over with her foot. There was no Stechkin holster and her heart lifted a little.

It was growing lighter in the east, a hint of dawn. She found a rutted road and walked down it, smelling smoke. As she walked, the smoke grew thicker and more acrid, mingling unpleasantly with the morning mist. A figure came toward her out of the fog, stumbling, a girl in a pink nightgown. Her face was smudged with ash and she was barefoot and grossly pregnant. She looked about fourteen.

She stopped when she saw Lucy. "Everything burnt up. I'm lookin' fer Ollie. Have you seen him anywheres?"

"No. But there's no one alive in that direction." Lucy grabbed the girl gently by the shoulders and turned her around on the road. "Is Ollie your husband?"

The girl was pale, with a wandering in one of her close-set, slaty eyes; there was something subtly wrong with the proportions of her face. "My brother," she said. "Papaw ain't give me no husband yet."

"Papaw?"

"The Cade. I have to carry the first fruits of the Father afore I get me a husband. But it's all burnt up now. The hell devils took it all away." This last syllable rose into a cry. "He has prophesied the end and the end has come!"

And more of that as they walked along, the idiot fragments of an insane faith. Like most such, the main part of it was that the old guys got to fuck all the young girls. The girl said that there were a good number of babies who were cursed by God. The girl hoped that hers would be one of the keepers, as she called them.

After some minutes, they came to a large clearing. On either side were fenced fields decorated by dead cattle and one white horse on its back with one leg in the air. There were mortar craters all around. Ahead, a large wooden structure was burning. Clumps of women and children stood around in nightclothes, wailing around the corpses of men. It looked to Lucy like a scene from Bosnia or Chechnya or Guatemala, someplace far from West Virginia, at any rate. The girl ran to one of the groups of women. Lucy sat down on a stump. She found that her head was still completely empty, all volition gone. A time to wait, then. She watched the dawn start to burn away the mists.

Then it seemed that men in black uniforms appeared as if by magic, poking warily into the smaller houses and mobile homes scattered around, collecting the women and kids. Then vehicles appeared, ambulances, trucks, and vans. A fire engine rolled in and firemen began putting out the fire. A man with a submachine gun told her to come along and she did, and joined the wailing women and children sitting on the ground in a circle, being guarded by black-uniformed men.

Lucy dropped to her knees and said, "Let nothing disturb thee, let nothing dismay thee, all things pass, God never changes, patience attains all that is strived for, she who has God finds she lacks nothing." And repeated, over and over, St. Teresa of Avila's own prayer, not the sort of thing that was ever voiced in the maniac religion that Ben Cade had established on Burnt Peak, but after a time she became aware in a distant way that the wailing had stopped and even the children had grown quiet. All the women sank to their knees, surrounding Lucy as she prayed. Thus her father found her as the sun poked over the edge of the mountains.

The hospital had arranged for beds to be brought into Giancarlo's room, so that his brother and a parent could sleep there. Nothing was too much trouble for their most famous patient. When Lucy and her father arrived there, morning sun was lighting the windows. Zak was asleep and Marlene was sitting on the edge of her bed, fully dressed, her head in her hands.

"What's wrong?" Karp said.

"You keep asking that. You should say, 'Anything more wrong?' I would reply, "Still the same amount of wrong, Butch.'" Marlene rubbed her face and looked at them. "Why are you staring at me like that?"

"They killed forty-two people, Marlene, your guys did, plus losing three of their own."

"What are you talking about?"

Karp raised his voice. "Oh, for God's sake, *tell* me you're not going to compound this by pretending innocence! You brought a bunch of murderers down here for a goddamn vendetta. The FBI already knows about it."

"You told them? You ratted me out?"

"Oh, for God's sake! You thought you could *conceal* it? You didn't think anyone would *suspect*? Are you *completely out of your fucking mind*?"

"Oh, fuck you! They murder your son and you fart around with your clever legal tricks . . . what the fuck kind of man are you?"

"How could you, Mom?" said Lucy. "Forget the Cades, how could you do that to Tran?"

Now Zak was up, a look of dismay on his face. "Stop shouting," he shouted. His parents continued to scream at each other, joined occasionally by Lucy.

"Yeah, stop shouting," said Giancarlo.

"I can't believe this," screamed Karp. "She still doesn't *realize* what she's . . ."

The whole family now did a double take, and in an instant the four of them had swarmed over Giancarlo, to the extent that the various tubes allowed.

"Oh, baby," cried Marlene, "you're back. How do you feel?"

"It hurts, Mom. It hurts like a *bitch.*"

Karp dashed out into the hallway bellowing for nurses, for doctors, for analgesics. Lucy and Marlene were weeping and clutching one another. Zak was holding his brother's hand.

"I caught a big fish," said Giancarlo.

"I saw it," said Zak. "Then you got shot. You got a bullet in the brain, but they took it out."

"My head doesn't hurt, just my back."

Nurses arrived, and Dr. Small, now the happiest non-Karp in McCullensburg.

"Can you move your toes?" asked Lucy.

"Yes." Giancarlo demonstrated.

"You're going to be fine," said Marlene, touching the boy's face.

He smiled at her, the famous GC smile. Then this faded and he asked in a puzzled voice, "Why don't you turn on the lights? Why are we sitting around in the dark?"

Karp and Lucy stood together on the roof of the medical center and watched the helicopter lift off, carrying Marlene and the twins back to civilization and a more advanced level of medical care. They watched it dwindle into a red speck. He put his arm around her shoulder.

"Let's go to Rosie's," he said. "It's catfish day."

They walked through normal small-town streets. The news vans were gone, after a frenzied week of reporting the aftermath of the Burnt Peak War and the simultaneous recovery of the Miracle Twin. At Rosie's the Karps got the kind of service that Edward VII used to get at the Café Royale. Everyone loved the Karps in McCullensburg.

"Why did they let her go?" Lucy asked. "I thought she'd be in jail for sure."

Karp shrugged and sipped his iced tea. "Well, she denies everything. And what proof do they have? Her prior connection with Tran? That's not a crime. A helicopter trip for him from Bridgeport to here and back? The maps from Dan? Suspicious, but also not a crime. No money has changed hands that anyone can see. The Viets have vanished except for that old housekeeper, on which they have nothing. They took all their weapons with them. If they had Tran or his people and they could get them to implicate Marlene, it'd be a different story. But they don't even know their names."

"But she did it."

"Yeah, you know and I know how it went down because we know her. But the law deals in facts. Okay, let's say they decide to bring her to trial. Ernie Poole is a good lawyer, probably better than Stan Hawes, when you get right down to it, so it's going to be fought. That brings up the politics of it. Does Stan Hawes want to prosecute the grieving mom of the Miracle Twin in Robbens County? For eliminating a family that's terrorized this county for a hundred years? Could he even get an indictment? Hey, much easier for everyone concerned if it's a gang war massacre. It's not the worst thing that ever happened in Robbens County, and at least the bad guys lost for a change. The FBI will do their national manhunt and come up empty."

"It's still wrong."

"Yes, it is. The law's an imperfect instrument. I recall a couple of years back they had a case out in some Midwest town, probably just like this one. They had a fellow who was just bone bad—an arsonist, a tire slasher, a vandal, a bully, a rapist. He'd been in and out of jail a couple of times, and each time he got out, he headed home and kept behaving the same way, or worse. One day a group of guys came up to him on the street, broad daylight, middle of town, and beat him to death with pick handles. No arrests were ever made. Do I deplore it? Yes. Do I also understand it? Yes. We do the best we can. Meanwhile, the instigators of this disaster are going to get a trial, a scrupulously fair trial, and I confidently expect they will spend their entire remaining years in prison. So I have to be content with that."

"Will you try the case?"

"I'll get it started. I want to see George in a courtroom at least. But Stan can carry it out as well as I can. Old Bledsoe isn't going to stand for any delay, so I figure ten days to can Floyd. Lester will plead if he's smart. After that . . ." Karp shrugged.

"Back to the City?"

"I guess. I hate my job."

"So change it. What do you want to do?"

"What I've been doing here, minus the crazy stuff. Prosecuting cases. I want to be like Domino's Pizza, we deliver hot—no politics, no social work, no supervision: somebody gives me an ass, I put it in jail."

"If they're guilty."

He grinned. "Picky, picky! And what about you? You're leaving today. I presume you'll stay in the City for a while."

"Yeah. I need to marshal the neurological resources of New York to focus on Giancarlo."

"You think something can be done?"

"I don't know. I already talked to some people. Occipital-lobe injuries are funny. Sometimes it comes back, sometimes there's partial impairment, sometimes it's dark for life. At least he's alive. And cheerful, considering. It's funny: there's no one I know that it's less fair to make blind than Giancarlo, and at the same time there's no one I know who could take being blinded with less bitterness than Giancarlo. He's talking about getting a guide dog and taking up the piano. A lot less bitter than Mom, which isn't hard."

"Yes. That's going to be an issue."

"You and her."

"Yeah. I knew she did sneaky and probably fairly dirty stuff for years, but this is different. It's murder for hire, when you cut to the chase. I don't know if I can . . ." He stopped and closed his eyes briefly. "Anyway, I shouldn't be talking to you about this kind of stuff. We'll work it out."

Or not, he thought. "What about you and her?"

"I don't know. I can't look at her and she can't look at me. It's not just the killings. It's her, the way she thinks, what she does. I love her, but I can't be in the same room as her anymore. A failure of charity, I know. It's something I still have to work on."

They finished their meal and he walked Lucy to her truck. A hug and a kiss and she was gone. Karp walked across the square and into the courthouse.

She drove to Dan's brother's place and found Dan in the back, in a deck chair, in cutoffs, with a cooler of beer within easy reach and a thick astrophysics text propped up on a board athwart the chair arms. She marched up to him, removed the board and books, and plopped herself down on his lap.

When he was able to breathe again, he said, "Does this mean you've decided to be nice to me?"

"It could be. Or it could be I am planning to plumb new levels of cruelty and this is the softening-up phase."

"I'm betting on the latter. When are you splitting?"

"Now. You're the last soul in McCullensburg I will see, forever."

"You can't leave without telling me what that Chinese writing on your shirt means."

"No. It says *zhi si bu wu,* meaning roughly 'unable to understand until death.' It's from a Tang-dynasty story about a hunter with a pet deer who gets along with the hunter's own dogs. The hunter warns it that not all dogs are like his pals, but the deer doesn't listen. It runs off, meets a strange pack of dogs, and gets eaten, without ever understanding why. It's an idiom used to refer to an incorrigibly stubborn person."

"You got that part right. So . . . will I see you in Boston, or what?"

"Oh, yes, I certainly hope so. But I don't know how long I'm going to stay in school."

"What will you do instead, and will they need a computer geek?"

She laughed. "I don't know. I'll let you know when I find out."

"So we just, you know, go on like this? Necking? And, you know, raising the tension to the heart?"

"I hope so. I'll understand, however, if you feel the need to consort with women of easy virtue."

"You'll wait there patiently, like a stained-glass window, huh?"

"Yes, until you ask me to marry you, at which point I will say yes."

"What if I marry someone else? One of those easier-virtue ones?"

"Then I'll dance at your wedding and stifle my disappointed tears, and then join the Ursulines. But if you wait, I will show you delights beyond the range of your adolescent fantasies. We will have to honey-moon at the Mayo Clinic, you'll need IV tubes, to replenish your bodily fluids, which I will have *sucked* from your pulsing flesh."

"You are such a *lunatic,*" he said, after which she did suck a little fluid from his mouth.

She then leaped to her feet. "So long and God bless you, Dan Heeney, until we meet again." She ran out of the yard.

He stood up and watched her. Later, that was how he most often remembered her: running down the narrow lane to her truck, with her long legs, and those floppy shorts and the clunky boots kicking up the gravel, and the grin she gave him over her shoulder, and the head of the great black dog hanging out of the window as the truck pulled away.